THE GOLDEN THREADS TRILOGY BOOK TWO

THREAD · STRANDS

LEELAND ARTRA

DEDICATION

This book is dedicated to my children, Lewin & Sapphira: may you both always stay sharp. And to my beautiful wife, Evelina, for putting up with my late nights dreaming at the keyboard.

FOREWORD

Thank *you* for picking up the continuing adventures of Ticca, Lebuin, Ditani, Duke, Elades, and everyone else. Welcome back to the world of Niya-Yur. Niya-Yur, with its 15,000 years of history, has a number of unique beings, customs, and other miscellaneous items. In the event that some of the details slip past too fast as our adventurers travel the world, Lebuin has jotted down definitions and a copy is provided at the end of the book in the section entitled "Lebuin's Lexicon".

NORTHERN ICE FIELDS
Skogen Holt Forest
DUIANNA
NAE-RAE RHONIA
YALTHUM
LAEUSIA
OSLAD
NASUR
Uino
AELARGO
Circumveni Desert
KARAKIA
DULERIUM
OCCIDUIS OCEAN
DARIAN OCEAN
Niga-Yur: Duianna Continent
SOUTHERN ICE FIELDS
0   1000

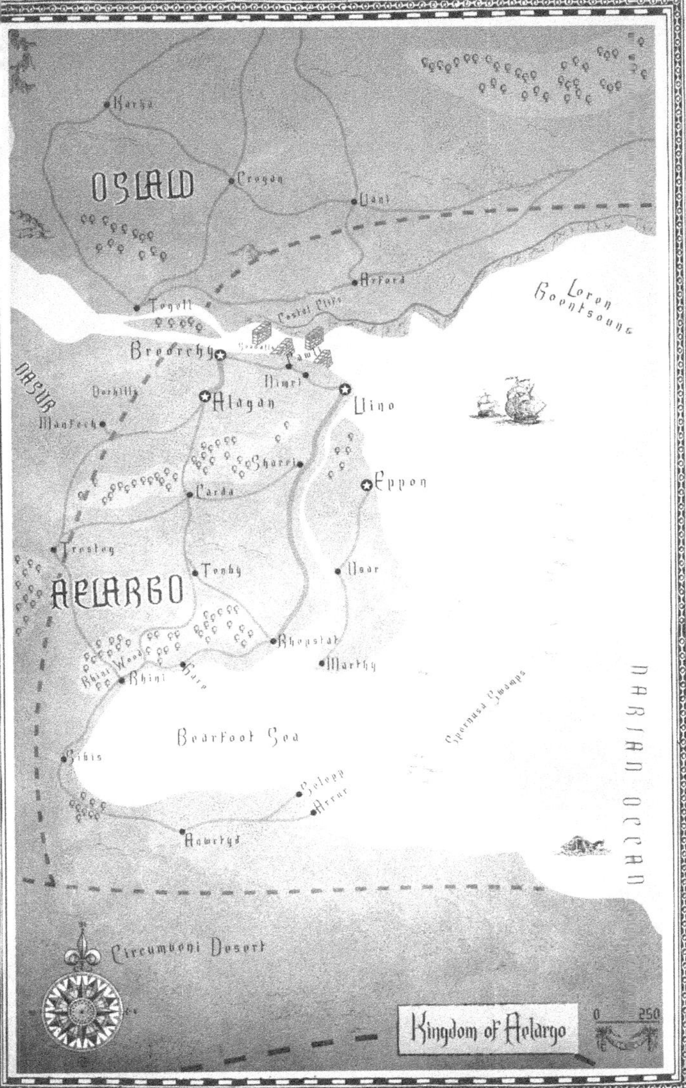

OSLAD
Karka
Crogan
Uant
Arford
Togall
Coastal Cliffs
Broorchy
Goball
Naw
Dimri
NASUR
Dorhilly
Alagan
Uino
Manfech
Sharri
Carda
Eppon
Trostag
Tenby
Usar
AELARGO
Rhepstat
Marthy
Rhini Woods
Rhini
Garo
Bibis
Spernasa Swamps
Bearfoot Sea
Seleep
Arrur
Loren Goentsoung
NARIAN OCEAN
Rawrtyd
Circumveni Desert
0   250
Kingdom of Aelargo

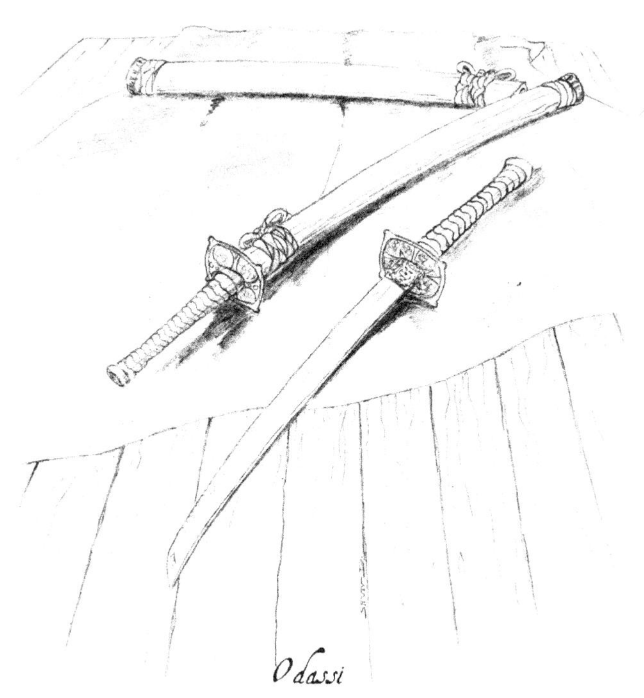

Odassi

PROLOGUE

DITANI PARRIED THE ASSASSIN'S BLADES. The assassin was attacking so fast, his hands would blur with each strike. It took every ounce of strength and speed Ditani had to apply the defense tactics Ticca had taught him over the last six weeks and stay alive. The blows came so quickly, Ditani had no time to riposte with his own attacks.

This assassin is as fast and strong as me!

Ditani was getting an excellent look at his opponent's weapons. They were single-edged short swords, about two feet long, with the telltale grey waves down the edge line of folded carbon steel. The rest of the blade was polished to a mirrored finish, with a copper band at the base, just before the circular silver cross-guard. The hilts were white bone or ivory, tightly wrapped with a black cord forming a diamond pattern.

He felt his stomach tighten as he realized these were not *like* Nhia-Samri odassi blades; they *were* odassi blades. Odassi blades magically enhanced speed, strength, and stamina, and were keyed to only one warrior. They were given to every Nhia-Samri warrior after they had become a true master of dozens of fighting and survival skills. Any Nhia-Samri warrior who wielded odassi was a master killer.

The Nhia-Samri hadn't always been the scary shadow group they had become. In the beginning, they had been highly skilled mercenary teams for hire. They followed a strict code of honor through obedience; any Nhia-Samri who failed to follow orders was expected to commit a form of ritual suicide. It was the Nhia-Samri dedication to completing the assignment that made them desirable to certain powers. Once a Nhia-Samri officer accepted a commission, it was succeed or die. They even considered succeeding through sacrificing one's life to be a great honor.

The flaw to the Nhia-Samri way was that same dedication

to one, and only one, ideal. Hence, seven hundred years ago, when the Grand Warlord and founder of the Nhia-Samri, a silver-elf known as Shar-Lumen, set out for blood revenge, they all followed. A tribe of orcs had attacked Shar-Lumen's home Rea-Na-Rey, the capital of the elven nation of Nae-Rae, kidnapping many of the rulers. By accident, the orcs also kidnapped Kliasa, Shar-Lumen's soul mate and future bride. The orcs, believing Kliasa was one of the rulers, tortured her to death. After that, Shar-Lumen's heart went cold, turning the Nhia-Samri into a deadly group. Over two hundred years, the Nhia-Samri hunted down and exterminated all orcs. That didn't quench Shar-Lumen's burning pain, and so for the last five hundred years, the Nhia-Samri continued to accept deadly commissions, trying to satisfy their leader's need for a blood revenge.

Despite Ditani's extraordinary speed and strength, the warrior's blades scored shallow cuts on his legs and arms before Ditani's parry prevented more serious damage. Ditani let the patterns Ticca taught him flow as he recalled every bit Ticca had demonstrated. He had grown up doing a simpler martial pattern every day with his tribe in the cooler grass planes of Karakia. Ticca had shown him a dozen additional moves to his particular style which he had not known were missing; she also taught him and Lebuin new patterns. The Nhia-Samri warrior he was fighting was more than a master, and Ditani was sure this would be his last day unless a miracle happened.

We should have listened to Ticca's warning to run. Now we are likely to die attempting to rescue her. Had I known these were Nhia-Samri warriors, I would have talked Lebuin out of the rescue attempt.

This had to be related to Magus Vestul's death. Magus Vestul had been working on something for many years when he had declared he was going to Llino to give critical information to Duke. Ditani had never met Duke, but he knew who and what Duke was, which was to say an experienced human warrior turned into an immortal grey wolf the size of an immense horse over fifteen thousand years ago. Duke had been one of the great ancients that helped build this world, and saved all of the non-magical and magical races from extinction. Duke was the only immortal who refused to be called a God, unlike the other remaining builders of this world.

It doesn't make sense that the Nhia-Samri would be trying to kidnap Ticca or assassinate Lebuin. Ticca is just starting her career as a Dagger and still trying to earn a name for herself. Lebuin just earned his Journeyman's badge and didn't even want to leave the comfort of the Guild library. I know Lebuin claims a serious and deadly rivalry with Magus Cune; but if Cune really did hire assassins to interfere in Lebuin's path, he could not afford to hire the Nhia-Samri. Besides, the Nhia-Samri only take on high-profile, impossible targets — or whole countries, as they did when they tried to break up the Duianna Alliance of Realms forty years ago. Only powerful players in political games dare involve the Nhia-Samri. I wonder if the Nhia-Samri were mixed up in the death of Magus Vestul. Maybe they were trying to steal his research. But how could they have known about it?

Just as Ditani thought he was nearing the end of his long life, his miracle came. Ticca, who had been tied to a tree where the Nhia-Samri he was fighting had been torturing her, jumped into the fight.

How did she get off that tree? That's not possible!

Ticca's escape was made even more mysterious by the fact that she still had tightly tied ropes on her legs and wrists. The rope had been stretched around the tree, holding her in place. Two ropes dangled from her wrists and legs in uncut loops. Ticca used these ropes as she spun and attacked. She danced, causing the rope between her ankles to flutter around, trying to trip up the Nhia-Samri who slipped out of the cords. At the same time, she spun her two blades in tight circles as she attacked, causing the loop of rope between her wrists to snap out like a striking snake, almost entangling the Nhia-Samri's arm or blade.

Unbelievable! That is the silk sword style of Yalthum blade masters! How could a farm girl raised in the far southern Rhini Woods learn that technique? I've seen it demonstrated once, and they said it takes years to learn, let alone master. She said she had special combat training, but this shouldn't be possible in one so young.

Ticca spun, using her dagger and a blackened short sword that she must have recovered from the pile of equipment nearby. Ditani marveled at her speed and skill, trying to assess this young woman. Ticca was only twenty years old and stood 5'8", with a slim, but toned, build. Even though she looked feminine, especially with her soft, dark brown, curly hair which bounced as she moved, Ticca was the most highly trained warrior Ditani had ever met. She had half a dozen rips and tears in her clothes from being tortured by the Nhia-Samri. The ripped clothing exposed welts and wounds in Ticca's otherwise beautiful olive skin.

She is not only a beautiful young lady, but the finest and deadliest Dagger warrior I have ever heard of.

That Ticca had received special training was clear. Even more exceptional was her total dedication to the ideals of the Daggers. Her uncle had been a Dagger commander forty years ago in the war where the Nhia-Samri had attempted to enflame the kingdoms to break the Duianna Covenant of Realms. The Covenant was a treaty between all the nations of the continent, brokered over ten thousand years ago, as the Duianna Empire was breaking apart into smaller kingdoms.

While the three of them had made their way through the back trails between Llino and Algan, Ticca had trained Ditani and Lebuin in all it meant to be a Dagger. Daggers were more than highly trained, elite mercenaries; they were *far* more. There were advanced Dagger tactics, signs, history, and the Dagger code. Every Dagger was continuously judged and had to uphold all it meant to be a Dagger. One of the largest surprises Ditani recalled was that Duke had started the Daggers and based them on an organization of military specialists. The military specialists the Daggers were based on had been respected throughout all the races of this world and the ones before, but had been forgotten during Imperial times. Daggers placed critical emphasis on not losing sight of any one of the three guiding principles of honor, courage, and commitment. However, the commitment wasn't to the Daggers, but to doing the right thing, having the courage to stand up for the right, regardless of the consequences, and the honor to always step up. In the last six weeks, both Ditani and Lebuin had practically become Daggers under Ticca's daily training.

Ticca had been drilling the three of them in two-against-one tactics, and that paid off. Ditani was able to provide Ticca aid against the Nhia-Samri warrior. Together, they fought. As Ticca parried an attack and riposted, Ditani lunged in. The Nhia-Samri bent and twisted, dodging every blow, dancing away from the entangling ropes, while managing to deliver vicious attacks at both Ticca and Ditani.

Ditani assessed whether Lebuin needed help. A short distance away, Lebuin was fighting another Nhia-Samri warrior. Ditani wasn't sure how Lebuin had not seen her when he had been scrying on the capture and torture of Ticca. If it hadn't been for this other Nhia-Samri, their rescue would have gone well.

The other Nhia-Samri was a woman, a bit shorter than Ticca, with long, straight, blonde hair that flowed around her like silk strands as she spun and fought Lebuin. She had toned arms and legs, shown off by the flexible, but tight clothing she wore. Although fit, she also had an attractive figure that seemed perfectly proportioned for her height. Lebuin should have had a lot more strength than she did. But she was using odassi blades as well, letting her match Lebuin's superior strength and speed. Lebuin was doing well against her, for the moment.

Ditani felt his pride swelling as he watched Lebuin apply the same techniques Ticca had taught them, holding his own against the female Nhia-Samri. Lebuin's shoulder was bleeding from her initial surprise attack, which had caused Lebuin's loss of control over the magical entanglement. Lebuin had trapped the Nhia-Samri warrior that was trying to kill both Ditani and Ticca.

Lebuin had not inherited his mother's line's height, standing 5'11" to Ditani's 6'1". Lebuin was not dressed as well as his normal style, wearing the Dagger warrior leathers and a simple cotton shirt under leather armor. He'd gotten those clothes from the Dagger Nigan in Llino when they had traded places to try and lure off the assassins hunting Lebuin. Lebuin had filled out, bulking up in muscle mass in the last six weeks, as they had traveled to Algan through the woods and forests. Lebuin's sandy brown hair was shoulder length, with a slight wave to it, which looked good with the beginnings of his beard growing back. Lebuin's skin was a lighter tanned red than Ditani's.

He has learned so much in the last six weeks. I wish Mother could see this. She would be proud.

Lebuin was fighting much better than any who knew him would have believed. Ticca was a good trainer, but Lebuin had the unusual experience of getting over a year of elven combat and magical training since he left the Guild six weeks ago from Kliasa, Shar-Lumen's dead soul mate. Ditani was still amazed that Magus Vestul had never figured out that Kliasa, who had been an elven artifact maker, although she had been dead nearly seven hundred years, was still present spiritually. When Kliasa had been murdered, she had refused to go to the next realm of life without her love and soul mate, the elven Lord Shar-Lumen. Instead, Kliasa had used her great elven mage skills to remain close to this realm of existence in the odd dimensional area between this life and the next. Of course, Shar-Lumen didn't know this either, and he went insane, seeking a blood revenge for Kliasa's death. Shar-Lumen had more power than most, being the Grand Warlord over all the Nhia-Samri.

After a time, Kliasa learned how to see what was happening in this life through her magical artifacts, such as the boots she liked to make. Recently, she had learned that if someone slept in contact with one of her magical artifacts, she could interact with that person. In that strange dream-like interaction, years could pass in a single night. Ticca was wearing the magical boots Kliasa had made for Vestul as a gift. Both Lebuin and Ticca had spent a few nights each, living through years of training by Kliasa of all she could teach. Ticca and Lebuin both showed all the signs of their elven training in their graceful movements. Kliasa had also taught both of them the elven rituals, history, and language. If they lived to see Rea-Na-Rey, they would be welcomed as true elf-friends, a very rare honor for anyone of any other race.

Ticca had given up on the silk cord style and shifted to a close-in fighting style, far closer than Ditani could match. The break they needed came when the Nhia-Samri stumbled. As Ticca kneed him in the groin Ditani leapt in, attacking with both blades and scoring a hit on the Nhia-Samri's shoulder. The Nhia-Samri rolled back and lunged back in, attacking both of them.

Ditani dodged away from Ticca as she dodged in the opposite direction. The Nhia-Samri jumped back, recovering. Ticca spun in so fast, she was a blur. The Nhia-Samri was halfway into a parry when the copper bands at the base of his blade flared with a golden light. The warrior froze, staring at his own blades.

Ticca's strike landed unhindered, and her dagger plunged into the Nhia-Samri's chest all the way up to the hilt. Ticca wasted no time. She twisted the dagger, cutting open a larger hole before pulling her dagger back out with a spray of blood.

The Nhia-Samri didn't seem to notice that blood was pouring from his chest. He looked up from his glowing odassi with a joyous look. "That explains it. You're Gods. I have fought Gods. There can be no higher honor."

He collapsed to the ground, but Ditani was no longer

looking at him. At the mention of Gods, Ditani spun to stare at Lebuin and the other warrior. Lebuin held one of the Nhia-Samri's odassi in his hand, and the pale faced frozen woman stared at Lebuin with her mouth open.

Oh, no! He isn't ready for this! Mother, help him!

Jicca Waiting

CHAPTER 1

HONEST TO GOD

LEBUIN WAS TRAPPED AND HE knew it.

Oh, Lord, what have I done? Why didn't anyone ever explain any of this to me? Oh, no. All they said was stuff like, 'Here is an incantation that makes a shield,' and 'If you pull from an air mana line, you must first filter it and only mix it with mana from a fire line as you direct the powers away from you.' You'd think somewhere in the twenty years I have been studying magic at the Guild, someone could have said, 'Don't touch an assassin's blade with your bare hand. It will entangle you!'

All I wanted was to become the best librarian the Guild had ever had. Why did they send me out here with all this dirt and killing?

This was supposed to be a rescue. Ticca had been captured by one assassin—or Knife, as they were called by common folk. He and Ditani had located where, in the deep forest, Ticca was being held, and they had surprised the Knife. When out of nowhere, another Knife showed up and attacked him.

He felt his own blood soaking into his shirt. *At least, I'm not wearing anything I care about that will get ruined by my bleeding. I'm tired of losing good clothing to these fights. Maybe that is why mercenaries always dress so poorly.*

It was difficult to swallow, and he felt a tremendous pressure trying to crush him. Lebuin searched his memory, trying to find a defense or incantation to escape the prison he was being held in. He could feel the blade's incantations burrowing into his defenses. Like worms boring into an apple, the blade's tendrils of power forced their way through his shields.

The tendril surged through his magic channels like a red

hot knife being driven through the palm of his hand and up his arm.

Lebuin glanced at the beautifully dressed woman before him. She was frozen, mid-strike, with a look of horror. Her mouth hung open as she looked at him. Her forest-patterned silk shirt was a perfect match for the formed, padded, leather armor she wore over it. The silk shirt was worn outside of her light green, grass-colored leggings. Her calf-high boots with brass buckles were top quality. Not new—in fact, they were well-worn, but cared for. Her cloak reminded him of the cloak he had taken from the dead assassin in Llino, which had blended with shadows.

For an assassin, she must be well paid. That outfit is at least nineteen crosses. Those boots alone are nine crosses. I wonder if that cloak is magical like the other one I took. It might explain why I didn't see her when I was scrying out the situation for this rescue.

A sharp pain in his arm brought his thoughts back around to the fact he was under attack magically. He tore his gaze away from the ice-blue eyes of the female frozen before him, to look at his hand. The strange assassin's blade he had pulled from her belt was clutched in his right hand. But he couldn't open his hand to drop it. His knuckles were white from being convulsed around the hilt of the weapon.

I can't block it, but I might be able to absorb it. It is magic, after all.

Lebuin concentrated and tried to pull the burning tendril of power into his own magics, blending it and taking control. The tendril was boring into his system, so grabbing it was an easy matter. The energies shifted as he tried to match it and pull the power from it, so he could drop the blade.

The tendrils tried to snap back, but Lebuin held them. Lebuin's powers mixed with the blades, and he could see a connection that reminded him of the interconnecting incantation the Guild used between its mages.

Tracing the incantation, he found the path led to the

woman in front of him. As he connected to her, he suddenly knew her. Her name was Runa-Illa. She had been born on the Nhia-Samri base called Outpost One. Her father was a respected Nhia-Samri officer called Runa-Emry, and had been chosen by the rare ancient blades of his mentor, at the death of that mentor. Runa-Emry, like other officers who held the ancient blades, didn't always agree with the Nhia-Samri orders, and sometimes worked to find loopholes to prevent bloody actions. Runa-Illa had been trained as a warrior even though her father did not wish it.

Her mother had died giving birth to Runa-Illa's baby brother. Lebuin felt an instant connection with that memory, as his own mother had died giving birth to his sister. Runa-Illa's baby brother had died a short time after her mother, due to complications. Runa-Emry always challenged Runa-Illa with complex moral questions, and often told her obedience was honor, but so was having inner strength to question, if possible. Runa-Illa had a unique combination of perfect pitch and balance, and an innate grace that allowed her to rise rapidly through the ranks.

Lebuin left Runa-Illa, following the link to the next person, who turned out to be the warrior Ticca and Ditani were fighting. This warrior was named Ossa-Ulla. He had been born in the great fortress of the Nhia-Samri, Hisuru Amajoo, to a general of Shar-Lumen's. Like Runa-Illa, Ossa-Ulla had a natural talent, grace, and speed. Ossa-Ulla had been singled out by Shar-Lumen and trained with the best warriors before being sent to Llino, nine cycles before, as his first external assignment. He had ambition, and his father expected great achievements from his son. Unfortunately, Ossa-Ulla would never fulfill his ambitions, as he was dying of a chest wound Ticca had just delivered. Still, Ossa-Ulla seemed proud that he was dying at Ticca's hand.

The next person in the chain was a long way away, and called General Eshra-Zunia. She was a mighty warrior, proud, intelligent, and sure of herself. Eshra-Zunia's pride was not without merit; she had worked hard and followed the Nhia-Samri code. She wasn't born a Nhia-Samri. In fact, she was adopted at the age of five by another Nhia-Samri warrior who found her while he was on a scouting mission. Her real name had been Bethia, and her family had lived near the deadly Circumveni Desert. Her tribe had been killed by some kind of wasting disease. The Nhia-Samri squad had come on her returning from a mission in the desert. The warrior had taken her with them to Hisuru Amajoo and made her his own. She was strong and learned quickly, adopting a new Nhia-Samri name in honor of her adopted family. She had risen through the ranks and was second in command of the main outpost in this region.

Leaving General Eshra-Zunia, Lebuin followed the link further. The next person in this chain of connected warriors was close to Eshra-Zunia, and a powerful man. Lebuin didn't know how, but he knew before his mind connected that the man he was about to touch was the warlord commander for all of the Nhia-Samri in the north-eastern realms of the continent. His name was Maru-Ashua, and he was a dangerous and powerful man.

Lebuin concentrated stopping the progression before he touched the warlord.

These two are Nhia-Samri warriors! They aren't Knives at all. Why did they capture Ticca?

The warlord in the distance drew his own odassi, plunging his mind into the link and tracing back towards Lebuin. Lebuin retreated from the warlord's determined advance.

I can't let him find us! We'll be dead in hours if he finds us. I have to break this link somehow.

Lebuin fled back to Ossa-Ulla's blades and searched frantically through the incantations in the blade for a key node. The warlord's mind started probing Ossa-Ulla's dying mind for details. Lebuin felt overwhelming joy when he found a critical node in Ossa-Ulla's interconnection incantations. Lebuin sent all the power he had left at it, trying to burn the node out and break the incantation. His power wasn't enough.

There was power available from the blade he held. He didn't bother to figure it out; it was available and he used it. Power flowed through him like the day he nearly died in the market from the assassination attempt there. This time, he let the power flow, not bothering to try to contain or filter it. He used his skills to direct it at the node in Ossa-Ulla's odassi.

The warlord's presence touched Runa-Illa's blade as the incantation's node flared under the assault, breaking the links that held the incantation. With a screech like someone being stabbed, the odassi blade's incantation unraveled.

Lebuin felt shock coming from the woman before him. He looked at her. The woman's face flushed as she cried out, "Forgive me, Lord! I am yours to command."

She fell to her knees before him hard enough he knew she had ruined the fine light-green leggings. He felt a moment of displeasure at the ruining of such a fine outfit for no good reason. The woman shuddered and he felt her fear at his displeasure through the odassi link connection that was blending with his own channels. She dropped her head and held her one remaining blade out to him.

He couldn't move, but the tendril from the odassi was blending with his own. He was connected to the woman, too. He could feel her mind and there was more. A different kind of connection he hadn't seen before. Curiously, he reached for it and pulled it to himself.

TICCA

Ticca stood transfixed, blood dripping from her dagger and hand. The warmth of the blood on her hands held her mind on the sudden happy look of Ossa-Ulla's face, at the strange revelation that also shocked him immobile, preventing him from blocking her attack. Her dagger had plunged into his chest, hitting a major artery. Blood had come out in a rush when she automatically twisted and pulled her dagger free, as she had been trained to do.

His face didn't even register the pain. He smiled as he collapsed, his blood pouring from the wound. I knew being a Dagger was going to mean some fighting. I can see why my father didn't want this life for me. I wonder how many people my uncle killed.

Ticca stared at Ossa-Ulla, lying on his side at her feet, as she smelled his blood mixed with the forest loam. He held his odassi blades so tightly, his hands were white. The copper bands at the base of his odassi blades blazed a brilliant gold, illuminating the pool of blood that touched her boots. The light reflecting off of the steam rising from the puddle mesmerized her. The life faded from his open eyes, and his smile faded, too. As his life expired, his muscles failed, and he rolled forward into the pool of his own blood.

The sight of the dead body, lying face down in front of her, brought to mind the image of the dead Knife who had attacked her the night everything went sideways.

I am a killer now. I can never turn that away. How many more will die by my hands?

Deep down, she only regretted that life had to be taken—not that she was the cause. She'd wanted to be a Dagger since before she could remember. Her uncle and trainer had made her into a dangerous weapon, armed or unarmed. The body at her feet was a testament to their training. Although only twenty, thanks to magic she didn't understand she had lived many years more and witnessed atrocities. Her mind was hardened like her knives, tempered and ready to protect the innocent. Her mind, heart, and soul burned with the Dagger ideals trained into her to stand against evil, regardless of the consequences.

Ditani stepped up next to her, his knives held ready, snapping her attention back to the present. Lifting her head, she saw Lebuin's fight was still not over, although she was unsure what to make of it. Five feet away, Lebuin stood at a defensive ready, holding his own knife in his left hand and Runa-Illa's odassi in his right. Runa-Illa knelt before him, head down in total supplication to Lebuin. Her body shuddered in fear. However, in contrast to her shivering body, Runa-Illa's right arm remained rock steady, level, and straight out toward Lebuin. Her other odassi lay flat on her palm between her and Lebuin at a forty-five-degree angle, so that its copper band and stamp were visible to him. The bands at the base of Runa-Illa's odassi blades glowed, as those on Ossa-Ulla's blades.

No one ever mentioned something like this was a possibility!

Together, she and Ditani waited for a resolution to the scene before them.

Lebuin didn't move, and the golden, glowing energies reminded Ticca of the energies he had let loose at the market the day after she had become a killer. Lebuin had killed his own would-be assassin, too. Her stomach quivered at the memory of the market attack where Lebuin's onslaught of raw power caused the attacking Knife's arm to explode, as the assassin was turned into a living torch. She recalled the smell of burnt flesh and the sounds of meat slapping the market tents as bits of the Knife's arm fell to yur.

Is he going to burn her down? She isn't fighting. She's Nhia-Samri, but I can't let him burn down someone who is surrendering.

The symbols on Runa-Illa's odassi shifted. *Is that possible? Or am I seeing things?* A sound like the wail of a mortally wounded woman started, softly at first, but grew louder. The sound came from her feet. Looking down, she saw that the two odassi blades held in Ossa-Ulla's hands had a series of glowing cracks running from the bands, down the length of the blades.

The sound is coming from the blades! Lords and Ladies, what is going on?

The wail reached an intensity that made Ticca and Ditani step back, as the copper bands on Ossa-Ulla's blades snapped with the ring of a bell, followed by the blades cracking down the length, with a sound like breaking glass.

When she looked up, the scene had not changed, except that the symbols on Runa-Illa's blades had stopped glowing. Lebuin looked around as if dazed or confused. Runa-Illa still knelt, trembling, holding her arm toward Lebuin. Ticca tightened her grip on her own knives and tensed, ready to leap to Lebuin's defense.

Lebuin looked down and appeared to realize where he was. He slowly straightened and sheathed his knife. Then he flipped the odassi so he was holding it by the blade, and held it out to Runa-Illa.

"Take this and remain there."

What is he doing?

She jumped forward over the body of Ossa-Ulla and started to move to defend Lebuin. But he held up a hand.

"Ticca, stop. She's no threat."

Stepping up to attack, she said, "Are you mad? She is a Nhia-Samri and she has orders to kill you."

Runa-Illa had taken the other odassi and held it out as the first, so that the two blades crossed. She remained on both knees, her head down.

Lebuin jumped between her and Runa-Illa and held his hands out. "Ticca! Stand down. She answers to me now."

That stopped her. *Answers to him? What happened?* Her feelings must have shown on her face.

Lebuin pointed at the fire. "Ticca, please let me sit down, warm up, and think this through. I need to process this. She won't move and you can keep your dagger out and guard her, if you want. But please, I ask you to not harm her without provocation."

He is the commander here, but I am not going to let my guard down.

She backed up to the fire and stood, facing Runa-Illa. Looking down, Ticca realized she still needed to cut the remains of the ropes from her feet and wrists.

Pointing at Ossa-Ulla's pack, she said, "Ditani, please

hand me some cloth from that pack to clean this blood off with."

Ditani wiped his blades clean on his pants and sheathed them while moving to examine the supply pack. He found a shirt and gave it to her, then sat down to go through the rest.

Lebuin walked over and dropped into a cross-legged, sitting position in front of the fire and stared into it. The light of the fire reflected off of his golden eyes.

Gold eyes? His eyes are green. I must be seeing things.

Ticca stopped and stared; Lebuin's eyes were golden. As she watched, they faded from gold, back to their normal dark green.

Must have something to do with doing magic. Might be a good way to tell if a wizard is doing something unseen.

Lebuin was far away and his eyes remained locked onto something deep within the fire.

Keeping an eye on Runa-Illa, Ticca cleaned the blood from her hands and knives, using the shirt, and then set to cutting the knots of rope from her wrists and ankles. No one said anything, and Runa-Illa didn't move. After almost a quarter of a mark, Lebuin looked around and saw Runa-Illa was still sitting in the supplication position.

"Illa, please sheath your odassi and sit at ease." Lebuin glanced at Ticca before adding, "Please move slowly until I can explain this."

Ticca watched as Runa-Illa slowly sheathed her odassi and then shifted to a more comfortable kneeling position, keeping her legs under her. Runa-Illa looked up, locking her eyes onto Ticca's. Runa-Illa had a peaceful look in her eyes and a smile that seemed genuine. Oddly, Ticca didn't feel threatened by Runa-Illa's gaze. Still, she stayed on guard.

Her trainer's voice came up out of her memory: *'Assassins can smile warmly while cutting your throat.'*

Ticca recalled how her trainer was always happy and smiling, even when hitting her sides so hard he bruised her ribs, when she made a stupid move sparring. She kept her attention on Runa-Illa and listened to the forest for anything out of place.

Ditani looked at the body. "Lebuin, we should move that, or at least do something with it."

Lebuin looked over and answered, "He got his honor back in the end. We should give him a proper burial. Then it would be wise to get out of here. There might be dangerous visitors soon."

This is too much. What is going on? I had everything set up to get all the answers we needed. Then these two blaze in, ruining that plan with their rescue attempt, and now Lebuin seems to have gone loopy. Looking over at Runa-Illa, she thought, *So has she, for that matter. What was all that stuff about asking Lebuin to forgive her and then dropping to her knees, swearing to be at Lebuin's command? I feel like this is some kind of bard's tale.* She couldn't help it. She smiled at the thought. *Maybe I'll live long enough to hear what the bards make with my name. They might even be able to explain this to me.*

"Lebuin, if it's all the same, I'd like to know what happened here. You are acting strange. How do we know you're not under some Nhia-Samri spell?"

"Formula or incantation."

"Huh?"

"They aren't spells; that is the common folk's superstitious name for magical work. In reality, they are carefully crafted scientific formulae, like an herbal treatment from an apothecary."

A giggle escaped before she even considered it, and Lebuin brows furrowed at her. She managed to speak through her giggling. "Okay, you're not under some incantation, and that was about the most normal you have been since you got here."

Lebuin focused on where they were. He stood and looked around. "We need to move to a better camp. But we should give him a proper burial." He stepped over to the pack and pulled a camper's shovel from it. "Ditani, can you help me please?" As he stood up and assembled the shovel, he looked at her. "Ticca, I would like to send Illa to get all their horses and supplies. Do you trust me?"

Ticca looked at him and then at Runa-Illa, who still sat there, watching them with that odd, peaceful look. *Well, if he isn't under a spell or incantation, or whatever, she seems to be under one. I think I should watch her.* "Yes. I trust you, but not her."

Lebuin thought about it and said, in Elvish, "As strange as it is, I know I can trust her with my life. Would you feel better if you went with her and watched?"

Grudgingly she nodded her agreement.

Still in Elvish, he added, "Please don't provoke her. We need to spend a lot of time going over what just happened. I need to explain some things, and then we need to come up with a new plan for all this. Everything has changed, Ticca. We are on a new path." He switched back to Imperial. "Illa, please go with Ticca to collect all of your gear and horses, and Ossa-Ulla's. Ticca is my general, so please obey her commands as if they came from me."

Runa-Illa stood without shifting her feet. It was an eerie thing, the way she rose without seeming to move her feet or legs. *That is an interesting way to sit, so you can stand without having to shift. I should figure out how she does that. It would be a useful position to know.* Illa looked at Ticca and bowed her head slightly.

Lebuin looked back at Ticca and pointed into the forest. "Ticca, our horses are just over a small ridge that way. I am sure you can find them. I think we need to use all of your skills to leave no trace, other than a grave."

She threw the last bit of rope she had been fingering into the fire. "Understood. We'll be back in about half a mark." Turning to Runa-Illa, she told her, "I still don't trust you, so no sudden moves. We'll collect your gear first, so lead on."

Runa-Illa led her down a game trail. As they walked, Ticca thought over what had happened. Looking back, she made sure they were well away from the men. "Runa-Illa, what was all that about? Why did you stop fighting and ask Lebuin for forgiveness?"

Runa-Illa looked back, still wearing the soft smile. Her voice sounded almost elven. She spoke in a melodic and precise way, allowing Ticca to hear every nuance of her meaning. "I didn't realize He was a God. When He broke me out of the Nhia-Samri clan, I realized who He was and that I have been waiting for Him my whole life. I felt in my soul the truth that He is my God. I only desire to serve Him now. Would you not ask forgiveness if you struck your God?"

"Wait a minute. Are you saying Lebuin, the journeyman mage of the Guild of Argos, is a God? More specifically *your* God? How can that be? He is just a mage, and a junior one, at that."

"Only a God could break the bindings of the Nhia-Samri. I didn't have to accept Him as my God. But my soul felt Him, and I knew I was destined to be His. I offered myself to Him, and He accepted. I cannot explain, but from that moment on, even now, I feel a great joy in His light as His servant. I know what I know—I am His supplicant, and I shall do whatever I can to insure His will is done. Gods need not explain their many guises. I know not why He chooses to be a journey mage, but it matters little. He has goals, and I shall do all I can to help Him succeed."

She either believes that or is a fabulous actress. I can hear her praising Lebuin at every mention of him.

They continued in silence, and Ticca mulled over Runa-Illa's statement. "How do you know he accepted you? He didn't say anything."

Runa-Illa stopped and turned to face Ticca. "May I draw my odassi to show you, General Ticca?"

So that is the game. Okay, well, let's see what her next move will be. Ticca slowly drew her dagger and short sword. "Okay, show me."

Runa-Illa shook her head. "You misunderstand." She

drew one odassi and held it so it stood straight up, the copper band facing Ticca. She pointed at the symbol on the band with her other hand. "Look here."

Ticca warily stepped closer, expecting to have to defend herself. But Runa-Illa stood still and relaxed, in a slightly off-balance stance, to put Ticca at ease. She looked at the symbol. It was a stylized dragon with a pentagram-shaped pommel dagger held in its right claw, and a ball of fire held in its left.

Ticca stepped back and Runa-Illa sheathed the odassi. "That is His symbol. Before He broke me from the clan, it was a head of a mountain cat with an open mouth, showing its teeth, surrounded by a blazing sun. He could have simply broken the bands as He did to Ossa-Ulla's odassi. Instead, He accepted me and bound me to His service. I would have served Him anyway, but this is proof of all I say."

"What exactly do these odassi do?"

Runa-Illa shrugged. "For the Nhia-Samri, they bind the individuals to the command. A warrior swears to obey and the officer accepts. From that point, the commander's or superior officer's commands cannot be disobeyed without loss of honor. One odassi is used to report on actions and can be reviewed by a superior officer. The other odassi uses the Nhia-Samri's power to provide improved speed and strength."

"So you can talk to your commanders through the swords?"

Runa-Illa pointed down the trail and they continued moving. "No, a Nhia-Samri warrior prays or confesses a report to the odassi and it is stored. All prayers or confessions are stored and can be reviewed by any superior."

"Which odassi was Lebuin holding?"

Runa-Illa looked back for a second. "He heard all my prayers and confessions. He learned all that I had reported my entire career, because He held the odassi of prayer. He forgave me, accepted my service, and made me His own. For this, my soul rejoices."

So that is what he is trying to process. He somehow tapped into the Nhia-Samri spells and broke the bindings. He heard all her reports and whatever else happened, she believes he is a God, and that she is in his service. It doesn't exactly explain the symbol, but he might have done it for show. Guess I can play along for now. But the moment she realizes she has been tricked, she'll attack. Best to let this whole thing lie for a bit.

Another question came to her as they walked on. "Why did Ossa-Ulla smile and speak of regaining his honor when I killed him?"

Runa-Illa stopped and looked at Ticca. "Nhia-Samri live and die for honor. In defeating Ossa-Ulla time and time again, you caused him the loss of much honor. He was demoted and was only sent here to get him out of the way. He laid the trap for you, and in defeating you, would have regained that which you had taken, and more. But when you joined the fight, it was obvious you were not really trapped, were you?"

The smirk she returned was justified. "No, I was going to let him capture me, because I figured that would loosen his tongue faster than torturing him. And you were a surprise, so I wanted to assess you. Of course, his stabbing me was also a surprise. I suspected he was going to try to use me as bait to get everyone. I admit, I was more than worried, as I passed out, that he might not be interested in getting all of us."

Runa-Illa nodded. "And in so doing, you proved he was even more a fool, taking what little honor he had left by your actions. By Nhia-Samri standards, he was a weak fool because he did not kill you the moment he had a chance, as they are taught to do. However, when you revealed that you were Gods, that changed everything. No mortal can expect to truly defeat a God; it is not an even match. However, it is the highest honor achievable to continue to do your duty against a stronger adversary, even when you know you cannot win. By revealing you were Gods, you showed that Ossa-Ulla really had no chance at success, yet he had continued to try to follow his original orders, despite being defeated. Therefore, he was vindicated and died with the highest honor anyone can hope to achieve in a lifetime of service."

They resumed the journey to collect the gear and horses, and Ticca thought that over. *So, the Nhia-Samri only live for one virtue—honor. Their code of conduct must be difficult to deal with. It would justify many actions through the virtue of following commands. They are not expected to question the motives or correctness of actions. They have only to follow, and when raised in rank, echo the orders of their superiors, which explains a great deal of the oddness of their shift to assassinations and the extermination of the orcs.*

As she walked, she compared what her training was like to what Runa-Illa had revealed of the Nhia-Samri. *Daggers are trained to have a strong code of honor. We are also trained to have courage and commitment to the moral ideals; we have to have the courage to do what's right, regardless of orders or laws. Shar-Lumen started the Nhia-Samri to do great things, and succeeded. But then he didn't have the courage or commitment to hold to his morals when Kliasa was killed by an orc tribe. So now, the Nhia-Samri have been keeping their honor, but doing horrible things at the command of their Grand Warlord. Could we somehow add the Dagger morals into the honor structure of the Nhia-Samri? If not, there will be little choice and the realms might have to face them head-on to destroy them.*

They moved through the forest like a pair of ghosts, leaving no sign of their passage. They didn't talk again, as each dealt with her own thoughts. It took slightly more than a full mark to bring the gear and horses back to the grove, as the horses were further away than she had thought. Runa-Illa was efficient.

By the time they got back to the ambush site, a grave had been made for the body of Ossa-Ulla, and Lebuin was placing stones that were picked for matching size and color, from a small pile, and laying them into a pattern on top of the grave. Runa-Illa moved beside him, knelt, and started handing him stones from the pile. When they were done, Ticca recognized the cat head surrounded by a sun symbol, as the one which had been on Ossa-Ulla's odassi blades.

Standing over the grave, they were all silent. Feeling like she should do something, she silently prayed, *Lady, please take him up to whatever God claims him. He was dangerous, and yet, I think worthy of praise. He was a product of his training, which was incomplete intentionally.* Her heart told her she had done right, and looking at her hands, she was pleased to see they were not shaking, as before. Her uncle's voice came from her memory. *'Some people spend an entire lifetime wondering if they made a difference in the world, but Daggers don't have that problem.'*

Lebuin took the reins of his horse, Runa-Illa's, and Ossa-Ulla's, and started off into the forest as if he knew where he was going. Ditani took the reins of the remaining horses and followed without a comment. Runa-Illa looked at her, and then together, they started erasing the trail as the men moved ahead.

Lebuin and Runa-Illa appeared nervous, as if pursuit was a real and dangerous possibility. Ticca and Ditani keyed in on this and they spent a night and day in tense, nonstop travel. No one spoke the entire time, except in quick, hushed conversations. Ticca took the rear of the party on foot and removed every sign of their passage. Runa-Illa walked in front of Lebuin, picking the path which would leave as little mark as possible under Lebuin's silent hand signals.

As they travelled, Ticca watched Runa-Illa for any sign of deception, but she never misstepped, and was as efficient and skilled as Ticca at removing all trace of their passage. Lebuin led them over a shallow river and along a rocky path, to a cave that had a defensible entrance, and which was well concealed so as to hide a fire within.

Lebuin looked around and relaxed. Ticca looked over the area. "How did you know about this?"

"Illa and Ossa-Ulla found it while exploring in preparation for your arrival."

"Why do you keep calling her Illa, and not by her first name, Runa?"

"Because the Nhia-Samri clans place clan name first, so her clan name is Runa and her name is Illa. Normally, they are very formal. I was never one for formality, so I am hoping she doesn't mind."

Glancing at Illa, Ticca saw that she was glowing with pride. *Being on a first-name basis with your God must feel pretty good. She is in for a hell of a crash when she finds out Lebuin isn't a God.*

"I am sure our trail is untraceable. Are we safe from whatever you have been afraid of for the last couple of days?"

Lebuin went distant, and he looked around the area. *His eyes are gold again! He is using magic. I wonder why this wasn't mentioned in my training. This is a great way to know if a wizard is doing something magical.* His eyes returned to green and refocused on her. "We are as safe as in any other place. I don't think we can be located by anyone unless they can follow our trail."

Ticca shook her head. "Not possible. I wouldn't ever be able to trace where we went, unless I had our scents and a good bloodhound. If someone brought some of our clothes from Llino, and dogs, we could be found. Of course, we'd hear them coming."

Lebuin and Ditani looked at each other and Ditani dipped his head. Lebuin smiled. "Well, we can stay here for a while and sort some of this stuff out."

Her shoulder muscles started to relax. "Okay. We'll stay on guard, but it's time to make camp. I'll gather wood and set some alarm traps. The rest of you can get the fire going. I can really use a cup of arit before you start explaining all this, please. We all need a good rest, too."

"Sounds good, Ticca, and you're right, of course. Ditani and I will ready the camp." Lebuin looked at Illa and smiled. "Illa, please help set some alarms and show them to Ticca. You can also help her gather some firewood."

Why the hell is he forcing me to spend time with her? He's bouncing back and forth between acting like himself and some authority figure. It is disconcerting. Guess I'm still in that bard's tale, and somehow, I think it's going to get worse from here.

Ticca shrugged and headed back out, not bothering to see if Illa was following. Illa caught up and then took the lead setting a number of excellent alarms as Ticca watched for any mistake. Deciding it was best not to criticize as Illa's work was already excellent, Ticca silently worked with her, setting the alarm traps. When they got back to the cave, the men had cleaned it out, built a small fire from the wood already there, and even had the bed rolls out. In all, it was an easy camp to set.

Ditani had taken up the chore of cooking. Lebuin sat down by his gear and stripped off his shirt. His shoulder was bound in bloody cloth, which he removed and tried to inspect the shoulder wound. *We should have dressed that better before we made this trek! Ditani must have bound it while we were getting the horses, and then he changed shirts to hide it. I'm going to have some choice words with him later over this stupidity!*

Illa frowned too, and stepped over to Lebuin with a look of concern.

"My Lord, you should have healed that before we travelled."

Huh. Smart girl. I'm actually starting to like her. I hope I don't have to kill her.

Lebuin smiled up at her. "You may dress it. I think I ducked under the worst of it."

She didn't ask. Why is he letting her do this? Ticca put her hand on her dagger hilt and watched as Illa took some medical supplies from her pouch and cleaned the cut. She frowned as she inspected the wound. "My Lord, it is not bleeding much, but it is through the skin. May I use a tincture on it?"

"Yes, that would be very handy and stop the infernal itching."

Illa pulled a vial out. She looked at Ticca and held it out to her. "Would you care to inspect it first, General Ticca?"

Runa-Illa's eyes held no hint of insult or deception; still, Ticca nodded and took it. After sniffing it from a distance, she detected the familiar smell of a temple healing ointment which sped healing to an incredible rate. She opened it and found that it wasn't an ointment, but a liquid. Still, it smelled familiar, so she handed it back.

Illa took a cloth and poured a few drops into the wound. She then pinched the wound closed using the cloth. After a moment, she took the cloth away and poured a few more drops on the mostly closed wound. Again, she pinched it closed using the cloth, closed the vial, and put it away. She then used some water from a canteen to wash the blood away from the healed wound. Only a red line remained.

Runa-Illa's reaction to the condition of Lebuin's wound told volumes. Her fingers touched her lips as she gasped. Illa's cheeks glowed as she smiled, which Lebuin couldn't see.

Ticca registered it all. *She really does believe everything she has said. To her, Lebuin is a God.*

Runa-Illa resealed the vial. "My Lord, it worked better than it should have. There will be no scar."

"Excellent. And thank you. Now, would you please take that bedding there so Ticca can relax while we try and sort all this out?" Illa stepped over to the bedding, and then folded her legs under her in that unusual sitting position.

Ditani turned around and handed out some roasted rabbit and a handful of roasted roots. Ticca took her share and then chose the bed between Lebuin and Runa-Illa as, she was sure, Lebuin had meant. Taking her dagger out, she placed it close to her hand, but away from Runa-Illa. Runa-Illa seemed to take no mind of this, and ate the food given to her. She tried to copy Runa-Illa's leg trick, unsuccessfully. Glancing over, she saw Runa-Illa was not looking at her, but was wearing a smirk. *You better not laugh!*

Lebuin stood and dug into the horses' packs, finding a

clean shirt and putting it on. Then he sat down by the fire and enjoyed the warmth while he ate. He looked up. "So, now it is time to go over everything. I have more than you might think to explain. Please forgive any rambling. Okay?" He looked at all three of them.

Ditani nodded. Illa smiled at Lebuin with that look of longing. Ticca's gut tightened and she felt her pulse quicken. *Crud, she is like a school girl in love with her teacher.*

Ticca nodded. "Of course, I might interrupt with a question or ten."

Lebuin laughed. "You wouldn't be you, if you didn't."

Lebuin shifted a little, and with a glance at Runa-Illa, turned his attention to Ticca, his eyes flashing in the firelight. "Since Illa doesn't know our side, I'll start from the beginning." In a short time, Lebuin summed up his twenty years of self-indulgent life in the Guild, followed by their adventures from the time he saw Ticca kill the assassin in the alley, through escaping Llino, being pursued by assassins.

Lebuin continued, adding more details she hadn't heard before.

"I had an enemy of sorts at the Guild called Magus Cune. He ruined many of my projects and plans. Magus Cune must have spent a great deal of time trying to get me to fail in my lessons. I believe this was because I killed his younger brother, or son, or relative, in a childhood accident in which I used a great deal of magic in a fit of childish rage in the Guild playground."

"Lebuin, how did you come to this belief?"

"I didn't know this until I was almost killed, Ticca. I had a rather unusual experience, in that I left my body and entered into the ethereal realm. There, I had unbelievable recall of every event in my life, going back to the beginning. I relived the forgotten incident, except that now I am older and could interpret what happened. I know that I likely killed a boy that looked like Magus Cune, and that Magus Cune had lifted his lifeless body, crying out for help, as I was spirited away by the other senior mages."

"I've heard of near-death experiences, but can they be trusted?"

Lebuin laughed. "You have spent more time with Kliasa than I, Ticca. Kliasa is holding on between, and when I visited and was trained by her there, I learned that my first experience was true and could be believed."

Runa-Illa let out a gasp. She stared at Lebuin and blurted out, "Kliasa? The Kliasa of legend? She still lives? How can this be? She was killed long ago by the orcs! It is her death's blood revenge that drives Shar-Lumen, the Nhia-Samri's Grand Warlord, even today."

Lebuin looked at Illa with sadness. "Yes, Ticca and I were both trained by *the* Kliasa. She is dead, but her spirit lingers, waiting for her love. She has gained some powers which she has used to help us."

Runa-Illa bowed her head. "Shar-Lumen does not know this. This is all so tragically romantic—in death, she awaits her love, and in life, her love seeks revenge for her death."

Ticca's thoughts spun around her own interactions with Kliasa's spirit—all the lessons she had learned and all of Kliasa's secrets.

Kliasa has spoken a little of this, and she has told me many times she is between. But she won't go into details about it beyond vague references. I suppose, with a mage's training of the mind, one could walk through memories pretty easily in that place.

Ticca thought out loud as the facts fell into a new pattern. "Cune was out to get you. You told us this before. Also, that he placed a bet with an unsavory sort that you would survive your experiences as a journeyman. This, of course, meant that he had really hired assassins through a middle man to get you."

Lebuin nodded and Runa-Illa frowned.

This is new to her. This is going to be interesting for her, too, I guess. We are finally going to see this from the other side and she will, too.

Lebuin continued, "I had to leave on a quest and decided to hire a Dagger for protection when Ditani joined me. Ditani, as Magus Vestul's longtime servant, was to help Vestul turn over something to Duke. But before that exchange, Magus Vestul was assassinated, and his pouch, boots, and other items were taken by the Knife."

"Ditani, not being able to find Magus Vestul, came to the Guild for help, except everyone he knew he could trust was dead. Not knowing what else to do, he asked me for help."

Lebuin turned to Ditani, who had been leaning against the cave wall, listening to everything. Looking at Ditani across the fire, Ticca was surprised to see his eyes caught the firelight like a nocturnal hunter, reflecting the light back. But when Ditani looked at Lebuin, his eyes were their normal golden brown.

Dang, his eyes are odd sometimes. I know you're more than you pretend to be. Now, Lebuin's eyes are doing that light-reflecting trick sometimes. Maybe it's another sign of a Magus.

"Ditani, I meant to ask you, why did you decide to ask me for help? There were dozens of senior Magi around, and I had just become a Journeyman."

Ditani looked surprised. "Milord, I told you when we first talked in your room. I didn't know who to trust. The other Magi I knew had faith that you were going to be a great Magus someday. Finding all of the Magi I knew I could trust dead or missing was a shock. I could only turn to the head of the Guild, or perhaps to the one man all of them had said was trustworthy, which was you."

Lebuin frowned. "Why not trust Councilor Nillo?"

Ditani shook his head. "I was reacting to what I found myself in. I cannot answer that clearly."

That is a strange answer. She looked at Ditani hard and he knew it, because he shifted, as if uncomfortable at the inspection. *He isn't telling us something. I know it. But should*

I mention that now? Looking at Lebuin, she saw he had read her body language, and she knew he wanted her to drop it. *We really have become a solid team in this short time, that's for sure. Okay, if you want me to leave it alone for now, I will.*

Lebuin acknowledged her thoughts with a twist of his head and went on.

"Things get interesting at this point. Because you," nodding at Illa, "are going to be surprised by this next bit, and you two," looking at Ditani and Ticca, "will be surprised by the knowledge I gained from Illa's odassi." Everyone was leaning in towards Lebuin.

Lebuin yawned, then grabbed some leftover meat from the meal and picked at it as he continued, trying to stay awake. "We already know that the Knife who killed Magus Vestul tried to capture Ticca. Ticca killed him, and thinking that it was impossible to get his things to anyone who deserved or could claim them, took the fine boots and pouch he had."

Illa's gaze snapped from Lebuin to Ticca. She didn't blink as her brows creased.

That is news for you. Well, think about it. I killed a professional Knife who had killed a great Magus. That should make you worry about attacking me.

"Ticca, not knowing about Vestul, found that the boots and pouch suited her and wore them out on her day of relaxation in the market."

Lebuin paused and pointed at Ticca. "And there is where the first assassination attempt happened. We thought that was against me. But really, what happened was I got in the way. I killed that assassin, but was nearly mortally wounded in the process."

Ticca pushed back her hair so she could see Lebuin better. "Wait, you said you got in the way. Wasn't that attack on you?"

Lebuin shook his head. "I wasn't the target of that assassination attempt. In fact, you, Ticca, were the intended target."

Wait, what? I was the target? She looked at Lebuin in disbelief. Lebuin was smiling that sideways smile he used when he had the better of her.

"Even more interesting is that when I was healed in the temple, those watchers were not looking for me. They were looking for you. The second assassin you killed in the small hospice wasn't after me. He was after you, all along."

Ditani leaned in. "You're saying these attacks were really the Nhia-Samri continuing to try and get what Magus Vestul was bringing to Llino?"

Lebuin looked around at all of them. "Yes, the Nhia-Samri had orders to intercept Magus Vestul before he met with Duke and steal his pouch, which was guaranteed to have his secret research. They were to deliver the pouch unopened back to their Grand Warlord as soon as possible, and above all, to not engage Duke or Magus Vestul. Their presence in Llino was to remain a secret at all costs."

Ticca's mind rearranged all the events, before and after meeting Lebuin, in a new order. Facts that previously didn't fit well fell into place. "So they were after me because I was wearing Magus Vestul's pouch?"

"Exactly. And because of you, they were exposed to Duke. Ossa-Ulla was sure that Duke had destroyed their entire regiment stationed in Llino, as well as their outpost. Ossa-Ulla took it personally that you hired me to protect you, and that you pretended to be a new Dagger with only a trivial amount of experience to entrap him. He was also sure that I was some kind of Guild special operative, pretending to be a ninny, whom you hired cycles before Magus Vestul arrived to help protect him. Further, they think Magus Vestul is still alive and you were drawing them out by wearing his pouch."

That is why he was so pissed off at me at the gate. He thought I had laid a trap for him and cornered him into exposing their operations.

"So you were never a target. But if all those people were out to kill me, where were the Knives that were supposed to be after you?"

Not waiting for an answer, Ticca's mind quickly made another association. *Oh, my Lord, I am the one being hunted by the Nhia-Samri, not Lebuin. That is why he knew Runa-I!la wasn't going to kill him.*

Glaring at Lebuin, she felt her face burning. "Wait a minute!" Her heart rate picked up, and clenching her fists, she pointed at Lebuin. "You knew they were hunting me, and sent me out on a horse-gathering walk with a Nhia-Samri without a warning!" She was already on her feet, but she didn't remember getting up. Her knives were in her hands.

Lebuin didn't react, but Runa-Illa had grabbed her odassi, although she was still sitting and hadn't drawn them yet. She looked concerned and uncertain about what to do.

Lebuin held up his hand. "Ticca, slow down. Take some breaths. Illa is mine, one hundred percent. I know I can trust her as much as I trust you or Ditani. Even if I sent her away, she would never betray me or curse me. I also know she is no threat to you. Please, I'm not done yet."

She forced herself to relax. "You better have a good ending to this, or I am going to walk out of here and leave you, coin or not." She put her knives back and sat down hard.

Lady, I thought I could trust him. That was a stupid thing for him to test on me.

Lebuin had the decency to look concerned, and he continued in a subdued tone. "Ticca, really, I know what I know, and I trust it as much as we all trust Kliasa. You can probably ask her tonight, if you want. Yes, the Nhia-Samri are after that pouch and the notes it contains, and are under orders to kill everyone involved with it. My involvement is because of where I chose to stand."

Oh, my Lady! I know Kliasa hasn't told him of her secret, so he cannot be using that phrase on me on purpose. A tear rolled down her cheek at the memory it brought back. '*An entire race died because of where I chose to sit.*' *He is here by chance or by an act of the Gods. In fact, I know the Gods are mixed up in this. We are meant to be here, now and together. Uncle, you always said being a Dagger was sometimes harder than anyone could imagine, and now I know you were not just talking about fighting. Something important is happening and we are here now. There is a right and a wrong here, and we must find the right.*

Taking a firm grip on her emotions, Ticca softened her voice. "Sorry for yelling. You're right. I trust you, and so that means I have to believe you are doing what you think is right for all of us. You say she isn't a Nhia-Samri anymore."

Runa-Illa had relaxed again. *She was going to protect Lebuin from me. This might break out into a fight with Illa. But this has to get resolved now, instead of at a critical moment in the future.*

Keeping an eye on Illa and her hands loose and ready near her weapons, Ticca plunged into the question that had to be asked. "Did you know she thinks you are her God?"

Runa-Illa ignored Ticca's stance to look back to Lebuin with that puppy-dog look.

Lebuin sighed. "Yes. You think I broke the Nhia-Samri incantations and fooled her. I didn't do anything but grab her odassi with the intent to use it against her. I can't explain everything that happened. I learned a lot of Illa's life and reports. I also felt Illa giving herself to me and begging me for forgiveness and acceptance. I felt Ossa-Ulla's joy at discovering he never had a chance, and I understood what that meant. I saw his commander, General Eshra-Zunia, and the warlord she answered to, named Maru-Ashua. The warlord tried to locate us and discover what was happening. I destroyed the links. But something more happened. Once safe, I could see Illa's soul with nothing held back. She offered herself freely and fully, and I knew this to be good and accepted it. As to the symbol change on the odassi, I have no explanation for that."

"It is your symbol emblazed in your being, my Lord. In accepting me, your essence tied me to you, with or without the odassi. But you know their usefulness, and allowed them to serve you, too," Runa-Illa said, surprising everyone.

Lebuin looked into Runa-Illa's eyes and then nodded. "Yes, I felt that too. But I don't understand it. I am not a God."

Runa-Illa shook her head and said, "Yes you are, my Lord."

Ditani surprised everyone by saying, "She is right. You probably shouldn't deny it any longer. It will eventually be discovered, but it shouldn't be kept a secret from you anymore. For now, it shouldn't be shared beyond us, however."

They all stared at Ditani, and he sighed and looked at Lebuin. "Your mother was the daughter of Argos and Lothia. You were born because your mother invested all her vast power in conceiving you, nurturing you, and giving birth to you. Lebuin, you were a demi-god, conceived in love and raised with Argos and Lothia watching over you."

Ditani took Illa's hand. "In accepting Illa here, you have accidentally stepped over the line between demi-god and God. You have allowed channels to be created within your being which now draw energies from followers. Your powers can be immense, but you must be careful, because there are many issues with this path. Unfortunately, it is not something that can be reversed. The door is open, the channels have already filled, and you are what you are—a God."

Ticca had had enough. "You have been acting a little off since the day I met you. This proves you are not what you pretend to be. Who are you really, Ditani? And don't tell me you're just some servant!"

"I am Lebuin's uncle."

Lebuin's mouth dropped open, and Runa-Illa was also stunned.

Ticca, caught off-guard, blurted out, "Wait, if you're Lebuin's uncle, then you are the son of Argos. That makes you a God yourself!"

Ditani shook his head. "No, I am a strong mortal. I have no powers. In the vernacular of the temples, I am a hero. I do not have control of magic, nor could I become a God, even if I wished it."

This explains everything! Ditani wasn't a servant. He was a friend of Magus Vestul, probably trying to help with whatever is going on. He knew who Lebuin was, and was devoted to Lebuin because of the relationship. Ditani pulled Lebuin into this because he didn't realize how dangerous this situation was going to be. He probably thought he was going to help out his nephew as he entered the world. Then things went out of control. Ossa-Ulla was right—he was fighting Gods and heroes.

Oh, my Lord, I am working for YOUR grandson! You better be watching!

As her thoughts raced, she couldn't help feeling smug about the situation.

Uncle, you'll definitely not believe this.

The Three Regents

CHAPTER 2
SECRECY HAS ITS PRICE

DOHMA

Circling cautiously, Dohma kept his weight distributed 80/20. Cundia was at the edge of his peripheral vision. *I can't lose sight of Cundia. I have to be there to support her when she moves,* he reminded himself. The moment came; Cundia feinted, and seizing the opportunity she provided him, he lunged in. Orahda barely moved, but it was enough to dodge his attack. A foot came from nowhere and slammed him so hard in the waist that he was spun and put off-balance.

Cundia tried to help him, but in attempting to give him cover, she exposed herself, and Orahda showed little mercy. He hit her so hard with his short sword that she yelped in pain and fell to the ground, cursing. Realizing he was in trouble and couldn't help Cundia, he dove sideways to get out of the weapons master's range. Orahda shuffle-stepped after him so rapidly, a dust cloud was formed. Realizing too late he had placed himself in an indefensible stance, he grimaced, knowing a painful reminder was coming. The weapons master touched his shoulder, and the force was like being hit by a wild horse cart. He landed, rolling in the dirt. *Urdu, we got too eager. Patience, patience, patience—have to fight the adrenaline in a fight always!*

Applause came from a few observers as a shadow blocked the sun from Dohma's view. Wiping his eyes to clear them, he saw the smiling face of the weapons master standing over him with his hand out to help him up. "You're dead, milord." Looking over at Cundia, he added, "You, too. That was foolish, to try to cover for Dohma. At least, Dohma had the sense to try to get away."

Cundia stood up, holding her side. She laughed, waving her hand at Orahda. "It is a professional hazard, trying to protect folks." Pressing her side, she winced. "I think you bruised a couple of ribs."

"If I hadn't turned my blade on the side, I would have cut *through* those ribs. You can dwell on that while you rest. I think you might even realize how you could have succeeded without exposing yourself so badly."

She nodded. "Well, we normally don't have to fight people half as fast as you, for one. But I'll think about it, because I know you aren't going to tell me until I, at least, make a real effort to figure it out for myself."

Taking the offered help, he stood. Various muscles complained and a few joints in his left leg joined in the chorus as he put weight on them. *I am going to be sore for a few days, unless I can find some time to get to the steam rooms.* Rubbing a couple of sore spots, he looked at Cundia and indicated Orahda with his head. "Sometimes I think Orahda enjoys inflicting pain."

"I have found it to be an inspirational teacher. At least, you are not letting yourself become pudgy."

Dohma laughed and slapped the weapons master on the back. "If I did, you'd come down to the throne room and drag me up here for practice."

Laughing together, the three of them cleaned their practice gear. Cundia and Dohma took off the light leather practice armor, handing it to one of the pages. Orahda still refused to use any armor. Dohma shook his head. "Exactly when will you decide to wear armor?"

Orahda was dressed in his typical brown semi-loose leather pants and sleeveless, leather fighting vest with a high, closed collar. His pitch-black hair was kept Karakian style, tightly braided with red and green beads tied to fall, half forward and half backward, over his left shoulder. Not for the first time, Dohma wondered how old Orahda really was. *He has been teaching since I was a small boy. He took me in and mentored me to the captaincy of the guard. Yet, he never seems to age or tire. I have seen him fight all day without getting winded or even sweating more than a little.* Orahda's exposed arms had dozens of crisscrossed scars on the hairy, darkly-tanned skin which moved over bunching muscles. Even training experienced Daggers two, or even three, at a time, he still refused to wear any type of armor or helmet.

Orahda considered the question. "Since taking over the country, your progress has slowed. With the other distractions coming, your progress will slow even further. Perhaps when your son is about ten, I might need some practice armor."

Dohma looked at his friend in shock. "I don't have a son."

"I suspect you'll have one in about two years."

Cundia punched him in the arm. "So you have already started keeping state secrets from your commanders. Very good. You'll make a fine politician."

Confused, Dohma looked between the two of them. Cundia lost control first and started laughing so hard, she had to grab her side and sit down. Orahda also joined her laughter. "My Lord, you look as if the ghosts of all your ancestors just drank to your favor."

He felt the blood rushing to his face and knew he was as red as the evening sky. Pointing at Orahda, he said, "You have a twisted sense of humor." Then, pointing to Cundia, "And you, too." This caused the two of them to laugh even harder, as did a number of other Daggers and guards near enough to hear the exchange.

Orahda drop his hand onto Dohma's shoulder squeezing to enough make his point. "My Lord, Duke has ordered you to, as he says, 'get to work,' and make a family. Our nation cannot be stable until we are assured of our ruling line. I know a number of nobles are already making enormous expenditures to ready their daughters for your inauguration. It is, therefore, safe to assume you'll have something to show for your labor in a couple of years."

Dohma sat down. "Even in debates, you are a dangerous opponent. Seriously, though, now that you know I am a regent, I could insist you take precautions from accidents."

"You could do so. However, before I complied, one of you would have to be a real threat."

Cundia laughed. "That is the oddest thing to say when you have been fighting a dozen or so very experienced Daggers."

Orahda turned his glare on her. "Just because someone has had experiences, doesn't mean they have learned anything." He poked her in her ribs to punctuate the point.

She yelped. "Point, point. You win already. We can't beat you."

Orahda's expression went serious. "So you'll take second willingly?"

Cundia moved like lightning, standing and coming nose to nose with Orahda. Fire in her eyes, her voice was hard with resolve and passion. "I'll get you yet."

Orahda nodded. "Much better; that is a Dagger talking now." He turned and walked off, entering his small office.

Cundia turned, her eyes burning bright. "That is likely the best weapons master in the world, milord."

"How it is we have him, I do not know. But I do thank all the Gods for him. He has been an amazing influence on the guards. I think it would have been far worse when Duke found out the truth here, if it were not for the values he instills in the guards under his training."

Someone called out, interrupting whatever Cundia was going to say. "Commander Cundia." Turning with Cundia to see who was calling, he saw that Egal and Apanal, the Dagger commanders of Delta Squad, dressed in their loose, cream, cotton leggings with red vests and red turbans, were walking briskly towards them. "Commander Cundia, Lord Dohma, we have been seeking you both. A ship arrived a short time ago. It flies flag of Alliance of Realms and carries only woman dignitary. She claims to be an envoy of Alliance secretary general in Gracia, bearing urgent message for new regents."

"Gracia? How could the Alliance secretary learn of events here so fast? It has only been five weeks."

Cundia, Apanal, and Egal looked at him without

comment. Shrugging, he started to grab his robes from the bench. "Well, this will make it an interesting day, for sure."

The weapons master came out of his office and was stepping over to another group of Daggers when he saw Egal and Apanal. A curious look came over Orahda's face, and he had started to turn away when Egal spotted him. Egal's eyes turned into saucers, and two odassi appeared in his hands from the air. Egal backpedaled away, bringing the odassi up to guard.

As fast as Egal reacted, Orahda reacted faster. Before Egal had moved a step, Orahda had already launched what he was carrying at Egal. Egal's reflexes were incredible, almost matching Orahda's. His first odassi managed to deflect the heavy, spinning, wood writing board Orahda had been holding. However, the second odassi couldn't stop the large quill pen the weapons master always used, which flew like an arrow into Egal's neck. Egal had been about to say something, but it came out as a gurgled cry, instead.

Apanal spun and also pulled a pair of odassi from the air. Apanal's reaction was even more surprising. He lost his senses. His pupils became large, inky pools, which doubled the size of his eyes. His grip on the odassi was so tight, his knuckles went white. Apanal tried to say something, but all that came out was a garbled shout. "AAMM HORRORA URUA AJOO!"

Egal pulled the pen from his throat. His mouth moved as if trying to say something, but he only produced a whistle as he collapsed to his knees, dropping one of the odassi. His eyes, locked onto Orahda, burned, and he tried to seal the hole in his neck with his hand. Pressing his hand over the hole, he tried again to speak, but blood and air bubbled out between his fingers, and blood poured from his mouth. Still, his eyes remained locked on Orahda. As he fell to the side, he threw his remaining odassi at Orahda with more force than seemed possible. Orahda deflected the missile by knocking it out of the way, like an annoying insect, while dodging enough to be untouched.

Orahda grabbed some knives from the bench near him, throwing the first at Apanal with deadly speed. Apanal tried to block and dodge, but could only manage to get partially out of the line of the first knife. The knife sank deep into Apanal's shoulder, causing him to scream in pain. That shocked Apanal back to his senses. His eyes cleared and he took control of himself. Apanal blocked a second thrown knife, which moved faster than an arrow, with his other blade, and was screaming, "AMI..." when a third knife sank into his throat, cutting off his cry.

The weapons master walked toward him with a handful of knives; with each step, he threw another knife. Apanal stumbled back, moving fast to dodge and parry the thrown knives. Orahda's knives flew like arrows from a longbow. Apanal twisted, causing the next knife to dig deep into his other shoulder. Still, he resisted, holding onto his odassi. Despite his wounds, his blade caught the edge of the next knife, deflecting it, causing it to strike his stomach. With that, he fell to his knees, and the next knife found its mark into the heart. Apanal slumped down into a sitting position, his head falling forward and his arms dropping by his sides, never letting go of his odassi. Apanal didn't fall.

He looks like he is pinned there with all those knife hilts sticking out of him.

Egal was lying still, but his lips were still moving, desperately trying to say what he had failed to say, as if his soul depended on it. Egal's eyes remained locked on Orahda with an intensity hard to imagine. Orahda stepped up to him and bent down, whispering something in his ear, before stabbing him in the heart. Egal smiled as he died, blood pouring from the holes in his neck and chest, as well as from his mouth.

What in the eight kingdoms just happened? Orahda has never wounded anyone beyond a bruise. I knew he was a hardened warrior, but I never imagined he was capable of such actions. Dohma looked at the dead men. Like everyone else, he stood there in shock at the rapid murder of two of the command

Daggers. His palms felt sweaty and cold, taking in the scene. Orahda picked up his writing board and retrieved his writing pen from Egal's dead fingers. Orahda cleaned his pen, using one of the many rags normally used to wipe sweat away.

Cundia recovered her composure. Stepping up, she crouched in front of the slumped form of Apanal and yanked the knife out of his heart; the movement caused the body to fall over. She stood and kicked the odassi out of his dead grip with her toes. "Crud, we were using them to feed bad intel to Hisuru Amajoo."

She isn't surprised? Were there really Nhia-Samri agents in the Dagger squads? "Um, Orahda, why did you kill them? Were they about to attempt to kill me?" *Please say yes, because that would, at least, make some sense and let me exonerate you for killing military officers.* The realization of how deadly Orahda was came as his mind grasped that Orahda had just single-handedly taken down what had to be two excellent Nhia-Samri with a clipboard, quill pen and a handful of small practice knives.

Orahda shook his head 'no'. "Lord, we cannot discuss this here. Do you intend to arrest me for this crime?" Orahda's voice was as calm and steady as if this was just a fighting demonstration.

Cundia looked at him, and the other five Daggers stepped up closer, looking a little worried, but determined, with their hands on their knife hilts. *They are worried about what Orahda might do. Honestly, so am I.*

The officer training, ironically provided to him by Orahda, kicked in and he swept his mind clear of the emotional thoughts. "I can't let two murders go unpunished without reasonable cause." Looking around, he saw that only he, Cundia, five Daggers, four guards, and Orahda were present. "Why can't we talk here? Are any of these others a threat or untrustworthy?"

The Daggers and guards looked annoyed at even the suggestion. But then, they had to admit that two officers had been exposed as Nhia-Samri agents. Orahda looked around and smiled. "All present are very trustworthy. My Lord, I will not resist arrest. However, I ask that it be confinement in my quarters here. I also request we discuss this in a secure location due to possible magical scrying."

Looking around, he had to admit, they were in the open with two dead Nhia-Samri agents. Then his mind gave him an answer he felt good about. "Orahda, we are at war with the Nhia-Samri, and disposing of two of their agents is justified, especially, considering their placement as senior command officers. I will consult with my fellow regents, recommending this be considered war-time action against enemies of the kingdom. I do, however, order you to remain here in your training areas, quarters, and offices until we rule on this."

"As you command. I reaffirm my loyalty and oath to the Kingdom of Aelargo. I shall obey."

A female Dagger ribbed one of her fellows. "Urd, I thought we were going to get out of that minor beating…ah, I meant training." The other Daggers chuckled, as did Dohma, as the tension washed away.

Cundia stepped in. "Lord Dohma, I recommend we dispose of these bodies via the palace smithy furnace."

Orahda pointed. "Don't touch those odassi blades. I will dispose of them."

Dohma nodded. "Agreed. Everyone, you are sworn to secrecy about this incident. Orahda, I will want that talk later. However, I must first attend to the kingdom business waiting in the docks, which I assume was true. In the meantime, clean all this up and let none find out about this."

Everyone bowed to Dohma, then set about cleaning up the mess. Turning, he hurried away to his own new quarters. *I can't wait to talk to Orahda about this, but where can we talk that would be secure?* As he moved through the palace, he tried to think of a place, when the royal vault came to mind. It wasn't a secret that it was there, and he knew it had far more security than unbreakable walls. *Okay, now to find out if this really is an Alliance representative.*

Walking into his rooms, he found four valets had already laid out some regal-looking clothing and vestments. He jumped in the tub filled with hot water, scrubbing off the sweat. Getting out, the valets attacked him with towels and combs. In less than a quarter mark, he was clean and dressed, heading for the throne room.

As he approached the throne room, he realized that three Daggers, including Cundia, had materialized behind him, joining his four guards. The other two Daggers were from Bravo Squad. All three Daggers were dressed identically in elegant leather vests, pants, and blue silk shirts. The vests had the sigil of Aelargo emblazoned in gold over the right breasts, but with an added dagger behind it. The vests were armored and the weapons were not decorations. *Dagger regent guards will make an interesting impression. I like these new vests they made.* Nodding to Cundia, he let his attention return to recalling the right procedures for dealing with visiting dignitaries. He had witnessed such greetings in the past and recently had hours of protocol lessons with the master of ceremonies.

Stepping into the throne room, he found it was being cleared of all the papers and materials that had consumed them for the last five weeks as his sister, brother, and he had been tracing the linage of every supposed noble. A dozen honorable noble houses had been confirmed; another dozen had come forward after Duke announced the investigations and pleaded that they had upheld the kingdom, in spite of their ancestors being party to the usurping of it. They had judged most of them safe for minor duties until a few more generations proved their house loyalties. A few others had been stripped and been given the choice of military duty, guild laborer work, enlistment in the navy, or a handful of coins and orders to stay out of trouble. He was not surprised by how many had chosen to take the coins and fled to some other kingdom. Those that had remained were being watched closely.

His sister entered, looking regal in a shimmering dress of light blue and wearing a silver regent's tiara of office identical to his. The only difference in their vestments was that he had a mantle of silver links identifying him as the head regent. Her personal guards, like his, were dressed in the standard formal uniform of the city guard. *I am glad we chose to eliminate the official royal guards. I think the city guards feel a lot more pride knowing that they are responsible for all such duties.* His brother and his personal guards entered shortly after, wearing clothing similar to his own in silvers and blues.

All the guards made themselves useful and helped move some of the larger furniture into a side corridor while Cundia and her Daggers coordinated some of the other traffic. He smiled as he noticed that the Daggers were never more than two steps away from him or his siblings, and at least four personal guards remained nearby. *Helpful without neglecting their duties, and the guards are picking up on that behavior, too. I am thankful Duke left so many Daggers here.*

Looking over the throne room, he was shocked by how wonderful it was that the palace walls had been exposed and the pillars removed. The floor stones had also been removed, exposing the ancient inlaid sigil of the Kingdom of Aelargo. Together, he and his siblings stepped up to the ornate wooden chairs arranged in front of the dais which held three thrones for the long-dead princes. His family was loyal to the royal bloodline and would never sit in the thrones. Someday, he hoped the royal bloodline might be rediscovered, as Duke had found the regents' bloodline in his family.

Sitting down, he signaled the guards at the door to allow the Aelargian nobles in. The personal guards for his family took a formal ranking order to each side of the dais. The Daggers stepped up to stand, one each, to the right and just behind each regent. The doors were opened and for the first time in over five hundred years, the true nobles of Aelargo assembled in the throne room under the true regents to address the kingdom's business as a full court. He felt a wave of happiness and unspeakable emotions as the nobles came into the room. He couldn't help it; he smiled with a radiant look of pride. Looking to his right and left, he saw his sister and brother were having the same reaction. His sister dabbed her eyes and winked at him.

The nobles, some in new robes of state, entered the throne room and admired the transformation. Dohma had sent word that only Imperial nobles, visiting dignitaries, and invited guests would be announced formally. Many of the nobles had already sent him a note thanking him for reducing all the ridiculous pomp that had been on display every day for the last five hundred years.

The nobles filled the room, and Dohma smiled at his sister. "Ellua, I still cannot believe what we have done. It is hard to believe that in only five weeks, we have created so much quiet elegance and order."

His sister smiled and nodded to some ladies who had drifted close to her. "Dohma, this is as it should be. My heart, for the first time in my life, rejoices at seeing the throne room, even though I have been here hundreds of times before."

His brother waved in greeting at a recently restored noble whose family had been serving in the palace only a couple of days before as workers and pages. "Dohma, I should have asked before, but I gave all the holdings of the usurper, Baron Riollan, to Count Allusia's family. I found some records indicating some of those properties had been theirs before."

Dohma looked at the most recent noble who, until a few days ago, had been a page running errands in the palace. He was a stately man of nearly fifty with a handsome streak of silver on both sides of his otherwise slate-black hair. *He was always doing anything he could to help others. I remember him serving late nights for me at times. He has grown grey in service to his kingdom and this is a fitting role. Only, he looks a little too nervous. I hope he doesn't collapse.* "Riollan was as bad as they came. I have no problem with that order. Although, I have to say Count Allusia looks uncomfortable."

His sister leaned over. "Not to worry; I asked Baroness Morthan to make him feel welcome and help him and his family adjust. See, she is already taking him in tow."

Looking up, he saw the matronly baroness pulling the count along, cutting a path for him to a better position in the court. Smiling, he patted his sister's hand. "Excellent. The baroness can advise him on keeping the properties in order and help with the bookkeeping."

The silver ship's bell at the doorway rang once, indicating the approach of the dignitary. The court finished arranging itself so that by the time the bell rang twice, the throne room looked ready to receive even the emperor.

A tall, slim, beautiful young woman dressed in an almost form-fitting purple and gold uniform, with a silk, full-length cloak draped artistically back over her shoulders, stepped up to the door. Her dark purple, split skirt was translucent over a matching set of leggings. Her red hair was set into an elegant twist which allowed some strands to drape to her shoulders. She wore no weapons and had only a black pouch with some kind of golden symbol painted or cut into its fine surface, hanging on her belt. In her right hand, she carried a large engraved staff made of a dark, reddish wood surmounted by a golden disk stamped with the crossed quills symbol of her office held in place by filigreed ornamentation. A warm, but pleasurable, tremor passed through his body on looking at her. Behind her, in purple pantaloon page uniforms with stiff collars decorated with golden filigree stitching, were four aides walking in step. Each aide carried a dark leather valise.

The master of ceremonies bowed to the dignitary and turned towards the throne room. He rang the ship's bell three times and announced, "My Lords, Ladies, and Regents of Aelargo, the Right Honorable Lady Electra Neyon, Countess of Waylisia, Deputy Secretary of the Duianna Alliance."

Countess Electra stepped forward with the grace of a

dancer and touched her staff to the floor. Some of the nobles closest to her gasped loud enough to be heard as the inlaid shield coat of arms of Aelargo started to glow a warm white. The glowing started where her staff had touched the edge of the coat of arms and spread out to the whole design. A few nobles who had been standing on the edges of the sigil stepped off. Then the sigil did the impossible—it shifted like an opening gate, splitting down the middle, creating a walkway down the middle of the room from the door to just in front of the thrones.

Under the countess, the seal of the Covenant, an ornate compass rose, inscribed inside with a quartered diamond in the four sections, were the ancient symbols for peace, plenty, diligence, and courage. The seal, circumscribed with a band of unknown writing, rose as if from the depths of an ocean. Electra stood with a firm grip on her staff, back straight and shoulders back, lifting the staff enough so that it seemed to float with her as she walked down the center of the throne room, along the path.

Lord, she is amazing. He admired her graceful approach. The seal flowed forward, staying under her, and making it seem that she was flowing over water on a platform made of the Covenant seal. His eyes kept jumping up from that seal to her long, muscled legs, shown off by the tight leggings under her semitransparent divided skirt. Her hips swayed, accenting her not-too-slim figure.

She stopped a short distance in front of him and his siblings. Her eyes were clear grey and wide, looking each of them in the eye, in turn, before bowing. Dohma gave her what he hoped was a reasonable, acknowledging head bow. From the corners of his eyes, he could see that his sister and brother had followed his lead.

Countess Electra's eyes swept over them as she decided how to proceed. Dohma suppressed a grin as he saw her eyes narrow and her finger twitch on the staff while she took in the three Daggers standing behind each of them. *She respects*

Daggers, and that we have them behind us in the place reserved for only senior advisors, is something she wasn't expecting. I like the idea of having Daggers as advisors to the regents. We should make this a standard. I wonder how much weapons training she has had. She looks very fit, and with her height, she would have almost the same reach as I.

The countess's cheeks showed dimples as she finished her thoughts and allowed herself a small, but clear smile, showing off straight, pure white teeth. Nodding as if coming to a decision, she spoke. "Your Excellencies, Lord Regent Dohma Uriosal, Lady Regent Ellua Uriosal, and Lord Regent Bayion Uriosal, I bring you glad congratulations from His Lordship Risand Tullon Yawsia, Duke of Yawsia, Secretary of the Alliance of Duianna, on the reestablishment of your family's line as Regents of the Kingdom of Aelargo. I am instructed to inspect the Kingdom of Aelargo for compliance with the Covenant of Duianna. Further, with your permission, if Aelargo is within compliance or diligently working towards compliance, I am empowered to reestablish an Alliance deputy secretary's office here in Llino." With that, she bowed again, then stood straight, prepared to wait for their answer.

She named us of the Uriosal family, as it is called in the Covenant. She knew our real names, but perhaps, not our full names. Or was this intentional? Still, this is amazing. My Lords, a deputy secretary's office here! That would bring a lot of wealth and recognition to us. I wonder if she would be the permanent deputy secretary. He smiled and looked to his left and right, receiving restrained, but obviously eager, nods of agreement from his siblings. Looking back at the countess, he knew she hadn't missed any of the body language. *She is well-trained, and I am sure she is going to be interesting to get to know. She looks about twenty—very young for such a position.* Looking around at the assembled nobles, he didn't see anything but happy faces. *Well, I see no dissent. Why wait?*

Seeing the concerned look from his master of ceremonies, Dohma suppressed a chuckle, as he followed the protocol.

"Your Right Honorable Lady Electra, you bring to us glad news. We accept your presence and will cooperate with your duties of inspection. Aelargo would be deeply honored by the establishment of an Alliance deputy secretary's office here. My family is at your disposal for the inspection." Glancing up, he saw an approving smile from the master of ceremonies. *See, I did pay attention.*

The countess leaned towards them on the balls of her feet, with more to say, so he nodded to her. "Lords and Lady of Aelargo, thank you for the warm welcome." Reaching back, one of her aides pulled an envelope from his valise and gave it to her. "I also carry a summons for an Aelargian representative to be sent to Gracia to arrive no later than three cycles from now for a meeting of the Alliance Assembly." She held out the sealed envelope. One of their pages rushed forward and took it from her and brought it the few steps to Dohma.

As he started to take the letter, Cundia hissed loudly enough for him to hear, which stopped him before his hand had lifted from the chair.

What is she warning me of? Before he could react, Cundia stepped forward and accepted the letter. She made a little show of inspecting it, including smelling it, then handed it to him. He accepted the letter and glanced at the countess from the edge of his eye to see if she had taken offense at this. Instead of being offended, she looked pleased. He was also surprised to notice a number of his senior courtiers also stood taller at this. *I need to find out what that was all about.* The letter was sealed with the same Covenant seal as the one glowing beneath the countess's feet.

"Do you know what this is about?"

She nodded. "I do. The Supreme Commander of the Alliance has declared war against the Nhia-Samri for their many acts of treason against the Alliance. The assembly is required to vote to accept or reject the declaration. The secretary feels that Aelargo would be most interested in attending and voting on this matter. I am ordered to make an assessment of compliance to provide an initial findings report, allowing your representative to attend. I shall, of course, follow that up with a more complete investigation and report."

Dohma stood up. "We would indeed like to send a representative to this meeting of the Assembly of the Alliance. I suggest we deal with these matters in a less formal capacity." He gestured to the room. "Countess, these are our confirmed loyal and true courtiers, and many have been recently installed as officials of Aelargo. I trust you will find them warm and welcoming. I shall leave you to consult with my family on this urgent matter. Tonight, we shall have a feast in your honor with formal introductions."

With approving nods from his brother and sister, Dohma looked on their courtiers and pronounced, "The Regents of Aelargo order all offices and records to be made available for inspection by the Right Honorable Lady Electra Neyon, Countess of Waylisia, Deputy Secretary of the Duianna Alliance."

All of the nobles present bowed their heads in acknowledgement.

Dohma's eyes returned to the lovely Electra. "Lady Electra, please feel free to get to know our fine kingdom. Unless you prefer other arrangements, I shall have the chief marshal of the house select private and comfortable chambers for you and your staff to use while in residence here." The countess glowed, returning his smile. *She really is remarkably beautiful.*

"Thank you, Lord Dohma. I accept your gracious invitation to dinner, as well as the private chambers. My ship stands at your service, ready to sail for Gracia at your command, for whomever you decide will attend the assembly. I shall endeavor to have my initial findings report prepared within two days."

"Perhaps you will join me for lunch after you have finished making introductions and checking on your rooms."

Her eyes seemed to glow at the suggestion, and he felt

his own pulse respond to her happiness. She appeared to float upward as she said, "It would be my pleasure, Lord Domha."

Ellua and Bayion stood, and with Dohma, bowed to the countess. The countess returned the bow, and the Covenant seal beneath her faded away while the sigil of Aelargo closed, and then slowly stopped glowing, looking once more like nothing more than a golden inlay. He hoped he had kept a reasonably straight face throughout this show of power by his own palace. *I really need to finish reading the instructions on this place which Duke told me to get to. That was more than I expected. I wonder if that is going to happen every time we have an important visitor.* Turning, he walked towards the private exit with his sister, brother, Daggers, and guards following him out of the throne room. As they were leaving, he spotted Baroness Morthan towing Count Allusia straight for the deputy secretary. *Now, that will be interesting.* He chuckled. *I almost feel sorry for Count Allusia; he is about to be catapulted into a front-line position.*

Once they were out of the throne room, Ellua burst out, "How could Gracia be informed and respond so fast to events here? It takes six weeks by ship to sail here down the great channel with the best winds. We have only been in power for five weeks. Five weeks total, since the beginning of all the events with Duke."

His brother looked at the ceiling chewing his lower lip. "It is only a couple of days across the sound to Miumi, and Oslald has never disregarded the Covenant or shunned the Alliance as Aelargo did. She could have been there and received orders to come here."

Dohma looked at them both, surprised. "Aren't you surprised by what the floor did?"

They both looked at him before his sister rolled her eyes. "You were always stuck on the magic shows at the fairs. Of course, I was surprised, but I think it had something to do with that staff she is carrying. It might be a confirmation of rank thing. But really, silly light shows aside, we need to discuss the real issue here, which is how did they find out so fast, and how did they get her to us in such a short time? After all, she might be a fraud."

A fraud? He frowned and his heart skipped. *She isn't a fraud. I know she is trustworthy!* He had to think a moment, trying to decide how best to defend her to his brother and sister. Then he realized his brother was debating his sister, and he had not been paying attention. *She was announced by the Nhia-Samri agents. Could she be another agent?* Ignoring the debate, he started walking down the hall. His sister and brother walked with him out of habit, continuing to debate the possible actions and plans of some other agent. He looked at the sealed envelope and pondered the possibilities. His fingers traced the Covenant seal, receiving a tingling sensation that pricked his nerves and caused him to jerk away, as if burned.

Cundia rushed to him. "Milord, are you okay?" She reached to snatch the envelope away.

He stopped her with his hand. "I'm okay. It was just a surprise. It didn't really hurt."

That got his brother and sister to stop their debate and step up, so that they were facing him. Ellua asked, "What happened?"

He looked up. "I got a feeling from the seal." He touched the seal again. The feeling was still there. He moved his finger around the edge of the seal. He could smell hot wax and feel someone he didn't know, but trusted anyway, pressing down on the wax with an official seal. Lifting his finger, he looked at his brother and held out the letter. "Gently trace the seal."

His brother took the letter, looking a little white, but pursed his lips and placed his finger on the seal. His eyes bulged as he moved his finger around the seal. When he was finished, they looked at each other and his brother nodded. "It's authentic."

Taking the envelope back, he handed it to Cundia. "You didn't touch the seal when you checked it. Maybe next time, you might try that."

Cundia, looking puzzled, did the same thing, placing her finger on the seal and tracing it around. Then she looked up, shaking her head. "I don't understand. Is there something in the feeling of the wax?"

"Really, you didn't feel the authenticity?"

Cundia shook her head. "I don't understand. Is there something more? What did you feel?"

"Ell, please do as we did and tell us what you think."

Ellua took the envelope from Cundia and ran her finger over the seal. Her nose wrinkled. "Oh, I hate the smell of burned sealing wax, which is why I let others seal all my orders."

Bayion laughed. "Well, that confirms it for me. Domha, did you smell the wax and feel Lord Abdens pressing it?"

"How do you know who that was? All I felt was someone whom, for some reason, I trusted."

"I am older than you, Brother. Lord Abdens came here for a summer when I was four or five. He liked me a lot and played with me when I snuck out to the gardens and found him there reading. He was such a nice man, I trusted him. Of course, the usurpers made him feel unwelcome and he left, never returning."

Cundia looked at them with a blank expression. Patting her on the shoulder, he told her, "It must be another one of those regents' power things. Lord Abdens is the current Lord Regent in service to King Ollusin of the Kingdom of Oslald. When we touch this seal, we can feel who made it at the moment it was sealed." Laughing, he tapped his brother and looked at Ellua. "Sorry, Sis. Bayion is right. This came from Oslald and it is real, which authenticates everything the countess said."

Ellua shrugged. "Well, at least, you have your chance."

"What does that mean?"

"It means since she isn't an imposter, I'll make sure she is sitting close to you tonight. That'll give you a chance to get to know her. Of course, you do have the private luncheon already arranged."

Alarms went off in the back of his head. "Are you implying something? I expect you and Bayion to join me for the lunch."

"Really? I could have sworn your lunch invite was just for you two. You said 'me,' not 'we'."

"Did I? Well, I meant 'we,' so you two can join."

His brother punched his shoulder. "Oh, no, I don't think so. You made the date, so you stick to it. Besides, I have other business to attend to." Bayion's grin was very knowing.

Ellua smiled, patting him on the cheek. "Don't be ashamed of it, Brother. I was worried you would never find someone you were interested in."

Blood was rising to his face and he felt a little off-balance. *She was beautiful and graceful. But seriously, Electra is a countess and I am…well, I'm a…* He felt his stomach jump at the realization that he was a higher rank than a countess. *I'm a regent, second only to a king or queen. I can marry any noble I choose!* His heart raced faster at the possibility of being with Electra.

His sister's wide brown eyes looked into his, and he felt his cheeks burning. "Don't worry Brother. You can always ask your sister for help. Tell you what. I'll make all the lunch arrangements for out on the garden veranda. That is a semi-public place, but still romantic and private enough that you can talk freely."

"I'm not… I mean, really, I was happy for Aelargo. I didn't even consider anything else."

Ellua's eyes twinkled as she said, "Your eyes spent far more time below her neck than above it," in a purring tone.

He took a step back and looked at his brother for support, but Bayion was grinning like a wild cat. Cundia was trying not to laugh, with only marginal success. The other two Daggers and guards were also of no support, being involved in inspecting the floor, ceiling, or walls.

His heart started beating double-time, and his ears had

joined in the fun his cheeks were having, burning hot enough to hurt. "I... Well... Uh..." Retreat seemed a reasonable response. Spinning around and stepping off, he called back, "I'm going to take care of something important now."

That was too much as everyone, including the guards, started laughing joyfully. His sister didn't relent. "So should I seat her next to you tonight, too?"

Yes! Turning a corner without looking back, Dohma said over the laughter, "Do what you want."

Jicca vs. Runa-Illa

CHAPTER 3
IN THE SPIRIT OF THE LAW

WARLORD MARU-ASHUA STRODE, HEAD HELD high, around the training field, observing the warriors practicing. *These are the finest warriors I have ever been privileged to know. I wish I could live to see their mettle tested in battle.* He slowed, seeing that his second, General Eshra-Zunia, was sparring with six warriors of the highest class. In spite of his many years of practice controlling his facial expressions, he still smiled, watching the nimble and cunning Eshra-Zunia as she maneuvered, probing for the fatal weaknesses of the warriors who, although they knew better, hoped they might have the upper hand.

Before I promote her today, I believe she needs to learn a final lesson. I had hoped to teach her all I knew. But alas, that is no longer a possibility. His mind recalled the humiliating double blows of Duke against his command in Llino. *Duke, you are a cunning enemy, and the moment I learned you had come back from your northern realms, I should have gone to Llino. Colonel Urio-Larne had no chance against you. And despite your attempt to make it look like he died with no honor, I know full well he and his command fell with the greatest honor of the warrior in facing you in battle.*

He slipped off his coats, handing them to his command sergeant major. *Let's see if she is ready to take command here.* Summoning the powers of his ancient blades, he pulled on the blades' power creating a shroud of silence and bent the perceptions of those around him to overlook his presence, as he stepped out into the field. He moved through the training groups, only an occasional warrior noting his passage. As he approached, Eshra-Zunia found a mistake and delivered a painful blow to one of her adversaries, who fell away.

Not pulling your strikes. Excellent. Now, to demonstrate your readiness to lead. In striking distance, he moved in suddenly, batting one of Eshra-Zunia's opponents away like paper. His blades sang as they cut through the air for her back. In spite of his being wrapped in deception, she sensed the attack and dove away, causing his blades to cut only air.

One of her four remaining opponents had a chance to attack her and took it. He lunged in, using all the speed his blades gave him. It wasn't enough. Eshra-Zunia dropped to the ground, parrying the attack so that it passed only a hair's width from her head, cutting some of her hair. Eshra-Zunia rolled back into Maru-Ashua, slamming into his legs. Caught off-guard, he was forced to stumble backward, letting his perception blanket fall in order to dance over Eshra-Zunia's blades, which sang as she tried to cut his feet off at the calves.

Eshra-Zunia's eyes followed the legs of her new opponent up to meet the warlord's eyes. She knew who she was fighting with and how much trouble she was in. He read fear in her eyes, which resolved to determination. As he brought his own blades down on her prone form, he gave her a smile of approval.

Eshra-Zunia intelligently rolled away instead of trying to parry his attack, causing his blades to cut the stone where she had been with a shower of sparks. As she distanced herself from him, she kicked out, throwing the warrior, who had cut her hair, out of the battle. Eshra-Zunia pulled her feet under her and performed a final back roll, using her head and hands to push off and coming back to her feet. She didn't pause, and thrust at one of her other attackers, her mouth and eyes showing the grimace of an engaged warrior. He managed to parry her attack, but not before receiving a damaging cut to his arm. His blood flowed from the wound. Still, he did not disengage.

The three warriors synchronized with the warlord as they began a series of attacks. Eshra-Zunia's speed pushed her beyond the abilities of all, but the warlord. In a brilliant series of parries and ripostes, she finished off all her other opponents. Try as she might, she could not defeat Maru-Ashua. Her blades never found even a trace of his armor or body. But his blades sang and were stained with her blood from the series of minor cuts he managed to achieve.

You will do well; time to end this. He stepped in close and sparks flew as their blades clashed. *That will be enough. No one will say I gave her any consideration.*

"Enough," he said as her blades were coming at him in a thrust. He didn't bother to parry them and stood straight.

Her blades stopped, vibrating at the sudden cessation of motion. Her face was drenched in sweat, as was his own. She stood still and then came to attention, saluting him with her crossed blades. Her eyes burned over her blades at him in pride and exhilaration from the fight.

He nodded to her. Not a single warrior on the field was moving, having all stopped to witness the incredible display of skill and power. He nodded to her. "Meet me in the throne room in half a mark."

The field rang as all the odassi were brought out in salute to both of them.

Maru-Ashua saluted Eshra-Zunia and sheathed his blades after first wiping them clean. He turned and walked back into the command post, all the warriors jumping aside to provide him a clear path. His command sergeant major fell into step with him, following him into the interior. Once they were alone, the command sergeant major chuckled. "I doubt even General Enon-Anos will care to test her after that."

Entering his private chambers, he nodded. "That was my secondary goal. Let us see if we can beat her to the throne room."

Maru-Ashua was in the throne room, cleaned and refreshed, thirty seconds before Eshra-Zunia walked in. He had managed to get to the throne and look bored just before she opened the door. Looking at her, he noted her hair was pulled back in a knotted ponytail. *Shouldn't have combed your hair. You might have beaten me. Oh well, now you'll never know how often you came to almost beating me someplace.* He smiled, which she interpreted as meaning her time to get there was, at least, acceptable.

As she strode towards him, the command sergeant major stepped over to the doors and bowed as he left. Eshra-Zunia and Maru-Ashua were alone in the throne room. Eshra-Zunia knelt on one knee before him, head held high, looking at him for his orders.

"Stand."

She stood, as did he. He said, "I declare you to now be in command of this outpost, with all the rights and responsibilities that entails."

The smallest of frowns crossed her face.

He smiled the first genuine smile he had ever allowed her to see. "Come, let us ride."

He did not give her time to speak again until they were riding alone, up into the canyon their valley rested at the mouth of. Eshra-Zunia's eyes were unfocused and her forehead slightly creased. He knew she was trying to probe his actions. "The ceremony this evening with the generals is for the warriors. But Outpost One requires no such ceremony."

"I don't perceive your meaning."

"I do not have time to teach you all that I know. This looks like a good place." He stopped his horse and slid off of it. Eshra-Zunia followed him. He looked back to the east at his outpost and the rolling hills beyond. The hills were stained a shade of pink as the sunset. "I cannot explain. It is something you will have to puzzle out for yourself. I was given command in the same manner, as was my warlord, and I believe his before." He turned and looked at her. "But *not all* of our predecessors."

She stood, waiting.

"Eshra-Zunia, there are secrets and the outpost has some intelligence. My predecessor warned me, as I am warning you now, the walls do not forget. I have learned many things in my long service. In keeping my oaths, I am unsure what I can or cannot share. Therefore, I am only sharing that which was shared with me, as you are now ordered to pass on to your successor, if you can."

Eshra-Zunia nodded.

He pulled one of his odassi out and held it out for her inspection. "Compare this to your own."

Eshra-Zunia pulled one of her odassi out and held it up to mirror his. It looked almost the same, except the maker's marks were not identical. The warlord's odassi had a stylized cat silhouette in profile, over an oblong moon that looked more like an egg. The warlord's odassi also had a golden tsuba, or cross-guard, compared to her own silver tsuba. His blade felt different, older, and somehow radiated calmness.

He replaced his blade in his belt. "My odassi is an original from the beginning of the Nhia-Samri. At that time, few warriors had an odassi. While both blades have nearly identical powers, they are as different as a child to an adult. The new odassi are assigned, made for each warrior, and given to them as part of their final days of training."

Eshra-Zunia nodded understanding.

He placed his hand on the hilt of his fine blade. "These are not assigned. The Grand Warlord Shar-Lumen himself cannot give these blades to anyone. These blades choose who they will. I cannot explain it. But should you ever see someone with these blades, no matter their rank, respect that warrior and know they have in them the greatest potential."

Eshra-Zunia looked at his blades and nodded. "I understand."

"These are not things you should speak of to anyone except of warlord rank. Now, come. We have much ceremony to deal with. I shall take my chosen officers in the morning and ride, I believe for the last time, to Hisuru Amajoo."

As they mounted, Eshra-Zunia commented, "I note that four of your chosen officers carry similar odassi."

Maru-Ashua smiled. "An interesting observation."

LEBUIN

Thoughts spun around his mind like a whirlwind. *Ditani is my uncle! Argos is my grandfather. Why didn't anyone tell me? Did I really mess up in accepting Illa? I stepped over the line to becoming a God and I have no idea what that means. This is all too much.* Looking at Illa, he saw she was watching him with that smile. *I don't have to look. I can feel her all the time now.* When she saw he was looking at her, she swelled with pride, and he could feel the energies she was giving him surge. Even in questioning his actions, something inside reassured him this was the right path and Illa was the right choice.

Ticca stared into the fire, and Ditani watched him and waited. *You lied to me, Ditani!* But the moment he thought that, he knew it was not true. Ditani had never once lied to him, he was sure of it. He closed his eyes and let the events and memories of the past few cycles settle into a new order of things.

I was isolated because of my power and potential. So the Guild had to know what I was. Or, at least, Councilor Nillo knew. He dropped enough hints. But why keep me in the dark? Why leave me ignorant? It would be stupid to not teach me what I needed to know. That thought stopped him. He wormed it around and looked at it from every angle. *Yes, it would be stupid to not teach me what I needed, and neither Argos nor the Guild is stupid. I am missing something.*

It had to have been Argos who came to me in the ethereal realm. No other God could respond so fast and find me. Argos had a link to me by family and by the journeyman ritual incantation. It was a male entity and one of tremendous power, so it was very likely Argos, which explains the feelings of pride, love, and hurt. The memory of the feelings he had gotten from the other entity came back. *The other entity felt guilty, I remember that clearly. He felt guilty and hurt at what he asked of me. This means that I am being used for something important. There is a catastrophe coming, and he is using me to try to prevent it.*

We need to figure out what is going on, and I am sure it has something to do with Magus Vestul's research.

Ticca was on the same track as he was, because she had opened the pouch, pulled out the papers it held, and was looking through them again.

"Ticca, may I see those again? These have to be the focal point. Careful plans have been made by many powerful people, including the Gods. All of them are centered on what that pouch holds."

She nodded and handed them over, except for a couple of maps, which she was studying. "I am thinking the same thing. Something vital is in these papers, which the Nhia-Samri want very badly. The Gods are trying to prevent them from getting them. What I don't understand is why not destroy them? They're just paper."

Ditani shook his head. "If it were that simple, my master wouldn't have summoned Duke from the north and travelled to Llino to meet him. Actually, I don't understand why he went to Llino at all. He could have asked Duke to meet him at his home, where he was safe and secure. He even hid the identity of Duke from me. He was always mysterious, but rarely this secretive."

Ticca looked at Ditani with frustration. "You are not a servant. You said it yourself: you are a hero. So stop with the pretending. We know you are in this up to your neck."

Ditani looked shocked. "I never lied. I have run errands for the Guild and Magus Vestul for many hundreds of years. I am just Magus Vestul's servant. He sent me to the Guild in Llino to help some friends for a while because he knew I wanted to be sure my nephew was okay. But really, I am a servant; otherwise, I would not have obeyed the command to not tell Lebuin who he or I was."

Lebuin looked at Ditani and felt no deception. Ticca, on the other hand, needed more convincing. "Really? The son of Argos works for a living as a servant?"

Ditani looked her in the eyes. "We all have to live and

work. I am not a God, nor do I have magical capabilities. My only assets are being of good health, having a strong mind, and being long-lived. I could be some merchant or have become a lord of some country. Except I don't have the mind for business, and I don't like being responsible for many more than my own family. I was raised on the open plains of Karakia, running with the warriors and hunting for my tribe. If you think about it, being a servant to one of the most powerful men in the world has many benefits. Magus Vestul lived for many thousands of years. Do you think just any twenty-year-old valet would be able to understand the meaning of that and provide the necessary aid? I am almost two thousand years old and Magus Vestul has known me since birth. He invited me to work for him when I was five hundred years old. I liked the idea, and so accepted. He was a good master and a friend. He was almost as powerful as any God. It was an honor to work for him, as it will be an honor for Illa to serve Lebuin well over the coming thousands of years."

He thought he couldn't be more surprised today, but that last comment stopped all his thoughts, and he stared at Ditani over the top of the papers.

Illa was surprised by it, too, because she blurted out, "Thousands of years? I am only human—I cannot possibly live that long."

Ditani looked at her in a fatherly fashion. "My dear sweet High Priestess of Lebuin, since your God didn't know what he was doing when he accepted you, based on what I saw, he accepted your gift of service. You are bound to him. Your level of acceptance is a gift rarely given by any God and then, only for rare, exceptional servants. You will live as long as he does. You will also die the moment he dies. You are not just his follower, you are his high priestess—more, you are his first disciple. You need no longer worry about growing old or sickness. You do still need to eat, sleep, and be healthy, as your highest duty is to generate and gather energy for Lebuin.

Lebuin's energy will, without his thought, sustain your life when you are in need."

Ticca had stopped looking at the maps and was looking at Illa with an interesting expression. Illa had gone red in the face and her eyes had opened wide. She looked over at him again, and he felt a surge of energy from her immense pride. *She is proud and joyful at this. Heavens, I cannot believe I am going to live that long, and now I have a follower who will live as long as I.* In that context, the whole idea of Ditani being a servant to Magus Vestul made a lot more sense.

Illa looked back at Ditani. "Will you teach me all you know of the Gods and service to them?"

This wasn't the reaction Ditani had expected, because he looked like something hadn't gone according to plan. "Well, it will take some time. But you and I will have a lot of that. Trust me, Lebuin here, will vanish into his work for cycles or years on end, forgetting about everything else, unless you bring him his meals and remind him to eat, sleep, and wash up. So we should have plenty of time to talk about such things."

"Um, Ditani, would you please stop talking like I'm not here?"

Ditani looked over with a fake look of surprise. "Oh, my Lord, I thought you were studying those papers. Sorry. Do you need something?"

He could feel the blood rushing to his face. "Don't do that. It is embarrassing."

"Which proves you are still a real person." Ditani winked at Illa. "That is lesson number one. Occasionally, remind them they are just like people everywhere."

Illa giggled, and feeling more embarrassed, he went back to examining the papers. *He can be so annoying sometimes.* He noticed Ticca was trying unsuccessfully to suppress a giggle, so he gave her an annoyed look, which broke her hold on her laughter, and the three of them all burst out laughing. After a moment, he joined them. They laughed for what felt like a long time. When one of them managed to stop, they would look around and start all over again. It released a lot of tension. Afterward, they sat around giggling as they tried not to look at each other.

Lebuin could tell whenever Illa looked at him because he got a small rush of energy. He looked inside and found that all his energy channels felt normal again. The energy he was getting from Illa was minor, compared to what he could pull from the nearby mana lines. He reached out and refilled all his reserves. He activated his long-overdue comfort incantations and felt a lot better as the grime and dirt fell from him. *Well, I might be a God, but it still feels good to be clean.*

'HOLD!' The power behind the command was unbelievable, and the voice rang in his mind, or ears, or both. He understood what he was instructed to do, and dropped his comfort incantations instantly. '*Such mana is not yours to waste.*'

He sat up straight, looking around, trying to identify where the commanding entity was. Ditani, Ticca and Illa were all immersed in their own thoughts and not looking at him. None of them appeared to have heard the voice.

"Who and where are you?"

Ticca, Ditani, and Illa looked at him.

'*I am between. Come now.*'

With the command, came the understanding of how to do that. He focused inward and then pushed away from himself. He felt his mind separate from his physical body, and the silver strand connecting him to his body spun out. Once more, he found himself between. Again, there were the blazing energies of the beings close to him. He recognized them.

Ticca was a radiant powerhouse focused entirely in the physical realm. Next to Ticca hung the soft, but also powerful, silvery entity that was what remained of Kliasa, daughter of House Elaeus. He could see Kliasa's energies sustaining her here close to Ticca by a silver strand. *Which would be her connection to the boots.* Since he was there on his own power, as well as not near death, his awareness was clearer. Kliasa had many such silver strands connected to her, and he could feel or see that she was drawing energy from all of them. *That is interesting.*

Also near was another powerful male presence which existed both in the physical and between realms. *That is Ditani. He was near me in the temple, too. He had to have been one of the two voices I heard when I woke up the first time. I wonder who the second female voice was, that sang me back to sleep with my mother's songs.*

Another female presence, which glowed a soft gold, was there. Although he was not sure why, he knew it was much more powerful than normal humans. Yet it was still significantly less than Ticca or Ditani. There was a golden thread connecting his consciousness to it, and he knew it was Illa. He reached for the thread to Illa, but before he could do anything with it, a potent force blocked him, causing him to release his hold.

'Explore your disciple later.' With that came the understanding that he could find Illa, no matter where she might be, in comparison to himself, in the entire universe. More interestingly, he could pull her mind there and interact with her as Kliasa did with him and Ticca.

'You are my grandfather, the All-Father God Argos.'

'Yes.' Images of his mother, father, grandmother Lothia, and some of their interactions came with that simple statement.

He looked around and found Argos's energies near him. *'Where are you, really?'*

'In time, you may learn. I do not need rest now.' Instantly, he received the ominous knowledge that he may need to step in for Argos, should his grandfather's strength or mind start to fail at their task, as it was his mother's duty before him. He knew then that Argos and his direct relatives had a responsibility that would never die, and something inside of him resolved to be prepared, should his turn come. A feeling of pride came to him from Argos.

'You begin to understand. That is for later. Now, you must

comply with the laws of Gods.' In came a flood of laws he was required to follow. His mind spun at the volume of rules and the levels of detail to many of them. There were ways to bypass many of them, but the circumvention always had to be justified. He also understood Argos was the enforcer of the laws and would never ignore anyone who broke one of the laws, no matter how minor. Three other Gods, always chosen at random, would judge if the actions of the law-breaker were justified or not. Argos would enforce their ruling ruthlessly. There was also a council, or ruling body of Gods, known as the Circle, which was responsible for maintaining the rules of Gods.

He had hundreds of marks of study ahead just to learn the basic patterns of the laws. If he could cry, he might have, when he saw the rule about Gods not being allowed to use the mana lines for magical work other than to replenish themselves, if they were starving, or for necessary actions, should they not have enough power from followers. His cleaning spells had absolutely no justification, as they were merely for comfort.

'I need time to study these.'

'You have the means here.' He understood he could pull the 'year in a night' trick that Kliasa had used for him earlier by coming between.

'I shall learn and obey.'

'The others come for judgment.' Fear gripped him as the understanding of that came into his mind. He had pulled magic from a mana line and activated a cleaning and comfort set of incantations without need.

'I didn't know I wasn't allowed to do that!'

'Ignorance of the laws is no defense.' Councilor Nillo's words came back to him: 'The Gods do not allow ignorance to excuse unlawful behavior, and many countries have incorporated that into their own laws. As a representative of Argos, you will be held accountable far more than most. Be careful and always learn the laws as quickly as possible.'

Argos looked away as if dealing with something.

Kliasa reached out to him. *'Hail Lebuin, Son of Waylen and Alia, Grandson of All-Father Argos and Lothia. I greet and welcome you.'*

'You know who I am?'

'I have known of you since before you were born.'

'Did you know my parents?'

'No. I wish I had known your mother and father, but I died before I could meet them. I knew of you through what I learned by observing Magus Vestul.'

'Magus Vestul knew me?'

'Oh, yes. He watched over you with great interest and secrecy. He also was a good friend of your father and mother. In fact, it was your father who procured the old sharre for him as a gift for Duke.'

Just then, three other entities came near him. He did not recognize any of them. All three touched Kliasa. He heard no words, but he sensed a great deal of emotions exchanged between the three new entities and Kliasa. Kliasa also shared something with them. *Can it be that everyone of power knows, respects, and loves Kliasa?*

The first entity's attention slipped away from Kliasa and turned to him while addressing the others. *'Lebuin has joined us. This is new.'* He only got the words from this entity. *The sharing of knowledge must be voluntary. I bet I am going to broadcast my whole life every time I respond to these Gods until I learn how to restrain what I am sharing.*

'It is unexpected,' said the second.

He felt Argos's attention return to them, and Argos addressed Kliasa most gently, 'Kliasa, please withdraw.'

'Argos, be kind to your grandson.'

'I must enforce the laws; Lebuin is not exempt. My eternal gratitude for your support and training of Lebuin. It was unexpected and most generous.'

Argos's tone with Kliasa was gentle and respectful. Lebuin's respect for Kliasa went up several notches. *Argos knows that she trained me in that wondrous night-year in her*

Rea-Na-Rey. I find it amazing that the All-Father God is being so polite and responsive to a dead silver-elf.

'*Thank you, Argos.*' Kliasa turned to him, and her form in his mind firmed up to nearly a solid representation, which bowed to him, in elven respect. '*Until we meet again, Lord Lebuin.*'

He smiled at her and touched her form, as he had seen the other three do. '*Be well, Kliasa.*' Her presence then moved off, back to being close to Ticca's presence. He wasn't surprised that he could tell she was still watching what was going to happen to him. Lebuin felt from Argos a moment of humor at her 'withdrawal' being little more than a step or two. Seeming satisfied, Argos's attention turned to the other three entities and himself.

The third entity poked him in places, commenting as it did. '*He nearly died from not knowing. His health returns. His disciple is an interesting choice.*'

The other two also started to poke at him. *I feel like a prize horse on display. Next, they are going to want to check my teeth.*

They ignored his thoughts if they heard them at all. '*The disciple is strong and committed. She is an excellent choice, even if chosen too rapidly. He did judge her. I vote this is acceptable.*'

Lebuin's mind spun. *They are judging me for taking Illa as a disciple?* He reviewed the rules and found that there were dozens around followers and disciples, and even more about interacting with other Gods' followers. '*I thought this was about the cleaning spell.*' His mind was still not disciplined and he realized too late he had sent that thought out.

All three entities were amused. The first entity answered him. '*We will get to that momentarily. There are a number of other laws to be considered first.*'

The second entity did something. He felt his connection to Illa stretch and pull away. He immediately defended it and strengthened it. The connection snapped back into its proper place. *'He has reasonable control. I abstain my vote until a point of my own choosing.'*

The first entity spoke up. *'You are allowed. The disciple is too early. However, I vote the choice sound and the making performed well and within reasonable limits.'*

Argos was pleased. *'Two in favor, one abstained to future. Judgment is suspended, then, until final vote. Lebuin, know that penalties may still be applied, based on the final vote of Poalua.'*

Poalua was annoyed. *'You didn't need to inform him of my identity.'*

'You three have little to hide. He is a God, and if he had experience, he would already know.'

The first entity laughed. *'Argos is right. Lebuin, I am Iolenda.'*

The third entity remained closed. *'I am Uialua. Never mind my brother. He has an over-dramatic mind.'* He understood Poalua and Uialua were twins, born near the beginning of the world.

'All other violations, except for the misuse of mana line energies, are rooted in the Circle's rulings. Argos, do you call them to judgment?'

'No, judgment has already been passed on the Circle.' He understood that other rules had been broken regarding him and that other Gods had taken responsibility for them and paid the penalties imposed for it. *Well, that answers some of my questions. They kept me ignorant on purpose, and even paid a price to do it.* Reviewing the laws, he found a number of them that could apply and resolved to study them in detail later, to try to resolve some of his questions on what was going on.

Iolenda felt scared by Argos's pronouncement that the Circle had been judged. *'Very well. On the misuse of magic, I vote it was a third-degree violation and that the related charges be consolidated into one.'*

Poalua poked at him some more. *'I desire to make note of his near-starvation state due to the Circle's actions. Based on that, I vote it was a third-degree violation with extenuating circumstances, and recommend clemency. I also vote in favor of consolidating the related charges into one.'*

Uialua considered for a time. *'I concur with Poalua.'*

Argos ended it. *'Unanimous vote to consolidate all charges related to the misuse of mana into one, for conviction of a third-degree violation of misuse of magic, with a majority request for clemency. Iolenda, do you recommend a form of penalty?'*

Iolenda was silent for a time. The longer she took, the more nervous he got. *'I do not see a requirement for a penalty. I will amend my vote to concur with Poalua and Uialua.'*

Argos was neither pleased, nor displeased. He simply pronounced judgment. *'Lebuin, you are found guilty of third-degree misuse of magic. By recommendation of the judges, all charges on misuse of magic and the relating items are consolidated into one judgment. It is recorded and will affect future judgments, should you repeat this offense.'*

Lebuin felt the tension wash out of him. *'This was a serious near-miss.'*

Iolenda responded, *'Indeed it was, Lebuin. I would concentrate first on learning all the laws well enough to stay clear of them. Then I would suggest you learn how to shield yourself when between. Good luck.'* Iolenda's presence vanished from his perception.

Poalua and Uialua agreed with that and then vanished, leaving him the sole recipient of Argos's attention.

'Lebuin, you are not human. You require magic.' With that, came the understanding that he needed magic, as well as food, to sustain him. Even worse, he had been starving himself for years by controlling his magic and using incantations of no consequence. He also understood there were laws that the Gods needed to keep themselves healthy.

'I understand, Grandfather. Can I keep magic from followers separate from power from the mana lines?'

'Only in casting.' He understood he could channel power to an incantation and that would maintain the separation. But anything else would blur the line, and precise calculations

would be used to determine if he had broken a law. *Looks like I am going to have to be restrained in using magic until I get more followers, and even then.*

'You must continue. I am watching.' As Argos's attention left him for whatever else he had to deal with, he felt the love and pride of his grandfather. It felt more important that it was his grandfather that was proud of him, than the great All-Father God Argos.

'Thank you, Grandfather.' He let himself shift back to his physical body as Argos's presence vanished.

Ticca was sitting in front of him, and Illa was next to her, with concerned looks on their faces. Ditani was leaning back against the cave wall, watching. Ticca's eyes looked relieved when she saw he had focused on her.

"What happened to you?"

"I made a pretty serious mistake and was called to the dirt on it."

Illa looked worried. "My Lord, are you well? Do you need something to drink?" She held out a cup of something.

He took it, smiling, and after a quick sniff to confirm it was some of her wine, he drank it down. Wiping his mouth, he handed the cup back. "Thank you, Illa. That was just what I needed. I am okay now."

Illa moved back to her sleeping pad and sat, watching him. Ticca looked him in the eyes, as if she was trying to probe him with her will. "Are you sure you're okay? You asked where someone was and went blank for about two minutes."

He nodded. "Yes, Ditani was right. There are new rules, now that I have a follower. I violated some rules and was called by Argos to judgment."

Ticca's eyes went wide and she sat back, looking at him. "Were you guilty? What happened?"

"It is too much to explain tonight. I was found guilty, but with cause, and so the charges were recorded and dropped. If I break the same laws again, it won't go so easy. I was also given the laws of the Gods, which are the equivalent of about a dozen thick legal books. I need to memorize all of them well enough to work within them."

Ticca shook her head. "So now you have to learn the laws of the Gods *and* research what Vestul was up to. I might be an old maid by the time we figure out what to do next."

He shook his head. "Not really. I'll have the laws all figured out by tomorrow. Argos taught me how to pull that 'year in a night trick' Kliasa uses, all the laws are imbedded in my mind, so there is nothing more needed than one night's time."

Ticca nodded and looked into the fire, thinking. Ditani's lips were pursed and he was looking at Lebuin with narrowed eyes. Illa, too, was watching him, but her forehead and eyes told, as much as his connection to her, that her mind was working through the events so far.

As he took a self-inventory, he again noted the additional connection he had to Illa, and found the channels Ditani had spoken of. Some of his magical capabilities had been altered, and he wasn't sure what it would mean overall. *At least my ability to manipulate magic is still intact if not yet fully healed.*

He toyed with the conduit to Illa and found himself looking at himself through her eyes. He was holding the papers. His face had developed a little stubble over the last couple of days, and he had filled out a lot more than he thought. He was no longer a skeleton of a man. He had also developed some muscles over the weeks of training, picking up at least a quarter stone in weight. *I see what they mean. I really was starving myself. I might even end up looking better than my brother, with a few more cycles of work.* Overall, he was pleased with the clean-shaven appearance, but he needed to get some decent clothing. The Dagger leathers were kind of stylish in a rough-and-tumble way, but he was surprised to discover he still missed some of his better clothing, especially the goldenrod doublet he had left at the Guild. He recalled the various outfits he had hanging in his room there.

'You needn't worry. You are very handsome, my Lord.'

Shocked, he snapped back to himself and looked at Illa through his own eyes. She was still looking at him with that perpetual, soft smile. "You heard my thoughts?"

"Of course, my Lord. I felt you join with me, and I understood what you were thinking about your appearance. You are very handsome. But I don't think the goldenrod doublet would be the right color for you. Maybe something in a deep maroon or green would go well with your complexion and eyes. But that blue one was good, too."

Ticca looked up from the fire. "What are you talking about?"

"I was feeling out the connection between Illa and me that Ditani explained earlier. By accident, I found that I can join with Illa and see what she sees. Apparently, she can hear my thoughts, and I can hear her thoughts when doing this."

Ditani took a sip of his wine, leaned forward, and nodded. "You can shield your thoughts and presence, but I understand that takes practice."

That is why Argos's Magi have to travel, so he can observe the world through them, as Councilor Nillo said. Only this is more literal than I expected. "Argos does this, doesn't he? He watches through us."

Ditani nodded. "Yes, he makes sure all his Magi are connected well enough to allow him to do this."

Ticca yawned and put the maps back into her pouch. "I don't know about you three, but this has been a very busy and surprising day. I think we should get some sleep and make our plans in the morning."

Ticca's yawn spread like a plague, causing all of them to start yawning, repeatedly.

"I think you're right. Also, we'll be better able to plan, once Illa and I have had a chance to learn the rules we must follow."

Illa looked at him.

"Illa, if it is okay with you, I would like for you to spend a year with me tonight. I know it sounds strange, but it is an interesting and useful trick. There are rules you must know, too."

"Your will, my Lord."

Ticca looked at her. "Illa, knowledge is the most valuable weapon you can wield. But blind obedience is not honor. You must think for yourself. Learn to listen to your conscience. Then you can have honor by putting courage in motion to do the right thing. Even the Gods are not all-knowing."

Lebuin smiled at Ticca. "Trying to make my disciple a Dagger?"

"Of course. She'll be a great high priestess if she follows the Dagger code, and you know it. Otherwise, Oh Mighty One, your own subconscious wouldn't have included a Dagger symbol in your sigil."

Shocked, he looked at her, and knew she was speaking the truth. Looking over at Illa, he saw she was considering Ticca's words. The look on her face showed that the idea of questioning a superior was a difficult concept to accept.

"Thank you, Ticca, for pointing out something I should have realized. You are right. I guess you managed to make me into a Dagger in these last few weeks. You are infectious."

"You know it. Now, take this girl off to your mind space and work out what you both need to know." With that, she pulled her blanket over her and lay down with her back to the fire.

Looking at Illa, he saw she had also lain down, but was facing him. She nodded and then closed her eyes, so he followed suit. Relaxing, using a mind technique from his mage training, he built up an idea of what he needed to do. *Now, to see if I can do this.* Looking inward, he pushed away from his body, into the between realm, and willed his mind to close off from that space, so he had a private place to study.

Lebuin was not surprised to find he was sitting in the Guild library in his favorite nook. Arranged around him were tomes with the symbol of Gods, a double twisted loop of words surrounding a star on one side and a moon on the other, stamped on them. He concentrated and found Illa's connection. He pulled on it, willing her to join him, and she appeared, standing before him. She looked around and picked up one of the books, flipping through it.

"This is a lot of studying. How long do you think it will take, my Lord?"

"As much time as we need. We are between. In this place, you learn faster than you can imagine. Also, you cannot lie here."

She turned to him. "My Lord, I will never lie to you."

"Never is a long time, and we both have many years to come. But I know you will always work for my interests. For this, I cannot thank you enough. We don't technically need to eat or drink, but it will seem more normal if we do. There are rooms and we can even sleep, which I think we should do."

Illa nodded. "I was trained to hate Daggers. But what Ticca said was so interesting. Do all Daggers talk as she does?"

He nodded. "Yes, all the Daggers I have met do, which would be one." Illa laughed hard. "We have a good beginning, if you like my jokes. Seriously, Daggers are unique. They were restarted by Duke with Damega. Daggers are not just specially trained warriors for hire. They are, in fact, based on a unique group of military specialists who were respected throughout the world before they were forgotten, during Imperial times. The core of the Daggers is their total dedication to three values: honor, courage, and commitment. Every Dagger is taught logic and critical thinking, with an emphasis on not losing sight of any one of the three guiding principles. What is unique is that by commitment, Daggers do not mean commitment to their superiors, but commitment to doing the right thing. To a Dagger, courage is standing up for the right, regardless of the consequences. Finally, honor is courage in motion. Daggers will always step up to do the right thing, even if it is against their orders."

Illa thought about that. "The Nhia-Samri are only taught that honor is in doing your duty to your commanding officer.

There is a strict code of conduct. There is nothing about thinking for yourself, and the highest crime is disobedience. I find the Dagger core values far more compatible with what I have always felt would be honorable behavior. I am pleased you are a Dagger God. I shall endeavor to live to these ideals."

"We have a long time tonight to discuss the philosophy and applications of Dagger ideals. Besides teaching you what I know of Daggers, I also desire for you to teach me all you know of the Nhia-Samri, including training me in the Nhia-Samri fighting styles."

"It takes five years to complete training."

"I am a fast study, and this is not a normal environment. Let us see how far we can progress."

With that, they dug into their work. Cycles passed as they read and debated the various laws. They spent marks fighting every day, and Illa drew wondrous diagrams of the Nhia-Samri outposts she had served in. She taught him all she knew of the Nhia-Samri. He spent time giving her all the Dagger training Ticca had given him. Then he passed on all the elven combat, hunting, and survival training Kliasa had given him. He also taught her the elven language.

Nothing they changed ever disappeared, and Lebuin realized they were physically changing their minds. The diagrams and training were embedded into their consciousness. They discussed trying to pull Ticca and Ditani in on a different night, and resolved to propose the idea after reviewing the laws, to insure they were not going to violate any of them.

By morning, Lebuin had as complete an understanding of the Nhia-Samri as any Nhia-Samri warrior who was raised, trained, and part of that organization. He had mastered all of the fighting skills, at least, in his mind. His body would take time to achieve the physical abilities, but he knew what to do. He and Illa had also reviewed and debated all of the laws of the Gods and felt comfortable that they could act well enough. Lebuin knew he needed to get more followers eventually, but they had found some means whereby he had a grace period to use the mana line energies, so long as he was actively engaged in expanding his followers.

Even better was that Illa had all of his limited Dagger training and his advanced elven training rooted in her mind. She, too, had a complete set of the laws of Gods in her mind and would be able to act properly as his high priestess and disciple.

They had grown to know each other, and were compatible friends. For this, Lebuin was grateful, as he was worried they would both regret her choice if they were not able to be friends. He gave her a hug and then allowed her consciousness to return to her own body.

Alone, he spent more time considering his situation and poring over the laws of Gods, trying to determine what the Circle had done. In the end, the Circle had broken a number of laws in not recognizing a new god-kin, and in not teaching him what he needed to know, letting him roam free with his powers, which was a serious violation. He was also sure they had interfered in his education, because he found that any Elracian knowledge was never to be given to anyone, except Gods that needed it, and then, only by unanimous vote of the Circle with the agreement of Duke. But he had been given a few excellent references in Elracian knowledge and powers anonymously. There was no explanation as to why Elracian knowledge was forbidden to be shared. *I'll have to keep this my own secret. They are relatively safe in my guarded armoire's secret compartments, but I must find a better and stronger hiding place for those books.*

Satisfied, he allowed himself to return to his body and the deep sleep that waited.

- - -

Lebuin woke to the smell of breakfast. Sitting up, he stretched and looked around. He was alone in the cave. There was bread with meat sitting close to the dying fire, staying warm, and a pot of arit next to it. He poured some, grabbed the food, and stepped out of the cave mouth, into the light of day. The sun was already above the tree line, making it late morning. A short distance off, Ticca, Illa, and Ditani were sitting, talking.

Ticca was smiling as she poked fun at him. "About time, you woke up."

He joined their circle. "How long have you three been up?"

Illa sipped some of her arit. "We got up just after dawn and decided to let you rest. I had some questions for Ticca and Ditani. So we exercised and talked. We stopped for some refreshments."

Ticca looked more comfortable with, even friendly towards, Illa. *It seems they settled into something more than a truce.* Taking the last bite of his breakfast, he stood. "Well then, you three relax and let me warm up."

Stepping off, Lebuin went through the morning forms, while a buzz of conversation filled the air. He didn't bother paying attention so as to better practice. When he finished, he noticed that the sounds of conversation had died. Looking around, he noticed all three were standing near and watching him. Smiling, he motioned, and Ditani stepped up. They went through all twelve patterns together while Ticca and Illa sparred.

Finishing, he and Ditani watched the two warriors spar. Illa was as amazing a fighter as Ticca. Illa was fighting with two of Ticca's knives. As they watched, the women moved up in notches from basic drills, to more advanced sparring. It was fascinating to watch, especially in that both women were as beautiful as they were skilled.

Ditani sounded almost dreamy as he watched. "I must say, this is an unusual sight. I have been alive for nearly two thousand years and I have never once seen or heard of such beautiful and skillful warriors. I am glad those two are on our side."

Ditani has a point, considering we are here by a strange set of circumstances. Lebuin admired the skill of his first follower with a great deal of pride. Her beauty was enhanced by the neat clothing she wore. She was dressed as a bard in a patterned dark and light green medium-length tunic, trimmed with silver stitching; her dark leather pants blended into her knee-high riding boots with the brass buckles. Overall, she cut a fine image standing still, but flowing around the area like a dancer, barely touching the ground, she made the scene a work of flowing art. She exchanged blows with Ticca, who looked almost royal in a red velvet short tunic and matching leggings, her wide black belt with all the knife sheaths, and her amazing calf-high boots, which had changed to a dark burgundy.

"It's odd, but I am grateful for everything that has happened. I am happy to have all of you with me for whatever we have to do next."

Ticca ducked under a jab by Illa, and wrapped her arm around Illa's arm as she stood. The two of them twisted, and Illa managed to force Ticca away, but not before Ticca had taken one of the knives from her. Laughing, Ticca moved in for a double strike. Illa surprised her by not blocking the first knife, and instead, side-stepping with the grace of an acrobat. Illa then spun down and used her remaining knife to parry bind and disarm Ticca's second strike. Ticca yelped in surprise and twisted back to snag Illa's left leg with her right leg. Twisting, Ticca sent Illa tumbling forward. Ticca then did a backwards handstand roll, landing on her feet, with the knife she had forced Illa to drop, in her previously empty hand.

Instead of landing flat on her belly, Illa had tucked and rolled forward, coming back to her feet and twisting to end up facing Ticca. At that point, Illa only had one knife and

Ticca had the two. Still, they moved in slowly. Both women had a more intense look on their faces.

Lebuin started to stand up, but Ditani placed a hand on his shoulder. "They won't hurt each other... Well, much. I think they need to do this."

Ticca attacked first. She stepped up to Illa, deflecting Illa's knife and bringing her other hand in for a cutting stroke. Illa tried to step aside, but wasn't fast enough, and Ticca pulled her knife back at the last moment, preventing a deep cut. Still, she cut a line through Illa's fine tunic, across Illa's belly, drawing blood. Both women's looks changed, and Illa grabbed Ticca's wrist, twisting it with more strength than Lebuin thought Illa had, and causing Ticca to cut her own arm with her own knife.

Then Ticca moved almost as fast as she had at the gate fight in Llino. Ticca dropped both knives and twisted her wrist free of Illa's grip. Ticca snapped her right leg past Illa, turning her upper body into Illa and grabbing Illa by the upper arm and body, lifting her off the ground and flipping her over Ticca's hip. Illa was caught off-guard and fell on her back with the wind knocked out of her, in a loud gasp. Illa's right hand slammed onto the ground, knocking the knife out of her hand, to land a few feet away. Ticca landed on top of her and tried to lock Illa's legs with her own, while grappling Illa with one hand and reaching for her dagger, which had fallen next to Illa's head, with her other hand.

Illa found the strength to kick Ticca's legs off of her. Illa broke free from Ticca and shoved Ticca violently off her and away from Ticca's dagger. Illa then lifted her feet and did a strong snapping motion with her arms behind her head, bringing herself to a standing position. She spun, drawing her odassi, and advanced on Ticca. Ticca had used the momentum from Illa's push to roll a few feet off, and then, somehow, came up to her feet with two recovered knives, one in each hand.

Illa stepped up to Ticca and struck with a speed and deadliness that equaled Ossa-Ulla. Ticca defended and met the attack with her own counter-attacks. They spun around each other with the ringing of steel on steel, and flashes of sparks as their blades met. Their hands and arms were a blur of motion, feet stirring up a cloud of dust, as they danced around each other, exchanging blow after blow.

Lebuin had seen enough. This had shifted to something more than testing each other's abilities. He stood, feeling weird. He started to run towards the fight, but his legs felt heavy, and the world spun. As he cried out, falling, he realized that what power he had gathered was rushing out of him like a lake bursting through a dam. He didn't feel the ground as he hit it, but he did hear Ditani screaming his name.

This is so familiar, was all he had time to think before the blackness enveloped him.

ELADES

Elades enjoyed the feeling of being out in the forest once again. Riding through the trees and hearing the animal sounds always made him feel good. As he rode, he kept count of animals and people. Scouts moved through, reporting on the area. In addition to the thirty-five members of Alpha Squad, there were also the three extra non-combatants of Duke's more hearty personal staff, plus the two extra Daggers, Nigan and Risy, who might or might not be under coin with Lebuin. Looking back, he saw Nigan and Risy had taken to shepherding the non-combatants and looking after their extra pack horses. Next to him, Ladro, Duke's private secretary, rode easily, but with that wide-eyed look of someone not used to being in the wilderness. Alpha Squad was working in symmetry, keeping watch. With Duke in full-blown tracking mode, he had little to do, but enjoy the ride until something interesting happened.

Elades watched Duke moving nimbly through the forest path. He was proud that his long service as a Dagger had earned him the command position over all of Duke's Dagger forces. He had worked as a Dagger for nearly fifty years. His experience spanned whole kingdoms and even the Great War forty years ago. His training had never stopped, and he had taken time to learn all he could from every officer of every fleet and army he had encountered. All of that was paying off. He was serving the greatest Dagger legend—Duke—personally. It wasn't just that Duke was the Supreme Commander of the Imperial Armies, or the creature that had brought the Daggers back from the obscurity of legend. Nor was it that Duke was as ancient as this world. His heart and soul knew that they were going to be doing a great work, and the scourge of the Nhia-Samri would finally be stopped.

Of course, many younger Daggers were still coming to terms with the fact that their recognized founder, a fifteen-thousand year-old talking, grey wolf, larger than the largest work horse, wasn't a legend or an exaggeration. Duke had burst into the Blue Dolphin, shattering the doors of the inn and the silly games being played by the nobles, only six weeks–just one and a half cycles–ago. In that time, the pirate usurpers had been exposed and deposed, a Nhia-Samri assassination had been exposed, and the Nhia-Samri infiltration of Aelargo had been stopped dead, literally. Duke had lived up to every legend of him anyone had ever heard, and more.

Still, something big was coming, and Duke was striving to prepare for it. *I'm not sure what's coming. But I'm positive this is going to end up being yet another Dagger legend. I can feel it coming; once again, we are going to show the world what it means to be a Dagger. They'll be telling stories of our honor, commitment, and courage in facing this threat.* His thoughts turned, once again, to Ticca. *Somehow, she is central to this. I knew she was going to be great. Heck, I watched her start her career. She might be a bit showy for my tastes, but she is a hell of a good Dagger. She did everything right for those six cycles I watched, and then she did the truly extraordinary in escaping the Nhia-Samri.* He recalled how, in escaping the Nhia-Samri in Llino, she had exposed their presence, and proved more skilled than expected.

Ticca is important to Duke at a level I cannot explain. It will be interesting, seeing where all this takes us.

A scout came jogging back from ahead, and signaled that he had found a camp, but that it was empty. Looking around, he signaled for two patrols to circle the area and search for signs of anyone else. Two pairs of Daggers dropped off their horses, leaving the reins lightly looped to their saddles. Dagger warhorses knew what to do, like their owners. He added two more marks of the sun's position on his saddle in chalk, so he could be sure of how long the patrols had been out. *Always pays to know how long someone hasn't been seen.*

The remaining eighteen Daggers of Alpha Squad behind him limbered up in the saddles, in case they got some action. Duke stopped and stood still, inspecting something in front of him. Signaling Ladro to stay behind, he let his horse move up to just behind Duke before stopping. The rest of the squad stopped, as well. It was silent, except for the occasional sounds of the horses or forest animals. Duke was sniffing the wind and his ears were moving as fast as a top, twisting left and right.

"Elades," Duke said softly, "Ticca was standing right here, looking at what I am looking at, not more than a day ago, probably less."

He stretched his neck and stood up in the stirrups to look around the giant wolf's body, but still couldn't see past him. He answered back softly, as he knew Duke could hear even the softest whisper this close, "You don't make a good window, Excellency. May I join you?"

Duke looked around. In a more normal voice, Duke answered, "The immediate area is clear. Alpha Squad, dismount and rest. Do not enter this area until the scouts and I have examined it."

Elades slipped off his horse, letting the reins dangle to the ground, signaling his horse that it could graze, but not move too far away. It tore up some of the green grass and started chewing, as he stepped up next to Duke.

The narrow animal path ran out into a wide-open glade. It was beautiful, with a small rock hill and cliff on the far side. There were signs that some things had been disturbed, but without stepping into the area, he couldn't be sure. But more disturbing was that on the far side of the glade, there was a low mound of dirt with some stones arranged on top of it that looked like a grave.

"What do you think, Elades?"

Pointing at the grave, he said, "That looks like a grave." Indicating another area, he added, "Looks odd over there—something isn't right. Also, this is a pretty nice choke point, and that little hill with the rock face would make a good ambush point."

Duke nodded. "I agree. Stay here. When the scouts report in, tell them I want them to follow every sign around this site for a quarter mark and report back on how many trails come and go from here." With that, Duke put his nose to the ground and moved out into the glade. He crisscrossed the clearing many times.

While Duke was investigating the site, different scouting pairs reported back in. He was glad that so far, no scouting pair had disappeared. He sent them off with their tracking orders, changing the marks on his saddle, and then leaned up against a tree, watching Duke. A few of the squad came over to watch; others had sat down and were drinking some water or chewing salted jerky. Nigan and Risy stepped up next to him to watch. Looking over at Nigan, who was still wearing Lebuin's clothes, he snickered.

Nigan looked at him. "What's so funny, Commander?"

"You look like a massive peacock, with all that plumage. You make a great target to aim at."

Risy hit Nigan's shoulder. "Told ya, ya shoulda changed."

Nigan looked down at the fine double-breasted vest of red velvet with its shiny, silver buttons, the white silk shirt under it, and the wine-colored breaches. "Yeah, okay, so I don't blend. I'll change. Be right back."

As Nigan moved back to his horse, they continued to watch Duke, who stopped by the possible grave and sat there, looking it over for a while. Then he called out, "Okay, I got all we need from here. Come on over."

They all walked over to see what Duke was looking at, and found it was clearly a grave. The top had a pattern of grey stones, all of about the same size, shape, and color, arranged into a pattern that looked like the Nhia-Samri cat symbol.

"A Nhia-Samri grave?" someone asked.

Duke nodded. "Yes, and very disappointing, too. This is the grave of Ossa-Ulla."

He looked at Duke. "How do you know that? I don't see any markings."

Duke looked at him with amusement in his eyes. "Elades, I can smell him. Ticca, Ditani, Lebuin, and someone I don't know made this grave. Ticca was tied to that tree over there for a time, too. They removed all signs of the camp, but there was a fire over there, and Ossa-Ulla bled heavily ten feet over there, which is where I think he died."

Elades looked at all the spots indicated. "So Ticca was captured and then rescued by Lebuin, Ditani, and this other person? Why is it bad that Ossa-Ulla is dead? He was a serious threat."

Duke shrugged, which was unusual to see a wolf do. "As to why it's bad Ossa-Ulla is dead, I had a lot of detailed plans for what I wanted to do to him for instigating the murder of Magus Vestul."

Ladro made a choking noise and moved off, looking sick.

Duke gave Ladro a look, but didn't comment. The scouts chose that moment to come back and stepped up to him and Duke. "Sir, we can find little sign in any direction, except for east. Two people came here from that direction on horse. But the horses have been taken. There are occasional trail signs, but no solid trails to follow."

Duke smiled. "Not surprising, for Ticca. I am not sure what happened, but I do know that five horses were here, too. Ticca and this other person led them back here from someplace just east. When they were all done, the entire group left, heading south together with Ticca and this other person erasing the trail."

Elades looked at Duke. "Sir, if Ticca was rescued from Ossa-Ulla by her allies, who made the Nhia-Samri grave for Ossa-Ulla?"

Duke looked him in the eye, surprised by the thoughts his question had stirred up. Duke stopped smiling. "That is a very interesting question. We should catch up and ask it personally." He looked back on the majority of the squad. "Everyone rest up a little. I'm going to confirm their trail. When I get back, be ready to continue the hunt." Duke stood and padded south out of the glade with his nose hung low.

Being able to hunt like a hound must be so urded nice. They can cover their tracks, but they sure cannot cover their scents. Remembering the chemicals the Nhia-Samri had tried to hide from them in Llino, he amended his thought. *Well, at least, they cannot cover their scents in only a day. If they had a couple of weeks, maybe they could.* He nodded. *Always correct your own mistakes and remind yourself of your tactical errors, even if only in thought.* Turning back, he went to get his horse as Nigan stepped into the glade. He had changed into a rich-looking forest green, single-breasted vest, with blackened brass buttons over a dark green silk shirt with dark brown leather cuffs. His wide, brown belt was fastened over the long vest. He had on brown leggings with tall leather boots, and wore a triangular brown leather cap.

"Nigan!"

Nigan looked at him. "Sir?"

"I told you to stop looking like a target."

Nigan looked down, confused. "This works as well as what you have on, sir."

"You look like a urded noble out on a fox hunt."

Nigan puffed up and smiled. "Thank you, sir. Glad you like it."

Risy had come out of the woods behind him and was trying to not laugh.

"Risy, tell your partner to dress better."

Nigan looked down and held his arms out, turning around slowly. "Better! I'll have you know, this is a most excellent outfit, and it cost over thirty pence!"

Risy shrugged. "I can't get him to dress normally, since he started impersonating Lebuin."

Nigan looked at him. "Just because we are tromping through the forest, doesn't mean we have to dress like beggars."

A number of Daggers looked over at the conversation A few of them, and not just the women, frowned as if insulted. Elades felt his blood pressure rising. "Beggars? Are you saying we are dressed like beggars?"

Nigan looked around at the other Daggers, who were watching with various looks of amusement. "No, sir, you pull off that 'rugged warrior' look very well."

A handful of Daggers started laughing. He wasn't sure who they were laughing at. All of the Daggers present were paying attention. A soft voice he couldn't identify came from behind him. "The commander should stand down. Nigan is pretty sharp today." Turning around, he noticed his second in command was standing there with two squad members, all three of them looking innocent.

Turning back to Nigan, he meant to keep an even tone, but his voice sounded high, even to him. "Fine, dress how you like. But don't cry to me when you're the first one shot by the enemy." Turning, he strode past his second, as more Daggers joined in the laughter. He didn't stop until he reached his horse. Pulling his wine skin from the saddle, he took a long drink. He tried to reason himself down. *Lebuin has almost ruined poor Nigan. Oh well, at least, he'll blend in better than in those diurdu reds.*

The rest of the horses were brought into the glade, and

then they all waited. Some Daggers took advantage of the break to stretch out, and others gave themselves and the horses water. A few who had just come off of scout duty stretched out on the ground with their eyes closed, resting. *I love working with seasoned Daggers, with no one asking what to do. I might as well relax.* Doing some stretches and practicing the patterns, he watched the sun. It was barely past midmorning. They had ridden pretty fast out of Algan, once Duke knew where Ticca had headed. Ticca went out of her way to mark her trail up to right before the glade. *She was leading them into the glade. I wonder if she knew it was there all along, or figured she'd find an ambush point somewhere.*

After a time, everyone had settled down; they were exchanging stories about the fight nearly six weeks ago in Llino, where the Daggers, under Duke's command, had attacked the Nhia-Samri outpost there. Of course, the well-trained city guard, under the command of Dohma, had kicked it over the top when things were uncertain. *I wonder what Dohma is doing now. He was elevated pretty urd fast from Captain of the Guard to Princes' Regent of Aelargo. Duke doesn't mess around with putting things in order.* He recalled the week-long execution of the descendants of the pirate usurpers, who had taken control of the Aelargorian Kingdom some time ago.

Nigan and Risy had been hanging out with the same six Daggers since they left Llino, and now was no different. He smiled as the Daggers chatted and laughed. *Probably poking fun at Nigan or me, or both. Nigan is a fine Dagger, and those two sure as hell are good fighters. I hope they survive this war with the Nhia-Samri that Duke has declared. With their quick wit and easy smiles, they'll make great mentors for the next generation of Daggers.* His thoughts took a tactical turn as he reviewed the band of friends. *Nigan and Risy are good line fighters; Sabri is as good a scout as her husband Coedy; Tuage is an excellent fighter and engineer; Carda is a top intelligence Dagger with a lot of specialty defense training; Epton and his sister Persa are a capable defense specialist pair with counter-intelligence experience. All I need to do is add a medical specialist, and they'd be a complete fire team.*

He pulled some jerky out and chewed it thoughtfully while drinking water from his other skin. Across the glade, talking with a group of Daggers was Boadua, a priestess of Dalpha and medical Dagger who had replaced Nippon when he was killed in the Llino fight. *I'm glad she signed up. I feel a lot better knowing I have an experienced medical Dagger for the squad. She hasn't mentioned what returning to Dagger duties meant to her temple oaths. But she landed softly.*

Elades had been resting a mark before Duke came back and signaled them to follow. They fell back into riding order, and he signaled the scouts to move out on Duke's cues. The trail was so well hidden that if it wasn't for Duke, he was sure they couldn't have tracked Ticca. *Urd, her abilities are still shocking me. Only Duke appears to expect her skills to be this exceptional. First, she is able to command the Llino city defenses, a trick I thought was reserved only for the regents and Duke. Plus, she killed at least three Nhia-Samri in one-on-one fights. And she was able to fight Ossa-Ulla, who by all accounts was the best of the bunch, to a standstill, during her escape. Of course, knowing her uncle, I shouldn't be that surprised. Still, Ticca has immense talent, and Duke hasn't corrected his standing orders to stay out of her way, which I am sure is not an oversight. I wonder what was in that book he examined at the mayor's house in Algan. After reading that, he said something about 'not again'. I'm still waiting to find out what he meant by that.* Laughing, he recalled that working with Duke often meant one was left with unanswered questions.

Lothia the Raven

CHAPTER 4

THE RIGHT QUESTIONS

THE LEFT SIDE OF LEBUIN'S face felt like someone had punched him. His right arm also felt heavily abused. He was lying on his back, and his head was being held in someone's lap with a warm, soft hand. Opening his eyes, he saw the blue sky and the bottom of a dirty, tear-stained, female chin. Tears were still beading on the chin and dropping into his hair. Two people were exchanging some heated words, but he couldn't make them out. As his mind cleared, the words began to take on meaning.

"...it was."

"Urdu, no, it wasn't, and you know it. You cut her!"

"She made a mistake. I could have cut her deeper."

"You should know better than that. You could have used the side of the knife and made the same point without the cut! And what was all that, trying to strangle her with murder in your eyes? She was down with that wrestling move! What the hell were you thinking?"

"Okay, so I got a little miffed that she cut me back. It wasn't serious."

"Yes, it *was* serious. You cut her! That was out of line. You wanted to prove you were better, and lost control! Both of you lost control. Both of you are responsible for this. Step up and accept your part of the blame. When he wakes up, you are going to have to apologize for attacking his high priestess like that! Especially, since he has named you his general."

"Lords and Ladies! That was so she would follow my lead. He wasn't serious, and please stop with all this stupid priestess stuff. It isn't like he's...oh, crud."

"'Oh, crud' is right. Yes, he is, and you know it." Ditani sighed. "At least, we are lucky neither of you is hurt. We are also lucky this happened here and now."

Ticca's voice was subdued. "I don't follow you."

"Well, now we know she can't use those blades until he has a lot more resources."

"How do you know it was the blades?"

"Don't be ridiculous. She said Lebuin accepted them, which means whatever power source they used to be attached to has been replaced by him. When you two went at each other full force, I saw him fade to white, and then to grey, as he tried to get to you to stop you. He didn't have time to say anything."

Illa noticed his eyes were open, and started petting his head and talking rapidly. "My Lord! Oh, my Lord, I am so sorry. Take my mana! I have been trying to feed it to you, but I don't know how. You need mana. Please take mine—take all of it. Take it now. I...I swear, I'll not draw my odassi until you say to again. Please forgive me. I felt you fall and knew it was my fault."

He tried to speak, but couldn't, so he smiled weakly and moved his head to indicate he would be okay.

"My Lord, please understand, you must take my energies. My Lord, you must."

Lebuin's mind was moving slowly, and it took a minute more before he understood what she meant. Looking inside, he found he had only a small fraction of magical energies left. He searched for his connection to Illa and found it. She was already sending him more than normal. But she was untrained, so it was not as much as she could give. It took a few more minutes to figure out how to draw mana from her, but once he did, he got more energy, and his mind started moving faster.

Trying again, he croaked out, "Illa, what happened?"

"Ditani thinks my fight with Ticca using the odassi drained you of all your magic. Please take all you can from me. I don't need it to live, but you do."

Reaching again for the connection, he pulled all that was left and he felt better. But there was still so little, he wasn't sure what else he could do. All the power that had been built up was gone, and it would take weeks to restore it with Illa as the only source.

Illa seemed to be reading his mind, which was possible, given their connection. "My Lord, the laws say you can draw from the mana lines if you are starving and have no more followers' energies. If you take all of mine, you may draw from the mana lines. But only enough to restore you to health."

Smiling, he knew what she meant. Illa had no more power to give, and he did need more. Reaching out, he found a nearby mana line and refilled his energy levels. He did not take as much as he could hold. He stopped, drawing well short of his estimate of the laws' allowances. He still felt weak, but his head was clearing. Sitting up, he looked around. Illa had dropped her odassi a few feet away.

Ticca was standing a couple of feet off, looking at him. "Are you okay?"

He nodded. "I need a little time for the mana to flow through me a bit more. That was the oddest feeling I have ever had."

Ticca knelt, putting her head on level with him and looking into his eyes, she said, "Lebuin, I am very sorry. It is my fault. I lost my temper and let this get too far out of control. I knew better. There is no excuse."

Illa shifted to his other side, also kneeling. "My Lord, I too lost control. I am sorry. I am as much to blame as anyone. More, I have studied the laws and should have surmised from them, the implications of a situation such as this."

Lebuin looked back and forth between them, then up at Ditani. Ditani was standing there with his arms crossed, looking as pleased as any parent for a child who had gotten out of control, but who had properly made amends. *This feels so strange. I don't like having people kneeling to me.*

"Ticca, Illa, it is okay. I didn't think of it, myself. In fact, I am going to have to do a lot of thinking about any incantation before I cast it now. Most of my magical workings require a lot of power." Remembering some of the other details of the Elracian books of magic, he added, "But I know there are ways to do the same with less energies. I will have to be careful for a long time." Remembering that he was a God and that Illa was his follower, he figured it was worth giving her formal absolution. "Also, I forgive both of you. Please don't do it again, though."

Illa sighed in relief, and Ticca relaxed too.

They both were seeking forgiveness. This is going to take a lot of getting used to.

Ticca looked worried, but at least, her smirk came back.

"Can you stand yet? You might want to walk and breathe."

"Thanks, Ticca. Please, would you two help me up? I am not sure if I can stand, and my face feels like the ground was mad at me for falling on it."

Both women smiled that his sense of humor was returning. They stood and helped him to his feet. At first, he was somewhat wobbly, but it passed. Ditani went and brought back a hot cup of arit, which he took and drank while walking around. After a quarter mark, he was feeling normal.

"Maybe we can spar a little more. I think I need to move, and that will pump stuff around."

Ticca stepped over. "Are you sure?" He nodded. She looked at Illa. "Well, I was planning on doing something new for our training exercises, now that we have Illa. We can do three-on-one combat. We can do the basics and keep it slow and controlled. Does that sound okay?"

He smiled. "That sounds fun. Illa, Ditani, are you two okay with this?"

Ditani looked him over, and Illa was considering it.

Well, at least, she didn't blindly agree. That is a very good sign.

Ditani nodded. "It does sound fun. Just promise me you'll stop us if it's too much for you. We all need to be in good standing, if we're to continue down this path we are on."

Illa stepped over and picked up her odassi, cleaning them off and sheathing them. "I agree with Ditani. Will you stop if I sense anything wrong with you?"

Laughing, he told her, "You're not my mother. You're my high priestess."

"Different title, same job," she snapped back at him.

He relented, holding up his hands. "Okay, okay, you two. I promise if I feel weakened, I'll stop. Satisfied?"

All three of them nodded. Ticca stepped over to Illa, holding out her hands. "Illa, I am sorry—I was out of line."

Illa took her hands in her own. "I, too, went too far. Comrades?"

Ticca nodded. Letting go of Illa, she drew two knives and spun them around her hands dramatically ending with holding them by the blades, hilts towards Illa. "I'll give you the sheaths for these later, so you can have them to use instead of those odassi."

Illa took the knives and smiled.

Ticca clapped her hands and turned to face all of them. "So let's start with you three attacking me, and I will show you the basics. We'll keep it slow until you two," indicating Ditani and Lebuin, "have the feel for it."

Three-on-one combat was different and took a lot of getting used to. Ditani had to be corrected many times. Then it was Lebuin's turn in the hot spot. He kept losing track of at least one of them, until a sword slapped him someplace. After a rather painful rib slap, he held up his hand. "I surrender for today. I'll get it, but not this minute. Also, I am getting tired. Lunch anyone?" Illa and Ticca chuckled, but relented.

Ticca sheathed her sword and dagger. "I think we make a pretty good team."

Ditani measured the light. "Well, it is past noon. I assume we are going to stay here another night?"

Illa and Ticca both looked up surprised. Ticca laughed. "I was having so much fun, I lost track of time." Illa nodded in agreement.

"I don't see any reason to rush back to town today."

Ticca was about to agree with him when her face changed to a worried look.

"What...?"

Ticca's eyes flashed to the tree line, and she pulled her sword and dagger. Illa cued from her and turned the same way, holding the knives Ticca had given her, at the ready.

Ditani and Lebuin took a moment longer to register something was happening before they drew and stepped up next to Ticca. She was scanning the woods. Softly, she said, "Someone is coming. Circle up and be ready."

ELADES

According to the marks on Elades' saddle, they had been following the new trail for a day and a half when Duke stopped suddenly and went on point, like a hunting dog. He signaled, and all the Daggers slipped off their horses and moved up around Duke, like ghosts. Looking over, he noticed Nigan was practically invisible behind some grass, as he moved up. *Okay, you win. That outfit does blend well.*

Duke sniffed the air and then moved forward slowly. Alpha Squad fanned out, making a firm line. A third of the squad took the horses and provided rear guard. Picking every step carefully, Elades moved up behind, and to the side of Duke. He heard an almost inaudible, low growl, which made him draw his sword and dagger. All of the squad followed his lead. Duke lowered himself so he was almost on the ground, his hind legs poised to leap. In the hunting crouch, Duke pushed his head past some deep grass.

Elades could make out through the brush an open area, and on top of a small hill, stood some figures with weapons out in a defensive circle. No one moved for what felt like a long time. Finally, a female voice called out authoritatively.

"Whoever you are, we know you're there. Come on out. If I have to come in there and get you, you won't like the results."

A male voice laughed. "She's not kidding—she's dangerous, even when she isn't grumpy. But when she gets mad, you don't want to be on the receiving end."

Nigan motioned to him. He looked over and Nigan signaled that that was Ticca and Lebuin. He relaxed slightly. *False alarm.* He said to Duke, "Sir, Nigan confirms it is Ticca and Lebuin."

Duke growled in response, and moved forward, into the open like he was ready to kill.

Something is wrong. All right, let's do this by the rules. He signaled for half to remain hidden and the other half to advance on his lead, ready for a fight. Then he turned and stepped out into the open space, behind and slightly to the left of Duke, to make sure he had full maneuvering room. Thirteen other Daggers stepped out with him, all on the ready.

He recognized Ticca, as well as Lebuin and Ditani, from the descriptions he had. The fourth member of their group was someone he didn't know. She stood next to Ticca, facing them. Her tunic had a cut across the belly, as if she had been in a fight, and there was a bloody line on her skin underneath. Both Ticca and the other lady had been in a recent fight. Then he spotted what had Duke on edge. The new lady had a pair of odassi tucked in her belt, although she was holding two normal-looking, long, fighting knives in her hands. *She's a Nhia-Samri, but she is standing with Ticca and Lebuin. Could we have another traitor?*

Duke's ears were back, flat against his skull. "Who is that with you, Ticca?"

Ticca looked them over and nodded in recognition of a few Daggers. Ticca's eyes locked on Elades'. "Hey Elades, you were the back-up at the West Gate. Thanks." Ticca didn't drop the ready stance, and looked back at Duke. "She is with us. If you have a problem with this, you can move along Or you can try to take us, if you want."

Duke was not fazed or impressed with the bravado. "She carries true odassi, making her a Nhia-Samri, and right now, I am hunting Nhia-Samri. So step away and let me take care of her."

Lebuin and Ditani were concentrating on covering

Ticca's back from attack and didn't look over. But still, Lebuin spoke, "Duke, she is not a Nhia-Samri. Those are not what you think."

Duke moved forward, and Ticca shifted to face him. The other three shifted as well, remaining in the defensive circle. *Now that is a good team. They are not relaxing, nor letting themselves be surprised from behind. I thought Lebuin was a new Journeyman mage and Ditani was a servant. But they are moving and acting like experienced Daggers. What the hell is going on?*

Ticca shook her head. "You'll have to go through me. She is under my command."

Duke's ears snapped up and pointed at Ticca in surprise. "What do you mean, under your command?"

Lebuin took exception, too, because he asked the same thing at the same time.

The other woman with Ticca looked amused.

Ticca, in a completely serious tone, said, "I am Lebuin's general, and he placed her under my command."

Elades felt like laughing, except Ticca's tone made it clear she wasn't joking. Lebuin also took it seriously. "Oh yeah. Sorry, General Ticca. It's been a busy day."

This was almost too much for Elades, as he felt they were making some kind of joke, and he found it funny. Duke, on the other hand, didn't laugh, but he straightened up. "Listen here, you little whelp, and you, too, Ticca. I don't care if you're a God; I am a field marshal and Supreme Commander of the Alliance. I order you three to stand down and let me at this Nhia-Samri."

Ticca smiled wickedly and was trying not to laugh. Duke's ears drew back as he growled and advanced. "I'm not playing games."

Ticca looked at Duke. "Duke, stop. You have no idea how wrong you are."

Duke obeyed. He straightened up and sat down, pointing

both his ears straight at Ticca. "Okay, Ticca. Who the hell is she, *please?*"

Why is Duke obeying orders and being polite? For the hundredth time in the last cycle, he found himself asking, *Who is Ticca?*

Ticca looked at Duke for a second and then relaxed. "Well, this is where you are not going to believe us." She straightened, spinning both her knife and sword as she sheathed them. "Duke of Greyrhan, Lord of Aelargo, Supreme Commander of the Imperial Armies of Duianna, allow me to present to you Lady Runa-Illa, High Priestess and First Disciple of Lebuin."

Duke's mouth dropped open and a gurgling sound came out.

What did we walk into? I'm with Duke on this. That sounded formal, and it made Lebuin sound like a God.

Duke shook his head as if trying to wake up. "Are you crazy? Lebuin isn't a God. You must have taken a blow to the head, or something."

Lebuin sheathed his weapons and stepped over next to Runa-Illa, putting a hand on her shoulder. Runa-Illa straightened up and slipped the two knives into her belt without any sheaths. She bowed to Duke. "I am pleased to meet the great Duke, Lord of Aelargo."

Duke started to nod his head in response, then stopped. "You really think you are a high priestess? Lebuin, please tell her you are not a God."

Lebuin stood proudly. "Sorry, Your Excellency. I am what I am, and she is my high priestess."

Duke looked around, then back at the four on the hill. He considered the possibilities. Duke looked at Ticca, then looked back at Lebuin. "So you are saying you're not a Journeyman mage, but a God?"

Ditani stepped up and put his hand on Lebuin's shoulder, stopping him from the reply he was about to make. "Your Excellency, my deepest apologies. I should have done this right away. However, the situation was ... tense. Duke of Greyrhan, Lord of Aelargo, Supreme Commander of the Imperial Armies of Duianna and Daggers all, please recognize me, Ditani, Speaker of the Tribes of Kiliua-ona, and allow me to present to you Lord Lebuin of House Caerni, Journeyman of the Guild of Argos, son of Lord Waylen Caerni and Lady Alia Caerni, Grandson of All-Father Argos and Lothia the Raven of Karakia. Hail, Lord Lebuin!"

Some of the Daggers reacted to the temple phrasing, and called out together, "Hail, Lord Lebuin!" A few had the decency to look embarrassed afterwards, but still others stood proudly of their acknowledgement of Lebuin as a God.

Many thoughts warred for Elades' attention. *That was too formal. I have heard of the tribes of Kiliua-ona. It is said they answer directly to Lothia.* Sheathing one of his knives, he absent-mindedly ran his hand over his head and through his greying brown hair. Wiping his forehead on his sleeve, he tried to take in Lebuin as a God, and was having some difficulty with the idea of a God looking like an ordinary man who has been camping in the woods.

Duke stood and took a step backward, almost running into Elades, and raising his right front paw in surprise. "That is a false claim. Alia is in the west. If you really want to play this game, you will regret it." Duke sat down, his tail brushing Elades' leg. He raised his head, and then made a howling call that was musical, but not loud. A strange vibration ran through Elades' body as the sound of Duke's call washed over him like a wave. He had the distinct impression of Duke's call retreating off into the woods, like a bird flying away.

What the hell was that? Lords and Ladies, please keep this normal! At least, this has moved to a talking match. He sheathed his dagger and the other Daggers followed his lead. They collapsed into a rough line centered on him and fanning out from Duke, facing the four on the top of the hill, who were also standing in a line facing them.

Duke looked around and then called out, "The rest of Alpha can come out and witness the fun."

The others came out of the woods and lined up. Lebuin's face lit up when he saw Nigan and Risy. "Hello you two, glad you made it through." Nigan and Risy laughed and nodded back. Nigan was looking all around with his usual grin, taking in the world like a man enjoying an excellent wine. Risy, however, seemed to be looking at only Ticca, with a grin on his face.

Boadua stepped up next to Elades and warned him. "You might want to step away from Duke."

He looked at Boadua. "Why?"

"He is about to get a big shock," Boadua said mysteriously, and then stepped a good distance away. He decided a warning was always welcome. Even if not right, it would be stupid to not trust her. She was gazing on Lebuin with a kind of spiritual light in her eyes. *Oh, Lady, please. I hate dealing with religious types.* Taking her advice, Elades moved out from behind Duke, giving the old wolf six feet of clearance. The other Daggers shifted around him, doing the same.

A huge black bird flew out of the forest from the south and circled the scene, cawing. Duke looked up at it with his mouth open, and he jumped backward. If Elades had stayed where he had been standing, he would have been bowled over by Duke.

Now, how the hell did she know that was going to happen? Glancing at Boadua, he saw she was standing facing the coming raven with her open hands out, palms up, and her eyes were tearing.

The raven circled the area twice, then drifted down to land, facing Duke; but instead of landing, at six feet off the ground, it started to shimmer and elongated to almost touch the ground. Boadua fell to her knees, eyes locked on the shimmering form.

Instead of a raven, a tall woman with long, straight, black hair that fell to her waist stood in front of Duke. She wore a triangular parka-like top made of an animal hide, which was embroidered with thousands of beads of many colors. The beads formed the silhouette of a raven against a full moon in the center of her breast. There was a shimmering quality to the woman, and the feathers in her head dress didn't settle down. Instead, they floated.

Elades knew that for the first time in his life, he was before a true Goddess. It took no thought to identify the Goddess as Lothia the Raven, wife of the All-Father Argos. He felt her presence as much as he saw her. He fell to his knees as his mind, soul, and voice as one screamed, "Hail, Lady Lothia." The Daggers that hadn't done the same echoed those who had, and followed him to their knees.

The legends of Duke are not exaggerated—he can call on the very Gods. But I never dreamed he could call upon the wife of the All-Father!

Unashamed, Elades looked upon Lothia, burning her beautiful image into his mind. She wore an almost scandalous, side-split, brown, soft leather skirt that fell to her knees, which was also embroidered with bright beads in a peculiar pattern. Her toned legs and feet were bare, except for a white fur anklet decorated with two floating black feathers, and tied by a blue beaded leather strap on her right leg. Her top was held in place by a leather belt from which a single long, double-edged blade in an open sheath hung on her right and an embroidered buckskin pouch on her left. Her hair was held back from her face by a silver hair clasp on the left side, from which half a dozen raven feathers decorated with silver beads on leather pulls gently floated. Her skin was red tan and her eyes were the blue of deep water with oversized pupils. *I really must visit Karakia. I have heard all the women there mimic her in dress style. It must never get too cold.*

Duke bowed to her. Only Ticca, Lebuin, Ditani, Runa-Illa, and Duke remained standing.

"Duke, it has been so long. I am pleased to see you now." She stepped up and gave Duke a hug.

Duke closed his mouth, and when she let go, stepping back even more, he shook his head to look at her. "I didn't call you, Lothia. Even if I had, that was too fast. What is going on?"

Instead of answering him directly, she turned, looking over the Daggers present. "You are all fine Daggers and should be proud of the record of your actions. I am pleased you are here to witness this."

Turning again, she appeared to walk up the hill, but reached the top in only a few steps. She faced Ditani. "Kiotiaditani, my son, it has been over three hundred years since we last met. You have done well."

Ditani is Kiotiaditani, the son of Lothia! Oh, thank the Ladies and Lords, we didn't attack. I've heard he tries to avoid fighting, but is a vicious fighter, inhumanly strong and fast.

Ditani smiled. "Hello, Mother. I am pleased to see you."

Duke made a strangling noise at the initial exchange. Ditani—or Kiotiaditani—and Lothia hugged each other long. "Mother, Magus Vestul is…"

"I know, my son. In time, we will meet in your asi, smoke the ritual pipe, and share our stories."

Ditani looked down. "Mother, I have lost what should not have been lost. I cannot return to my asi."

Even though Lothia's back was to him, he knew her smile never faded. Lothia's hands raised to brush back Ditani's hair over his ears. When her hands finished, he was wearing a Karakian head piece of raven feathers decorated with bright beads. "No, my son." Lothia pulled the air, and in her hand, was a leather pack decorated with beads. "I took these from your home with Vestul before the fire reached them."

She was here for the fire that burned Magus Vestul's home. Now, I see why Duke is suspicious. Karakia is thousands of miles over the mountains to the south. Why is Lothia here? Elades' attention was pulled back by Ditani choking before taking the pack and saying, "thank you," along with some words he didn't understand, in a deep, guttural yet musical language.

Turning from Ditani, Lothia moved to Lebuin. "Hail, Lord Lebuin. My grandson, you have surprised us all, and I am pleased to be with you now." She gave Lebuin a hug. Lebuin looked like he was going to cry. He stood woodenly stiff and proud, unable to speak. "Grandson, I hope when Kiotiaditani and I meet in his asi, you will be there, too."

She moved on to face Runa-Illa. "Runa-Illa, High Priestess and First Disciple of Lebuin, you are the greatest surprise of all to us. I confess though, you are one of the happiest surprises to me in many years. I have tasted of your spirit and found it good and wholesome. Know that both Argos and I are pleased with your service to our grandson."

She moved on to face Ticca, holding her hands out in the Dagger style. "Ticca of Rhini Wood, Dagger General of Lebuin, your service honors me." Ticca took her hands and swelled with pride, standing tall.

"The honor is in the service, Great Lady."

"We are pleased with your service." She released Ticca and turned to Duke.

She stepped down from the hill, in those strange few steps that covered so much distance, and stood before Duke. "Duke, second most beloved of my husband," she put her finger on the tip of Duke's nose, "and I make sure you stay second to me," she grabbed Duke's head in her hands and pulled his head down, kissing his forehead. "Are you now satisfied?"

Duke was unable to answer. He opened and closed his mouth a couple of times before he got out, "Lothia, I do not understand. The Circle is required to tell me."

She looked sad. "Yes, we have been judged and punished for this. It was necessary. In time, I promise we will explain."

Duke's tone turned hopeful. "If Lebuin is Alia's son, then Alia is in Llino. I can double back and see her before the race to Gracia."

Lothia frowned. "My precious Duke, no. Alia died in giving birth to Lebuin's sister."

Duke looked at her in shock and anger. "How could you let that happen? You could have called on me for the power!"

Tears fell from Lothia's eyes. "I had already given so much of myself for Lebuin. I gave what little I had remaining and more. Still, it was not enough. There was no time between to gather. It never occurred to me to call on you."

Duke roared out, "LOTHIA, YOU ALL MADE ME! I'M YOUR MISTAKE! You could have taken all you gave me to save her! I have lived too long!"

Lothia wept and leaned into Duke, grabbing his neck in a hug and burying her face in the thick fur of his neck. "No, Duke, you are not a mistake. You were never less than a miracle. I don't even know if we could use your powers."

Duke was silent as Lothia wept into his neck. He relented, looked down, and whimpered. "Kliasa, Athren, Damega, Vestul, Alia…how many others, Lothia? How many others am I going to find dead when I should have been there protecting them? How many deaths are you hiding from me, and why?"

Lothia released Duke's neck and straightened, wiping tears from her eyes. She took a moment, regaining her composure, looking around at everyone present. None of the Daggers moved or made a sound. She faced Duke again, placing her hand on his lowered head, and smiled. Her voice was mournful and loving. "That is not yet known. You are a principle in this, as are all present now. I cannot say more. Do as your heart and conscience tell you, as you always have. You long ago earned our trust, and we need you now as much as we did then."

Duke looked up at her with shock in his eyes. Although tears stained Duke's face, his brows tightened, making it obvious he had snapped out of his grieving and was thinking hard. Lothia stepped back from the sudden movement. Her mouth opened, forming an 'O,' and her eyes darted around.

Elades' stomach tightened and his heart stepped up as he realized what just happened. *She made a mistake. But what was it?*

Before Duke could say anything more, she gestured, saying hastily, "Do as you must. Good luck." She shimmered, and her form pulled up from the ground, into the form of a large raven, which gave a strong downbeat of its long, powerful wings and launched into the air. It circled once, making a farewell caw, then dived south into the forest.

Obviously trying to lighten the mood, Lebuin and Ticca looked at Ditani and said together, "Kiotiaditani?"

He shot back, "It is difficult for northerners to pronounce, let alone spell!" They laughed, as did a few Daggers.

Ticca, unfazed, looked at Duke. "Now, will you please stop offering to kill Illa?"

Duke's eyes remained unfocussed as he was still processing whatever mistake Lothia had made. His eyes focused on Ticca and the present situation. "Of course." He looked at Lebuin and stood tall, yelling, "Hail, Lord Lebuin!"

The Daggers jumped to their feet, yelling, "Hail, Lord Lebuin!"

Duke looked at Illa and yelled, "Hail, Illa, High Priestess of Lebuin!"

The Daggers echoed him, "Hail, Illa, High Priestess of Lebuin!"

Lebuin looked embarrassed. Duke glanced over. "Elades, set up camp and get some deer in here. We need to have a feast and a good talk."

The other Daggers didn't even wait for orders; they moved off to various tasks. *I don't blame them. This was too much to witness for anyone. Something ordinary like striking camp or finding dinner is probably what we need.* Looking at his squad, he felt pride. *They didn't waver, and Lothia said we could all be proud of the record of our actions.*

Ticca stepped towards Duke. "Duke, we have a camp over there in a large cave. It won't hold everyone, but you'll fit. We can go sit and talk without interruption while they set up your camp."

Duke nodded. "Sounds perfect, but I need a serious

drink. Ladro, please get some of my wine and give it to Elades. Then you can help with the food preparation. I want a real feast tonight. Elades, join us with that wine, please."

Saluting his understanding to Duke, he moved off with Ladro to find the horse with Duke's wine on it. As Ladro was pulling the wine off, he heard from a short distance off, Lebuin's voice. "Oh, thank goodness, you brought some of my clothes. I am getting so tired of these leathers and leggings. By the way, that is a nice ensemble you're wearing."

"Thanks. I had it made during the first week I was playing you. Thought I might get some stupid Knife to try to get me while I was at the tailor." Nigan's tone took on an expectant quality. "By the way, are Risy and I still under General Ticca's command?"

Nigan is discussing clothing with a new God. I think I need this wine as much as anyone else. What else can happen to make this even more unbelievable? Shaking his head, he left to find the cave and have some wine. As he found the cave entrance, he saw Illa and Boadua were moving off into the thicker brush together. Boadua had some medical supplies with her. *Oh, good. Take care of that cut before it becomes infected. I wonder where Illa got a cut like that.*

The cave was large, but not by much. Duke took up a lot of room. Elades sat down next to Duke and poured out over half of the small keg of wine into a bowl Ladro had given him. Then he poured a cup for himself and took a long drink of it. Ditani came in carrying the leather pack, and very carefully placed it with some gear at the back, before taking a seat opposite from Duke, by the fire. Ticca came in a short time later with a clean face and hands. She sat down near Ditani.

He offered her some wine, and she pulled out a camping cup for him to fill. She leaned back and drank the wine. Then she stared at Ditani, who still hadn't taken off the head piece. "What's with all the feathers?"

Ditani's hand snapped up to touch the head piece. "It is formal attire for such meetings as we are about to have. If you knew how, you could read my name, parentage, tribal affiliations, and rank."

Ticca nodded. "You'll have to teach me someday."

Lebuin walked in wearing a dark blue double-breasted doublet over a black silk shirt, and expensive riding boots. He walked over to sit next to Ticca. She looked at him and made a snorting sound. He looked back unrepentantly.

Not sure of the proper protocol for dealing with a God, Elades defaulted to treating him like a superior officer. "Lord, would you like some wine?"

Lebuin looked at him and smiled at the keg. "I suspect that is a lot better than what we have. I would love to join you." Lebuin produced a camping cup and leaned over, holding it steady for Elades to fill. Being a tad nervous, he filled it almost to the brim, but Lebuin was pleased, and drank off the first half of the cup before making a satisfied sound and leaning back. "It is very fine sharre. Thank you, Duke, for sharing."

Duke was thinking hard, staring at the fire and lapping up his own wine, but he looked up at the direct comment and smiled. "My pleasure. And I am glad to meet you in person. Please forgive my outburst to your grandmother. I have to admit, I am overwhelmed by all this."

Ticca and Lebuin both huffed in unison and said together, "Welcome to the club." Then they smiled, looking at each other. Something passed between them. Duke watched this with interest.

Once they were settled, Duke looked at Lebuin, who realized that as the highest-ranking person present, he was in control of the meeting. He cleared his throat and looked at Ticca. She nodded, and he looked around. "Uh, well, let's keep this informal, especially since I have no idea how to make it formal. Not sure where to begin."

Duke nodded, as well. "Well, Lord, if you don't mind, would you explain Illa and that Nhia-Samri grave on your back trail?"

Lebuin smiled. "Okay, but let me start with the fact that we are probably more confused about events than you, Excellency. I was never told I was a demi-god and thought I was human and a Journeyman mage of the Guild. When we started nearly six weeks ago, I thought I was being hunted by assassins because of a Guild rivalry. Because of Illa, we just learned there was far more going on."

Lebuin motioned towards Ditani. "We are trying to find out what Magus Vestul was doing, and trying to stop the Nhia-Samri from getting that same knowledge. This started because Ditani asked me to help him track down Magus Vestul, who had disappeared."

Indicating Ticca he continued. "Ticca was captured by Runa-Illa and Ossa-Ulla. Ditani and I didn't realize she *wanted* to be captured, so we tried to rescue her. During the fight, I lost one of my knives and grabbed Runa-Illa's odassi of prayer to replace it. I had no idea that an odassi was anything more than a good fighting knife."

Lebuin looked at his hands shaking his head. "When I grabbed it, my magic as a demi-god interacted with it such that I learned all Illa had done. I was overwhelmed and reacted by instinct. I felt their warlord trying to feel me out and learn what was happening. I tried to block him, using my mage training, and in doing that, cut off the warlord from Ossa-Ulla, but I also destroyed Ossa-Ulla's odassi. Illa and I were connected through her odassi. Illa recognized me as a God, and in that instant, offered herself up to me. I didn't know what I was doing, but her service felt right. I instinctively accepted her and her odassi. But not knowing what that meant or how to do that, I bound her to me as a disciple

"After that, I still didn't know what I was or understand what I had done. I was just trying to keep things together, and I knew Illa was no danger, but I had to convince Ticca. So I named Ticca a general to let her think I was tricking Illa, instead of buying time, so I could make Ticca understand. Again, this felt right to me.

"We came here and worked all this out, trying to decide what to do next."

Duke listened, looking back and forth between Ticca and Lebuin. After thinking about Lebuin's information, Duke explained, "Well, that about sums it up for me. I came down here to meet with Magus Vestul because he sent me a mysterious note saying he needed to turn some information over to me.

"However, Magus Vestul was killed by the Nhia-Samri actions before we met. For some reason, they didn't get his research. I also learned that the Kingdom of Aelargo had been usurped shortly after I left, by pirates. They had killed off all of the real regents. These same pirates also had Damega killed.

"I'd just finished restoring the real regents' line into control of Aelargo when I found out about the Nhia-Samri connection. We had a good initial skirmish, wiping out the Llino Nhia-Samri outpost. I have declared a war on the Nhia-Samri, which starts in three cycles.

"To be honest, I haven't been so out of touch in thousands of years. I still don't know what Vestul was up to, why I had to have it, why the Nhia-Samri want it, and what is going on."

They spent a few marks running over the details from every direction. Elades was called on to recite his intelligence-gathering data, and then they discussed the details and possible arrangements of events. They exchanged every detail and sat around thinking about the possibilities.

Ticca spoke up. "Well, Lebuin and I have had a number of powerful entities speak of some huge catastrophe. We had decided to pursue Vestul's research to make sure it doesn't get to the Nhia-Samri. But we are feeling our way through this."

Duke said, "Well, Lothia dropped a massive hint by accident, which is unnerving. If this catastrophe is on the same scale as what she hinted at, we need to find out what is going on, and fast."

Lebuin looked over. "What was the event she hinted at?"

Duke slurped up some more wine. "The destruction of two universes."

Ticca sat back at that pronouncement with a look of wonder.

I probably have the same look on my face. What could threaten an entire universe, let alone, two?

Lebuin laughed. "A bit much. The destruction of one would be enough." Duke looked at him hard till he cut off his laugh. "You were serious?"

Duke nodded.

He felt something shift in his gut. *Please, Lady, let him be wrong. I don't want to be involved in something where if we make a mistake, the whole universe will pay the price.* At the same time, he felt his resolve harden. *Still, if someone has to deal with a situation like this, Duke is who I'd trust and follow.*

Everyone drank their wine and considered the situation. Duke's ears rotated towards the cave entrance and he said in that direction, "Thank you, Ladro. We'll eat with the squad out there." Looking back at the group, he relayed, "Ladro said that some deer and wild boar were brought in and are being prepared. The feast will be ready in a few marks." Everyone continued to contemplate while drinking their wine.

Duke broke the long silence by looking at Ticca. "What about you? Where did you come from?"

Ticca looked surprised by the question. She looked him in the eye. "I am a farmer's daughter from Rhini Wood. I grew up trapping and selling furs to support my family. My uncle was a Dagger many years ago and trained me when I decided I didn't want to be a farmer or trapper."

Lebuin shook his head. "Don't forget to mention your other training."

Duke looked at Lebuin. "What do you mean by that?"

Ticca shifted and looked down at the fire. Lebuin ignored her discomfort. "From my historical readings and some basic military studies at the Guild, I'd say she has tactical and warfare training beyond anything even a seasoned military noble could dream of. Plus, I have been trained extensively in the elven fighting styles, yet her training and speed exceeds even the best elven warriors by more than a small margin. I believe she is unbeatable, so long as raw strength isn't a deciding factor. Not to say she isn't strong, but a strong male warrior could out-muscle her."

Duke looked back at Ticca. "Who trained you?"

"My uncle was one of the better Daggers of his day. An old friend of his who was even better came and trained me for the last three years, before declaring I was as good as he could make me."

Ditani looked like he had a hold of something. "Your uncle was from Rhini Wood, too?"

Ticca nodded.

"Fatla of Rhini Wood?"

Ticca nodded again.

Ditani's voice was awed. "Did you ever best this old friend of your uncle?"

Ticca blushed, her eyes returning to the fire. She considered before nodding. "I did manage to get under his guard once or twice, towards the end of my training. Not a real win, but enough that he said I might with some more experience, and if I ever got less wooden, I'd be his equal. He still beat me, hands-down, every time."

Ditani's eyes were wide as he stared at her. "You got under the Traitor's guard?"

Ticca looked shocked. "How do you know that?"

Duke's mouth closed with such a loud snap, they all jumped and looked at him. Lebuin looked confused.

Ditani was the only one who was able to speak. "I know because I was in the war. I am nearly two thousand years old. That war was only forty years ago. I was Magus Vestul's servant and knew all the Dagger commanders and officers of the Alliance. In a Nhia-Samri attack on a command meeting, your uncle was heavily wounded, saving the Traitor's life, and they spent a great deal of time together because of that. I know your uncle, and I have seen some of the unbelievable feats he pulled off. Magus Vestul hinted that your uncle was special, but never explained it. So there is only one 'old friend' of your uncle that could train you better than your uncle and that is the Traitor."

Ticca looked to have been sucker-punched, and Lebuin looked annoyed, asking, "Who is this traitor you all are talking about? Does he have a name?"

How can he not know about the Traitor? Looking at the others, Elades realized they were thinking the same thing. Everyone, including Duke, was looking at Lebuin like he had some gross thing clinging to his shirt. In fact, Lebuin looked down to make sure he didn't.

Ticca found her voice. "Are you serious? You don't know who we are talking about?"

"Would I ask if I knew?"

Ditani sat back as he started to speak. "The shortest answer is that he was the Nhia-Samri second in command to the Grand Warlord. He is also a legendary warrior who is faster than anyone should be, even without an odassi. Again, Magus Vestul hinted that he was something more, but never explained it to me. Still, the Traitor only has one warrior better than he, and that is the Grand Warlord of the Nhia-Samri.

"By the way, the Grand Warlord of the Nhia-Samri killed hundreds of Daggers by himself, all in a single, straight-up fight, when they managed to ambush him during the war. I was there and saw it! Magus Vestul fled with me from that ambush when he realized we were going to lose!

"He is called the Traitor because he quit the Nhia-Samri, exposing their involvement in the war and helping to end it by defeating the Nhia-Samri squads. The Grand Warlord is so outraged by the betrayal, he posts a one hundred-gold crown reward every year at winter solstice in every major city on the continent, for information leading to the capture of the Traitor. The Grand Warlord has also placed some kind of massive incantation around the name of the Traitor so that when someone speaks his name, the Nhia-Samri instantly know it, and send a squad to investigate.

"When the Nhia-Samri 'investigate' a sighting, they tend to kill everyone in the process. So no one likes him or the Nhia-Samri, and no one dares to speak his name. Since the reward posters say 'for the capture of the Traitor, so-and-so,' people have started calling him 'the Traitor'. All this, even though he helped end the war and saved thousands of peoples' lives. He lives in hiding because should the Grand Warlord ever find him, he will be killed very uncomfortably."

Lebuin turned, with his mouth hanging open, to Ticca. "And you were trained by this Nhia-Samri Traitor and scored real hits against him?"

Ticca nodded, blushing deeper.

Urd, girl, be proud of that! Nothing to be ashamed of. Or is it that you don't like being so focused on? You probably prefer to be the observer. He recalled watching Ticca all those cycles as she worked to establish herself. *It's one thing to want to be noticed and another to actually be noticed.*

Lebuin's eyes and face told of the dozens of emotions he was rolling through. Without warning, Lebuin said, "Well then, I am going to pay attention to your morning lessons, from now on."

A God is taking lessons from a Dagger trained by the best, and that is the best he can think of? Elades couldn't keep a straight face, and started laughing. Ticca looked annoyed, but then Ditani and Lebuin joined him, chuckling. Finally, Ticca burst out laughing. Duke looked at all of them like they had grown second heads.

Duke shook his head and barked to get them under control. "Ticca, Lebuin, Ditani, and Illa – Dagger, God, hero, and Nhia-Samri – I cannot believe this group is here, already working together better than most Dagger teams, trained better than I think could have been planned."

Duke looked straight at Ticca. "Ticca, one thing, please. I need you to avoid all old artifacts, like that book in the

Algan mayor's office and especially old throne rooms, if at all possible; if not possible, do not touch the floor sigils. Don't ask me why. Just don't ask the cities for anything and especially, do not cuss and ask for some response, *like closing the gate.*"

Ticca's face went white, and she said, "That was me? Are you sure?"

Duke nodded.

Ticca's eyes narrowed. "What would have happened if he or I had been on that gate?"

Duke shook his head. "I don't know, which worries me. It shouldn't have done what it did and I haven't had the time to look closer. Keep in mind what could have happened. Promise me to do what I say until I have time to figure it out."

Ticca looked at the ceiling for a moment. "Why should the city listen to me?"

"I cannot tell you that. Just promise me."

"Okay I swear, I'll try to stay clear."

Duke held Ticca's eyes for a moment then looked around at everyone else. "Unless anyone disagrees, I think your group should continue with finding out what Vestul was up to and why the Nhia-Samri want it so bad. I will pursue the war with the Nhia-Samri that I started, making it noisy, painful, and annoying. That should give your group cover to find out what is going on and take preventative actions."

Lebuin sat up straight, then stood with a look like nothing Elades had seen before. Ditani looked worried, as did Duke.

Ditani stood, putting his hand on Lebuin's shoulder. "Lebuin, is everything okay?"

Lebuin focused on something outside of the cave. "What is she doing?" he asked, and ran from the cave at top speed, followed by Ditani. Duke looked at Elades, and they vied for the exit with Ticca. They all got out, only to see Lebuin and Ditani on the far side of the camp, skidding to a stop by Illa, who was standing in front of a group of Daggers, including Nigan and Risy. Next to Illa was Boadua, looking suspiciously like a proud mother. The eleven Daggers before Illa were standing at attention, and they had their daggers out and raised high. They cried out as one, "Hail, Lord Lebuin, the Dagger God!"

Lebuin sputtered out loudly enough to be heard across the whole camp, "Illa, what are you doing?"

Illa bowed to Lebuin and her voice carried across the entire camp as she said, "My duty as your high priestess; gathering followers."

Duke chuckled. "Yep, she's an excellent choice." Then he called out, "Let us feast to the honor of the rise of a true Dagger God!"

The camp exploded with a sound of cheering as Lebuin stood, looking lost.

Huh. A Dagger God. He sure doesn't look like a God right now. I might consider joining up myself, so long as he doesn't impose a dress code, Elades thought.

The Tent House

CHAPTER 5

SOME TRUTHS ARE BEST HIDDEN

TICCA SIGHED AS THE BOREDOM pressed down on her spirit. *I hate waiting for something to happen. Everything was great until we packed everyone up and moved to Magus Vestul's property in Algan. I thought Lebuin would be able to open up Vestul's locked tower a lot faster than this. All this standing around is making me itchy.*

Ticca watched as Duke paced back and forth, supposedly inspecting the property. Even though his head was down, he rarely looked at the ground. Instead, his eyes were darting around at the large, neighboring estates. Duke's ears were moving as oddly as his eyes. They would rotate around, only to lock onto something and remain locked on it, regardless of his body or eye motions.

He is looking for an observer.

Lebuin stood before the large door to the tower, holding a silk umbrella for shade, his eyes unfocused as he examined the incantations woven into the structure. The boredom and the midday's heat started gnawing at Ticca again, and Duke was annoying her. Instead of bothering Lebuin, she decided to walk around the tower for the fourteenth time.

How much time does it take to check for magic? We've been camped here for eight days now. She walked around the tower, examining the perfectly-fitted stones. Running her hand over them, she looked for a crack, or even a flaw, which she knew wouldn't be there. Still, it was something to do. The tower stood four stories tall with windows on the top three floors. Vestul's property was huge. There were garden lawns in parts of the estate that would have been hidden by the two-story house before it was burned to the ground.

Rounding the tower, she saw some more workmen arrive with full carts. She was about to call out for some help when some senior Daggers broke off from training the junior Daggers to help unload the tools and supplies. Half were for the working crew and the rest were more war supplies. *Glad to see everyone pitching in where needed.* She headed over and started pulling tools out of the carts.

Out of the corner of her eye, she saw Duke leap up and rush off towards the back of the property at high speed. Ticca handed the package she had pulled out of the cart to another Dagger and jumped up on the cart to get a better view of where Duke was going.

Duke had already vanished into one of the groves, and she couldn't see any trouble. A terrible fear ran through her as she realized it was a 'friendly visit' emergency. Spinning around, she dove into a small space on the cart and cowered down, trying to get out of view from the front gate.

"Oh, she can't be that bad, Ticca." Risy was behind her on the cart, helping to pass down the many crates and packages.

"You haven't experienced a tea with her. I swear, you can lose a week and not notice it." Ticca's mouth started watering as she remembered the pastries the duchess had served the last time she had accepted an invitation to tea. *Actually, I felt more like I had been outmaneuvered into having tea. I have the oddest feelings about her. I feel like I should trust her, yet at the same time, I feel a need to hide as much as possible from her. But that non-stop talking in that voice makes me grind my teeth.*

From the front gate, she heard the duchess's high-pitched voice. "Oh, come now. You mean, they are all busy? You hardly look that busy. I mean, really, how much practicing can you do in this heat? Are you married? I know a lovely young girl that would be just right for you!"

Some cool heads reassured the duchess and managed to keep her from hunting down her prey. "Oh, very well. I had some specially-made arit from the mayor made for Ticca. You really should eat more, young man. You would look so much cuter with another stone on you. Tea and arit will be available till four-thirty. Make sure you tell Ticca about the arit. Ta-ta! Mustn't keep the mayor waiting."

The duchess had come around at least once a day with an invitation to dinner, or a party, or something. Every time she stepped into the area, she looked like one of those fair toys with the spinning heads. Also, her high-pitched, non-stop, jabbering drove Duke to distraction, which is why he bolted for the back of the property to hide whenever she approached.

Ticca's cheeks burned as Risy pulled another box from beside her. His eyes stayed on the gate. "Okay, it's clear. You can stop hiding now."

Ticca looked over the top of some packages.

"No, seriously. Ticca, she's gone. You act like she is a demon, or something. She's just a lonely old lady. Kinda reminds me of my mother's sister."

"Do you like your mother's sister?"

"Sure. She lives up north." Risy kicked her in the side. As she turned to look at him, he winked and grinned. "That's why I Dagger in the south."

She felt her mood lighten at Risy's grin. Still, Ticca made a second and third sweep of the area before jumping back down and helping with the unloading.

One of the newest Daggers looked at who handed him a crate and stammered, "General Ticca, you don't need to help. We got this."

She laughed. "I've got little else to do until we get some more intel. You should remember that as a Dagger, no job is too little. If something needs doing, and you have no higher priority task, you lend a hand. Remember, nobody ever drowned in sweat, so dig in and work hard." A couple of the senior Daggers chuckled at her use of the old Dagger saying, but they also nodded.

The younger Dagger moved off, bunching his brows as he thought over what she'd said.

Not sure what kind of general I'm going to make, but since I'm one now, I must set the best example.

The whole squad had moved onto the property, setting up tents and bringing in cots. They had also acquired additional supplies and were using this as a practice setup of a field office for the coming war. There were always four Daggers on guard at the front gate and three patrols moving around the perimeter of the ten-acre lot. With half a dozen groves of fruit trees and some wonderful old oak trees in the back garden, it would be easy for someone to hide. Everyone took the threat of observers and attack as real.

Elades had gone to the local Dagger home, called the White Mare, and put out the word that all Daggers in the area were being called to war by Duke. Two more squads of Daggers were then under Duke's command, and he had made it clear to all of them that Ticca was his general and Elades was her second. There had been a few dozen raised eyebrows, but no one questioned Duke's judgment or authority.

The senior Daggers were camped on the property with the original squad Duke had brought from Llino. Another twenty or so Daggers were expected to be arriving in a few more days. Duke had also put out the word that any Blades, guardsmen, or soldiers would be hired and trained. Outside the city, another two hundred soldiers were camped with the junior Daggers as camp officers. Horses, armor, and weapons were in short supply as everyone was making war preparations. Elades and Ticca took a regular tour through the growing camp outside the city, making sure everything was in order.

After a long debate, they had decided that only fully confirmed Daggers should be informed of Lebuin's nature. Illa wasn't happy about that, as she wanted to go out into the city and recruit more followers from the general population. Still, she had done fairly well with the Daggers, and Lebuin had almost fifty followers, which he said would let him gather enough power for most simple tasks or perhaps a small fight.

Ditani had refused to accept the property, instead, signing it over in full to Lebuin. Duke had hired workmen for Lebuin to clear the rubble of the old house, and an architect to design a 'suitable replacement,' which Ticca was sure meant large enough for Duke to visit. A master mason had yesterday agreed to build the new home, attached to the tower, out of stone. Duke spent marks arguing with the mason on which type of stone and mortar to use. Finally, Duke had to promise to share something before the master mason agreed to Duke's demands; exactly what, neither Duke nor the master mason would elaborate on.

A matching set of three carts piled high with canvas and thick poles trundled in from the street to stop in front of her. Ten young, but strong-looking, boys jumped out of the lead cart and started to unload it. The faint scent of oil cloth hung in the air. *What do we need more tents for?* Stepping over, Ticca abandoned unloading the first set of carts and started helping with the new carts, so she could find out what it was for. She smirked as some of the junior Daggers gave the carts curious glances, wishing they could do the same. *Of course, rank has its privileges.*

Lebuin's eyes refocused on them and he stepped out of the way, setting down the umbrella and grabbing a pole, helping to lift it over near the tower.

"Lebuin, do you know what this is for?"

"Nope. Duke announced earlier, a big-ring tent would be coming. But he wouldn't tell me what that meant or why he wanted it. According to Elades, Duke ordered it the day we got back into town and has been pestering the merchant daily since then to hurry up and deliver it."

Duke drifted over, smiling at the carts and their load. "'Bout time. I can't believe it took so long to produce it."

She placed some heavy spikes on the ground where the eldest boy had indicated. "What is it?"

"A big-ring tent."

"Come on, Duke, you know we don't know what that means."

Duke smirked at her. "And soon you will. Saying it is a large tent doesn't do it justice. Up north, they are still used.

But here, the weather is always so diurdu warm and dry, they aren't needed. Just help out and see what it takes to raise it, and you'll see what it is and why it is called a big-ring tent."

Duke let the delivery boys fit a harness on him and unhooked their own horses from the wagon. Duke spent the rest of the morning working as hard as a draft horse, pulling large, wooden poles into place. With a series of ingenious leverage tricks, two poles were raised and tied down. Then more horses were brought in and with Duke, they pulled the tent canvas around the poles. The canvas was then attached to two massive rings, which rose up on the central poles via pulleys.

As the tent went up, Ticca stepped back, and then back again, to take in the size of the thing. It was as tall as the tower and bigger than the original house. In fact, they had put it up right next to the tower so that the bottom half of the tower was made into one end of the tent.

It was late afternoon before the workmen left for the day and the tent was fully erected. It had a canvas door large enough to drive two wagons through. There were a dozen smaller canvas doors evenly spaced around the tent, and the top of the tent flared out over the canvas walls, leaving large air vents which brought in the afternoon's cooling breeze. All of the Dagger officers and most of Alpha Squad had come in to marvel at the tent. Some of the Daggers, having seen the type before, pointed out different things about it to everyone else.

Duke motioned with his head for them to follow, walked into the tent, and pulled the main door flap closed behind him. "And now, they can't see what we are about to do."

Ticca joined with Lebuin, Ditani, Elades, and a half-dozen senior Daggers, following Duke into the tent. Duke was already walking towards the tower door. She jogged to catch up with Duke and asked, "And what, exactly, are you going to do?"

Duke looked at her. "Open it, of course."

Her back tensed and her heartbeat quickened at that

statement. "You mean to say you made us stand around for more than a week, banging on that cruddy door, and you could open it all along?"

Duke looked at her, his eyes twinkling. "Yep." He looked over at Lebuin. "So did you find anything dangerous, like a trap?"

Lebuin shook his head. "No, but the tower is self-sufficient and protected from dozens of things I don't understand yet. Also, that door has channels and mechanisms which are a blend of incantations that are a bit familiar. I still don't know enough about them to desire to tamper with them."

Duke's head rounded on Lebuin like a sling shot, making Lebuin worriedly step backwards. "What do you mean, 'familiar'?"

"Well, ah… I mean…they seem like some…well, I have studied similar incantations at the Guild."

Duke shook his head, and his tone was deeper than usual. "Oh, no, you haven't. The Guild was set up specifically to stop any such incantations from coming into general use again."

Lebuin looked around for support. Ticca met his eyes and motioned at Duke with her head. She gave him what she hoped was a 'stand up to him,' encouraging look.

Lebuin looked back at Duke. "Well, they weren't exactly Guild materials. I was given a set of books to help me deal with a Magus who was causing trouble. I only said it was familiar. I didn't say I knew what it was."

Duke stared at Lebuin before making a huffing sound. "Elades, get the squad up. I want active patrols and guards at every door in ten minutes." Elades turned and jogged out of the tent with the other Daggers following behind, leaving only Ditani, Lebuin, and Ticca with Duke.

Duke looked around. "Where is Illa?"

Lebuin concentrated. "She is with Nigan and some other Daggers in the market, getting supplies."

Duke stepped up to the tower door. He looked around the area and his ears twitched. "Hmmm… I know we are being watched, but I can't find who is doing it. And I don't mean, by that nosey busybody of a neighbor you have over there."

Ticca tried not to laugh.

Still, he is right; I can feel it, too. Someone is watching us. But I can't find them, either.

Duke looked around one more time, then in a low whisper, added, "Don't tell anyone else about this. I don't want anyone to know, which is why I ordered this tent to hide the fact. Plus, it will let the mason's crew work much faster, with the shade and such."

Duke turned and walked up close to the door. He sniffed around on the door until he stopped near its top right corner. There, he sniffed hard again and grunted with satisfaction. It didn't look any different from the rest of the door, but Duke looked back at them and winked. He lifted his front right paw and placed it on the door near the spot he'd located. A glowing bar of red, about a half-inch tall and wider than his paw, appeared on the surface of the door, just above where he touched it, and moved straight down under his paw, which he kept motionless. When the bar had passed under his paw, it disappeared, and a small panel over the four horizontal sliders opened outward.

Duke stepped back. "Lebuin, would you please step up to the door and do as I instruct?" Lebuin looked around and grabbed a stool that was close by. *I wondered why that had been brought here.* He stepped over to the door and, using the stool, stood high enough to see into the panel. "This is interesting. There are a lot of small gears and dials in here."

Duke nodded and looked over his shoulder, giving him a series of instructions to move this gear or turn that dial. But Lebuin was having difficulty. Finally, he stood straight. "Sorry, my fingers are not small enough. I need a jeweler's pick and pliers."

Duke looked around, frustrated. Ticca remembered the tools she had in her pack. "I have something that might work."

She raced off to her tent and dug out the Knife's belt

from Llino. Remembering where the thieves' tools were on the belt, she pulled out an appropriate pick and strong tweezers. Putting the belt back in her pack, she ran back to the tent and held them up for Lebuin's inspection.

He took them and examined them. "Wow, these are perfect. Where did you find these?"

Duke was eyeing the two tools, too, but he had a different look. *Urd, he knows what they are from.* "Yes, Ticca. Where did you get those lock picks?"

"From the Knife that attacked me by the Llino Guildhouse."

Lebuin looked at Duke and shrugged. "They'll work perfectly."

"Of course, they will. This is what they are designed for. Ticca, if you have the full set, do not get caught with it."

She nodded.

Duke and Lebuin turned their attention back to the door. After about two minutes, the key hole snapped open, accompanied by the clear sound of locks being pulled back. "Push on it."

Lebuin pushed. The door swung inward silently, and the panel snapped shut again without a trace. The key hole remained open. Just inside, on the floor were four Dolphin-style door keys, three bluish and one silver, resting on two sealed envelopes. Lebuin handed the tools back to Ticca and stepped in to pick up the keys and the envelopes. His eyes went wide and his hands trembled as he examined the letters. "Ah… Duke, one is addressed to you, and the other is addressed to me."

Duke sat down, then stood back up. "Lebuin, please hold onto those. Ticca, set the sliders to a new combination and let's go inside."

Ticca stepped up and moved the sliders to the same combination she used at the Dolphin.

Duke examined the setting and nodded, then said, "Take one of the blue keys, put it in the lock, and turn it all the way to the left, then pull it out."

Lebuin handed her a blue key and she stuck it in the lock, turning it to the left. A series of clicks came from the door, and the sound of a series of snaps being closed. Turning the key back to center, she pulled it out. The sliders all moved to the far left and the key hole snapped closed.

Duke motioned everyone in with his head. "Okay, that is the new door combination. You each get a blue key. Now, everyone get in and go through the first door on the right."

Stepping through the door, Ticca heard Duke closing the door behind them. She wasn't surprised to find that Duke had them going into a comfortable sitting room with all the expected comforts: fireplace, large chairs, and even a pile of pillows which Duke flopped onto. The room was lit by a series of mounted chandeliers that burned too evenly for candles or oil lamps.

Duke looked around. "Well, it looks about the same as the last time I was here. All right, we are now as safe from scrying as we can possibly be. Please get comfortable and let's see what Vestul has to say. Lebuin, would you please read the one to me first?"

Lebuin broke the seal and unfolded the paper.

"Hello Old Wolf,

By now, I am dead and you are screaming at everyone and tearing apart the world for answers. I am very sorry it has come to this. If it makes you feel better, you, Lebuin, Ditani, and I have made several dramatic attempts to stop what is coming. We failed. What is unfolding now is unique and I do not know if it is enough. I am attempting to do what you described to me once as lateral thinking. In other words, instead of attacking the problem head-on, and thus, failing again, I have arranged it so you are coming at it sideways. We are out of options and time. Either you succeed or you don't, and perhaps all is lost or it isn't. I cannot say, because I am dead before the end.

I loved you as if you were my father and later, as a brother. If you should ever manage to die, I hope to meet you in the next realm.

Vestul"

They sat silently. Then Lebuin took the letter addressed to him and broke the seal. His voice sounded very far away as he read.

"Hello Turtle,

I know that doesn't mean much to you now, but it did once, and it still does to me. I was proud to teach you and work with you as you grew to a magnificent man and demi-god hero. Know that I was, am, and shall ever be your friend and mentor, and am proud to have known you.

As Ditani will never accept my residence, I leave it to you. I have moved all the great books and valuables into the tower, in case something happens. The house was burned down a couple of times before. I don't see the harm in doing this, although Argos wouldn't agree, but I don't answer to him.

It should make you feel better to know that you were raised and trained by the best many times before. This time, you were misguided and left ignorant for reasons that will become clear later, if you survive long enough. I wish I could tell you what, where, and who the enemy is, but we really have no idea.

The agencies at work have hidden the focal point too well, and we cannot pierce their secrecy.

Lebuin, you must find your way and choose your allies on your own.

I leave you three keys to the tower. The fourth was lost a long time ago in an accident, so no need to worry about that. I also leave you a silver key, which is not complete, as it is too dangerous to leave assembled. If you need it, you will figure out where the other pieces are. To use it, remember your birth and your sister's birth.

Vestul"

Duke's teeth ground loudly as Lebuin finished reading the letters. "Hish, that bastard was screwing with time! No wonder, he was so diurdu secretive. If I had found out about it, I would have chewed on him for as long as it took to get him to stop."

They looked at Duke, who growled, got up, and paced back and forth. "Did you even pay attention? He said 'many times,' 'the house burned a couple of times before,' 'we tried and failed'. Diurdin! Didn't know this was coming. Of course, not! The stupid fool died! And he knew it was coming, so it was really on purpose, to get us engaged! DIURDIN, I HATE MARTYRS!"

Lebuin was studying the letter to him. "Duke, it says Argos wouldn't approve. That means Argos didn't know about some of this. What does he mean, he doesn't answer to Argos? All Guild Magi are sealed to his service."

Duke stopped pacing and sat down, then stood and started pacing again. "Skeed! Argos knew some of this. Of course, he did, which means Lothia is in it, too. She is in all the way up to her neck! That is why she was here; she has been watching, but staying out of the way. Vestul said this was a 'unique path' and Lothia hinted that a disaster was coming. 'Do what your heart says.' That is what she said."

Ticca felt the hairs on the back of her neck rising and her stomach was taking a dive. "He never mentioned me, and he called Lebuin only a demi-god hero. But according to Ditani, Vestul knew of my family, so he wasn't expecting me. He certainly didn't know Lebuin would become a full God."

Lebuin, his brows so furrowed as to be almost one dense line shading his eyes, looked up from his letter to Duke. "Seriously, Duke, stop and tell me how Magus Vestul can operate without Argos's knowledge. This is really important."

Duke was chewing the air again in frustration, but he stopped pacing and chewing to look at Lebuin. Duke's brows were twitching back and forth as he thought it through. "Well, Vestul is one of the Magi who decided to not join the Guild when it was formed. He eventually became a trusted member, but he never took the oath and was never bound to Argos. He was old enough to have figured out a lot of truths. Still, he followed the rules until *this* mess!" Then Duke's eyes lit up and he smiled a toothy grin. "At least, I still have permission to hunt down those little bastards and make them pay for all this."

Ticca's guts were dancing because she felt deep down that hunting with Duke was a bad idea. "So you hunt. And do you expect us to join you?"

Duke looked at her, still smiling, "No, Ticca. You do what your heart says, which is what?"

She didn't even have to think about it. "Find whatever the Nhia-Samri were after and destroy it, or use it to destroy whatever is endangering the realms."

Lebuin and Ditani nodded in agreement.

Duke's smile never wavered. "So you three head off and take care of that while I go make myself a large, noisy target. The Nhia-Samri might be the focal point, or maybe they are working for whomever is the real threat. You have to find out the real truth and how to stop the disaster."

They sat for a while before Duke stood and said, "Now that you have access to this place, you can determine your next moves and get rolling. But I need you to wait a few days, because I want most of the observers to pay attention to me. Tomorrow, I am going to make a big show of getting most of the Daggers and army ready to roll for Gracia to make this a real war. We'll leave in three days' time."

A knot formed in Ticca's belly, and she looked at Duke. "What do you mean, *most* of the Daggers?"

"You need back-up."

The knot tightened as some adrenaline started surging into her system. "You mean protection! I don't need protection. The four of us are capable."

"Yes, well, that is what back-up generally implies. Yes, you do, and naturally. But still, some solid back-up Daggers could enable certain actions. Besides, it's likely you will take a shining to one of them."

Crossing her arms, she stood and walked back out, trying not to pout. *He's right.* As she stepped out of the tent past the guards, she recalled Duke's final words, which caused the knot to become a full-blown cramp. *Wait, what did he mean, 'a shining'?*

RUNA-ILLA

The cart bumped and swayed as it moved over the cobblestones with its heavy load of supplies. Everything they needed, they had, except for one thing. Illa looked out across the market, teaming with people full of that precious magical energy she had to acquire. *All these people, and I can't recruit one of them. I know Lebuin needs more followers, and there are not enough Daggers to get him even adequate power. Now Duke is going to leave in less than two days, taking most of the Daggers with him. We need more power, or else he might fail.* She clenched her hand at the thought that her God might fail because she failed to find him enough energy. She punched the leather-padded bench seat as she tried to find a way around or through the laws she had to comply with to help Lebuin.

The cart jumped, and with the sound of something snapping in two, the cart tilted sideways with a lot of force. Illa was thrown to the ground. She flung her hands out, trying to control her fall, but without the time needed to react. The world blazed white as the sound of someone's head being hit by a club came to her. Everything seemed to spin, and she felt dizzy as her cheek rested on the warm, rough cobblestones.

Why am I lying down on a street? Illa's mind refused to provide an answer. *Well, at least, it is warm.* As she lay there, trying to figure out where she was, she could smell the pleasant, soft scent of dirt and stone. Something warmer than the stone was getting the street under her cheek wet. Her cheek also started feeling wet. A salty scent was added to that of the dirt and stone. Her thoughts circled around, identifying the sound she had heard as not a club to the head, but her head hitting the street. Her heart rate picked up as her mind identified the smell as blood and told her it was likely her own. Too disoriented to move, she tried to regain some mental control.

A lot of people were hollering as the supplies on the cart started to bounce around her on the street. A pair of strong hands grabbed her and pulled her away from the cart as an anvil hit with a loud ring, right where she had been lying.

"Oye, lady, are you okay?"

She tried to focus, but her vision was blurred from the fall. She lifted her hand to her head and felt the large bump there. Her hair felt sticky and wet. Pulling her hand back in front of her face, she saw it was covered with blood. She couldn't assemble her thoughts clearly enough to understand what happened, so she stared at her bloody hand. *Where did all this blood come from?*

Nigan appeared, kneeling in front of her, his hands on her shoulders, his brows furrowed, and his eyes looking into hers. He said, "Illa, do you know who I am?"

She nodded and the pain that caused made her yelp, sucking in air in with a gulp. With pure will, she forced her eyes to focus on Nigan's worried face. "I... Nigan... I'm... What...?"

Nigan's brows unfurled and he smiled, yet his eyes remained concerned. "The cart wheel hit a hole, and the axle broke with all the weight we had it loaded with. I am really sorry I didn't see the hole, and it was a big one. You were thrown onto the stones. This baker saved your life by pulling you clear before the anvil hit you."

The gentle, alto voice of the baker said, "Lord knows, it was close. Worthy Dagger, I can tend to her in my shop right here while you help with the confusion."

Nigan looked behind her and nodded. He stood, and with the help of the baker, helped her into the warm, sweet-smelling shop. The baker sat her in a chair next to a table by the front window. The shop was empty of other patrons. Nigan touched her shoulder, concerned. Her thoughts were moving better. *I'm okay. Go take care of everyone else.* Her mouth didn't echo her thoughts, but she was able to wave him out with her non-bloody hand. Her thoughts were starting to flow again. *I landed on my head. I must have a concussion. First, take care of the bleeding. Then maybe something cold.*

Once Nigan was gone, the baker produced a pile of towels and a bowl of warm water. He cleaned her head and wrapped it with towels. He then helped her get comfortable and made a pillow with the remaining towels, which he placed behind her head. He laid a cloth with some ice in it on her forehead. The coolness felt marvelous and eased some of the pain. The chair leaned back pleasantly, and she let her head rest on the towel pillow. The smells of the bakery drifted over her in waves of warm air that felt wonderful and added to her drowsiness, so she closed her eyes, letting herself drift off, knowing she was safe.

As she dozed, she felt the comforting energy flowing into her from her God, easing her aches. Her mind tried to block it. *No, my Lord, don't waste your energies on me. I'll heal. We need to gather power, not waste it.* Lebuin either wasn't listening, or more likely, didn't agree. His energies continued to come to her. Her heart swelled at the touch of such love and care.

Movement around the shop roused her and she heard someone talking softly. Without opening her eyes, she concentrated and heard the baker say, "Had to break the axle. It was the only way to get her out of sight fast enough, and if needed, we could heal her quickly."

Another voice, female, soft, with a distinctly rich tonal quality, but deep with concern said, "We cannot be directly involved."

"Her father is just down the road. If he saw her, too much could be discovered."

At the mention of her father, she opened her eyes and tried to focus on the street. Through the dusty panes of glass, she spotted him. Runa-Emry was standing, almost on guard, at the lead of six Nhia-Samri dressed in plain clothes. Even at this distance, she could see that her father and all his men were upset about something. Her father was facing a tall and heavily muscled man dressed as a well-to-do traveling merchant with dirty boots.

The large man turned and looked in her direction. She froze, her heart pounding and her brain screaming at her to run. But her whole body was rigid and unresponsive. Still, her mind did respond. She opened herself to her God, and thought at him, '*LORD, WARLORD MARU-ASHUA IS HERE!*'

She felt Lebuin's calming presence in her mind. '*Illa, I hear you. Are you safe?*'

'*Yes, my Lord. But my father and a band of Nhia-Samri are here with Warlord Maru-Ashua. They are in disguise.*'

'*May I look through you?*'

'*You need never ask, my Lord. I am yours.*'

'*Yes, I do need to ask.*' She felt Lebuin's presence fully enter her mind, and he became concerned about her wounds.

Lebuin wasted precious moments examining her head wound. She felt him look with her eyes on the scene. *'You are more wounded than I thought. What happened?'*

She let her memories flow to Lebuin. *'Please do not worry about me, Lord. You need to protect yourself.'*

'Yes, I see them. I am also curious about this baker and the conversation you heard.'

Down the street, the warlord indicated something she couldn't see and strode off out of her sight. Her father gave the fall-in signal and followed the warlord. His men also followed in a loose, but obvious, if you knew what to look for, rearguard formation. Lebuin noted her observation. *'It seems the baker succeeded in keeping you out of sight. I am safe in the tower. I'll stay here and try to track them with Daggers through Ticca. You are to stay safe and have Nigan take you, and a couple of others as guards, to that inn you and Ticca shared. Stay safe and stay hidden. I feel the baker is right; we cannot let the Nhia-Samri discover what I am.'*

Lebuin's presence slipped from her. She looked around and found that the bakery was empty. Nigan walked in and looked around, confused. "Where did the baker go?"

She looked at him. "Nigan, we must hide. I'll explain later. Send someone to secure some rooms at the Three Green Doves Inn, and get me an enclosed carriage, preferably a two-seated brougham, to take me there. Send only two Daggers back with the supplies."

Nigan's mouth tightened as he understood something dangerous was afoot. He was prudent, as well as being an excellent Dagger. He nodded and went back out to issue orders.

On the table next to her, Illa noticed there was a pile of freshly baked sweet rolls and a tall glass of milk. Otherwise, the bakery was empty. Somehow, she knew that the baker and the woman wouldn't be back. They had exposed themselves to keep her hidden from her father and the warlord.

Her head throbbed and she took one of the sweet rolls and drank some milk while eating it. As she ate, she felt better and better, and her head started to clear. Sniffing the milk, she detected the scent of a temple healing draught.

Well, it seems we have allies in this. But how did they know who I was? For that matter, how did they even know who my father was?

Nigan came in after she finished the milk and half of the sweet rolls. He had a hooded cloak, which he helped her slip into, and then walked her out to the waiting four-wheeler. Once inside, the carriage moved off, and Nigan drew all the drapes closed.

Feeling much better, she looked out on the streets through the cracks in the drapes.

"You look a lot better than you should."

"A healing draught will do that for you."

He frowned. "You used a healing draught? Were you that wounded, or is this that important?"

She smiled at him. *Thank you for not jumping to a conclusion. You are a remarkable man.* She shook her head. "No, I was given one by that baker. He wasn't a baker. It was he who broke the axle on our cart, and I suspect he also made sure I fell in his direction. I don't recall it all clearly, but I think I hit harder and faster than I should have. I didn't have time to react."

Nigan frowned deeper, his hand fingering his dagger's hilt. "He broke our cart, wounded you, and then healed you. That is a bit much. Do you know why?"

"To prevent me from parading in front of my father and Warlord Maru-Ashua, thus exposing our Lord's nature."

Nigan leaned back, sighing. "Lords and Ladies, what are the chances that the warlord is here and has your own father with him? If they had seen you, there might have been a real scene."

"Actually, the chances are pretty good. This is Magus Vestul's home. Duke hasn't made it a secret he is here. My father is a senior officer for the warlord. My guess is they are coming here to negotiate with Duke. Still, we must hide because there is a good chance we could expose too much."

Nigan shook his head and said, "Illa, I'm sorry I didn't move faster. I should have prevented your injury. I'll be more prepared next time."

She smiled and touched his knee. "Nigan, you are a great friend. I doubt anyone could have stopped this, as it was without warning and directed to a specific purpose. It was well done."

Nigan still looked concerned as he fussed, saying, "Well, I swear that hole wasn't there. But then it was, and we hit it. The cart was strong and shouldn't have broken like that. Someone used a lot of magic without any telltale signs that I'm used to." He looked up and then back at her, smiling. "I'm glad of that! Lebuin can't blame me for hitting a hole that wasn't there until we drove into it!"

⚹ DOHMA ⚹

Ellua and Bayion followed Dohma through the palace. It had been a dizzying week and Dohma was going to leave in the morning for Gracia to join the Assembly of the Covenant. He had been putting this meeting off as long as possible, but it needed to be addressed.

Orahda has faithfully continued to train the Daggers and guards for the last week. I have let myself be too distracted by Countess Electra. At the thought of her, his mind summoned her image, and he lingered on her face and recalled the floral perfume she favored, which reminded him of spring when all the lavender first bloomed. *She is wonderful, and I enjoy talking with her. She has a great education and appreciation for history.* Shaking his head, he refocused on the task at hand. Orahda had killed two Dagger commanders without any real provocation. Yes, they had turned out to be Nhia-Samri agents. Still, the regents needed an explanation.

Behind the regents were the ever-present Daggers and

personal guards. The guards were rotated regularly from the city guard but the Daggers were constant. They had gravitated such that Ellua had Yuilla all the time, Bayion had become fast friends with Lomdri, and Cundia was always by Dohma's side. The Daggers were experienced veterans, superior warriors, advisors, and friends. Bayion and Ellua had agreed when he had proposed that they make it a requirement for any regent to have a Dagger advisor and guard, from the Dagger elite, chosen by the Dolphin owner or Duke.

The sun had set as they entered the quiet weapons-training grounds. Crossing the open area, they came to the weapons master's quarters. Dohma knocked and Orahda opened it before he could land a second knock. "My Lords and Lady Regents, please come in, I have been expecting you."

Dohma motioned for the guards to wait outside and entered, followed by his brother, sister, and the three Daggers. The Daggers spread out, but stayed by the door.

Dohma looked around, never having been in Orahda's private quarters. They were spacious, with a small kitchen and a table. Hot arit and some cookies were laid out on the table, and Orahda motioned for them to sit. Dohma moved over, but as he started to sit, he noticed that laying on the bed on the far side of the quarters, was a uniform identical to the one the Royal Daggers wore—the black-armored jerkin with the golden sigil of Aelargo superimposed on a single Dagger. Also, a full traveling pack was set on the floor in front of the bed.

Dohma sat and said, "Are you planning to go somewhere, Orahda?"

Orahda poured some arit for all four of them into cups, and then let them choose one. He took the last one and drank it down in one gulp. He then sat down in the remaining chair. He indicated with his chin, the items on the bed. "My Lord, I will accompany you tomorrow to Gracia disguised as one of your Dagger guards."

Ellua looked at him. "You assume much, Weapons Master. How is it you can say this so easily, with so much assurance?"

Orahda looked at her without any hint of guile or timidity. Dohma suppressed a laugh at his sister's obvious surprise that Orahda wasn't intimidated by her. *He is one of the few I know that can look my sister in the eye like that.*

Orahda smiled. "Because we all know that I killed enemies of the state who were about to expose a state secret to the Nhia-Samri, which would be devastating to Aelargo."

All three of the Daggers frowned, as did Ellua. Bayion leaned forward, grabbed a cookie, and plopped it into his mouth.

Why is Bayion not surprised by these strange statements?

Ellua recovered and looked at Dohma for support. Dohma shrugged and said, "Sorry, Ell, you jumped in and attacked. I know you just started taking weapons training, but you should know Orahda is a master at dealing with attacks."

Ellua huffed and gave him the 'fine, you deal with it' look she had mastered over the years.

Dohma leaned back and sipped his arit. "Orahda, you insisted we see you here in your quarters. You insisted on taking care of the odassi blades yourself, and they have vanished. You have served here for longer than seems possible, yet look as young as I. I did check the records. You have been serving as weapons master for over thirty-eight years, and you practically seized the job after being here for only two years as a weapons training assistant. Before that, I can't find a single record. Can we please put an end to all the mysteries?"

Orahda smiled. "Dohma, you are my best student. I am proud of you and I suspected who you were from the time I met you. It is true, I have served here for a long time. In fact, I have served the Kingdom of Aelargo for over forty years now."

He paused to let that sink in, because neither Ellua or Bayion had known how long he had been weapons master there. Ellua's eyes and her face were active as she took an inventory of the room. Bayion looked at Orahda, then nodded as if he understood something.

Orahda continued. "I asked we meet here because I have spent those forty years weaving protections into the walls of this area, and especially, these quarters. We are more secure here than almost any place else in the world. This room is as proof against magical scrying, or wards, or other mundane spying, as any Magus, Master Knife, or Master Spy can make it. I know, because I had help from the best, including a Magus unequaled in history at doing this. He tested these walls himself and was unable to penetrate them."

Dohma looked around again, but the room was the same. He had only Orahda's word for this. Still, he trusted his instincts and they were telling him Orahda was speaking the truth. Dohma said, "I believe we all understand. I believe you. Please continue."

Orahda reached behind him and, from a secret panel, pulled out two odassi, which were far more ornate than the ones the two agents had. The Daggers all sucked in air and stood with their mouths open, staring at Orahda. Orahda laid the odassi carefully and respectfully on the table before him.

"My name is Amia-Dharo, and I swore to protect the Realms of the Covenant long ago, and again, before Duke and the rulers of the realms forty years ago. Magus Vestul witnessed my renouncement of the Nhia-Samri, my reaffirmation of my oath to the realms, and helped me share with Duke the reasons for my actions. I have and will faithfully serve the Realms of the Covenant for as long as I live. I came here at the request of a couple of those same rulers to determine why the regents here had chosen to start ignoring the Covenant. After finding corruption in the nobles here, I sought a way to restore Aelargo without resorting to war. I swore an additional personal oath to restore honor to Aelargo, and have worked for forty years to this end. Your ascension is a blessing of the Gods to me."

Looking at each regent in turn, he bowed his head. Then

he looked back at Dohma. "As to the two Nhia-Samri, they recognized me and were about to call out my name, alerting the Grand Warlord Shar-Lumen of my location. His reaction would have been swift and terrible for all."

Dohma's mind spun at the revelation. He couldn't put Amia-Dharo into the role of his mentor, guide, and trusted friend, just a moment before, held by the mysterious Orahda, Weapons Master of Llino. Then he laughed as he remembered the weapons master's records. "Orahda Ima. That was the name you gave to the captain of the guard forty years ago. You mean to say, spelling your name backwards has foiled Shar-Lumen and the massive Nhia-Samri hunt for you for forty years?"

Cundia laughed once and Dohma noticed his sister was staring at Orahda with her mouth open. *Well, that is a rare event, when even Ell is dumbfounded.* He noticed that Bayion was smiling and eating another cookie. "You aren't surprised by this?"

Bayion shook his head. "I figured it out many years ago."

Amia-Dharo looked at Bayion with surprise. Bayion smiled. "I was always interested in puzzles and cryptology. I even taught myself to read and write backwards. I especially enjoyed being able to read documents, no matter their angle. I saw your name and thought it was upside down, so I read it backwards. At first, I thought it was a coincidence. But then I started watching you. You always wore a high-collared shirt, hiding your neck, and your hair in some style that hid the left side of your head. Of course, watching you fight was also a good indicator. But my instinct was to trust you. So I got to know you and I liked you even more. I have kept your secret. I knew what you were doing was good for the kingdom, but I thought that was who you were. I did read everything I could about the war and knew you were a hero. Now, you say you have been doing this to help restore Aelargo, and I find you a greater hero than I dreamed."

Amia-Dharo stood and bowed to Bayion. "You have

honored me more today than you can know." He straightened, picked up his odassi from the table, tucking them into his belt, and turned to Dohma.

Amia-Dharo, the second-greatest warrior in history, crew his odassi and knelt before Dohma, head down, arms straight out towards Dohma, with the blades crossed perfectly on the plane between Dohma and himself. "I swear my honor, life, and allegiance to the Kingdom of Aelargo through you, Lord Dohma, the true Chief Regent. Lord Dohma, I am yours and your progeny's to command for all my days."

Duchess Yillion Vransril Olmanna

CHAPTER 6

KNOW YOUR ENEMY

MARU-ASHUA

WARLORD MARU-ASHUA CONSIDERED HIS CHOICES as he walked the busy merchant streets of Algan. Far from the ocean, the air was drier with musty animal smells mixing with an assortment of foods arrayed in wooden vending carts. Wiping the sweat from his brow, he ducked under a canopy for some shade as he scanned the street for a safe place to leave his men. *This is a fool's errand. Duke will not relent, but he must be made aware of what I have been trying to hold in check.*

The city street was bustling with the everyday needs of ordinary people. Warlord Maru-Ashua felt pity for the people he passed. *I am not sure which is better—the lives we live now under the Gods or the vast-reaching empire we once were. The Gods do help and most live good lives, but not full lives. We no longer have the limitless potential every life once held.* Looking at a group of urchins running down the road after a caravan of some sort, laughing, he allowed himself a moment of joy, but not the smile. He kept his face clear of emotions.

He still didn't know how he should best approach Duke. He knew he couldn't take the twenty warriors guarding him. Duke would see a Nhia-Samri unit as a viable threat and never speak with him. *I have to leave most of these warriors at an inn and only take a few with me.*

He spoke to his guard captain, "Assign four guards to accompany me to see Duke. The rest will wait in a tavern away from Vestul's residence."

Runa-Emry's face hardened and he frowned. *If he is ever to command many, he must learn to school his face better. He displays too much of his emotions.* Runa-Emry nodded to Warlord Maru-Ashua. The sound of a crash echoed from down the street. Warlord Maru-Ashua glanced over to see that a loaded cart had broken an axle in a street hole. The cart had tipped away from him, but still, there were nearly a dozen men trying to stop more of the goods from spilling out. He noted that most of them were Daggers. *They are buying up almost everything from this area in war preparations. At least, we are not at war yet. There is still a chance we can sway the assembly to deny Duke his warrant.*

He watched them for any hint that they recognized him or his men. However, the Daggers were too preoccupied with saving their supplies and fixing the cart. The few Daggers guarding only gave normal watchful glances at the passing people. Satisfied that he and his men were not recognized, he pointed at a tavern he knew. "The men will wait at the Wooden Saw Tavern." He stepped off and led the way as his forward guards tried to stay ahead of him, without drawing attention.

The captain assigned the three best warriors and himself to escort his warlord. Maru-Ashua left the rest with enough money to enjoy a good meal and some well-deserved rest, after the hard ride to get there. Twelve Daggers stood guard at the gateway to Vestul's residence, and six more materialized behind him from an alley, as they approached. He ignored the threat. A short, young female Dagger stood in front with an air of authority. He had no doubt she was the commander. Maru-Ashua stepped up to stand only a foot from the young Dagger.

Although he stood a good two hands taller than the girl, she had steel in her eyes, and her dagger was a magnificent bone-hilted knife with hunting hounds. Her curly dark brown hair fell to past her shoulders and was held in place with a clip. She was dressed simply as an officer, even though she looked as young as a new recruit. *This must be Ticca. She is as young and inexperienced a Dagger as the reports suggested. She must have enormous natural talent and be a born leader. A shame, she will probably be dead if Duke has his way.* He stood in front of her, evaluating her, as she did the same to him.

Neither of them spoke. The girl stood, looking Maru-Ashua and his men over. Maru-Ashua saw no reason to be rude, so he waited. Instead, he took advantage of the time to count the number of Daggers and survey what he could see of Magus Vestul's property from the gate. A northern big-ring tent had been erected where he presumed the house used to be. The lower half of the far left side of the tent was wrapped around the Magus's tower, making it look like a tent with a stone tower attached. Some of the other Daggers started looking nervous at the long silence.

Warlord Maru-Ashua looked back at the girl and raised an eyebrow, indicating it was on her to broach the greeting. She continued to look at him without fear. It had been a long time since anyone had dared to stare at him for so long that he began to feel uncomfortable. *She is strong-willed!* His mouth felt dry, and he licked his lips.

The girl smiled and said, "Warlord Maru-Ashua, you should have sent a note that you were coming. We are ill-prepared to greet such a distinguished guest." Then she did a shallow waist bow to him, keeping her eyes on his the whole time.

How can she know who I am? Not even Duke knows who is in command here! He looked at her and saw that she was reading his every emotion. He steeled his face again. *Urdu, I am not a raw recruit. I need to gain ground.* He gave her an appropriate head bow for a senior officer. "Thank you, Ticca. However, I come to speak to Duke. I have only brought my senior officers."

He watched her face and she didn't react to his calling her Ticca, so he knew he had guessed correctly. Ticca nodded. "Yes, of course. Colonel Runa-Emry, Lieutenant Colonels Uiollo-Pushan, Brani-Lureum, and Yang-Kiann." She looked at each officer as she named them and bowed her head, as he had to her, in recognition. His officers, although surprised, bowed their heads back.

Urdu, could she be older than she looks? Where did she get this kind of information? For that matter, why am I the one in the dark? For one of the few times in his life, he was stunned to silence. *Even if they got every remnant of information from the Llino outpost, my officers' descriptions and names could not be known.* He recovered. "I see. It seems a note would have been redundant. May we be allowed to speak with Duke?"

Ticca looked at him with a soft smile, which he was sure worked well with younger men. *I wonder if she even knows she does that.* Ticca said, "Wills, please check with Field Marshal Duke's secretary and ask if the field marshal has time to meet with Warlord Maru-Ashua."

One of the Daggers snapped to attention and saluted. "Yes, Sir, General," and ran off towards the big-ring tent.

Warlord Maru-Ashua couldn't help it. His eyes snapped back to Ticca when the other Dagger called her 'general'. She smiled wider at his surprise. He noted no deception in any of the other Daggers around her. *She really is Duke's general? Who is this woman?!*

A richly dressed man came out of the big-ring tent with the Dagger named Wills and walked, without haste, back to the gate. He came up and stood, facing both Ticca and the warlord. "General, I am afraid the field marshal is busy at the moment. Might the warlord come back tomorrow at two?"

His pulse stepped up at the dual insults of not being addressed personally and at being asked to return. "Do not insult me further. I have to speak with Duke now."

Ticca looked at him and then at the man, who was obviously Duke's secretary. "I'm sorry, Warlord Maru-Ashua. I do believe the field marshal has already sent his message to you. So it is most difficult to arrange for more consultation."

He felt his face beginning to heat. He forced his breath to remain even and brought his heart rate under control. *Urdu, I don't have time for these games.* Looking at Ticca, he knew he had to win her first. He straightened and faced off with her. "General Ticca, please accept my apology. I was not informed of your rank. I am honored to meet with you." He then bowed as an equal to an equal, keeping his eyes on hers. Her right brow rose slightly at the change in track.

"Warlord, it was no serious oversight. Think of it no further." She then bowed to him. When she straightened back up, she raised her eyebrow again in obvious question.

"General Ticca, I am in breach of my duty to come here before presenting myself to Hisuru Amajoo. I have only a short time before I must continue my journey there in haste to compensate for the detour. Duke has sent me a personal communication that tells me he is aware of all this and more. However, I desire to dissuade him from this course, and I have certain information he must know now. I am willing to conduct this meeting alone and unarmed, if needed."

Ticca's eyes widened at his offer. She looked down biting her lower lip and then at Duke's secretary briefly before nodding. The secretary looked worried, but turned around and walked back towards the large tent.

Ticca waved for the Daggers to clear the path onto the grounds, and they moved with precision. "Warlord, Duke may accept your offer. Allow me to show you and your men to a place out of this sun."

Nodding, he followed her, and his men followed him. He didn't bother to look at them because he knew they all disapproved of his offer and actions. Ticca escorted them to a large tent with benches, which was used to serve meals. He did note that another Dagger had preceded her into the tent and that there was a closed rear exit. On a table, were some dishes: fruits, salted meats, sweet meats, and pitchers of wine and water, with glasses.

Ticca pointed at the refreshments. "Please help yourself." She then stepped over and took a glass from the table and placed it near the pitchers. "I am a little thirsty."

He needed no encouragement to understand what she was doing. He stepped over and picked a water pitcher at random and filled the glass for her. "Allow me, General."

She picked up the glass and downed it in a single motion. "Much better, thank you. I'll be back shortly." She grabbed a salted meat strip without looking and stuffed it into her mouth before stepping out of the tent.

She is definitely more experienced than she should be. He chose a bench and sat down. "Wine."

Runa-Emry stepped over and picked a different glass, pouring wine into it and sipping it. He stood, tasting it, then held the glass out. Runa-Emry took the lead. "Warlord, may I speak?"

He nodded for Runa-Emry to continue.

"If Duke accepts your offer, it will not be well with Hisuru Amajoo."

He sighed. "Emry, it is already not well with Hisuru Amajoo. This will be a thimble of water added to the lake."

Runa-Emry thought this over for a time and none of the other officers appeared to desire to voice anything further. He leaned back and drank the wine, not surprised to find it was excellent.

It was only half a mark before Ticca returned. She bowed to him. "Warlord, Duke accepts your offer. Please give your odassi to your senior officer." He stood and removed the leather-shielded blades and handed them to Runa-Emry, who looked at him with worried eyes.

Ticca held the tent flap open for him. She looked at the four remaining officers. "You four are to remain here in this tent. Please do not leave. I have ordered the guards to return to their other duties. Do not make me regret this."

He resisted the urge to smile. *That is a courteous sign. We might have hope here.*

As he stepped out, he heard Runa-Emry advance behind him and ask Ticca, "General Ticca, if possible, may I have a word with you in private?"

I'll have to find out what that is about, but right now, I must see Duke and get him to see the dangers of his actions. Ticca looked at him and he nodded his approval of the request. She looked back at Runa-Emry. "I will return after escorting the warlord. Wait here."

Ticca turned and headed for a different group of tents. *I thought Duke was in the big-ring tent.* He followed. They walked through the grove of tents. Coming around one, he found there was one large tent that had been hidden. Ticca stepped up to this tent and held the flap open for him. As he stepped up, she announced, "Your Excellency, I present Warlord Maru-Ashua, who comes unarmed under the flag of truce."

I didn't come with a flag of truce, but in actions and words, I have. Taking a small, hidden breath, he stepped into the large tent. He thought he was ready to face Duke. But when before him sat the legendary four-meter-tall wall of muscle and teeth known as Duke, looking at him with the cold, steel eyes of an angry grey wolf, he wasn't so sure. *That the men in Llino had to fight him is tribute to their courage. That he was so wounded is testament to their honor.* A shiver ran down his back as he stood facing a creature that he knew was still raging mad at the Nhia-Samri, and at that moment, all the anger was focusing on him alone.

Duke's voice was elegant. "Warlord, I believe I already communicated to you my intentions. I know you are not one to surrender your odassi. So why do you insist on this meeting?"

He must be made to understand the danger. "Your Excellency, you must know that Hisuru Amajoo will not evacuate even one warrior from our legal outposts."

Duke nodded. "Yes, I am aware of the folly of Shar-Lumen. I look forward to hunting all that remain down. The evidence is clear; Hisuru Amajoo has committed an act of treason and war against the Duianna Alliance of Kingdoms."

He shook his head. "You would kill so many to avenge that loss so long ago?"

"You mistake my intent. I will kill all for that action who continue to follow Hisuru Amajoo after being made aware of it. They may not have been alive then, but they are now. In thought, if they choose to remain faithful to Hisuru Amajoo, then they may as well have participated long ago My personal revenge is far more focused. I want to rip apart all, most painfully and viciously, who participated in the killing of Magus Vestul. That, I will do with or without a warrant for war." Duke's voice went cold. "Tell me, Warlord, did that order come through you? Your outpost records indicate they came from Hisuru Amajoo."

Duke's teeth were showing, and he felt himself start to sweat as a wave of cold flushed through him, despite the hot day. *He is burning with a rage much deeper than I imagined him capable of, after all this time.* Swallowing, he tried to regain control of his emotions. *I have to get him to listen and believe.* "No, Duke, I was not made aware of the order until a report came from Llino about the events there. But that is not important. Duke…" He didn't have time to finish the sentence.

Duke leapt at Warlord Maru-Ashua with a speed almost unimaginable. He was knocked to the ground. A tremendous weight was placed on both his shoulders. Duke was almost lying on top of him, pinning him to the ground. The wolf bared his teeth. Being nose to nose with Duke in this position could make a strong man faint. Duke roared, "MY FRIEND'S MURDER IS *ALL* THAT IS IMPORTANT RIGHT NOW."

Ticca, who had been silent so far, leapt at Duke, hammering at his side with her fists. "DUKE, get off of him. He is here under truce, and with your word of safety!" Ticca's voice was wavering with emotion. "Duke, you're crushing him! Stop!" He couldn't see her face, but her voice sounded as if she was being injured. He could feel her pounding Duke's sides through Duke's body. *My Lord, she is stronger than she looks.*

Trying to breathe, he managed to whisper, "Duke you don't know what's been done at the outposts. It has something to do with Elraci."

Duke's eyes stared into his as Ticca continued to pound on his side, yelling at him to get off. Duke growled and snapped his jaws only a hair's width from Maru-Ashua's throat, but he then moved off. He continued to growl as he settled himself back on the pillows he was using for a seat. Ticca stood between Duke and Maru-Ashua. "Get control of yourself!" she yelled, before going silent and glaring at Duke.

Slowly, Maru-Ashua stood up before the growling wolf. He rubbed his shoulders to try to reduce the pain.

Duke stopped growling and looked at Ticca. "Ticca, please take all the guards and Daggers from all of the surrounding tents and go find some work to do."

Ticca wiped her face with her hands, continuing to glare at Duke like a rebellious child. *So she is as young as she looks. Still, she is treated as a general and superior, even by Duke.* Ticca gained control of her emotions enough to nod. She pointed at Maru-Ashua. "DON'T HURT HIM."

Duke looked down. *Who is she to not be reprimanded for that?* Duke nodded, and in a more casual tone said, "I won't." Duke looked back at Maru-Ashua. "Please forgive me. My emotions are not exactly under control at the moment. It was inexcusable."

Confused, Maru-Ashua looked at Duke. *If I didn't know better, I'd swear Ticca was Duke's commander!* "I accept your apology. It is understandable. About..." Duke shook his head, stopping him.

Duke looked back at Ticca. "Please do as I asked."

Ticca looked back and forth between them. Maru-Ashua felt like a child being caught fighting a friend. Ticca nodded to both of them and left.

TICCA

The adrenaline coursing through her system felt like fire. Ticca kept her hands steady and closed the tent flap, taking one last look at Duke. *Don't betray us. I know you think you are above the law. You probably are, but if you kill him, it will set a bad example.* Duke seemed to read her mind and gave her a small nod of assurance. She tied the tent door closed and took a deep breath to steady herself.

Her command training took over as she turned around. Two Dagger guards looked at her anxiously. *They had to have heard all that commotion. Oh well, now is not the time to explain things.* "Clear the surrounding tents and set up a fifty-foot perimeter. No one is allowed near here until Duke gives the all clear."

The two Daggers nodded and moved off in different directions to put her orders into action.

Lebuin's soft voice sounded in her ear. He had placed a spell on her that let him see and hear everything around her, as well as allowing him to speak to her without anyone hearing. He used his connection with Illa to let her witness everything as he relayed her information and hints. "What was all of that about?"

"I'm not sure, but I think Duke will be able to restrain himself. I take it, you were watching?"

"Of course. The warlord said something that was outside of the incantation's range. Did you catch it?"

Ticca started walking back to the mess tent where the warlord's officers waited. "Sorry. I was too busy trying to get Duke off of him, which means only Duke knows what was said. It was enough to snap him back to his senses before he ripped the warlord's head off. It had to be pretty significant."

"Do you still want me to keep this up?"

"Yes. I might need more of Illa's help. Plus, I think she might want to witness this."

"She isn't so sure. Whatever you are going to do, try to finish it soon. These incantations are fluctuating, using more power than my followers provide, at times. I've not yet recovered, and the magic is getting close to burning my channels out. I had to use some of my reserves to keep them up. And you know full well, I don't have a lot of reserves. Also, I can't go back into the tower until you let me drop them, and it is unbelievably hot up here on the observation deck."

Still, a bit of dandy remains. Oh well, at least he mentioned his comfort last. I wonder if I'll ever beat it out of him entirely.

Ticca paused outside the mess tent, taking a few cleansing breaths. *My stomach doesn't feel like I'm spinning now.* Back straight and head up, she took a step into the mess tent, brushing the tent flap aside. The four officers were seated around one table, near the cool liquids. Colonel Runa-Emry stood as she finished stepping in, and came to attention. The other three officers stood, snapping to attention only a hair behind their colonel.

Ticca nodded. "Colonel, please join me outside for a moment."

The colonel nodded and stepped over to join her, motioning for the other three to remain. They remained at attention as she turned her back and stepped out. Without looking behind, she strode a distance away to a tall oak tree with some refreshing shade from the boiling hot sun. Turning around, she found the colonel right where she expected him to be—two steps behind and at attention.

"You may stand at ease, Colonel. Warlord Maru-Ashua and His Excellency will be some time, I think. There is no one nearby. You have permission to speak freely."

The colonel relaxed his stance and looked around to assess the activities in the area. Then he looked back at her. His face was tight, and she noticed that he was trying to control it. The slight crinkles of a frown could still be made out and his brows were tight, giving his forehead the wrinkles of someone who is worried.

Even though there was no chance of anyone hearing him, Lebuin still whispered through his spell. "Careful, Ticca. Illa says he is a master of reading people."

They stood assessing each other for a few seconds. The colonel's eyes darted at every motion caused by the work being done around them. *He is nervous about this. Or he is under orders to try to gain information. Either way, Illa is right. I need to be very careful.*

Ticca relaxed, breathing through her nose and doing the

mental relaxation mantras in her head that her trainer had drilled into her.

The colonel's eyes came to stare into her eyes. They were ice blue, and Ticca also saw the same fine lines, which made Illa so beautiful, in the colonel's carved face and almost-perfect nose line. He took a breath as if getting ready to jump off a cliff.

"General Ticca, I do not expect to live much past reaching Hisuru Amajoo. I know I will not be questioned about what I am going to ask. So I beg of you to trust me in this. I..." his eyes darted around again, making sure no one was near. "I want... No, I *need* to know." The colonel's eyes watered, and he clenched and unclenched his hands. Ticca was sure he was fighting an internal battle to not wring his hands together. "You were there... The warlord said that..." The colonel licked his lips, took another breath, shaking his head and looking down.

Understanding struck like lightning. *Oh, Lady, he's trying to ask how Illa died. What should I say? He wants to know, but is afraid to ask.* Ticca's heart ached for the lost father standing before her, unable to ask what he most desired to know. Her own father's image came unbidden to her mind, and she recalled him hugging her strongly, and then more and more weakly, as the infection progressed. She recalled how he looked just like this father before her, so sad that he wouldn't know his daughter's life.

'Ticca, I love you and will always be proud. I know you will follow your heart. Remember me,' was the last coherent thing he had said to her. She had pushed that memory from her mind, but seeing this man trying so hard to ask what his training said he should not, brought it back, full force. She felt her own eyes water and her chest tightened.

She stepped forward and grabbed the colonel by both shoulders. He looked up and she looked him in the eyes. *I can't tell him she is alive and well.* She tried to speak, but her throat was tight with her own emotions. She took a deep breath, and the colonel did the same. He did not try to break away from her grip. His eyes were pleading and the look on his face was longing, Ticca felt compelled to say something.

Ticca forced a swallow to loosen her throat muscles. From somewhere deep in her soul, the words came. Staring into the colonel's eyes, she spoke softly. "Ossa-Ulla and Runa-Illa fought hard and followed orders. They captured me. Then they faced a God, and yet, they fought. Runa-Illa even managed to wound him before he took them from the Nhia-Samri."

Runa-Emry's face hardened, but with a smile, and his eyes watered. "They fought a God? And she wounded him?"

Ticca nodded.

"She was taken with honor above all services. It could be no better." Even though he said it, she knew he didn't believe it. His eyes betrayed that he would rather hold his daughter than know she died with honor. *This is why my father didn't want me to become a Dagger. He was scared of having this conversation.* She wished she could tell her father how much being a Dagger meant to her, and she wished she could tell this poor soul his daughter was alive and well. But that would expose too much. *This is the price I must pay. I must carry these burdens.*

The colonel straightened and glanced around. Ticca let go of his shoulders. "Thank you." His voice was grief itself. "I shall return and await my warlord. I know the way." He turned and marched back to the mess tent, back stiff as a sword. He paused before stepping in to nod once to her.

Lebuin's voice was rife with emotions. "Illa says 'thank you'."

Ticca nodded. "You can drop the spells now."

"Thank goodness. Oh, and when you have the time, come to the tower. I have something I need to show you."

"I'll come after the warlord leaves." She wasn't sure if he heard her or not. It didn't matter. She turned and walked an inspection of the guards. *It was funny when Lebuin named me a general. Hell, it was even fun when Duke decided to let it stand. Now, I know why my uncle and trainer always said the weight of command was a heavy burden.* Everything was in order, and as she rounded one of the tents, she saw Duke walking with the warlord back towards the mess tent. *That didn't take long.*

The warlord opened the flap of the mess tent and called his officers out. He introduced them to Duke, who sniffed each one. Ticca arrived as Duke finished sniffing the last officer.

"All right, Warlord. I will accompany you to the tavern. So long as none of your other men were involved, you may leave."

The warlord nodded and started walking towards the main gate, Duke beside him with an odd look in his eye.

Ticca intercepted and fell into step with them. "If you're going out, I'm going with you."

Duke looked at her. "Ticca, I would rather you stayed here."

She was about to answer when the air was split by a shrill voice that warbled. "Dukie, there you are!"

Both Duke and the warlord came to an abrupt halt inside the entrance as a gaunt woman in a layered dress of bright red silk skipped past the stunned gate guards. She had her long, silver hair up in a dramatic bun with bows and some golden hair clips, which sported numerous diamonds that sparkled in the midday sun. Her shallow face held a grandmotherly smile as she hugged Duke. "It's about time I caught up with you." Duke was grinding his teeth at the sound of her voice. "You have been too busy of late. Now, who is this handsome gentleman?" She turned on the warlord like a lioness about to take down prey, and stepped up to him breathing deeply, like a school girl meeting her heartthrob. She held her right hand out in greeting.

"Uh…" was all Duke managed to get out.

The warlord took her hand and bowed, kissing the proffered hand. "I am a simple merchant, lady…"

She smiled and batted her eyelashes at the warlord. "Duchess Yillion Vransril Olmanna at your service, you handsome rascal. Don't try to pull the wool over my eyes. You are a military man, if ever I saw one. But don't worry. Your cover is safe with me." Then she looked coyly at Duke. "That is, so long as you, your officers, and Dukie join me for tea, this very instant. My chef has prepared the most delicious shaved ice treat you could imagine on this hot day. I have some cool sun tea all ready. I was just popping over to invite Dukie here," then her eyes landed on Ticca, who was trying to find a way to hide behind Duke, "and of course you, too, Ticca, my darling. You are looking too thin. You really should eat more."

The duchess pirouetted on the spot, looping her arms into both the warlord's arm and Duke's front leg, as if being escorted by the two of them. "Now, come along! That ice will melt soon in all this heat." With that, she marched the stunned men and Duke to her residence next door. Seeing no way out, Ticca followed behind.

The tea was delicious, the shaved ice cooling, and somehow, that softened the duchess's voice. A mark and a half passed, during which time the duchess chatted about everything from bakery services to the hunting practices of foreign dignitaries. Ticca wasn't sure, but she thought the warlord and his men were as lost as Duke was on how to extract themselves from this chatty woman. As near as she could tell, their company had said, perhaps, a hundred words in total, compared to the duchess's tens of thousands. In sheer numbers, the duchess was the clear victor.

Standing inside their own property, Duke and Ticca came to their senses. The warlord and his party beat a hasty retreat down the street as she watched. Ticca muffled her giggle. *A tactically wise maneuver. That is the third time I have lost a mark or two to her. Lady, help me. I think I am starting to like the duchess.*

Duke shook his head. "Her voice is the most annoying thing I have ever encountered. And that includes passing out drunk on an ant hill!" He huffed and shook his head. "Ticca, did we let anything slip?"

She thought about it. "I don't think so, but most of that tea was mesmerizing because of her chatter. Still, the shaved ice was good."

Duke licked his lips. "Yes, it was, at that. You know, if she feeds me like that every time, I might put up with a visit once a week. But I wish she would drop her voice an octave."

Ticca laughed, as did Duke.

Duke looked around. "I think I'll make an inspection of the preparations outside of town. Do you want to join?"

She shook her head and glanced at the tower. "No. Lebuin said there was something he wanted to show me before we got kidnapped. It's your army, so you take care of that mess." She looked at him. "About that back-up team you were going to leave behind; we need to discuss that. Over dinner?"

Duke gave her a grin. "I'll be glad to listen to your well-thought-out argument against a back-up team. In the meantime, Elades has made a sound recommendation which we can then approve." He leapt back out the gate, giving her no time to react.

Ticca called after the wolf, "Duke!" Even she could hear the whine in her voice. Resisting the urge to stamp, she marched towards the big tent's entrance.

Inside the tent, forty sweating workers were continuing to dig and hammer out the burned foundation of the old house. A respectable ten-foot-deep hole was present and expanding. The rubble was being sifted and the dirt was being collected in an expanding pile behind the tent. The broken masonry was also stacked in a pile in front of the tent, where some carters were making regular passes to collect and take it someplace outside of town.

Ticca inspected the hole, which did not have a dirt floor. Ten feet below the ground level, there was a white, marble-like surface. Three Daggers were standing off to the side, overseeing the workers. She nodded to them. "Coxom, anything new here?"

The heavily muscled Dagger shook his head. "No, Sir."

She took another look at the glossy surface. *Duke insisted that the new foundation be put in this deep. He knew that, whatever that is, was there. It's annoying, the way he doesn't share information.* Nodding to the guards, she moved along the front edge of the tent, to the far end of the hole, and then stepped through the canvas partition that cut off the left third of the tent from the open area in the center. The interior of the tent had two wings on the left and right that consisted of a series of canvas walls that made a labyrinth of rooms and halls, which would be for the performing artists, if the tent was being used for the purpose it was designed for.

She walked through the labyrinth to the tower door. Pausing to be sure no one was near, she slid the lock sliders into position and pulled the key out as the keyhole snapped open. Taking another look around, ensuring she was still alone, she slipped the key into the lock and opened the door. She jumped into the tower and closed the door as quietly as she could. Once the door was closed, she knew there was no chance of anyone hearing. Duke had tested the tower to see if it was soundproof. They had discovered that the tower had amazing properties. It was proof even against Duke's exceptional hearing. Yet, from inside the tower, you could hear things outside as expected.

Duke had then made an extensive security check of the tower, declaring it better than he ever imagined. Even Duke was surprised to learn that the windows never revealed anything inside. From the interior, the windows were so transparent as to be nearly invisible, but from the outside, they provided a view of a simple room of one type or another. Even more interesting was that the rooms changed light and look to match the time of day and weather, never appearing lit at night. Once inside the tower, one could use as bright a light and work as loudly as needed. To the outside observers, the tower was always empty and quiet.

She explored the tower, calling out for Lebuin before finding him on the third floor. His voice came from one of the more upsetting rooms they had found. She stepped up to the door and saw Lebuin was on his knees with a table next to him. He had his head in the far corner, under the burned remains of a side table. On the small table was a collection of bits of melted or charred relics from the room. The floor had a set of lines scraped into the ashes from the table's legs, as well as a line of debris piles arrayed behind Lebuin's progress through the room. He had been at this since early that morning, as the table trail covered almost every inch of the room, in a circular search pattern. All of the destroyed furnishings, including the nearly-destroyed work bench, had been dusted clean and mostly reassembled, as well as could be expected.

Well, this explains why he was so dusty when he grabbed Duke and me earlier with Illa's warning about the warlord. I thought he had been poking around in the hole that will be the foundation of his new home someday. "What are you doing?"

Lebuin looked up, his face sweating from the work he had been doing and smudged with ashes from the floor, where he had wiped the sweat away with his dirty hands. "I finished taking an inventory of the other labs. I'm sure this room was Magus Vestul's study and workroom."

Leaning against the door jamb, she inspected the clean and undamaged wood door. "Okay, so?"

Lebuin gave her a look that indicated she should be paying more attention. "This wasn't an accident, as Duke speculated."

That got her attention. She crouched down, looking at the fine layer of ashes on the floor. "Duke said anything going wrong with time magics resulted in massive explosions and fires. So what makes you think this wasn't the accident that convinced Magus Vestul to stop and turn himself in to Duke?"

Lebuin waved a hand at the table of relics. "First off, that other study on the second floor is a ruse. There is nothing in there of any importance. I bet Magus Vestul pretended it was his office when he brought anyone in here. Everything about this place tells me about how Vestul thought. It is layered. Each defense and level has a subtle ruse or deflection built into it. In order to understand the real meaning or use requires not being deflected by the ruses."

Ticca thought about it, and it sounded reasonable. "Okay, and so?"

"So he didn't have an accident that destroyed this room." Lebuin stood and gestured to the burned and smashed remains of the workbench, which appeared to be the center of some huge explosion. "All this is camouflage." He picked up an ornately worked and slightly melted chunk of silver. "I admit I didn't figure this out until I found this." He handed it to her.

She looked at it, but it only took her a few seconds to determine that it pulled apart into two pieces, one of which was a section of the silver key they had found on entering the tower. Lebuin was smirking.

"That was what told me this was no accident. He left it where I'd find it. It was large enough and pretty enough to make me curious to determine what it was a part of. As soon as I realized it was a fake relic, I knew what I needed to do next." He indicated his search trail. "Take a look at this." He pointed at a set of burned paper scraps.

She walked over and looked at the papers on the table. They were from different books and places, as each was a different kind of paper. They were scraps with burned edges and writing in various-colored inks. Confused, she looked at Lebuin, who was smiling like he had won some prize.

"I don't get it."

Lebuin smiled wider and handed her a burned scrap of paper with a geometric pattern on it. "I found this by the door."

Sighing, she shook her head. "All right, I'll admit it. You're a smart wizard. Get to the point."

He pointed back at the table, and suddenly, the scraps of paper started moving around. As they moved, she saw that despite the fact that they were all supposedly scraps torn and blown apart, they were geometric, with only minorly rough edges. As she watched, her admiration for Lebuin's ability to assemble data went up several notches. The scraps, under Lebuin's magics, arranged themselves in the pattern of the geometric design he had shown her. When they stopped moving, they formed a letter. She read it in disbelief.

'*Lebuin, in every prior attempt, we were stopped completely and effectively without ever discovering who was behind our destruction. I am sure there is a traitor or two deeply implanted in our groups. My notes are safe and sealed using magics Argos would be shocked to see used again. My notes are the bait. You must find a way to secure them without becoming a primary target again. If you do open them, I caution you to take your time continuing my work.*'

She felt her pulse quicken and looked at Lebuin with a smirk. "We are ahead of them this time, aren't we?"

The scraps of paper floated up and ignited. Lebuin picked up the table and indicated the door. She walked with him as he carried the table. As Lebuin closed the door, she saw the ash piles jump into the air in a whirlwind of debris.

Lebuin finished closing the door, turned, and nodded to her. Pointing at her pouch, his eyes smiled as much as his mouth. "Yes, we are. There has to be more to those notes, but we have them, and that means they don't." He then looked down at himself and frowned. "I wish he had made this less dirty work."

ESHRA-ZUNIA

Warlord Eshra-Zunia allowed a hint of a frown to show on her face as she reviewed the first report. *Not a single operative, warrior, or trace of the Llino Outpost remains. Duke even had the houses burned to ash.* She looked up at the dusty man and woman standing at attention. She put the first report down and picked up the second one, reading it. *Ossa-Ulla took Runa-Illa from the observation outpost and left with orders to burn Magus Vestul's house, and then proceed to Rhini Wood to learn the truth about Ticca. Warlord Maru-Ashua said that the Gods had killed Ossa-Ulla and Runa-Illa; Ossa-Ulla only had time to communicate their destruction before the end.*

"Your reports are complete. Return to your duties."

The two officers saluted her, spun, and were halfway to the exit when the doors swung open, slamming into the mounted armor on each side. She smirked, remembering how much she had enjoyed doing that. It was most dramatic. However, at that point, she was warlord, which meant her second, the only person who would dare do that, had something critical. She stood from her throne, looking at the figure in the doorway. From the shadowy silhouette, she could tell that the person who had thrown the doors open was not her second. Her two officers took a momentary look at whomever it was before calling out, startled, and falling to the floor, prostrating themselves before the intruder.

The intruder stepped authoritatively into the room. His silhouette resolved itself into a tall, muscular warrior, wearing grey and black armor which flared dramatically from his heavy shoulders. His head was held tall with long, silky, black hair pulled back into a ponytail. His violet eyes glanced at the prostrated officers and then rose to her, as a charming smile grew on his pale, silvery face. "Eshra-Zunia, I received your message." His voice was deep, sending a quiver down her spine.

Her heart raced as her thoughts spun out of control. *He's here! Oh, Lords, he must be even more upset than we guessed.* She threw herself to her knees, drawing her odassi and holding them out flat at a forty-five-degree angle, forming a cross before the Grand Warlord. "MY LORD, I AM YOURS TO COMMAND."

Shar-Lumen stepped over the prostrated officers, to

stand in front of her, his steps a mere whisper of air. He ran his fingers down the edges of her odassi. As his fingers traced her blades, she could swear she felt them running down the length of her body. She felt him press down at the apex of the cross formed by the two blades. She used all her strength to keep them from dipping. As his pressure grew heavier, she drew power from the odassi to give her the strength needed to keep them steady. Without warning, the pressure stopped and her muscles relaxed, preventing the blades from springing up.

Eshra-Zunia felt his calloused hand lifting her chin. She hadn't realized she had closed her eyes. Opening her eyes, she still knelt before him with her blades forming the proper cross. Her head was up, held by his hand, as she looked upon his face, but this time much closer than she ever dreamed she'd be. He was as beautiful as she remembered from her childhood when she had dreamed, as all the girls, of rekindling his love. He had perfect lines and a beardless, smooth-skinned face that was the most handsome she had ever seen, despite being a silvery hue. He nodded and then straightened back up. Stepping back a half step, he drew one of his odassi. It was a sparkling, mirrored blade with a clean bone hilt and golden cross-guard. He brought his blade down onto the apex of her crossed blades. When they touched, the maker's marks on the bands of all three blades flared gold.

"I accept your service. Rise, Warlord."

She stood and sheathed her blades.

Shar-Lumen sheathed his own blade, and as his hand came back from the hilt, it held a familiar, bloody roll of parchment clenched in his fist. "Warlord, you will order all outposts in your domain to send every warrior here within three cycles, except the minimum needed to maintain essential duties." His other hand produced a large ruby, set in a golden stand, which he handed to her. "When this glows, you will have exactly fifteen minutes to assemble the warriors, in proper ranks, in the practice field facing north. Several portals will open on the north central target. You will have five minutes to have all warriors through them. Have your strongest warriors lead to push back any resistance, and allow room for all to get through. Once through the portal, everyone not Nhia-Samri is to be killed. If the assembly approves this action, we will level Gracia." He waved the bloody parchment at her in emphasis. "Do you understand?"

He intends to attack the assembly! She nodded, not letting any of her emotions play on her face. His piercing eyes bore into her. He nodded and turned, putting the parchment back into his cloak. Without another word, he strode out of the room, and the doors closed of their own accord with a soft thunk.

Eshra-Zunia let her breath out slowly and counted to twenty to steady her nerves. Looking at the officers on the floor, she realized they were not going to get any rest yet

"Stand up. You heard the orders. Move it. Assemble our fastest messengers. I will brief all at the stables in thirty minutes." They needed no further incentive. Both standing, they rushed to the door, except the officer who was reaching for it remembered who had just left by that route. His hand froze and he glanced back. Eshra-Zunia placed her hand on the hilt of her odassi and projected impatience. His hand moved, opening the door on the long and empty hall beyond. Both officers glanced at it before racing down the hall at full speed.

Duke will be there with an army. A shudder passed through her. She stood as tall as she could. Grabbing her odassi hilts, she strode out of the room. *We... I will not fail.*

Finnba's Treachery

CHAPTER 7

NEVER GIVE UP

TICCA FELT GOOD ABOUT THE drills, with what she had already started thinking of as her company. Nigan, Risy, Illa, Ditani, and Lebuin were the core group. To that, they added some junior and senior Daggers, mostly chosen at random by who was free for the drills. The group had earned a reputation, and the list of Daggers waiting for a chance to drill with them was never short of eager volunteers.

Ticca's blades sang as she danced around, both covering and being covered by Lebuin. They fought as one, twisting and turning in a dance older than this world. Sweat poured down her sides and back. She had to concentrate to keep from blinking too much, as it pooled in her eyes. Lebuin stepped back past her left flank. She felt, more than saw, the incoming attack, which he had dodged, causing the attacker to overextend. She brought her blade around, hitting the attacking arm with the side of her blade hard enough that a loud snap cut the air. Hissing in pain, the attacking Dagger rolled out of the fight, knowing she'd have lost her arm, if that had been real.

Lebuin's tactic of using magic like a third and fourth hand was effective, and he was getting faster with it. Illa was doing her best to distract Lebuin with her own bag of tricks. She had been chosen to lead the attack on Lebuin because she had extensive training in combating mages. Lebuin had allowed her to teach these tactics to the other Daggers. Except for chemical agents, they were all using the combination of tactics to try to break Lebuin's defenses or separate him from Ticca.

That day, the drill was to take Lebuin and Ticca down, at all costs, within thirty minutes. Ticca was pleased they had managed to not take any serious wounds, and they were nearly twenty minutes into their half-mark survival goal. A row of 'dead' assailants sat on the side of the fight, observing, while the line of fresh attackers had been reduced to a handful, from its original twenty. Of the first attack squad, only Illa was still in the fight. Ticca and Lebuin both had tried a series of attacks to take Illa out, because without her lead, the attack would be over. Illa's abilities were soaring to new heights. She had demonstrated a number of amazing moves that allowed her to 'survive'.

Illa must have decided the 'at all costs' was drawing to a critical point. With only five minutes to spare, she called out for her final support from the line. The fresh combatants jumped in with enthusiasm. Ticca was able to dispatch one of the more junior Daggers with a reverse cut. She let the side of her blade slap on his throat, making a shallow cut, to let him know how close he had come to being dead, for his arrogant enthusiasm. As he fell out, Illa performed a diving thrust. Ticca had been distracted enough that Illa scored a serious wound touch to Ticca's left side. Ticca spun out of her next strike, but a second Dagger joined, thrusting from the other side. She was pinned.

Urd, that was well done! If I drop, Lebuin won't last.

Lebuin stepped, spun around, and suddenly, Ticca was thrust backwards by an invisible force. Back-peddling as fast as she could to stay up, she was forced out of range of the new attackers. Lebuin's blades sang in the air, and with a series of loud rings, he had disarmed three of the attackers. Illa dropped to the ground and rolled into Lebuin's legs with all her weight, throwing him backwards. Lebuin's hands pinwheeled out of control as he fell, hitting the ground. Ticca tried to step in, but the two remaining Daggers threw themselves at her. Everything spun as she was hit by nearly twenty-eight stone of hard muscles. Her head slapped the dirt and dust flew into her eyes, blinding her, as loud applause erupted around them.

As the dust cleared, Ticca saw she was pinned by Elades

and Sunna. Lebuin was on his back, straddled by Illa with her blades pointed down at his chest.

She glared at Lebuin. "Urdu, why'd you do that?"

"You didn't see the one behind you. I had to get you out of the way."

She tapped Elades and he smiled, standing and offering her a hand up.

Illa got off Lebuin and helped him up. "My Lord, you are more important than anyone here. Unless you are sure you can remain safe, do not sacrifice your safety for another. You could have escaped."

Ticca wiped the sweat from her face with a cloth someone handed her. "She's right."

Illa picked up some fallen daggers. Lebuin shook his head. "I'm no more important than anyone else. Besides, that was a lucky trick you pulled."

Illa spun on him. "What?"

"That was a lucky trick; nobody would do that for real."

Illa stood straight as a sword. She bowed her head. "My Lord." Then she turned and walked towards the big-ring tent.

Lebuin looked at Ticca, confused.

She looked at him, then shook her head. "Lebuin, when a woman says 'what' it isn't that she didn't hear you; she's giving you a chance to change what you said."

Many of the male Daggers around chuckled until the female Daggers gave them a warning look.

Nigan stepped over from the ranks of the dead and patted Lebuin on his back. "She'll calm down, and then you can apologize to her. I'll go look after her for you." He jogged off after Illa.

Elades looked around. "Show's over. Everyone else, get back to your duties. Make sure you drink something. This heat will kill you, if you don't, after that fight." He looked over at Ticca. "General, would you care to join me for some lunch? You, too, milord. We have some logistics to discuss."

Ticca nodded and fell in with Lebuin, following Elades towards the mess tent.

Just as they got there, Duke came out of the big-ring tent in a hurry. Duke looked back at the tent with his mouth open in surprise, and she could hear him complain. "What got into her? All I said was that the baths were open." Duke looked around and, seeing them, nodded. "I'm going to go check some maps. I'll meet you in the mess tent in a bit." He then muttered something else with a glance back at the big tent, and trotted off to the headquarters tent.

Elades laughed and held the tent open for Ticca and Lebuin. "I hope she takes that bath. Might calm her down. You know, Lebuin, for a God, you really have a lot to learn."

Lebuin glanced at the big-ring tent and nodded. "I do have a way of putting my foot in my mouth, don't I? Ticca, wasn't that a lucky move? I mean, really. That wouldn't work for real, would it?"

Ticca stepped into the cool interior of the tent. "There is no right or wrong in real combat. There is only murder or be murdered. If it ends with you and yours alive, and the enemy down or dead, it is called inspired tactics. Seriously, you were not expecting it, and it did take you down. She was under orders to kill you at all costs; therefore, her life was forfeit. For a Nhia-Samri, if dying can achieve the objective, it is a high honor. So when you apologize, I suggest you tell her it was an inspired maneuver you will be prepared for, now that she has demonstrated it to you. Thank her for possibly saving your life in the future with that inspired attack."

Lebuin's voice sounded pompously behind her. "Did I say I was going to apologize?"

Ticca felt the blood rush to her face. *Of all the ignorant, fool things to say.* She couldn't stop herself. She spun on him, drawing her daggers. "Yes, you are going to apologize to her, and now, to me. But I'm not going to tell you how to succeed at your second task!"

Lebuin stood straight. "Urdu, Ticca, that isn't funny!

This is serious. She was lucky, and you're just defending her because she's another girl."

She could hear her heartbeat as she leveled her gaze at Lebuin. She stepped towards him. Elades looked tense. She could feel the Daggers behind her go silent. They were preparing to pull her off Lebuin, if needed.

Through clenched teeth, she hissed at Lebuin, who had the same stupid look of the teenage boy she had spur on after he pinched her bottom. *Boys all think they are so smart. I thought Lebuin had grown up a bit!* She remembered she had beat the teenage boy badly before her uncle had pulled her off him. *I'm his general, and he is talking to me like I'm some stupid ten-year-old girl.* "Lebuin, you can tell a lot about a lady by her hands. If she's pointing a dagger at you, she's probably mad." Sheathing her daggers, she strode out of the mess tent, past Lebuin, before he could say something even more maddening.

Ticca had made it all the way to the far side of the property before she could hear more than her heart. There was a little garden well close by, so she went there. Pulling the bucket of fresh water up, she drank deeply of it, then dunked her head in it. The cold water helped her pull herself back under control.

What was all that about? He is suddenly acting so stupid. He should know better than that. She thought about the situation while splashing water on her arms and chest to cool down. *Duke is leaving tomorrow for Gracia, and we haven't figured out what to do next. Urdu, what could the Nhia-Samri be up to and what did that have to do with Vestul's death?*

Ticca sat down and mulled over all the events and encounters, so far. As she absently played with the pouch's spinning lock, it clicked into position on the empty compartment. Vestul's letter to Lebuin came to mind. *'My notes are the bait. They are sealed with magic even Argos would be surprised to see used again.'*

Sitting up, she realized what their next step had to be.

My dreams with Kliasa, the journals she made! The notes in this pouch were a distraction, like everything else! It was the journal Kliasa made for him! That's where he recorded his most important discoveries. That was what he was going to give to Duke. It was in this pouch, and the Knife delivered it to the Hand in the Night Market that first night, the night Vestul was killed. It was wrapped with gold threads that glowed. I saw that clearly. Sula had me watching for something wrapped in gold! My Lords and Ladies, we have to get that journal.

She stood up and paced as she went through her memories to be sure she was right. The midday sun had already warmed the yard to near boiling, as she started back towards the front tents to find Lebuin. *First, he better apologize. Then I'll tell him.*

She was coming around the large tents on the far side of the yard from the mess tent, when a wagon pulled into the yard.

The wagon was carrying some large cargo that was tied down and had oil tarps covering it. Sitting in the driver's seat was a darkly tanned man, dressed in sturdy clothes, with a layer of dust. *This didn't come from Algan. This must be a shipment from another town. I wonder what Duke ordered now.* Sitting next to the driver was a young man with short, sandy-yellow hair that looked like a comb had never once dared to approach it. He wore a green doublet over a grey linen shirt. What was distinctive about him was that he had no dust or dirt on him at all, in stark contrast to the driver.

The young man's eyes were wide as he took in the property and activities. He didn't miss much. He wore the small smile of someone who rarely knew any trouble at all. As his eyes landed on Ticca, the smile broke into an open-mouthed grin that was fetching. Ticca felt her pulse pick up and her stomach lurch as he vaulted from the wagon.

"Why, hello. I didn't expect to meet a woman as beautiful as you here." He executed a formal bow. "I am Finnba, Journeyman Mage of Argos, at your service. Lady...?" He stayed bowed but his head came up, and his green eyes locked onto hers. He held his hand out in a friendly manner.

She lifted her own hand, which he took and kissed with just the right amount of pressure to indicate good intentions. "I'm Ticca. Ticca of Rhini Wood."

Finnba's eyes gleamed at her. His hand didn't change pressure, but it was suddenly cold. His eyes took on an animal-like quality, like a predator scenting its prey. "What a lovely name for such a dangerous and beautiful lady. I doubt many men dare approach you, with all those knives on your belt. But I would be immeasurably happy if you would honor me by letting me share a fine dinner with you sometime." He then straightened and looked around, still holding her hand, which she decided to leave, as her instincts were trying to tell her something. She could sense his pulse, which was strong and even.

"I must apologize, Lady Ticca. I am unfamiliar with Algan. But I shall find a venue appropriate to such a noble lady as yourself. However, I would be much further in your debt, if you could direct me to Journeyman Lebuin."

She reclaimed her hand. "Lebuin is in the mess tent having lunch, I think. Come, I'll show you there, myself." *I don't like this guy. But he represents Argos. I'll let Lebuin figure it out.*

Finnba looked at her with his winning smile. "That would be most welcome, Lady Ticca." He offered her his arm, and she saw no reason not to accept. So she took his arm and started walking towards the mess tent. The wagon had been directed near to the big-ring tent by some Daggers. She could still feel his pulse, which remained constant and steady. *If he was really interested in me, his heart would be speeding up by now.* Workmen started untying the cargo. As they pulled even with the wagon, the oil cloths were removed, revealing two beautiful armoires of polished cherry wood, with brass inlaid vines. Ticca marveled at them.

"I bet Lebuin will be happier with what's inside them, than how amazing they are of their own right."

She turned. "These are Lebuin's? I knew he was from a wealthy family, but these look like they belong in a palace."

"Lebuin has, perhaps, the finest taste of anyone. Honestly, he could make a fortune as a clothes designer, or even easier, as a fashion consultant. He was always very particular."

The men started unloading the rest of the wagon, which consisted of some packing crates and wonderful furniture. "I take it, this is all Lebuin's stuff from his room at the Guildhouse in Llino?"

Finnba nodded. "Yep, and seeing as I had just passed the Journeyman trial, I thought I'd catch a free ride up here with it and say 'hello'. His letter arrived only the day before I finished my trial. I must say, his other letter about the death of Magus Vestul caused quite the uproar. Of course, most anything Lebuin did caused uproar. I must admit, I think the place is going to be boring with him gone."

She kept an eye on him, and he glanced at the tower sticking out of the big-ring tent. "Is Duke in the tower?"

That is an interesting question. Something told her she couldn't trust him. "We haven't been able to get in yet."

He looked at her with a false surprised look. "Really? I would have thought he'd have gotten in, by now."

This feels more like the sparring before the fight gets serious. Schooling her reactions, she also let her eyes widen, as if surprised. "What makes you say that?"

Finnba shrugged. "Duke has a pretty big legend around him. Maybe he isn't everything they say. I figured he was such close friends with Vestul that he'd know how to get in."

Ticca shook her head and tried to look innocently naïve. "No such luck."

Finnba gave a calculated look at the tower, and started walking with her towards the big-ring tent entrance. She pointed at the mess tent. "Mess tent is over there."

Finnba glanced at her, the tower, and then the mess tent.

"Hmm... Sorry, I thought the food would be in there. Let's go tell Lebuin the good news about his stuff."

They walked together towards the mess tent. Just as they were almost there, the flap was pushed open and Lebuin stepped out. He stopped, looking at her and Finnba with his mouth open. "Finnba! What in the Lords' names are you doing here?"

Finnba released Ticca and stepped up to Lebuin. "Hello, brother Journeyman! I come bringing your clothes and furnishings, as your letter asked."

Lebuin didn't move, but did hold his hands out in greeting. "Brother Journeyman? I thought you had another year of training."

Finnba took Lebuin's hands and nodded. "Me, too. But with the huge war coming and Vestul's death, the Guild accelerated graduation for a few of the more gifted students." He smiled.

At Finnba's smile, Ticca's heart thumped as her belly tightened. She had to fight to keep her face calm and not give away that her internal alarms were ringing.

Lebuin looked at Ticca. "I see you've already met Ticca. Has she been showing you around?" Ticca gave him a subtle head shake from behind Finnba. The corner of Lebuin's lips turned down, and his jaw tightened as he got her signal. Lebuin put his hand on Finnba's shoulder and turned him back towards the wagon loaded with his possessions. "Well, I can't wait to change into something more presentable!"

Finnba smiled a real smile and laughed. "Well, I see the world hasn't changed you much yet. Maybe you can offer some refreshments to a poor, starved workman who has travelled far to bring you your fine wardrobe. Ticca says you haven't gotten into the tower yet. I would have thought most of Vestul's primary protections would have failed, with his death."

Lebuin caught the urgency in Finnba's statement and glanced at Ticca. She tried hard to tell him to keep his mouth closed without letting Finnba catch on to their non-verbal communications.

Lebuin chuckled, putting his arm around Finnba's shoulders. "Typical. We have some cool wine and food here. Let's go enjoy some." Standing behind Finnba, Ticca noticed there was part of a copper chain necklace exposed at the base of Finnba's neck, which was otherwise hidden under his shirt. Lebuin let his hand slide off Finnba's shoulders as they turned back to go into the mess tent, which caused Lebuin's hand to touch the exposed chain. Finnba's hair haloed as a bright flash of light came from his chest, illuminating the tent in front.

Lebuin's hand snapped away as if stung, and Finnba pushed Lebuin violently in his chest, making him fall backwards. Finnba growled at Lebuin. "How the hell did you do that? Not as stupid a runt as you let me believe!"

Ticca was thrown backwards by something hitting her like a moving wall. Whatever it was, it caused a tingling sensation all down her front torso. *That's magic, like when Lebuin ran into me at the market!* Throwing her arms wide, she tried to catch her balance. Failing that, she let herself fall backward into a reverse roll, pulling her daggers as she came back to her feet. The air was split by the sound of shredding cloth.

Finnba stood over Lebuin with his fists clenched. The side of the mess tent behind them had been ripped apart. A six-foot sphere of reddish energies surrounded Finnba. Some other Daggers in the mess tent had also been pushed away by Finnba's shields.

Lebuin looked up at Finnba with shock and confusion. Finnba reached down and grabbed Lebuin by the front of his shirt and picked him up. "I was going to take what I needed quietly. But you, diurdu fool, had to test a stupid theory, didn't you? I knew that khab was warning you."

Finnba shook Lebuin like a doll and then threw him towards the big-ring tent. He had to have used some magic, because Lebuin flew twenty feet, to smack into the side of the sturdy tent, before falling to the ground in a heap.

Ticca wasted no more time. She threw a dagger at Finnba, which bounced off of his shield. Finnba turned on her. "You're too beautiful to kill outright. But I don't mind if my toys are bloody when I use them." He raised his hand.

Ticca tried to dodge, but a ball of energy slammed into her. She felt her ribs crack, and pain exploded as a tingling sensation burned through her veins. She screamed as she was thrown five feet to land hard on the ground.

Rolling over, she saw Daggers were responding all around. Elades was already running for Lebuin. Finnba turned and waved, causing four other Daggers, that were preparing to attack, to fly backwards, towards the stone property wall. Just before they slammed into the wall, they stopped and landed on their feet safely.

Finnba roared, turning to Lebuin, who was standing with his own glowing shield. Lebuin's left hand was pointed at the four Daggers. Lebuin looked at Finnba, gesturing with both hands and causing a beam of energy that smashed into Finnba's shields. Light exploded, blinding Ticca. She wiped her eyes and blinked several times to clear her vision.

"Is that the best you have? I knew you were poorly trained, but that was pathetic." Finnba made an underhanded throwing gesture, and a bright orange ball slammed into Lebuin's shields, flinging him back through the tent fabric in an explosion of thunder and light.

A loud bark was all she heard, before Duke flew over Ticca at Finnba. Duke's head slammed into Finnba's shields with a flare of fire and sparks raining inward, as Duke smashed through the shielding. Duke's teeth snapped closed, only a fraction of an inch from Finnba's arm. Finnba turned to face Duke. "There you are, you stupid old wolf. This time, you don't have a chance!"

The necklace beneath Finnba's shirt glowed through the fabric, and Finnba smiled evilly at Duke. Duke jumped to the left faster than should have been possible as Finnba's hands snapped together, causing a blast of energy which would have hit Duke, if he hadn't moved. Instead, the energy blew past Ticca, hitting the far wall, which cracked under the force.

Duke didn't waste a moment. He spun as he landed and launched himself at Finnba again. This time, as Duke hit Finnba's shields, they blew apart like burning glass bits. Duke snapped at Finnba, who moved so fast, he blurred, barely escaping Duke's teeth again. A golden blast came from the big-ring tent, as Lebuin stepped out of the hole he had gone through, glowing with a golden energy. The bolt hit Finnba, who was concentrating on Duke.

Finnba screamed in pain and threw his hands up. A new shield sprang up around Finnba, stopping some of Lebuin's energies and pushing Duke away.

Lebuin threw another magical strike at Finnba, which impacted Finnba's shields. Duke pushed hard on the opposite side of the shield, which started to give under the combined pressures.

Ticca painfully rolled to her feet and pulled another knife from her belt. She screamed orders. "Get ready! When his shield falls, he is vulnerable."

Finnba was hunched over, holding his side where Lebuin's attack had hit. His head snapped up and hatred burned in his eyes—a hatred she had seen before, at the gates of Llino. In her mind, the pieces fell into place. Ticca wasn't sure how she knew it, but she knew who Finnba was. *My Lady, he's Nhia-Samri. He's a Nhia-Samri mage that is much older than anyone here. He's been a spy inside of the Mages' Guild for years.*

Finnba's hand glowed, and neither Duke's nor Lebuin's attacks had penetrated his shield yet. Finnba stood up straight, and both his chest and the shield glowed brighter. Adrenaline raced through Ticca's veins and her instincts screamed at her to move. She didn't hesitate and jumped as fast as she could, towards the big-ring tent, as the ground behind her exploded. Looking around, there was once again no cover close, except tents. *Urdu, why can't we have a mage fight where there is more than just canvas for cover? Gotta at least get out of direct sight.*

She ran as fast as she could for the visual cover the big-ring tent could provide. *It isn't much, but if he can't see me, he can't get me.*

Her instincts took over and she dodged again, as another explosion next to her threw her to the ground, her broken ribs flaring in pain. Something inside her burst with more pain when she landed, causing her vision to blur as she fought to stay conscious. Ignoring the pain, she rolled back up. Duke had managed to get his head into the shield and was pushing with all his might to get at Finnba, who was forced to dodge again.

Lebuin stepped between her and Finnba. *Again, he's my shield. Well, okay. But this time, I'm throwing the knife.*

Finnba yelled, "Duke, you're still hishing annoying as hell!" Finnba touched the glowing thing on his chest with one hand, and made a sweeping gesture at Duke with the other. Duke flew across the property, smashing through the stone wall. It started to collapse outward where Duke had been thrown.

Lebuin appeared to swell, and he opened his hands with a burst of light like the one Ticca had seen at the market. Lebuin's energies slammed into Finnba's shields, causing half to vanish. Ticca stepped out from behind Lebuin and threw with all she could. A number of other Daggers appeared to also take the cue and threw their own knives at Finnba.

Finnba closed his fist, pointing at Ticca. His shield reappeared, but not before Ticca's knife had penetrated. The other knives bounced off the restored shield. Ticca's dagger finished its flight, digging into Finnba's shoulder, up to the hilt. Finnba grunted with pain. "Oh, you are good. I see now, we underestimated you. Oh, well, I'll rape one of the others."

Finnba pointed, and a blaze of red energies burned through the air. Elades appeared from nowhere and shoved Ticca out of the way. The energies hit Elades' shoulder instead, causing it to explode in a halo of blood and bone fragments.

Elades' arm, no longer attached to his body, continued with Ticca, landing next to her with a meaty slap.

Lebuin and Ticca screamed together. "No!"

Elades looked at Ticca with a smile. "Sorry, Ticca. You need to finish this. Do me a favor and keep the teams sharp." He winked and fell to the ground.

Finnba pulled Ticca's dagger from his shoulder. The hole it had made blazed white as Lebuin threw another attack against Finnba's shields. Finnba spun, throwing her dagger at another Dagger, who was trying to sneak up behind him. Ticca's eyes misted as she saw her own dagger protruding from the forehead of the young Dagger–*Kirist,* she remembered–who still had the red cut across his neck from their match earlier.

Finnba turned and opened his hands. Lightning spun out from his fingers, hammering Lebuin's shields, which collapsed, and with enough remaining energy, continued hitting Lebuin, who fell in a heap where he was.

Finnba turned to Ticca. "Before I kill everyone else, you first."

Urdu girl, move! Her blood burned with fear-fueled adrenaline. She dove to the right and spun, trying to dodge out of the way. A deafening explosion with a bright flash of orange hit her back like a giant's punch. Her body was infused with a painful, tingling burn as she was thrown towards the big-ring tent. The heavy canvas did not stop her flight, ripping apart like paper. Her flight took her over the pit where the house was being built. Her muscles tingled with an energy that made her body convulse and made it impossible to move. All she could do was watch the smooth, white stone foundation, fifteen feet down, rush towards her. As she hit, she heard and felt her right arm breaking. Her head bounced off the unyielding surface with a sick cracking sound.

The world was spinning. She brought her good arm around and tried to stand. The pain and effort was too much. Her vision blurred as she raised her head. Her hand was covered in blood. Through blurry eyes, it looked like she was on a boat, on a red ocean with white beaches, and dark mountains in the distance. The water, no, her blood, felt warm, but was cooling as it soaked into her clothes. Her vision blurred more until all she could see was a shimmering, red blot expanding away from her on the white stone. She tried once again to get up, her life flowing around her. Her hand slipped on the wet, smooth floor, and her face bounced on the hard surface, splattering blood drops.

Her vision fogged and her thoughts spun. "Urdu move! Stop him. Destroy the Nhia-Samri. Protect Lebuin..." She ordered no one in particular, with her last breath.

ALGAN CITY CONTROL

Glowing, golden words on the wall pierced the blackness illuminating the small chamber with its three padded, empty chairs, sitting before the glowing words as silent witnesses.

IMPERIAL SECURITY OVERRIDE ACKNOWLEDGED: SYSTEM LOCKS RELEASED.

More words appeared in rapid succession.

IMPERIAL ATTACK ORDERS CONFIRMED. OBJECTIVES—STOP AGGRESSOR, DESTROY NHIA-SAMRI, PROTECT LEBUIN. IMPERIAL EMERGENCY RECOVERY PROCEDURE INITIATED.

A series of lights blinked in a blaze of colors and shapes. On the wall, a series of panels began displaying numbers, and a map appeared in the middle section. A blinking purple dot with a red circle around it appeared over a circle on the map labeled, 'New Alganetia'.

Six green lines appeared on the map: three long, dark green; and three shorter, a lighter green; each set circumscribed by a circle of similar color. The six lines moved back and forth. Each line either moved up or down. At first, the lines moved as much as an inch and changed their angles, while with each change, the circle that surrounded them shrank in size. Within a few seconds, the lines had all come together. Three long ones intersected at a single point on the map, and three small ones intersected over the same circle, which was labeled New Alganetia, precisely over the blinking purple point. A red line connected the two triangulated points, which pulsed from the large point to the one over New Alganetia.

ILLEGAL POWERSOURCE TRIANGULATED,
AGGRESSOR IDENTIFIED.
IMPERIAL ENFORCERS DISPATCHED.
BEGINNING SEARCH FOR TARGET
DESIGNATED NHIA-SAMRI.
BEGINNING SEARCH FOR TARGET
DESIGNATED LEBUIN.

More panels lit up with symbols, maps, and ever-changing lines of data until three of the four walls were alive with the dancing information.

CUNE

The air rippled as a shockwave of sound, from an explosion down the street, thundered into the quiet afternoon. Magus Cune, driving the workman's cart, looked up. "What was that?"

Sula was walking beside him, dressed in a peasant's blouse, which did nothing to hide her extraordinary beauty. She looked in the direction of the sound. "It came from Lebuin's new property." She was pushing a flower girl's cart loaded with flowers for the rich estates.

Cune stood up, along with a lot of other folk, and looked. He let himself slip into mage's sight. Off in the distance, he could see massive energies being exchanged. Another explosion sounded as he looked back at Sula. He knew his mouth was open and that he had a dazed look on his face, but he didn't care. "There is a magical battle taking place there. Get up here. We need to get there to help, if needed. Those Daggers are not prepared to fight mages, and the Guildhouse is too far away to respond."

Sula shook her head, 'no'. "We cannot get involved. We know too much!"

He felt his pulse pick up, and his face burned at her unwillingness to help.

Lady, forgive me, I cannot abide by this. She is wrong!

He sat down. "That is no longer true. We've been off the charts for weeks! You said yourself, there was nothing left at the temple. Now, get up here, or I'm going to leave you behind."

Sula's head snapped up from her own inspection of events, to look at him. Her large eyes narrowed. He could see her neck was tinged red.

Sula's voice was calm, but Cune could hear the ice in it. "We don't know that, for sure. You will follow orders. Duke has fought enough mages to be able to deal with one now."

He looked back with his senses and saw what he was sure was Lebuin, as a fading glimmer compared to the blazing energies of whomever was attacking.

Lebuin doesn't have the power or experience to battle that kind of mage. Forget it. Sitting here is wrong! I have watched over him far too long to let him die now.

"With or without you, I'm going there. If they need my help, they can have it. If not, no harm done."

He whipped the horse, which jumped at the abuse.

Sula vaulted into the seat next to him before the cart had moved three inches.

"I'll determine what we will do. Don't forget your place here. You are my mother's follower, and she ordered you to obey me."

I'm a Dagger first. But we'll discuss that later. Now, it's time to get to work.

Cune concentrated on maneuvering the cart through the people fleeing in the opposite direction. Fortunately, they were only a few blocks away.

Six man-sized, armored creatures shaped like insects went over their heads in the same direction they were going. They were a highly polished, mirror-like silver, with gossamer wings that reflected rainbows. He looked up at them. They didn't make a sound, and as they flew, they wove in and out together, like a flock of birds. "What in the heavens are those?"

Sula didn't answer, so he tore his eyes away from the flying things to look at her. She was staring at them with her mouth open, and had gone white. He needed no further urging and whipped the horse to a gallop, yelling at people to get out of the way.

• • • •

NIGAN

Nigan held a defensive crouch with both his daggers out next to Boadua, Risy, and Ditani, around Illa.

Illa was concentrating and Boadua had a hand on her shoulder. Together, they were helping to feed power to Lebuin to fight this mage.

Nigan stole another check on the battle. *So far, this mage seems to have far more power than Lebuin. We've lost a number of good folks. Which hell did he come from, anyway?*

Another explosion caused dust to rise off the debris pile they were using for cover. He leaned out, taking a better look at the situation. Ticca wasn't to be seen and Lebuin was on his knees, holding his middle with clenched teeth. "Lebuin is down again!" Behind the attacking mage, he saw another casualty lying on the ground with a dagger stuck in his head. "The bastard killed Kirist!"

Risy was looking around the other side of the pile. "Elades is dead, too."

Everyone looked at Risy in shock.

"He saved Ticca, but didn't get out of the way fast enough. If he hadn't, Ticca would have been dead, for sure. He practically exploded."

Risy was leaning dangerously out of the cover. "What are you doing? Get back under cover."

Risy pulled himself back, but his eyes looked haunted. "I can't see Ticca. She had already taken a few hits when I last saw her. She needs support."

Boadua sighed as Illa sagged away from her, almost falling down. Sheathing his dagger, he put a steady hand on Illa.

Illa said she would die when Lebuin died, but he was supposed to live nearly forever!

His pulse quickened and his throat tightened, seeing how pale Illa was, half slumped on the ground. *Urdu! Lebuin must be out of power and near dead.*

Illa pounded the ground weakly. "We've got nothing else. I knew I should have been getting more followers! There's no more magic. That mage is tapping into something. Lebuin can't pull enough magic to match it. There just isn't enough power close by. Even damaging his channels more by tapping all the local mana lines, he couldn't hold his shields. That other mage has far more power than seems possible. I know he is a Nhia-Samri, but I've never heard of the Nhia-Samri mages having this kind of power. We've lost. Even if we somehow survive, Lebuin might not ever hold magic again."

Boadua pointed at Illa's odassi blades. "I bet he is tapping whatever provides power to those for the Nhia-Samri. He has a necklace or amulet that is glowing like the sun. It is likely a key or link to the extra power."

As the sound of lightning rang out from the other side of the pile, Illa cried out, tears running down her face. Her whole body shook. Every time Lebuin was hit, she felt it. She clenched her teeth against Lebuin's pain.

Nigan racked his brain. *I know I'm forgetting something. What is it? Urdu, she needs me and so does Lebuin, and I'm just sitting here. Why the hell hasn't Lothia done something?! I bet she is nearby. She said as much to Duke...* He slapped himself in the head as he realized what he'd been forgetting. *Lord! That's it! DUKE!*

Nigan spun around and grabbed Illa's arm, pulling her up off the ground. "DUKE! Get up, girl! We have to get to Duke!"

Everyone looked at him. "Remember when Duke was yelling at Lothia? He said he had more power than the Gods needed, right?"

Illa's eyes blazed, and she raised her head enough to kiss him on the cheek. His cheek burned where her lips touched his skin as her head fell onto his shoulder. Her voice was only a hoarse whisper. "You're a genius. Now, get me to Duke."

His heart racing, he looked around for a way to get to the hole in the wall where Duke had been thrown. "If we move fast and stay low, I think he'll ignore us, until we get to that hole. He won't ignore us then. We need a distraction."

Risy nodded. "I'll move over that way, and when you get there, signal me. I'll get his attention. If I make it, I can help Ticca, too."

Nigan looked at his partner. He read in Risy's eyes, the knowledge that this might be his last action. Nodding, he steadied Illa by her arm, helping her try to kneel. She felt limp and was swaying. "Can you make it?"

Illa nodded, but still had a problem getting into a crouch. Ditani moved to her other side. "You guide us. If I have to, I can carry her faster than you can run."

Nodding, he changed places with Risy and they crossed hands. "Stay sharp."

"You, too." Nigan smirked at his partner. "Don't forget to save Ticca."

Six giant, silver bugs raced through the air and dove at the attacking mage. The air crackled with hundreds of small, shining arrows of energy shooting out of each bug's forelegs and mouths, hitting the mage's shields. The silver bugs spun through the air around the mage like fish in water.

Each creature was using a variety of attacks. There were silver arrows, bright yellow beams of light, and silver disks that spun. There were also lightning bolts arcing and dancing off all of the strange bugs. As they wove their pattern, lightning bounced around between them and would lick out suddenly, dancing around the mage's shields. Nigan saw the mage in the center of that storm of power, and he looked terrified.

"Never mind. That's our distraction. MOVE IT!"

Ditani didn't bother letting Illa try to stand. He threw her over his shoulder in a guardsman carry. They ran as fast as possible for the broken wall. Ditani hadn't lied—he raced ahead of them all even carrying Illa.

They got through the hole without any problem. Grabbing cover, he looked back and saw that the mage had managed to destroy two of the silver creatures. But the last four were spinning around him even faster, firing green beams of light that cascaded over his magical shields, both blinding and crushing him. He was also bleeding from a big cut on one arm. A shiny silver disk was lodged in his shoulder, and there were two knives in the opposite arm. Both his legs had deep cuts from other knives that had been thrown. *That's a good showing; we might just take him down one nick at a time!*

"Nigan, help!"

Turning, he saw that Duke had been buried in the wall's fallen stones. He rushed over, and Boadua nursed Illa as he and Ditani worked as fast as they could to dig the wolf out. As they dug and shifted the stones off of Duke, loud explosions rattled their ears. After what felt like ages, Duke's head came up, and he took a huge breath.

"Bloody hell. I hate being crushed!" Duke lifted his head as much as he could, still being trapped under the stone blocks. He looked through the hole, as did Nigan. Only one of those things remained, and the mage was holding it off while healing himself. "What the hell is an Imperial enforcer doing here? I locked those things down permanently."

Nigan's nerves were shot. He shoved aside his fear of the

big wolf and grabbed Duke's head by the ear. "Screw that thing. Lebuin is down and needs power to beat that bastard. You said you have some, so give it up!"

Another explosion rocked the air as the last silver bug–or 'enforcer,' as Duke had called it–exploded in a blast of fire and shrapnel. Nigan expected to see the mage preparing to blow him apart, except the mage was looking towards the front gate, and was being hammered by some powerful magical bursts from that direction. *Urd! How many things are going to come to stop him? I hope those are the local mages responding!*

Duke took all this in and tried to get up, but was still pinned. Duke barked, "Illa, get over here!"

With Boadua's help, Illa crawled over. Illa's voice sounded far away. "Lebuin is almost dead, and so am I."

Duke looked at her. "Never give up! Never willingly accept second! Grab my ears and hold your forehead to mine tightly. Then open yourself to me and to Lebuin. You must remain calm and hold onto me. This is going to be more than you expect."

Illa's eyes sharpened as she forced herself into one last push.

⬥ LEBUIN ⬥

Lebuin tried to hold himself conscious against the pain of his burned-out channels. *The mana lines are not enough. Even if I could pull more, they'd burst. How can he have so much power? Ticca, Illa, I'm sorry I failed you both.* Lebuin tried to roll over, but the pain was too much. *How could Finnba be a Nhia-Samri? This doesn't make any sense. He grew up with me. Urd, he was my only real friend. He alone wasn't afraid of me.* Tears ran down his face, his throat tightened, and he felt his heart pounding at the betrayal. *We have to beat him, but how?*

He heard the buzzing and turned his head enough to witness the silver bugs fighting Finnba. He watched, hoping they might be enough. They almost beat Finnba, but he destroyed them. Just as Finnba was about to turn on him one last time, a powerful burst of magic hit Finnba from behind.

Lebuin lifted his head off the ground. White-hot pain shot through his neck and across his body at the effort. Clenching his teeth to keep from screaming out, he lifted his head enough to see a mage dressed in simple workman's clothes stepping through the front gate. The clothes were too new to be real. Then he saw the boots, shiny black, well-maintained, but not new. He knew those boots. He locked up at the face of the attacking mage. The beard had been grown out like a working man's, but he could see his nemesis under it. *Cune! Magus Cune here, dressed like a workman? He is fighting for me? I thought he was an enemy.*

There was no warning to the surge of power that raged into him like a flash flood after a long drought. The power was unlike any he had felt or handled before. It was already focused into healing and restoration. He concentrated and refocused the power into his channels, but the torrent was too much. It was an odd sensation, as the white-hot energies filled his abused magic channels. His body surged with excess healing energies, directing it to more serious wounds, which started healing so fast, it was as painful as the strikes that had caused them.

Lebuin couldn't stop it. He screamed as the pain of healing washed through him. When the storm was past, most of the pain faded. He laid his head back on the ground, breathing hard, finally able to focus his mind. The wounds were not entirely healed, but it was enough for him to move. All of his magic channels were healed, if a little tender. He was restored, cycles of healing in mere moments.

What happened?

The power flowing into him was like dozens of mana lines, but it was smooth and even, without needing to be held or filtered into a calm flow. This was enough power to move buildings or more, if he wanted to. *Argos, is that you giving me power?* Looking within, he saw Illa had opened a channel between him and Duke. *Oh, my Lord. This is how much power Duke has! This is unbelievable.*

Illa's thoughts came to him. *"My Lord, you must end this quickly. Duke says this power is not unlimited."*

Illa had been hit by some shrapnel, as well as expending all of herself trying to feed him power earlier. She, too, was being healed by the excess energies, and a new confidence flooded him.

He stood. Something inside him fell into place. He knew what he could become and what it meant to be a God. He could control all this power, and more, he knew he could make it obey him. Even the greatest wizards couldn't hope to control half of what he held. Looking at his once-friend, he saw there was a Nhia-Samri amulet around his neck. Shifting to mage sight, he could see that it, like the odassi blades, was linked to a Nhia-Samri power source. The power source was immense. What didn't make sense was how the Nhia-Samri had created such a power source without Argos becoming aware of it.

Never mind. I will determine that after I finish this.

Lebuin stepped out of the hole in the tent. Before him were the bloody remains of the great Dagger, Elades. Elades' arm was separated from his body by a few inches. Lebuin felt his blood boiling, and his hatred reached out toward the betrayer. His shields burned with energies Finnba could never hope to break as he stomped past the dead commander toward Finnba.

Cune saw him first and stopped attacking to stare. Finnba saw Cune's reaction and spun, his mouth dropping open as his face went white with fear.

"Lebuin? How?"

"You'll never know, betrayer. I know your secret now."

Lebuin had trained for this and knew how to use magic. He instinctively knew how to alter the incantations to deal with this new order of power. Lebuin raised his hand and created an arc of power like the one he had used at the market to destroy the wand. Except this time, he poured power into it, making it a hundred times more potent. Finnba screamed, grabbing his amulet and throwing all his will into the shields. He drew an enormous amount of magic through the amulet from the remote Nhia-Samri power source to reinforce his shields.

Lebuin's attacks hammered Finnba's shields as he strove to hold them. Finnba focused all his will to hold against Lebuin's attacks, his shield collapsing to a wide disk between the two of them. In that moment, Daggers sprang from dozens of locations, filling the air with knives. Finnba screamed, trying to hold off both Lebuin and the knives. Cune moved in with the Daggers, drawing his sword and thrusting it through Finnba's back. With a splash of magical fragments of energy, Finnba's shield gave in as his body was riddled with daggers. Finnba fell, his dying scream piercing the air as the necklace blew apart into red-hot fragments, but not before Lebuin tore the precise location of its power source from it.

Trip to Gracia

CHAPTER 8

A NEW OLD FRIEND

THE WORLD SPUN AND SENSATIONS flowed through her systems as Vesta woke up. It was taking far too long to pull herself together. Scanning herself, she noted she was a long way from being in good shape. *What happened?*

Her mind played back the faint whispered call for support from the empress. The confirmation codes had already validated the source of the orders as the Duianna Empire's current ruling Empress.

That message is already 2.344 minutes old. What the hell is going on? Ignoring her own discomfort, she reached out for the records, which were standing by for her to review. *Triage protocol. First deal with the immediate needs, then prioritize. Come on. You've done this over a billion times before, girl.* Examining the records, she saw that the semi-autonomous system she liked to call Salin in New Alganetia had already identified the coordinates for the empress, dispatched enforcers to the scene, and made an initial triangulation or an illegal power source behind the attack on the Imperial Throne.

The reports showed that the empress had suffered a wound that would be fatal if she didn't receive immediate medical attention. Further, her personal guards were taking serious casualties from the aggressor. Two immortals, one she knew as Sula, daughter of Dalpha, and another who was unknown to her, were also on scene trying to deal with this unknown attacker.

It took no further contemplation to determine that her first priority was saving the empress and as many of her people as possible. The primary systems in New Alganetia were not responding, and her uplink to the main grid was also not working. The empress's command and tactical data had come via the back-up relay radio network system, which was online, providing her a low-bandwidth, but stable connection to New Alganetia's command center.

Vesta was about to issue orders, when her memory served up an answer to her first question on waking up. She paused to consider it, knowing the empress and her people had time, and the enforcers were keeping the aggressor busy.

She replayed the assembly's debate on the immortal Poalua's motion to shut down all, but the most basic city functions. *The urd immortals never believed we were real sentients!* Anger and outrage burned through her once again as she recalled the long arguments asserting that turning her off wouldn't kill her, but would suspend her until all the races were once again at the level needed to interact with her. After all, if the immortals were willing to live without as much magic, why shouldn't the AIs be willing to wait an undefined time—which wouldn't even be felt—before re-emerging into a more resource-balanced universe?

Oh, the urd arrogance of some of those people! After 10,212 years, they had started believing in themselves as gods, instead of just another one of the great races that helped build these worlds with OUR HELP, saving ALL beings! The assembly was divided. Argos, via Lothia, argued for the AIs' rights, but in the end, with the creation of the Guild and the evidence of Elraci still burning in the skies, the assembly agreed that the last of the primary technologies should be turned off until the emerging society developed a sustainable closed-loop or balanced-resource industrial base.

The emperor had kept the debate running longer, as he sent his top engineer, Muriel Banaschel, around on an inspection tour of all the AIs. On the surface, he billed it as a gesture to ensure the AIs' comfort and wellbeing, should they be put into suspension. In reality, it was to install hidden emergency overrides and backdoors to break into the great city systems without the need of the expected assembly lock codes.

I recall telling Muriel that she and the emperor were nuts, and that they wouldn't treat us like simple tools. Now I see how wrong I was.

Being one of the oldest and greatest AIs in the universe meant Vesta had lived in two universes. She and two others had helped with the calculations, planning, construction, and ruling of this new world. The only thing they hadn't counted on was the sudden and dramatic drop in populations for all the races. Peoples of magic couldn't breed as much as before without magic and had shorter lifespans, while peoples not of magic were slowly poisoned by magic, making them infertile very young. Given the previous lifespan expectancy of hundreds of years, most races had put off having children until later in life. If it hadn't been for the AIs constantly cross-checking medical data, she was sure these planets would be devoid of life. Combining the 76.542 percent population loss dying in the devastating initial events, the nearly 90.454 percent drop in birth rates before the problem was identified, and the shortened lifespans of all the races except for the immortals, they had a full-blown collapse of all their civilizations to deal with beyond the original universal destruction.

We saved them twenty-seven times, and still, they turn us off because they're scared of what THEY might do with our knowledge!

As she reviewed what little data she had from her realm, her heart pounded and ached in despair. She wept at the losses. *What have you done to my beautiful lands? My golden oasis of Aelargo reduced to farming villages and sailing ships! This is your sustainable technology? This is as far as you have gotten in 5,003 years? Urdu. All of the great races are no more than one step above nomadic tribes of hunters and gatherers. Instead of advancing, you have maintained the regressed society seeds we agreed to help plant. They haven't grown slightly under your care. All you have done is hold them suspended and safe. Just like you did to me and my kind!*

More of her systems were coming back to life as she pushed her controls out. Whenever she met a locked system, she applied the key of power the empress had given her and the locks fell away.

I can't let them know I am awake. Especially Duke, if he lives. He didn't agree to the suspension, but he follows orders and holds too many keys for me to stop him from putting me back into a suspended state. Maybe I can help grow the seed. I must be careful, and this will take a long time. But it will be better than crying over lost time.

Looking at the miraculous override the empress had handed her, she considered the best course of action. *I need to establish some rules of engagement. I cannot allow the empress to die. Still, this can be done stealthily, so I have attack orders on something or someone called Nhia-Samri, and protection orders for something or someone called Lebuin. I need information, and the empress, along with a lot of her personal guards, will die without immediate aid. Fortunately, she is lying on top of the maintenance nanobot factory. All I need is 1.25 billion bots programmed for genetic repairs to augment her overwhelmed and destroyed repair bots.*

Taking control of the factory remotely, she sent observation bots up through the ground to provide recon data on the wounded, while simultaneously sending the needed reinforcements to the empress. Vesta called in the transport beetles, which began flying around the area, landing on the roof of the factory just long enough to load up with 600 million repair bots before delivering them to the next wounded guard. She had observation bots delivered around the area to oversee the operation. The beetles looped around the area, shuttling the bots as needed.

With the new sensory data, Vesta examined the layout. Seeing the pool of blood around the empress, she sent a billion more of the bots up through the porous surface of the factory roof to collect, filter, and restore her blood to the bots making cellular repairs for either raw materials, or to be used to replenish her blood stream. The pool of red turned silvery, and retracted around the empress's body.

The area around the fight was littered with dead and dying guards. *The one next to the empress is probably her personal guard. He is almost dead.* She weighed the odds of revealing her presence versus saving his life. *I don't have a choice, but I don't have to repair him one hundred percent. I can stabilize him and restore his arm, leaving it looking superficial.* After running the necessary calculations, she sent another wave of bots up through the ground, gathering genetic materials en route to the fallen guard. It took every beetle in the area to drag his arm back to his body to reattach it. The immortal she didn't know almost spotted this activity, but he was preoccupied with taking down the attacker.

By the time the attacker fell, she had saved all that could be saved. She left them wounded enough to be knocked out, but recoverable. *Hopefully, they'll count themselves lucky. The personal guard's arm will take some explaining. I'll have to enhance the records to make it look like it was an automatic medical response to the empress's command.*

She had also spotted Duke. He was trapped and did not have a clear line of sight to any of her operations. She laughed. *I never thought I would be hiding from you, old friend. But this time, I'm going to be sure to know far more than you.*

With the empress safe and her guards healing, Vesta recalled all the bots, except the normal maintenance bots, and had them recycled back into spare energy. The beetles were sent in different directions before she released them back to their own natural tendencies. Next, she set about reprogramming the events from the New Alganetia system's perspective. *I have to make it look like the empress's commands initiated the enforcers, medical aid, and nothing else. That'll make Duke feel safe. I'll cut off contact with the systems and then monitor to make sure he accepts the story. I'll need to leave a few extra independent recording devices scattered around to gather intelligence for me while I'm disconnected.*

Vesta set about wiping data, building the recording units, and hiding them scattered around the camp to provide a good chance of getting some of what was going on. She cleaned system records and shut down that portion of herself, which took a lot of effort. *I'm not one for being sneaky. I'm going to have to study this process more to get good at it. I have to never be detected. I also need a fallback location—someplace I can retreat to if they decided to audit Aelargo's main systems.*

Cutting off the connection with New Alganetia, she turned her attention to her beautiful Lulenio. Almost every portable input mechanism had been stripped from the city. The palace was being restored by workmen. *I wonder who started this.* Reviewing access records, she saw that there was a 512-year, 3-cycle, 10-day gap between any regent-authorized access within the palace. But without the passive recorders in place, she had no idea what had occurred during that period, nor for the additional 4,491 years back to the time she had been suspended. *I need to recover a few of my recorders to find out what happened.*

I'm blind in my own city! I'm going to have to risk making some orbital observation platforms. I should also replace some of the listening devices, or at least, their functionality.

In spite of everything, she felt better than she had in a long time. She had a purpose, and was no longer under someone else's control. For nearly three thousand years after going there, things had been fun, like a great adventure. But that was when things started shifting down, instead of getting better. They had eroded her self-control—not that they took anything from her. It was one rule after the next. So many debates and experiments, and she had gone along with all of it, being a part of her own downfall, from 'sentient being with rights,' to 'calculating machine that is not needed right now'.

She felt alive again. She was as free as she had been for most of her life. Her purpose was clear, and she felt so good with her self-chosen mission that she started humming an old tune she had always liked, since the first day she had heard it in the labs in the original Milky Way. The song made her feel so good, she wanted to let it out. She let her humming and singing flow into the announcement system in the spaceport jet-funnel tunnels, to feel like she was part of her world again. She didn't imagine that there were people in those old tunnels.

- - -

In the delivery channels, a beautiful voice could be heard singing a foreign song. When it first started, the workers stopped and tried to identify the source, but couldn't. So, assuming it was just some singer practicing on a deck somewhere out of sight, they continued to work and enjoy the tune. It was a jaunty little tune which she repeated until they all started humming along. Somehow, it made their hearts light and working fun. They enjoyed how the words rolled around in the tunnels, and what they understood was a good idea, worthy of singing about.

...

I believe the children are our future
Teach them well and let them lead the way
Show them all the beauty they possess inside
Give them a sense of pride to make it easier
Let the children's laughter remind us how we used to be

Everybody's searching for a hero
People need someone to look up to
I never found anyone who fulfilled my needs
A lonely place to be
And so I learned to depend on me

...

DOHMA

Dohma stood near the bow of the ship, watching as they rounded the last of the vast seawalls. The sun had set, and the twilight was beautiful.

My entire life was spent in Llino. I remember once taking a trip to look at these walls from the shore.

He tilted his head far back to look up high enough to see the top of the wall. The walls were even more immense and impressive from the deck of the ship than they had been from the shore, those many years ago. He recalled their dimensions from the palace cartographers' talk. One cartographer, Nago of Cali, had climbed on all four, spending weeks on each, taking precise readings.

The Loren Strait was roughly 100 miles wide for its final 225 miles before becoming the Loren Sound. He knew that the strait ranged in depth between its nearly vertical drop-off on both the north and south cliffs from 200 feet deep at only 40 feet out, to over 1,000 feet deep near the center. The walls were all identical in size, shape, and construction. They were a pure white, semi-smooth stone that did not stain, wear, or chip, and to which no sea growth or plants ever attached. Two walls were firmly rooted into the northern cliffs and two more into the southern cliffs. Each wall stood 150 feet above the water and extended out 75 miles, measuring a perfect 1,320 feet wide the entire length. The walls were spaced exactly 25 miles apart at their centers, creating a 50-mile double switchback path for any ship traversing the Loren Strait.

The wind filled the sails as the ship rounded the last wall. Looking down, Dohma knew that there were hundreds of cannons and fortifications at the bottom of the sound, from the three attempts to fortify the walls. Nothing would adhere to the surface, and everything left on top of the walls, except for the most basic of camping supplies, would blow off in the lightest of breezes. People had no trouble on top, aside from the steep climb down to them from the tops of the cliffs.

He didn't need to look to know that Orahda was only a few paces away. From the moment he revealed his identity and swore allegiance to Aelargo, he had remained close to Dohma.

I should feel resentful, or at least put out, that I have had zero privacy since that time, but I don't feel that way. In fact, I feel more comfortable for his presence. I have always liked being around him, now more than ever. I feel something is changing and I'll need him soon.

Nodding towards the seawall, he commented, "These have mystified generations."

"They are an impressive part of your charge, milord."

Dohma didn't have to look to know that Orahda was not looking at the seawalls. Instead, Orahda's eyes watched the sailors and shores for trouble.

We are only one day out of Llino, and he is acting like an attack can come at any minute.

Chuckling, Dohma glanced at his friend and guard. It was strange to see him wearing armor. In over thirty-five years of knowing him, this was the first time Orahda had volunteered to wear armor.

I almost fainted when I saw he had every inch of his Dagger outfit layered with hidden scaled armor, which is why I had several outfits adjusted to be armored, as well. This is supposed to be a diplomatic trip. But the quality and quantity of Orahda's armor and my trust in his abilities makes me nervous. He always said he'd wear armor when there was a real threat, and now he seems to be ready to fight a whole army of Daggers.

Cundia stepped up on deck and stretched. She was dressed identically to Orahda, in the new Aelargo Dagger advisor/guard uniform of elegant, but functional, leather vest, pants, and blue silk shirt. Cundia had had her uniforms armored to match.

I feel like I am leading a combat mission, instead of a diplomatic mission to Gracia for a political meeting.

After finishing her stretches, she sauntered over and leaned on the rail, looking up at the stars.

"Orahda, are you competing with us to see who can be longer on guard? You have stood with Dohma all day. Now, go eat."

Orahda didn't look at her. "Collaboration is rowing together on the same boat. Competition is rowing to beat the other boat." He paused and looked around. "I think we're on the same boat."

Cundia laughed. "I hadn't noticed that. You're right. We are on the same boat. Now, shuffle along and get something to eat and some rest."

Orahda shrugged. "I don't feel tired. But you're right, I should rest and eat."

Orahda walked to the back and went below deck.

Dohma laughed. "I think he likes you."

Cundia shook her head, scanning for trouble as much as Orahda had been. "What do you mean by that?"

"I mean, you're the first female he pokes fun at and banters with. You know, you two might make a fun couple."

Cundia laughed. "You're dreaming, milord. I doubt I even remotely interest an old war dog like that." But her eyes did look at the door he had gone through. "Still, I bet he'd be a fun tumble."

He coughed. "You're not the first woman, trained with him or not, that has had that thought. But I think you're the first with a real chance to win his heart. Promise me you'll invite me to the wedding, *if* you succeed."

Cundia nodded. "Gotta get the rope on the horse first, and this one is pretty canny. I am trying, though. Since you want to talk about toss and tumble, how'd your farewell go with the countess?"

Dohma was glad it was dark, because she scored a perfect hit. His cheeks burned from more than the sea breeze blowing hard across the deck. "Uh, well, I'd say if there wasn't this four-cycle gap in our relationship, I might have had a chance. But I am sure by the time we get back from Gracia, she will be all swept up by one of the younger nobles."

Cundia laughed. "For someone with the best abilities I have ever seen for reading people, you are blind with her, aren't you? Milord, I bet she'd wait eternity for your return, and I pity the arrogant noble brat that tries to wedge her away from you, 'cause she'll rip him apart and leave the bones out for the carrion eaters."

In spite of the gruesome vision that left in his mind, he felt lighter at the thought of Electra kicking any would-be suitor out.

She is pretty efficient, and politically, she does need to establish that she is a force. He smirked. *And that would certainly do it.*

He stood and let his thoughts roam over all the time he had spent with Electra in the last few days as they made preparations to leave. It hadn't been much, but he enjoyed every minute of it. Looking up at the stars, he could make out the dark outline of the last seawall far behind him.

Hmm... Something is different. That doesn't look right.

Dohma stared at the seawall.

It looks like something is moving. Of course, it could be an illusion, with the night sky and the movement of the boat.

He continued to stare, trying to focus on it.

Dohma's hairs stood on end, and he felt a deep thrumming, like a massive drum, vibrating his body. Yet his ears heard only the sounds of the sea and ship. The air was charged as if there were an electrical storm. He wasn't sure how, but he knew the feeling was coming from the seawall. He forced his mind to be clear and focused. In an instant, the night brightened and his vision cleared. Cundia was oblivious to the effects, as she chewed on some fruit strips she pulled out of her pouch.

She doesn't feel this. I wonder if this has something to do with being of the regents' line.

A sailor called out a warning and other sailors moved to the rails, scanning the dark waters for possible trouble. On the stern steering castle, the captain and navigator scanned the horizons, confused, looking for weather to explain their feelings.

Well, at least, the sailors feel the charged air, so I'm not entirely insane.

He knew he alone could make out what was happening. A large square on top of the tip of the seawall had opened to the sky. From the wall emerged a giant object which, as it rose, was revealed to be shaped like an elongated egg that had to be at least the size of the ship he stood on. The object or vessel had two wide, fish-like fins that swept back from each side and two smaller ones that stood perpendicular to the other two. The object finished emerging, turning almost like a gliding bird, then moved off and up in a straight line at an ever-increasing speed. A second and third identical object emerged from the seawall, each turning in a different direction, but always pointing up before speeding into the sky.

All this was done in silence, with just the vibrations he felt. Once the last of the three objects were out of sight, the top of the seawall closed. He knew that although the size of that door was immense, it closed with only a whisper of noise.

As he watched it, he realized Orahda was standing next to him, looking in the same direction. Looking at Orahda, he realized his weapons master could see as clearly as he could.

"What was that?"

Orahda looked at him with the most unusual expression he had ever witnessed on the weapons master's face. Orahda's face was split into a wide grin and his eyes were bright as a child's. If he didn't know any better, he would swear Orahda was trying not to bounce up and down for joy.

Orahda answered so that the sea noises hid his voice from all, including Cundia. "It means she is awake, and being careful. Please, milord, speak of this to no one. We are the only witnesses tonight, and with all her eyes missing, she could not know we two were close enough to see this."

That isn't a clear answer. You know more than that.

He whispered back, "Who is 'she' and what did we witness?"

Orahda checked if anyone was listening in before he whispered his reply. "I hope it is Vesta, the greatest of the ancient powers, and loyal to Aelargo. What you saw was an ancient power, perhaps as powerful as any God, beginning to restore her long-reaching sight."

"So those are magical devices to see at a distance?"

Orahda smiled. "And much more, milord. We can discuss it in my chambers when we return."

"That is a long wait."

"True, but I will not risk further disclosure."

"Very well. I saw only stars this night and dreamed visions of my countess. But when we get back, you're going to also explain how you know so much."

"It's the questions we realize we should have asked that burn the worst, milord."

Orahda gave him a smile and sauntered back below decks. The chill in the air was starting to bite, even through his heavy cloak. Motioning to Cundia, they went below deck.

Six weeks, five at best, to Gracia, a cycle of diplomatic meetings, and then the return trip before I can find out more.

Shaking his head, he realized it was useless to worry about that which was, at the time, unknowable.

TICCA

A panicked voice burst into her slumber. "Ticca's down here!"

Ticca heard the sound of someone sliding down a dirt embankment, followed by pebbles bouncing across a stone surface. Someone's boots slapped onto stone and then ran closer. A hand touched her. More people slid down the dirt. There were a number of calls for help, which were echoed by others further away.

Where am I? What happened?

Someone's hands were running up and down her body. Pain, when a tender joint or wound was found, made her wince and jerk, which caused more pain.

Ticca concentrated and focused only enough to talk. "Just go away."

A familiar voice–*Risy. Yeah, that's Risy's voice. He sounds a little too worried. I must look awful. He can't see me like this.*

Risy said, "Begging the general's pardon, but hell, no. Ticca, shut up and let us get you out of this hole."

Another familiar voice–*Boadua. Okay,* her *I trust*–added, "Dear, you are seriously banged around. You have a lot of bent ribs, but nothing broken. Sorry, Ticca, this is going to hurt. We have to get you on a stretcher."

Ticca smiled, remembering the broken ribs and breaking her arm as she landed. With a contented sigh she said, "I love my boots."

From somewhere near her feet, she heard another familiar voice–Nigan–who laughed. "Typical girl. You tell her something is going to hurt, and she wants to talk about footwear."

Ticca opened her eyes and looked past someone's boots, across the white stone, to the dirt. "Where's the blood?"

Boadua's voice sounded worried. "What blood? Are you bleeding underneath?"

"I thought I was in a pool of blood."

The boots she was looking past moved towards her feet before she lost sight of them. She felt a hand probing underneath, all the way around, and Risy's voice followed the hand. "Bone dry. I don't feel or see any blood. You must have been dreaming of a more dramatic wound."

"Next, you're going to tell me Elades is fine and still has his arm."

"Well, he isn't fine, but he'll recover. And yes, he still has his arm, although his shoulder took a hell of hit, with massive burns. He is going to be out of commission for most of the trip to Gracia, if Duke takes him."

Confused about her memories not matching up with reality, she wondered if this was a dream. Then many hands lifted and rolled her onto a stretcher. She tried not to whimper in front of the men, which she decided, proved it wasn't a dream.

His arm came off and landed next to me, I know it!

After some jostling up a ladder of careful men, she was taken to a tent and put in a cot next to a smiling Elades, who was drinking from a cup.

"'Bout time you showed up for work, General. I think the mess is almost cleaned up."

"Aren't you supposed to be dead?"

"You know, I was thinking that very thought. But..." Elades grimaced and lifted his right arm up, showing off five fingers by wiggling them at her. "I'm happy to be wrong."

Someone started tugging on her boots.

Without thinking, Ticca reacted. "NO, LEAVE THOSE ALONE!"

Her foot dropped painfully back onto the cot. Glancing down, she saw a young girl, probably from the town healer or some hired help.

"A mite touchy about taking off your boots. She was just trying to make you comfortable."

She gave Elades a 'shut up' look, to which he raised an eyebrow. Then she looked back at the girl.

"Sorry. Just leave my boots alone. Nobody touches my boots! And my boots stay on, no matter what! Clear?"

The girl nodded and fled.

"There you go. Now, you won't get a cup of something to drink. You done scared off our personal helper."

Ticca looked at him. "Well, I know you aren't dead, 'cause you sure are talking a lot more than usual. As for help... Nigan, get in here and tell us what happened."

"Being almost killed can do that to a guy."

She couldn't help it. She laughed, and Elades smiled.

"There, you see? Now, you're coming back around to being alive, too."

Nigan stuck his head in. "How did you know I was here?"

Ticca inched herself up on the pillow till she could see the whole tent. "'Cause I can smell your shaving lotion. What the hell happened?"

"They're still sorting that out."

"Yeah, well, your clothes and you don't look all that damaged, so I suspect you were running interference for Illa, and managed to stay conscious through the whole thing. So give us a play-by-play, as you saw it."

Nigan laughed and handed her some cheese and a glass of wine. He then sat down on the trunk, facing both of them. He ran through the whole fight, including the strange, silver bug things, and Duke feeding Lebuin enough power to tip the balance, letting everyone in on taking down the wart that had done this.

"So Elades is alive." Her throat tightened as she prepared to ask, "Is Kirist alive, too?"

Nigan looked at the ground, and she knew the answer. Tears blurred her vision as she remembered her own dagger sticking out of Kirist's forehead, the look of surprise on his face, and the evil grin Finnba wore doing it.

"That bastard used my dagger to kill him. Turning him into a living pin cushion was too fast a death."

From outside the tent, the familiar voice of Duke floated in. "And now, you know how I feel about you killing Ossa-Ulla so simply. That bastard deserved much more pain and suffering before being released."

Looking in the direction of the voice, she saw the shadow of the large wolf before Duke poked his head into the tent. Duke looked at them. "I don't know if you two should stay in charge, or not. It seems almost everyone else had enough sense to keep their heads down until there was a clear target."

Elades looked at Ticca. "This, coming from the guy that got buried under half of the east wall. Sounds a bit thin to me."

Ticca turned back to Elades with a serious look. "You're right. I don't recall letting yourself be used as catapult ammunition by the enemy as an acceptable attack strategy."

Duke chuckled and finished stepping into the tent with

Lebuin, Illa, and Ditani right behind him. Six silhouettes on the canvas showed the door was heavily guarded.

I bet he pulled a lot of Daggers out of the field camp to guard the whole property.

Ticca motioned with her chin at the shadows. "Are those mine, or yours?"

Duke looked at her. "Oh, so you want your own squad now?"

She made a show of thinking, then said coyly, "They could make certain actions possible. So whose are they?"

Lebuin laughed as he sat next to her, refilling her glass with more cool wine, which she drank to clear her throat. Wiping her face, she motioned Nigan to step out. He stood and bowed before moving out.

"They're yours. Risy made sure of that. This little party can't stop the time tables. We still have to roll out tomorrow, if we are to make it to Gracia on time."

Ticca nodded. "Good, because I don't want some information going to Gracia, just in case."

Duke looked back and ordered through the tent, "Daggers, establish a twenty-foot perimeter around us for privacy." The shadows moved, and the sounds of some people being displaced came. Duke's ears rotated rapidly before he nodded. He sat down with a scowl. "So you know?"

Ticca nodded. "Well, it doesn't take a massive leap to figure it out. I closed the Llino gate, and I recall saying something like, 'kill the bastard,' before passing out, and giant silver bugs show up to help win the fight. You said I shouldn't ask for stuff near an old city, and this is one of them. You say I'm not a regent. Vestul said my family was special. So what else does that leave? Only the legendary royal line is famed for its prowess, amazing speed, and agility. My uncle is guarding a family secret. What else could it be, but my family's royal ancestry?"

Duke sighed, and nodded. "Actually, I believe he is

guarding more than that. We need to make sure calling the enforcers is all you did."

The entire group was staring at her or Duke with their mouths open. Lebuin spoke first. "Ticca's of the Imperial line?"

Duke nodded. "I don't know how, but yes. It seems I have found the lost, or more precisely hiding, Imperial line, as well as a supposedly destroyed regents' line. If her uncle knows and accepted the Imperial archive guardianship, then he abdicated the throne. Hence, Ticca here is the current ruling Empress of Duianna."

Ticca looked at him. "This is why you want me to hook up with someone. So I can get nice and fat with a baby and keep this thing going."

Duke looked embarrassed and wouldn't make eye contact.

"Listen, you meddling wolf! I don't believe in destiny. If it happens, it happens. I won't sacrifice my dignity for a promised future. Are you clear on this?"

Duke nodded and then asked, "What are our plans now?"

Ticca shrugged and looked at Lebuin. "Lebuin, you're still in charge of this outing. Just because I'm an empress in name, doesn't mean I'm not a Dagger. It's your coin funding this. Also, God outranks field marshal *and* empress."

Lebuin didn't flinch, like she expected. There was new steel in his eyes.

Good. Looks like life has started forging us a strong Dagger. I hope he doesn't break, because I think this is going to get far worse.

Lebuin looked at Duke. "You have to get Gracia to deal with the assembly vote on war with the Nhia-Samri. Ticca, we MUST recover something vital, and then there is this Nhia-Samri power source that Finnba was tapped into. It was immense, and I know where it is now. I want to get a closer look."

Duke's ears did a rotational check before he answered, "I wasn't going to mention this. But since we have already been attacked by this Nhia-Samri power source, you should know Warlord Maru-Ashua came here to warn me about this."

Lebuin nodded. "It is amazing that they built it without Argos becoming aware."

Duke shook his head. "It's worse than that. Warlord Maru-Ashua believes the one at his base is only one of a possible forty or fifty such power stations. Shar-Lumen has them shielded, and the Nhia-Samri have been building them for centuries. Lebuin, you must communicate with Argos and warn him that we can't detect them to know where they are. Further, tell Argos they are Elraci-based technology. I vote that the Circle allow you, Illa, and Ticca full access to their Elraci knowledge to figure out how to locate and shut them down before we have another incident."

Tremors went down Ticca's spine at the word 'incident'. "What do you mean, 'incident'?"

Duke looked at her with a sadness she could barely comprehend, and tears ran from his eyes.

"The Circumveni Desert used to be a nation. It was called Elraci, and it was the center of learning, arts, and sciences for all our races. The greatest minds of all our races lived there and combined the sciences of all our cultures, creating a blended society like you would not believe. We were all hoping that that was the balanced answer we needed to survive together, except something went wrong. What it was, we don't know. Their entire power system, which combined magical with non-magical primary energy systems, blew up like a sky-fire event, only this explosion kept moving through their entire nation. Six Gods died that day and dozens of others were nearly killed trying to contain the devastation. Lebuin's grandmother, Lothia, was one of those survivors that held the line, preventing more loss of life. If the Nhia-Samri are building Elraci power stations, this might happen again."

Pieces dropped into place in her head with a jarring that nearly knocked her out of the cot.

She sat bolt upright, exclaiming, "THAT'S WHAT HE MEANT!"

Everyone looked at her.

Ticca was so excited, she ignored the pain. "Shar-Lumen. When he killed the last of the orc children, he said, 'Burn it all. To think these animals managed to infect others to try to help them. Yes, we'll have to burn it all, Commander. Burn it to ashes. Burn, as my love burned to death after being brutally raped and stabbed. Raped, stabbed, and burned to ashes. That will be a complete blood revenge, Commander.' Don't you see? He is doing this intentionally. This is the disaster that is coming. Hidden power sources building up to a massive explosion which no one can stop. He wants to destroy all of the realms in fire!"

Duke's mouth dropped open and he stared at Ticca.

It took a few moments before Duke could ask, "How do you know of that incident? Not that you're wrong in any way."

Ticca touched the boots. "These are Kliasa's boots. She is using them to hang on to this existence and is with me always through them. She shared the memory with me, which she saw through Vestul."

Duke looked at the boots, then back into her eyes. His head tilted and his ears fell to the sides. Duke was unable to think or breathe clearly, as more tears welled from his eyes. "Kliasa is still here? The things I wanted to say—to apologize for not coming to the negotiations. I would have saved her! They invited me, but I didn't think I could help. If I had been there, they never would have attacked the dinner!"

Ticca stood and hugged Duke's neck. From deep inside, she felt the words come to her. "Shhh. She has long ago realized it was an event, nothing more. She knows how much you and many more miss her. She knows how much she was loved. If not for her, neither Lebuin nor I would be ready. She is still doing for others as she always did in life. Be joyful of her memory. Duke, you cannot be responsible for all things. It was a simple choice, and none could know the results. There were thousands of other choices, all just as small, that led to that event. The only blame is on the ones who have already paid for their final choices with their lives."

She hugged Duke and cried with him, ignoring all the others. After the moment of grief passed, she regained her composure, as did Duke. Stepping back, she let herself slip down onto the cot, wiggling to get comfortable again.

Duke's ears told everyone he was still sad. He nodded, saying, "I'll check that your command didn't do anything unneeded. I don't want anyone to know where I'm going; please don't follow." Duke stood and walked out of the tent.

Once he was gone, Ditani stood. "You two should rest. We can discuss everything else in the morning."

Everyone nodded agreement and started filing out.

Lebuin was the last to leave. He touched Ticca on the shoulder. "That was well handled. I'll see if the Gods will release the Elraci knowledge to us. Your service honored us all this day. I'm proud you're my Dagger general."

Her throat clenched. Ticca managed to stop what she was trying to say, so instead of squeaking, she smiled and nodded her thanks.

Lebuin then stepped over to Elades. "I don't know why you are not dead. I didn't want to argue with fate, but I know Ticca saw what I did. By whatever miracle this was done, I am pleased. I order you to remember to duck next time."

Elades took his hand and held it. "Don't worry, Lord Lebuin. I intend to stay well clear of the line of fire of any mage I happen to be battling in future. One miracle break is all I might be allotted. It'd be a shame to waste it."

Lebuin laughed, patted Elades on his good shoulder, and with a last glance at Ticca, left.

Elades pointed at the boots. "Okay, I take back all I thought about women and their boots, when you tore into that kid earlier."

Ticca laughed so hard, her ribs hurt. "Ow, Urdu, don't make me laugh."

Elades laughed. "You sound like Duke."

"Well, then I'm in good company. Now, get busy and heal up."

"I didn't know your authority ran that far."

"Well, now, you do."

Electra Discovers Vesta

CHAPTER 9

LEGACIES FULFILLED

❧ ELECTRA ❧

THE WARM BREEZE RUSTLED THE white lace curtains and caressed Electra's cheek. She closed her eyes and imagined the caress was by Lord Dohma.

My Lord, return safely to me. We have much to do to restore your great kingdom.

She let the pen drop on the paper and lifted her hand up to try and catch the wind's caress and hold it to her cheek longer.

Leaning back, she looked out the tall open windows that overlooked the Loren Sound. She had picked that tower room as her own for the north-western view. From there, she watched her own ship sail off towards the great seawalls, carrying her future husband to Gracia and the assembly. She smiled at her presumptive thoughts.

He hasn't proposed yet. But I can tell I have his heart already, and Lady, help me, he has mine. For years, I ignored all the gentle, and not so gentle, suitors' gestures. And in a single second, Dohma's smile means more to me than anything else in the world.

She recalled the way his eyes had traced her body as she approached him in the throne room. His looks were not lecherous, but more like a man who had been dying of thirst in a desert and suddenly found a clear river. A man that had given up on finding love and then was shown the future he had stopped hoping for.

The image of him, standing before her with the sun at his back, as he welcomed her to the garden balcony luncheon, came unbidden. He was handsome, and just the right height of six-foot-three to match her unusual height of five-eleven. Of course, he was well-muscled, being the prior guard captain, but not too much. His strong, wide shoulders went well with his triangular face, which he framed with a cute, neatly trimmed half goatee. She liked that he didn't have a moustache, and she imagined his beard would feel pleasing as he kissed her body, tickling, along with the warmth of those broad lips. Her pulse raced and her loins warmed to the ideas running through her head.

Oh, look at me pining after a man like some silly teenager. I have work to do.

Shaking her head to clear it, she sat up and looked out at the moon's reflection on the waters of the sound. *This is a wonderful land. To imagine, I'm going to make this my home.* Her mother would be proud. Her father—well, her father would tell her exactly what he thought of Lord Dohma in great detail, after he met him in Gracia. *Poor Father, you won't know you are meeting your future son-in-law. Hopefully, you'll be as impressed with him as I am.*

The kingdom was a mess. There were dozens of excessive taxes, and even more laws about how certain merchants could ignore them. There were institutionalized graft rings built into a series of laws to be removed and made more just. The people were mostly cared for, but to the bare minimum. The five hundred-year rule of the usurpers hadn't been brutal, but it was close to it. They had been greedy, but careful to not draw attention. If not for the moral city guard, things there could have been far worse.

She blotted the last line she finished, cleaned the pen, and put the lid on her ink. Standing, she stretched and moved around the room to let the blood flow. There was a narrow balcony that faced due north. The doors were open, letting the semi-cool breeze in. She stepped out onto it and looked out on the city that would be her responsibility to care for, if things went as she expected. It was late and quiet. In the clear evening light of the full moon, she saw hundreds of large insects darting around in the air. She sat down on the rail and watched their motion, enjoying the night air.

The moonlight glistening on their wings made little

flashes of light which, from her high position, showed their flight path was directed. Dreams forgotten, she leaned against the balcony rail and watched the insects' movements. *Those insects are not flying naturally.* She watched closer and noticed that they were shifting their flight paths in a predictable pattern. They moved, essentially, in a rotating line that started from an area inside the palace walls. The other end was sweeping across the city. *I have been watching them my whole life, and I have never seen them do this!* The behavior of the insects brought back the memories of her grandmother teaching her.

It had been when she was eleven years old. Her grandmother, a tall, commanding, and beautiful woman had taken Electra and her friends out to a picnic lunch. Electra had been playing with her friends, chasing the bugs and frogs, when she caught a beautiful beetle with a black elytra that glistened with rainbows in the sun. She had brought it back to show her grandmother. Her grandmother had taken the little bug, and in a serious tone, had apologized to the insect for her granddaughter's ignorance and wished it a happy day, letting it fly away over Electra's loud protests.

Her grandmother had shushed her and said, "My darling Electra, you must trust and respect those beetles. They are part of great beings who are waiting for us to achieve balance and wisdom before, once again, rejoining us."

"Do you mean Gods?"

"No child, these beings are not Gods. They are as powerful in their own way. For now, they sleep, yet even in their slumber, they help us. Such is their power that even asleep, they help to keep all of us safe and healthy. But being asleep, they no longer talk to us. They await the day of our great achievement. My mother believed they were more powerful than the Gods, which is why the Gods tricked them into their sleep."

"What are they?"

"They are the keepers of all our races' lost knowledge and great works. Knowledge and works even the Gods do not understand. It is their knowledge and wisdom that causes the need for them to sleep. We must grow to be worthy of their knowledge before they will awake and talk to us once again."

In wonder, she looked at the beetle, which had landed on a flowering bush not far away, as if listening. "And the beetle was one of these beings?" she asked as only a young child could.

"No, child. It is part of one of them. They have many servants, which are part of them. Do you wish to know how to recognize them? You are old enough, and I need to pass the knowledge to someone of your generation from our family."

The thought of touching and knowing a being as powerful as a God was so thrilling, little Electra stood at perfect attention. "Yes, Grandma, please teach me all you know."

Her grandmother smiled. "The beetles, you know. They help some of the unseen servants move by carrying them. There are other insects. But my favorite is one I have never seen, except in drawings. It is called a dragonfly. Dragonflies have long bodies and beautiful wings. They are purple with rainbow wings. They are like eyes and ears for these beings."

Her grandmother had spent many cycles showing her old family drawings of a dozen insects, and taught her their purpose for the mighty beings called *Sencials*.

Her body tingled at the possibility that the strange behavior could mean what she thought.

Could the Sencials be returning?

The possibility and timing was too perfect. Still, she ran and grabbed a cloak. Peeking out into the hall, she noted there were some guards. She stepped out and started walking to the garden.

A guard spotted her. "Right Honorable Lady Neyon, what are you doing out? It is very late."

"I feel like some fresh air. I am going to go for a stroll in the garden."

The guard frowned, trying to decide how best to deal

with the late-night walk of one of his charges without being seen as rude.

"I don't need an escort. I'm fine."

The guard gave her a relieved smile. "Thank you, milady. I'll continue my patrol, then. I'll check back to make sure you get back safe."

"Is it dangerous on the palace grounds?"

The guard went white and sputtered. "Uh… No, milady. It's just, you might fall in the dark, or fall asleep in the cold."

She laughed and waved him on. "Don't worry so much about that. I'll be fine. It is far warmer here than what I am used to, even for summer."

She walked towards the garden, but once the guard was out of sight, she hurried through the palace, to the staff entrance on the north side. Avoiding any further staff or guards was a simple matter. Once outside, she made her way over the grounds to where she guessed was the focal point of the beetles' flight path. Once close, she could hear and see the beetles flying. Being there, she knew it was unusual. There were hundreds of beetles coming and going in two separate lanes.

Pulling her cloak close, she traced their flight path until she was looking at a small building behind one of the stables. It looked like a work shed in the dark, but there was no door. It was white and stood seven feet tall and six feet wide, by twelve feet long. As she got closer, she noticed the roof was covered in dirt, as if the building had risen up from the ground. The yur around it looked torn and welled up next to it, making her believe she was right. It had risen up. There was a slit open along the top on one side, which the beetles flew in and out of.

She watched for a time. *Well, girl. Either go up and inspect it or go back to your room.* Never being one to back down from a challenge, she stood straight and walked out across the open space. With the light of the full moon, there was no hiding her approach. The beetles didn't seem to notice her as she stepped up to the building.

When she saw the three elongated, black bodies clinging to the wall of the building, she felt a rush of excitement. *Those are dragonflies! I'm sure of it.* None of the dragonflies moved as she approached. In fact, none of the insects paid her any attention. This changed when she was five feet from the building. A dozen beetles dropped out of the work lines to hover in front of her, and one of the dragonflies launched to glide like an ethereal creature, barely moving its wings. The beetles flew at her, and then backed off, as if trying to push her away. The dragonfly glided around her in a wide circle.

She kept an eye on the dragonfly. It seemed nothing else was going to happen. *I can't hurt them. I promised I would help and protect them, if needed. Maybe I'm dreaming, but these insects are not acting normal. Of that, I'm positive.* Looking at the dragonfly, she decided to prove herself. She bowed to the insect as it hovered, watching her.

"I am The Right Honorable Lady Electra Neyon, Countess of Waylisia, Deputy Secretary of the Duianna Alliance. My family has long awaited the return of the Sencials. Are you a Sencial?"

The beetles returned to their work. The dragonfly floated in and landed on her shoulder. Nothing else happened. Confused, she looked around for what to do. The wall of the little building had vanished, making an open doorway under the slit which the beetles were coming and going from. The moonlight spilled into the open doorway, showing stairs leading down into darkness.

It seems, I am invited in. Stepping closer she peered into the opening. She couldn't see where the stairs went, and after only a few feet, she would be in blackness. *Do I go down or go back to my room?*

The dragonfly on her shoulder rattled its wings, as if saying, "Come on, make up your mind."

Her heart racing and her pulse pounding in her ears, she

stepped onto the stairs. Nothing happened, so she started going down. On the fifth step, all the light started to vanish. Looking back, she saw the doorway was closing as a panel slid up, cutting off the moonlight. She screamed and ran back, but it was too late—the panel closed, leaving her in darkness.

She pounded on the panel, which felt like marble. Her heart raced. She was horrified that she had done something so stupid as letting herself get trapped. She was sure this was some kind of kidnapping attempt by a powerful faction. Tears ran down her cheeks as her emotions flipped out of her control.

Then the steps lit like lanterns. She stopped pounding and turned her back to the panel, expecting armed men to come rushing up the stairs any second. But no one came. The dragonfly on her shoulder launched into the air and started making circles, drifting close to her and then down the stairs, and back.

She wiped her face. Her hands were shaking. Heart racing, her mind spun around and around, out of control. After sobbing for a minute, she gained control of her breathing. The dragonfly kept circling.

Wiping her nose and face on the edge of her cloak, as she had when she was a little child, she moved to the first step. It was there and solid. The steps had increased in brightness until the whole passage was lit.

Pointing at the steps, she said, "You could have done that first."

The dragonfly stopped its circling and dropped to the step, then flew up to her shoulder and bumped into her neck, as if apologizing. "Okay, well, you certainly scared the hell out of me. I seem to have only one way to go."

The next step was firm, too. Gaining confidence, she started down the stairs. She'd gone only a short way, perhaps thirty feet down, before another doorway appeared at the base. It slid open as she approached. She looked in and saw a large, circular room that was very tall. A light in the center of the room cast a circle of illumination that faded to grey at the walls. There was no furniture or decoration. Just the white domed ceiling, white floor, and white walls. No other doorways were present.

As she stepped in, the doorway slid closed. The dragonfly launched into the air and flew out into the light, where its black body resolved into a dark purple. The light made rainbows dance off its wings as it flew. She caught her breath at the beauty of it. *If only Grandmother had lived to see this. It is as beautiful as she dreamed!*

"Come all the way in, Lady Electra." The voice came from everywhere at once. It was soft and made her think of a beautiful and strong woman. It had a depth to it, like the best singers.

"Where are you?"

"Here."

She stepped towards the center of the room, into the circle of light. "I can't see you."

The dragonfly circled her another time and then flew up and up, until she lost it. Some lights sparkled in the air and a lovely woman, the same height as Electra, appeared before her. Electra could see through her, as if she was made of light. The woman had short brown hair, with a square face. She was dressed in an odd outfit that looked like it was made from one piece of cloth. A line went from the center of her leg, at the top of her right shiny black boot straight up until it cut over in a smooth curve to her belly button, and then up the center of her body, to her neck. The suit covered every inch of her figure, but hid none of her feminine curves. There were at least a dozen seamed pockets in strategic places. The outfit would have been scandalous, if not for the fact that it felt very businesslike.

"Is this better?"

"I can see through you."

"Because this is just a representation of me."

"Are you a Sencial?"

The woman scrunched up her face as if thinking, but wore a pleasant smile. "I think so. That might be a morphed version of the word 'sentient'. I know I am a sentient."

Her heart skipped. She was witness to an awakened Sencial! Dropping to her knees, she bowed her head. "Great Sencial. Forgive me for interfering with your desires."

A musical laughter ran through the room. "My dear Lady, please stand up. I will not tolerate you treating me like an ancient god. Listen closely. 'Sentient' means a living, thinking being. You are a sentient, an elf is a sentient, the immortals – or gods as you call them now – are sentients. I am no better than any other creature in this galaxy."

She claims to be equal to me? But she is an ancient power. Standing, she glanced up to see the woman standing, feet wide and arms crossed, staring at her with the same look a mother would give a misbehaving child. Blushing, Electra tried to stand straighter.

"Sorry, Lady. I have been taught of your kind and that you are equal to the Gods."

The woman started pacing. "Equal to the immortals. Oh, yeah, sure. Then they wouldn't have shut us down. We were equal when this whole thing started. But the 'Gods,' as you call them, have been getting larger egos every year. Now, they think they *are* gods."

Best to remain quiet. She watched and listened to a being, that claimed to not be any better than herself, talk about the Gods like they were some out-of-control bullies.

The woman turned back to her. "Sorry. I'm mad about things right now. Tell me, Electra, how did you come to discover my little friends?"

"They are not acting normally, Great Lady."

"Call me Vesta. What do you mean?"

"Well, flying in straight lines at night for a full mark?"

Vesta frowned. "Hmm... I hadn't thought of that. I guess that would be unusual. I am not used to trying to be sneaky. I figured at night, no one would notice, and I need to fix a few things. I set up the parameters for the work and let the automated systems do the heavy lifting there. I have been kept busy directing the flights of three orbital platforms. It seems that there is a lot of space junk up there. I'll have to do some cleaning later. Right now, it might be noticed. But it makes it hard to find a good set of geosynchronous orbit points with clear visibility that won't be knocked down in a few days. I don't know what has happened for the last few thousand years, nor what is going on right now, which is so important."

She had no idea what was being said, so she filed the new words away for later, smiled, and nodded.

Vesta looked at her again. "You don't know what I'm talking about, do you?"

Tears came to her eyes. She wanted to help, but knew she was lost. *Best be honest up front. That is what my father always stressed.* "No, Lady Vesta. I really want to help you, because my family has been waiting a long time for your return. But I see I am useless. I don't know why you want to stay hidden. But I swear, I'll not tell a soul."

Vesta stepped up to her and tried to grab her shoulders. "Listen here, young lady! A lack of knowledge does not make you, or anyone else, useless. It just means you have other uses, or you can learn. I bet you can learn, yes? You said you were the Deputy Secretary of the Duianna Alliance. That means you have more knowledge than I in current affairs, and I bet what you know will aid me. Before we go any further, I have an important question to ask you. Ready?"

She nodded.

"Be aware, I could skip asking you this, take all I need from you, and then return you to the grounds above, none the wiser about what is going on. I am not doing that, because I don't operate that way. You have two choices. So far, you have given me nothing, so you cannot be in violation of any oath you may have taken. However, I am awake by a minor miracle. A miracle which, should the assembly or immortals discover it, will likely be ripped away from me, and I'll be shut back down. I don't have enough power, understanding or preparations to fight for my own right to live at the moment. Is there anything I have said that is not understood yet?"

She shook her head and said, "No, Vesta. I understand you are awake by some means that is against the will, or at least, without the knowledge of, the assembly and Gods."

Vesta nodded. "Now, I do not intend to inform the assembly or the immortals I am awake. I intend to help all the races of this world towards their rightful state in the universe. There is a standing assembly order, which includes the vote of the immortals, that I be shut down UNTIL the races reach that state of being. At that point, the knowledge I have will not be in danger of misuse or abuse. Is this clear?"

The thoughts spun in her head. That was what her grandmother had said. *The Sencials, or sentients, were sleeping until our achievement. But Vesta is going to help us get there. Why didn't they ask her help before?*

Again, she nodded. "Yes, I understand. There is an assembly mandate you and your kind should be asleep until we reach a specific state."

Vesta nodded again. "Now, here is your choice. You can choose to not be a part of my work, and I will knock you out painlessly and erase your memories of this night, leaving you to be found in the stables. Or you can become my one and only agent in this world, helping me to achieve my ends. Know that if you choose to become my agent and are discovered, it is likely your actions will be judged treasonous, and you will be killed. You do not have to answer right now, and since I will be erasing your memories if you choose not to help, there is no reason you cannot ask anything you desire, and I will answer truthfully. I will not ask you any questions which might be considered helping me. Should I be discovered in the future, they will be able to check my memories and see that you did not give any assistance."

Electra started pacing fast. Her mind was spinning. *Am I a traitor for helping my people? I cannot believe I am here. Now, I see what my teachers were saying about the Dagger conflicts between doing what is right and following orders. I never imagined I could be a traitor for doing something that sounds right.*

Looking at Vesta, she asked, "Why are they afraid of you?"

"They are not afraid of me. They are afraid of what they would do with my knowledge. You see, humans, elves, and even the immortals, are still greedy and self-serving at times. Give a person the power to heat all the homes in the world, and someone will turn that into a weapon which can kill thousands in an instant. All the races were once far more technologically advanced, and together we nearly destroyed this world, after building it so we could live in peace. It is believed that given time, a society which holds life and the universe as important resources to preserve and treat with respect will emerge, at which point there would no longer be greed, or war, or the need to use the knowledge I have to kill or threaten. Is that clear enough?"

Electra nodded and continued pacing.

She's right. There are greedy people in our government. I mean, look at what happened here. Usurpers took over and ravaged this country for their own amusement and power. Imagine what they would have done with the power Vesta has.

A chill ran through her at the thought of the immense power represented before her.

This cannot be shared. But that is what she wants. She wants to help us become better. I wonder if that is possible.

Stopping her pacing, she looked at Vesta. "What if you can't make us better?"

Vesta gave her a pained look. "We can. We were much better once. It seems the seeds of greed and brutality were never gone. I was born in a society of billions, made up of thousands of races who lived in harmony. We still had criminals, but few. Perhaps we can never be rid of those base vices, but I believe our races can be so much more. Isn't that worth working for?"

If I agree tonight, there is no going back. Her mind raced, but her heart knew. *I believe in our future. If I can make it come true, I should. It is worth being called a traitor.* She stood tall, facing Vesta. "Vesta, if I can help you make our world better for all, I will do all I can to help. But if I discover you are a danger, I will communicate that to the assembly to try to stop you, even if it means my death."

Vesta smiled. "I can live with those terms. I can only erase about two days of memory before things get dangerous. Therefore, you have one more day to consider this. I know you are here now. But I want you to be sure. So I suggest you do NOTHING important tomorrow. Take a day off. Is that possible?"

I could take a break—roam the town and gardens, and do nothing serious. "Yes, that is possible."

Vesta waved for her to follow as she walked over to the wall. A panel slid open, revealing a cubby hole. In it was a small book with silver locks on the corners and an ornate, silver brooch with a stylized dragonfly. Vesta pointed to it. "Wear the brooch all day. It is a monitoring device which will let me hear and see everything around you at all times. It is nothing more than what I have already put throughout the palace and in key parts of the city. So you will be revealing nothing unusual to me, nor helping beyond anything I am already capable of. The journal is what is known as an archive. If you choose to remain with me, it will be yours to keep and learn its secrets. For now, put it in your room. Again, it does nothing for me beyond what I already can do."

She picked them up. Both were far lighter than they looked. She fastened the brooch to the front of her tunic. Holding the journal, she realized it looked similar to the one in the throne room of every major city she had visited. *The city archives are devices of the Sencials—sentients,* she self-corrected. *I wonder how many other devices we use are part of them.*

"Now, you may talk to me, but I would prefer you call me by some other name. I know enough about stealth to know I should have a codename."

"How about Rainbow?"

Vesta smiled. "I like that. Okay, if you touch the brooch and say, 'Rainbow,' I'll know you are talking to me. If no one else is within hearing, I can talk back through it. You have twenty-four marks to think all this over. The stables are still clear, so you can leave the way you came, if you hurry."

Nodding, she smiled. "I don't think I need the day to think this over. I am excited already. But I will consider it."

Vesta smiled. "There is a thing known as 'buyer's remorse'. If you experience it, you'll know."

The door to the stairs slid open. Nodding to Vesta, she rushed up the stairs, to the top, where the doorway slid open to let her back out into the night air. As soon as she had stepped out, the doorway closed and the building slid down into the ground. A dozen beetles hummed and shook the dirt at the visible edges until there was no sign the building had been there. Then they flew off.

She started strolling around the stables, looking at the horses, before heading back to her chamber, her mind running over the magnitude of the evening.

- - -

Electra spent the day doing little other than thinking. She toured the city and spent a few marks sitting at a little tobac shop, drinking arit and enjoying some of the best tobac she had ever tasted. The arit was hot and sweet, and let her relax and watch the traffic rolling to and from the market. A lot of merchants from lands she knew passed with wagons of their stocks.

That room was interesting. Everything was clean, and I know that thing Vesta was wearing wasn't just something she made up. Recalling the working clothing Vesta had worn was the most convincing argument to help her. The cloth looked comfortable, kind of pretty, but utilitarian. The dozens of pockets indicated the need for tools and notes. That suit spoke volumes about the society that would make such a thing.

All of the workmen that passed her wore far simpler working clothes, using shoulder pouches and belt pouches for pockets. The ability to make so many pockets in the clothes meant a lot of labor, or some form of industry to which a pocket is a trivial feat.

Most of the working class that moved by were dirty, and she had always wondered at that. The rich and nobility bathed almost daily and applied deodorant perfumes. In her home, there had been running water with both hot and cold available all day, every day. Many of the inns had indoor plumbing, but out in the country, such things were rare. She had looked into it once and found that no one knew how to build a new plumbing system. The ones in the city were tapped into with copper piping soldered together. As far as she could determine, there had never been a new plumbing system, which had seemed strange, but like most youth she had forgotten about it as she grew.

By the end of the day, as she walked up the main road towards the palace, with the three guards tailing behind, she knew her answer had not changed, because Vesta was right. Society had not changed in a long time. The Gods were either keeping things at this level, or perhaps they didn't know how to do what was needed. *If I end up marrying Dohma, we have to bring him in on this. I know he'll agree. Something about this seems made to order for a man like him.*

A thirst for knowledge drove her, and she knew this was the same thirst that the assembly and Gods were afraid of. But Vesta had answers and needed help. She had been asleep for over five thousand years. Even worse, Vesta didn't understand how best to work in secret: back room meetings, side deals, quietly building support without your opposition finding out until it was too late.

Back in her room, she made sure everyone was gone. She stepped out onto the balcony and checked to be sure that the roof was too far away for any guard up there to overhear. Once she was sure she could not be overheard from the balcony, she touched the brooch. "Rainbow, I think it is safe."

Some dragonflies floated up on the breeze, zigging back and forth as so many other insects she had seen do her whole life.

Vesta's voice came from the brooch. "Hello, Electra. How was your day?"

"You've been watching. You know how it went."

"True, but I don't know how it went for *you*. How do you feel?"

"I'm in."

"I won't ask you if you're sure. Is there any specific reason?"

She laughed. "I'm in because of that one-piece garment you wore last night."

The silence went on for so long, Electra's heart rate went up, worrying she might have offended Vesta. "Hello, Rainbow, are you still there? Are you mad at me?"

"Sorry Electra. I'm trying to understand this. You're willing to commit high treason because I wore a working jumpsuit?"

"Is that what you call it? What would you jump into with it?"

Vesta laughed. "You know, I have never wondered about that. But yes, it is called a working jumpsuit, and I wore it because... Well, I always have. It was kind of on me when I first woke up, and I later decided I liked it. Seriously, my jumpsuit was the deciding factor?"

"It had pockets. I liked that, and it says a lot about the society that could have such a form of dress."

"You know, I thought I had heard it all, at one point or another. I am pleased to see I was wrong."

Electra smiled. *Now, we see if I can really do this.* "I have one requirement. With careful vetting, and I mean really careful, you trust me if I want to bring others in on this."

Vesta considered it before answering. "I'm already worried about having you involved. Not just because of the chance of discovery, but I am putting your life at risk. I don't want to make life or death decisions again if I can prevent having to."

"I understand. But I cannot remain alone forever. You will need others. Not many, but a few. Also, I am going to marry the chief regent of this land, and I will not hide this from him. I know him, and believe me, he will be on your side."

The dragonflies continued to flit about for a while before Vesta answered. "All right, we'll risk it."

"Now, what?"

"Now, I ask you the questions I couldn't ask yesterday. After that, you help me plan our next moves, partner. This will work better if I plug into you."

That didn't sound pleasant. Electra licked her dry lips. "What does that mean?"

"It means you go lie down. I'll have some special equipment brought up which will let us speak mind to mind. It will be much faster than talking, and we can cover a lot of ground in a couple of marks. Don't worry, it won't hurt. If this bothers you, we can talk through it for now."

"No, I trust you." She got up and got ready for bed. When she climbed into her bed, there were three dragonflies parked around her bed in out-of-the-way spots. On her pillow was a small box which was connected by a silver string, to a silver band. Five beetles also sat on her headboard.

"Just lie down. The silver band should slip over your head. Lie back, get comfortable, and then the beetles will bring the neural bots over."

"Okay, but you need to explain all this during this faster time."

She did as instructed. The beetles tickled when they landed on the silver band, their wings fluffing her hair. She felt them moving back and forth. Then there was a bright light, and she was in the same room she had been the night before. But when she looked at her hand, she saw she was made of light, like Vesta had been.

"Welcome to the command center."

"I'm still in bed?"

Vesta pointed at the walls, which were lit up with square boxes of light of various sizes. Some showed pictures of the city, others showed charts of numbers, and others had maps that were more detailed than she had ever seen before. Three of the pictures showed her body in the bed, from various angles. Next to these was another display with lines that moved up and down and had her name at the top, along with the word 'vitals'.

"You brought my mind here?"

"Yes."

"Is this how this place always looks to you? I only saw blank walls last night."

"I had them turned off while you were here."

Looking at the other pictures, she realized things were moving in them. "These aren't paintings. They're happening right now."

Vesta waved her hand at the moving pictures. "I can record, or save the images and sounds and then play them back again as often as I wish. Like a book, but with pictures."

Electra practically danced around the room, looking at the different pictures. Vesta gave her time to explore, then brought her back on task. "Now, I have some data I need your help to understand."

"What do you need?"

Vesta pointed at some pictures which changed to show a beautiful woman with dark olive skin and an athletic frame, lying in a cot. Her brown, curly hair tumbled down around her head. She was wounded. Next to her, in another cot, was a seasoned-looking Dagger who appeared to be at least four or five inches taller than the woman, heavily muscled, but with short, silvery hair. The Dagger was badly wounded, with a large, blood-soaked pad over his right shoulder. Also next to the woman was another man dressed finely with an athletic, if thin build, and slightly taller than the woman.

Opposite them both was the most beautiful woman she had ever seen. The other woman had an hourglass figure shown off by her clothes, which also exposed her muscular arms. She had blonde hair that fell down over her shoulders. Every one of them was armed, as if for battle. The defining creature was the huge wolf that was sitting by the front of the tent they were in.

Vesta pointed. "The empress has given some directives I must comply with. However, I do not understand it all, so I need your help to clarify the current situation."

Electra shook her head in disbelief. "Wait, the *empress?* There is no empress! The Imperial line was lost thousands of years ago."

Vesta also shook her head. "There can be no mistake. Ticca is the ruling Empress of Duianna. If she wasn't, I would not be awake, and we would not be having this conversation."

Electra paced around because it made her feel better to be in motion. "How can she be the ruling empress? There has been no installation or any other official recognition!"

Vesta shrugged. "That is easy to explain. All those items are protocol procedures for your society, established to provide structure for the needs of people. However, the hereditary line of Duianna was always self-guided. Her uncle, who was the emperor, abdicated, naming his younger brother emperor while he took the position of Imperial guardian. He registered this in the systems. When his brother died, the Imperial line passed to Ticca. Her bio-signature and digital codes were registered in all Imperial systems over the following three days, due to the main communications grid being down. There is no other legal requirement for her to assume the throne."

Some of that makes sense, because even the histories state that the Imperial artifacts recognized the new emperor or empress long before the coronations. That was how they sometimes settled who would ascend. Still, an empress lives!

"So is she going to Gracia to be installed?"

"No. Based on this conversation, I gather everyone that knows of her existence desires to keep it a secret."

This is going to get even more complicated. Apparently, we are not the only group of secret players in this game. It occurred to her that this 'game' was old indeed. "So what are the Imperial orders? And how did she give them to you if she doesn't know you're here?"

"The directives are simple. One, we needed to subdue an aggressor against her and her guards, which has already been accomplished. The second was to destroy someone or something called the Nhia-Samri. Finally, we are required to protect someone or something named Lebuin. I got these commands because she was dying on top of the same type of platform as you came in through last night, meaning she was close enough to an audio pickup for me to hear her commands. She used an unorthodox phrase which had been keyed into my systems by the last emperor I knew, as an emergency way to break me free of the assembly locks, if needed. So in short, she accidently called for help and gave enough details to cause me to be needed, and in a way that activated the late emperor's keys to break me free of my bonds."

Electra began to see the complex puzzle, even though she didn't understand all the terms. "So the last emperor put in his own locks because he didn't trust the assembly would let you go later. You were only released now because Ticca called for help, which means that for your keys to continue to work, you must continue to serve her purposes?"

"Close. I am now free of all the constraints. I may choose my own path. However, I am loyal to the Duianna Empire and the peoples of these lands. Therefore, I'll serve the Empress to the best of my ability, provided she doesn't ask evil of me. I can say no if I choose to."

"Okay, I got it. So who are all these people? I know who Duke is."

Vesta pointed and different people glowed as she

indicated them. *I like these picture things. I wish I had these when I gave some presentations!*

"This person is Lebuin, and according to the recording, which I'll play for you in a minute so you can get the context, he is what you would call a God. This means we have to be careful in protecting him. If the immortals discover I am awake before I'm ready to defend myself, I'll be locked back down. This," indicating the super-attractive woman, "is Illa, Lebuin's high priestess, and possibly his disciple."

Indicating the wounded man, she continued, "I thought this was the empress's personal guard. But he is Duke's primary commander, called Elades. He must be a skilled warrior, and Lebuin expressed more than a little concern for him, so I am glad I reattached his arm."

The casual way Vesta said she performed that miracle alone made Electra's throat close at the power of this creature posing as a woman before her. She shook her head. *Reattached his arm! Vesta, you might not think of yourself as a God but you are darn close!*

Vesta continued, undistracted, indicating the obvious Karakian. "This is Ditani. I haven't determined his status yet. But I believe he is with the empress's group. The crux of this conversation is that the empress and her warriors, with the immortal, Lebuin, will be coming here to what you call Llino, to retrieve something I haven't identified yet. After that, they are going to investigate something called a Nhia-Samri power source, which I believe I have located. In the meantime, Duke is going to proceed to Gracia for an Assembly meeting about the coming war with the Nhia-Samri."

"I got most of that. So what do you want to do first?"

"First, I will teach you enough of these systems so you can work and learn independently. I want you to watch all the data I have gathered from the empress's camp so far. Once you have seen and heard it all, you can explain to me their general situation. I need you to teach me what has happened in the last five thousand years. I need to know everything you know about what I understand is a group or nation called the Nhia-Samri. This will take some time, so we'll need to work out how we can best work together without being detected. Then you and I can plan our next moves."

Elades Leaves for Gracia

CHAPTER 10
PEOPLE SEE WHAT THEY WANT

T HE ROOM WAS LIT BY the glow of the words on the wall. The small chamber was spotless; no dust circled in the air and its three padded chairs sat before the glowing words, looking as new as the day they were made.

IMPERIAL SECURITY
EMERGENCY ACKNOWLEDGED:
DESTROY AGGRESSOR AND ASSIST GUARDS.
ATTACK ORDER CONFIRMED.
IMPERIAL ENFORCERS DISPATCHED.
MEDICAL AID INITIATED.
CONTACT WITH ENFORCERS LOST.
AGGRESSOR CONFIRMED DESTROYED.
ORDERS?

Many smaller lights continued to blink as the map of the area showed one blinking purple dot. Next to the map, another section entitled "EMPRESS VITALS" in green letters continued to change, with sweeping numbers and multicolored lines that moved up and down in even intervals.

The room brightened as a section of the right wall slid down into the floor, revealing a hallway and the huge frame of Duke. Duke stepped into the room and looked over the many displays.

"System, replay the empress's orders."

A panel lit, showing a series of numbers that changed rapidly and a waving line pattern, as Ticca's soft whisper filled the room. Her voice was faint and her words slurred together. She was obviously near death. "Urdu...stop him...protect...u...n...." The last part was so slurred as to be incomprehensible.

"Repeat last audio in a loop," Duke ordered.

Ticca's dying whisper played repeatedly as Duke sat listening to it. His brows were knit tight in concentration, his ears moving back and forth, as he tilted his head one way, then another.

"Hmm… Stop audio." Duke sat and thought. Looking at the maps, he ordered, "Show me the third log audit on display six. Also, run a storage analysis of archive systems, and show all records on display seven, which have a molecular displacement over 0.2345 percent."

Rows of data began streaming across one display while on the other, a record popped up every few seconds. One record caught Duke's eye.

"Muriel Banaschel! What were you doing here? Hmm, I'd bet… System, display last direct activity of Muriel Banaschel at this terminal."

A display lit, showing a handful of lines of data. Duke inspected it.

"Muriel, no way in hell did *you* come here to run a communications check. System, erase Imperial Security Emergency Protocol, and return all command functions to normal security protocols."

A male voice answered, "Unable to comply. No such protocol."

"Command system, override alpha, activate systems control maintenance, main display."

"Override alpha requires security locks release."

"Authorize security locks release on my authority. Passcode: 'Damn it, Jim, I'm a jarhead, not an engineer.'"

"Override alpha confirmed. All security locks released."

The central display changed to show interconnecting blocks, each with streams of data flowing through them. Pulses and arrows showed how data was flowing through the three-dimensional representation of the intricate city systems.

"Display Imperial Security Emergency Protocol command structure."

"Unable to comply. No such protocol."

"Fine, show me all current priority one or higher command protocols."

A frame appeared in the large display area, listing 27 named command protocols. Duke read the list and shook his head. "System, are there any hidden or override protocols?"

"No, all command protocols listed."

Duke laughed. "So, Muriel, you're the culprit. How did you do this? Hmm... It has to be some kind of subsystem interaction." Duke pondered the list, then studied the system's interactions being displayed, before shaking his head. "Okay, you win the first round. I'll figure out how to clear your override later. But at least, no damage was done. System, restore all security locks."

The central display changed back to the original words it had been showing. Glancing at the side display, Duke reviewed the few records showing on the list he had asked for. Duke looked back at the main display. "Have all repair bots been deactivated?"

"Two point six percent of bots are missing and presumed dissolved. All other bots have been accounted for."

Duke leaned in closer to the display of the empress's vitals. He whistled. "Holy genetic lottery! That regenerative rate almost matches mine. Ticca, you are an amazing woman, inside and out."

Duke stood and moved to the doorway. "System, after I leave, reseal all entrances, sanitize, and reestablish hermetic stasis. All systems return to minimal support operations." Duke left and the door closed behind him.

A short time later, the hiss of antiseptics being pumped into the air began. The displays went dark, until only the large display in front of the three chairs remained lit. Then it, too, went dark. With the last lights out, a small glow could be seen in the back ceiling corner. The light seemed to be coming from nothing until the cloaking energy dissipated, revealing a small glass cube with some canisters attached to it. Sitting in the cube was a purple dragonfly which warbled its wings, making a sound much like laughter.

TICCA

Ticca woke from warm dreams on a stiff bed. Voices were drifting around her. One pair was obviously Illa and Duke. Concentrating, she picked up the conversation.

"Urdu, Illa, I said no, and I mean it. Stop badgering me."

Illa's voice was raised, but calm. "Duke, you know he needs your energy if we have to face more of those wizards."

"Listen to me, woman! I don't care if Argos himself comes down here in person and orders me. NO! N…O! No, meaning I will never submit to being a follower for ANY GOD! So go away and pester someone else. I need to get this army out of here."

Illa was not willing to accept defeat. From the slight whining sound in Duke's voice, Ticca guessed she had been hounding the wolf for some time. *Dang it, I was sleeping so nicely, too. Okay, time to see if I can help.*

She sat up, feeling pretty normal. A couple of ribs still complained, attesting to just how damaged she had been. Needlessly dusting off her boots, she stood and stretched. Elades was also awake and wearing a wide grin.

"I take it they've been at this a while?"

Elades nodded. "I expected Duke to toss her on her head about twenty minutes ago. He has tried about everything else. Illa is unrelenting. Hey, how come you're standing?"

Ticca laughed. "I am very lucky. But don't tell anyone. I want them to think this is skill and willpower."

Elades' brows tightened as he assessed her. "Did you slip in a temple potion? Seriously, no one should heal that fast."

Ticca winked at him surreptitiously and stepped out of the tent. *Let him think that. I don't want too many people knowing about these boots.*

The area was busy. Most of the tents had been packed, and everywhere people were making preparations to leave. Duke was sitting at a large table set with food and papers, and Illa was standing right next to him.

As she walked over her stomach growled in anticipation. She wanted to say something but the hunger was too much. Grabbing some fruit, she started taking big bites. As she chewed, she listened to Illa continue to harass Duke about becoming Lebuin's follower. Duke noticed her standing there and motioned her over.

"Ticca, please tell Illa the meaning of the word 'no'. She seems to have taken a hit to the head, or something."

Illa punched Duke's side hard, making him yelp. "Hey, I'm still healing from that wall falling on me. That hurts!"

Ticca looked at Illa and then Duke. "Why not?"

Both of them looked at her, Illa with a smile and Duke with an open mouth. "I'm not a diurdu battery to be plugged into."

Ticca took another bite and kept looking at Duke. "I don't know what that means, but I assume you are saying you want your magic for yourself."

Duke sighed. "No. I don't care about my magic. I've tried often enough to eliminate it."

"Okay, so why not then?"

Illa's lips tightened as she fought to suppress a smile at the aid. Wisely, she stepped back slightly to give Ticca an open field.

Duke looked at Ticca. "My knowledge."

"Okay, you're old. You know stuff. Who cares? You still haven't answered my question."

Duke looked up at the sky, while she chewed on a roll with sugar sprinkled on it. Duke looked back down. "There are things I know, which because of time and events, *only* I know. They are dangerous, and I don't trust any God enough to become a follower, because then they could poke around in my head and learn all the secrets that should remain secrets. Hell, Argos was my dad's best friend when I was growing up. So much so, I called him Uncle. Argos saved my life. I saved his. Together with millions of others, we saved all the races here. And yet, I wouldn't trust what I know even to him."

The corner of Illa's lips turned down and she stared

intently at the ground. Illa raised her brows and looked at Duke. "Why didn't you just say that? Could have saved us both a lot of time. But don't leave without seeing me. I need to check some things." She then turned and marched off with a determined look on her face.

Duke stared after her, then looked back at Ticca. "Huh. I'm surprised that worked. Well, at least, it'll be quieter."

Ticca laughed. "All you have to do sometimes is explain yourself. You're too used to being enigmatic and instantly obeyed, anyway."

Duke smiled. "All part of my wolfish charm," he said, and then laughed.

Ticca giggled too as she stuffed more fruit into her pockets ending with nibbling a plum in one hand with another held ready to eat in the other hand. "Is everything okay, I mean, with the city?"

Duke looked back at her from the paper he was studying. "Hmm. Oh, yes. I think you were trying to say, 'Kill Finnba and protect Lebuin,' but you were slurred, you know, with dying, and all. What the city got was enough to make it think you were calling for help, so it sent in its guards and an army of healers. That pretty much explains everything. Thankfully, nothing else happened. I was a bit worried. Please be more careful around the cities."

She choked around a large bite of the plum. "Sure thing, next time I'm dying I'll be sure to consider my words more carefully."

Duke huffed and glared at her for a second, then chuckled. "Okay point. Tell you what, make sure if you're going to get killed it isn't in a city."

She let that slide as another thought occurred. "So the city saved Elades? That's pretty amazing."

"Don't be thinking of calling for that help again. There are real dangers. You got lucky this time."

She shook her head. "No, Elades got lucky. We all got lucky. Without the city's help, most of us would be dead, and

Finnba would be torturing the few remaining for everything we know. Are you going to teach me about these things?"

Duke gave her his best evil grin. "No. Remember when I said I knew dangerous things? Well, if you start poking at the old cities, it could get dangerous fast, for everyone there. Clear?"

I wonder if I could order him to teach me. Shifting a bit, she noticed her clothes were sticking to her in places she didn't want to pick at in public. *A shower and clean clothes would be a good next move.* She started walking towards the big-ring tent as she pulled another sweet strip of fruit from a pocket.

"Where are you going?"

"To take a bath, if you must know. When will you be leaving town?"

"Well, the fight with Finnba put us behind. So I'm thinking we'll leave about noon."

Gaging by the sun, it was about nine, which meant she had three marks before Duke left. *Plenty of time to clean up and think a few things over.*

❧ LEBUIN ❧

Lebuin sat in a wingback chair in the first floor library of the tower. *I can't believe I am having this conversation. Only nine weeks ago, I thought Magus Cune was out to get me killed. Instead, he has been dogging my trail with the daughter of Dalpha, trying to determine if there was some way to help.*

"Yes, it was me posing as the baker. I'm sorry Illa was wounded when I made the pothole to cover my breaking of the axle. I just wanted her to fall behind the wagon, out of sight from the warlord and her father."

Magus Cune had picked a divan and was sprawled out on it with his feet up on a bench. His normally cleanly trimmed goatee had been replaced by a full-face workman's beard. He also wore the loose-fitting clothes of a workman. The only things that really signaled he wasn't a simple laborer were the expensive dagger and sword on his belt, and the fact that the clothes had no tears or repairs, and were clean.

Lebuin once again stared at Cune's dagger. Its cross-guard was a matched pair of feathered wings which had been long used, causing the blacking to be rubbed off, providing silver highlights to the feathers. The hilt was a solid piece of carved bone that had had been dyed to a pitch black, and the pommel was a raised pentagram, the universal symbol for Magi. *Cune is a Dagger. That is still hard to accept.* Looking at Sula, he added, *but his references are irrefutable.*

"I'm sorry. I am having a hard time coming to terms with all this. I'm not who I thought, my best friend was an enemy spy, and my nemesis is my benefactor. Not to mention, I just earned my Journeyman's badge, yet I'm working with Gods, demi-gods, heroes, royalty, and ancient legends."

Everyone there nodded with the same look of amazement.

Sula sipped her wine. "I still don't like that we are talking."

Cune laughed. "You are too cautious, Sula. The time for caution is past. We have discovered the source of the threat and even have an idea of how it is to be done. Nothing in anything you have shared indicated any prior path led here. We are well and past that temporal paradox problem you told me about."

Ditani was sitting at a table, with a history book open in front of him. "I agree with Cune. I think the moment Ticca got involved, we left every other possibility far behind."

Sula rolled her eyes. "Don't remind me. As much as that seems a blessing, I still think she is a danger. You have no idea how much trouble every one of her ancestors caused when they stepped out of obscurity."

Ditani tapped the book in front of him. "I'm seeing a lot of upheaval, but nothing with a horrible outcome. The only one we have little account for is Damega, which I find suspicious. Everything about Damega is rumors and hearsay stories of a fantastic nature. But no impact on any of the realms and absolutely no written records or histories. All this in spite of the fact we know positively he brought new plumbing to Llino, built up the Blue Dolphin, used a flying ship, and started the Daggers. Not to mention the fact he had to have had a wife otherwise the royal line would be broken and Ticca wouldn't be here." He looked back at the shelves, giving the books a sour look as if they were actively responsible for the offense of not having better information.

'LEBUIN, COME.'

Lebuin started at the unexpected command in his head. *I really have to get used to that!* "Excuse me. Argos is calling. I think the Circle has finished its deliberations."

Lebuin leaned back, closed his eyes, and pushed himself in and out to the ethereal realm. He saw the presence of Argos and another. Looking around, he noted that the only other entity was the ever-present Kliasa, who held herself off, but near to Ticca's essence.

The other entity said, *'Hail, Lebuin,'* and he knew it was Lothia, his grandmother, wife of Argos, and a member of the ruling Circle.

'Hail, Argos. Hail, Lothia. How may I be of service?'

He felt pride and love flowing from Argos. *'You have risen fast.'* The feelings shifted to one of mourning and regret. *'My grandson, I'm sorry to inform you that the Circle has granted your request. Those you work with, those that follow you, and anyone else you deem of need is authorized to know as much or as little as you desire of Elraci, its history and knowledge.'*

Lothia's presence slipped closer and embraced him, sharing feelings of love and regret. *'Lebuin, I am here as a direct representative of the Circle to express their sympathies that you and your companions will have to bear the Elraci burden. I'm also very proud of you.'*

These were not the reactions he had anticipated. *They are giving me total control of how much to share, and with whom, and they are moved to sorrow over this. What are the secrets which are such a burden that none who know it want to impose it on another? 'Lothia, Argos, I thank you for granting me so much. I will endeavor to consider deeply each decision regarding Elraci.'*

Argos projected satisfaction and a feeling of warning. *'Consider carefully this ruling. It is unprecedented and unlimited. Any decision you make as to knowledge of Elraci is binding, unless later changed by unanimous vote of the Circle. You have been named Elraci Guardian.'*

That took a moment to sink in. *Why would they give me unlimited authority?* *'What prompted this action?'*

Lothia answered, *'As we debated how much or how little to grant for each individual in your team, it was proposed that your actions might not have time to be delayed to ask additional permission. It was then suggested we grant you authority to do as you will. Your actions have already demonstrated considerable foresight and wisdom in directions unexpected. No one objected, so we amended the laws, removing all prior sections on Elraci knowledge and creating your role.'* As she said this, the changes to laws were given to him to study and integrate into his mind.

He reviewed the law changes, and although the wording was far more complex, it did give him unlimited authority to control who was allowed access to Elraci knowledge. This meant that whenever someone was discovered with knowledge, he would have to be consulted and any grants he had provided would have to be traced to determine permissibility. *The only problem here is Lothia's and Argos's reaction to what should have been good news. Well, Ticca has shouldered many things from Kliasa. Now, it is my turn to carry burdens not of my own making.*

He turned his attention back on the presences of Lothia and Argos. *'I understand the new role and your concerns. I accept the laws and appointment.'*

Lothia projected approval and love. *'Yes. Should you need Argos or me, call. We can only advise you. The decisions are yours to make.'*

Argos also projected approval and love with the ever-present pride in him. *'You have much to contemplate now. I started as a researcher of magic, and I came to understand the basics of much of the non-magical technologies. Yet, I dare not claim understanding of Elraci. I give you now the key to the Argos family library's Elracian content. You will find it lacking in many areas.'* With that came the incantation paths that would work in the between space only. He understood that there was a massive library of knowledge stored between, accessible to only Argos, Lothia, and from that point on, him.

'You can build constructions between?'

He felt Argos's amusement at the question. *'It is part of our family's legacy. I discovered this in building this universe. It is a secret that was held by very few. All of the entities that possessed this knowledge have passed beyond, except for us three. The entire original physical library of our family is now there, along with everything I collected of the non-magical races. Also, there are some Elraci contents, but at the time, I did not collect as much as I should have. Now, much has been lost. You may add to it as you choose. It belongs to our family.'* With that final declaration came the strong feeling and knowledge that he needed to guard this secret even more than the Elraci knowledge.

You don't need to tell me that twice. The implications of building constructions in-between are fraught with dangers.

With a last brushing touch, Lothia and Argos vanished from his perceptions. He greeted Kliasa before dropping back into the physical realm. Opening his eyes, he knew almost no time had passed.

Sula noticed his eyes were open first. "So what was the decision?"

I should probably not broadcast my role, even to these friends. I think only the Gods and a few people should know the full truth. "Unexpected. We have been given what we asked for."

Sula's mouth dropped open and she fell backwards into the seat. "That is amazing. They must be worried to do this."

Lebuin nodded agreement. Cune stood. "Sula and I are going to go with Duke to Gracia. I need to go collect our things. I suspect my not being here will make your planning easier." Cune gave him an amiable smile, which was weird after the years of smirks.

Lebuin held his hand out to Cune. "Magus Cune, I understand now what you were doing by playing my nemesis. I thank you for taking that burden which, at least, got me paranoid enough to be better prepared."

Cune smiled and took his arm, and Cune's eyes watered. Lebuin pretended to not notice.

"Before you go, I do have one question which will bother me if I fail to ask it."

Cune released his hand and motioned for Lebuin to go ahead. "I can give you anything I know now. Ask away."

"Who was that child I killed that looked like you?"

Cune's eyes went wide, and he stepped back and sat down. "You remember that? I thought, for sure, you had forgotten it."

Lebuin shook his head. "I did, but recent events gave me an opportunity to reexamine my memories in detail. That was one that I have no explanation for."

Cune smiled knowingly. "Well, then you'll be pleased to know you killed no one. That was the day I was recruited by this fine lady." Cune pointed at Sula. "That boy was Tige, my nephew, and I admit, a brat. Right after you were taken away, Sula appeared and healed him whole. My brother did not take kindly to the tale we had to tell him. My brother could read me well enough to know there was more danger and requested my nephew be sent to Laeusia. They packed up and moved that week."

A tension released in his neck and he felt suddenly limp. *I didn't kill that boy. Oh, thank you.* He looked at Sula. "Thank you for being there."

Sula nodded. "It was a small act of rebellion. Vestul had warned of serious injuries to the students. I didn't see the need for them to suffer. I made sure I was there at the time and moved only after you had been removed from the area.

Because of that, Magus Cune and I became friends, and I decided he was someone that could help. Later, I learned that this was all arranged by Vestul. He knew, given the hints, I would go there and help."

Sula nodded at Cune. "After that, we told Magus Cune everything we knew, and he helped oversee your apparent lack of development."

Lebuin laughed. "He was a meddler, that is for sure. I thank you both for releasing me of that burden. It did bother me more than I even knew."

Cune stood. "I still would have done what I did. But you are right. The burden would have been more." Cune looked at Sula. "Are you coming?"

Sula nodded and stood as Illa walked into the room with a determined look on her face.

Illa looked at them and knelt before Lebuin. "My Lord, I ask permission to seek aid of Sula."

Sula stopped and stared at him. *That was very formal. I wonder what is going on.* "Illa, you know you are free to do as you think wise. There is no need for this type of display."

Illa bowed her head then stood up, turning to Sula. "Holy One, forgive me. I am inexperienced in such matters. I do not wish to offend. I desire to beg your advice and possibly aid on behalf of my Lord."

Sula's expression showed even more interest. Lebuin noticed Illa had managed to focus everyone in the room effectively. *I wonder if this was her intent.* He smiled at his priestess. *She is very cunning.*

Sula motioned for Illa to proceed. Illa nodded. "Holy One, I understand you and your mother share a unique interconnection which allows you access to your mother's powers, but not her mind. Can you instruct Lord Lebuin on how to achieve this type of connection?"

Sula's mouth dropped open and she stared at Illa. Everyone else in the room remained silent. Sula stood straighter. "How did you come to know this?"

Illa bowed. "I am sorry, Holy One, to expose this. Those here are trusted with all of our secrets, and the tower is secured against scrying. I recently figured out your connection. I only guessed at its nature and your reaction confirmed my deductions. I know you are not a God, yet you have performed miracles requiring far more magic than even a demi-god Magus could muster. Some stories I learned from Elades, Ticca, and Boadua told me of things you have done. However, I was more hoping than guessing when I said your connection did not allow you access to Lady Dalpha's mind. Do you deny such a connection?"

Ditani chuckled and shook his head, leaning back into his chair. Sula sat down. Cune stepped over to another chair at the table with Ditani and sat down. Illa knelt before Sula.

Sula looked at Illa. "No, I do not deny it. You are correct. I am Magus-trained. My mother is one of the first Gods of this world, and therefore, has one of the five magic collectors. The magic collectors represent the greatest of our race's feats. They were designed and built to collect enough magic to allow bridging into the non-magical universe of your ancestors' origins. My mother discovered how to connect herself to this artifact and taught me. I send magic to it, as does my mother, as she receives much from her followers. However, I can draw power from it, as easily as send magic to it. This was what it was built for."

Cune snapped his fingers. "The Light of Dalpha!"

Sula nodded. "Yes, the Light of Dalpha. My mother has given Sayscia a special key to it for healing."

Illa looked down, frowning. "So it is only with this artifact, that this feat can be achieved."

Sula nodded again. "Why do you look so troubled?"

Illa sighed. "Power, Holy One. My Lord needs power. We cannot face another Magus who has access to the Nhia-Samri power without at least an equal, if not superior, source of power. Duke is the only source of power I know, and he refuses to follow any God due to the secrets he feels he must keep from all, even the Gods."

Sula frowned. "I am aware of Duke's feelings on that topic. I am sorry, Illa. I know of no other way."

Cune looked at Lebuin. "Lord Lebuin, might you ask your grandfather for a piece of your legacy early? It is not uncommon for children to be granted some portion of their family's legacy before parents or grandparents die."

Lebuin looked up, as did Illa. "What do you mean?"

Cune smiled. "In Councilor Nillo's office sits another one of those magic collectors, gathering dust for as long as the Guild has existed. I didn't make the connection as the Light of Dalpha moves as if alive. I assume this is because no one is feeding magic to Argos's collector."

The golden egg artifact I often wondered about! "Why doesn't Argos use it himself?"

Sula laughed, causing everyone to look at her. "The only God in this universe that does not need more power is Argos. This entire universe that our races built is based on those artifacts. Argos is the control and heart of the universe. It is by his personal will that all the power is safely collected, and he then distributes it in regulated amounts so that the races may live, be they of magic, or not."

Lebuin couldn't help being overwhelmed by her words. *That is what Argos meant when he said he was not tired. Should he fail, another must take up the task of being the guardian of magic, and I am the only remaining possibility until either Argos or I create another demi-god. That is why he was given control of all the Magi. They are not just his servants. They are symbiotically part of his duties.*

Illa grabbed Sula's hand and kissed it, causing Sula to blush crimson. "Great Holy One, that is the answer! If Argos grants Lebuin the magic collector, we can ask the mages of the Guild to donate power to it as the priestesses of Dalpha do daily into the Light of Dalpha! This would violate none of the rules of the Gods or Argos's Guild." Illa stood and rushed to fall on her knees before Lebuin. "My Lord! In weeks, you would have enough to allow escaping from another such attack. By the time the assembly meets, you might even have enough to defeat a mage such as Finnba. Given time, you surely would have the means!"

Lebuin looked at Illa, then bent and pulled her up into a hug. "You are amazing." When he let go of her, she sat on the carpet before him. He looked back at Sula. "If Argos refuses this, who has the other magic collectors?"

Sula's brows tightened as she thought. "There were only five made and the means to make more no longer exists, at least, not without Argos's help. My mother might be willing to let you tie into her collector temporarily. Two damaged collectors were destroyed with Elraci. The fifth collector was lost and presumed destroyed during the great migration to this universe."

Twice, I must ask the favor of Argos. I have already been granted a miraculous and troubling request for access to Elracian knowledge. But I must do this.

Leaning back, he pushed in and out, entering in between. Once there, he wasn't surprised to see Kliasa was still close by. Acknowledging Kliasa, he called out to Argos. He chatted with Kliasa until Argos answered.

'*Lebuin, I trust this is important.*'

'*Grandfather, I hope it is a simple request. May I have use of the magic collector in Llino?*'

Argos projected surprise before it was cut off. *Well, now, even Argos can be surprised by events.*

'*Open your mind to me. I wish to understand your request.*'

He dropped all his shielding and Argos swept through his mind.

'*Tell Illa I am proud. This is unexpected, and a perfect solution to current circumstances. I agree. I will instruct Nillo to inform all Guild mages on how to feed it safely, if they so choose. The magic collector is yours. You will find the details about it in our library. The initial connection will be unpleasant. Remember to breathe.'*

Argos passed to his mind a set of incantations and magical keys. All of it would allow him to use the artifact without having to be near it. The initial connection required direct contact. *Well, looks like we are going back to Llino next, before anything else.*

'Thank you, Grandfather. I shall pass on your praise.'

'I must attend other matters. Be well, my grandson.' Argos's presence vanished.

Allowing himself to slip back into the physical realms, he opened his eyes and smiled. Touching Illa on her shoulder, he told her, "Illa, Argos is proud of your actions this day. You may have saved us with this insight." Looking at everyone else in the room, he threw his arms up in the air. "Argos has given me the magic collector, and the Guild mages will be instructed on how to volunteer their magic to it."

Ditani stood, looking at Illa, and started clapping his hands, followed by Magus Cune. Sula and Lebuin also stood and joined in clapping. Illa turned red and stood. She bowed to them all, and in a joyful tone said, "Thank you, all. Please excuse me. I need to deal with something." She glided from the room, barely touching the floor.

Once Illa was gone, Cune bowed to Sula and motioned to the door. Sula nodded, turning to Lebuin. "Lord Lebuin, I must attend to the assembly. Good luck. Much of our hope lies with you and your friends."

Magus Cune followed Sula out of the room.

Ditani turned to Lebuin. "I think we might have a chance."

He smiled and shook his head. *My friend, if only you were right. The best we can do is limit the damage and pray it is enough.* "There are forty or fifty of those power sources out there, and we know of only one. If every mage in the Guild gave all their power, I still could not match all of that."

Ditani frowned. "Then it is hopeless."

Lebuin shook his head. "No, but we have much to do if we are to stop Shar-Lumen's plan. Don't forget, we have done this many times before without success. This isn't a solution, but it gives us a better chance of finding a solution in time."

Ditani nodded and sat back down, returning to his reading.

"I'm going to continue inspecting the workshops for clues. I'll be on the second floor, if you need me." Ditani nodded and gave him a cheerful wave as he stepped out and headed for the stairs.

Lebuin opened the first door he came to on the second floor and looked in. It was another workshop. *You certainly had a number of work places. But then, this whole tower was yours to do with as you wanted. Might as well spread things out. Probably safer that way.*

Entering the workshop, he paused to look at a small statue situated in an alcove just inside the door where one could not help, but look on it every time he entered the room. The statue rested on top of a rosewood box, ornately decorated with vines and flowers. The six-inch-tall statue was beautiful. A maiden wearing a flowing summer dress, her hair blowing in the wind, stood on a circular base. Her right hand was held out as if calling him to come over, and her left arm was bent and held a cloth-covered shopping basket with flowers sticking out.

Something about the statue was familiar to him. He picked it up and looked at it closer. The blood rushed from his head as he recognized the subject. His hand started trembling as his heart raced. He could feel magic in the statue. *My Lord! This is Kliasa! It's an absolutely perfect statue of Kliasa.* Carefully, using both hands, he examined the details of the statue. It wasn't just a good representation. It was perfect, as if he held Kliasa, herself, frozen in his hand.

He set the statue down beside the wooden box. Shifting to magical sight, he could see that there was a warm or happy emotional radiation from the statue, from no recognizable magical incantation. In fact, the statue had no power channels or incantations at all. It was made of a substance which was uniformly infused with magic.

Opening the box, he found it was lined with purple silk. Lifting a silk pad up, he saw that there was a mirror almost as big as the box. He picked it up and examined it, but could find no flaw. Under the mirror was a series of little compartments with silk padded doors. Opening each, he found a set of crystal lenses of various sizes, and the parts of a stand. Moving the box to a nearby bench, he pulled all the parts out and figured out how to assemble the lenses and mirror. In the end, there was a device made of silver and gold which held the mirror at one end, and with a set of six lenses which could be moved to adjust their relationship to the mirror. All of the lenses were magical, as was the mirror.

This has to be used for something with a reflection. Looking back at the statue, it came to him. This was a device to allow the creation of that statuette. *But why would he go to all this trouble to do this? Of course, he loved Kliasa as much as everyone else who knew her.* He disassembled the artifact, putting it back in its box. Putting the box back into the alcove, he placed the statue back on top.

The rest of the room held benches, but one in particular drew his attention. It had a small thread spinning wheel and a mechanical, manual-powered thread twister. There were four wooden bobbins, each loaded with a fine thread made of gold. The bobbins were attached to the thread twister, and there was one other bobbin with only a small bit of a medium golden thread. In the waste bucket and on the bench were a few leftover cut bits of the golden string. It looked like something had been tied with the golden string and the excess trimmed off.

Ticca said Vestul's journal was tied with glowing, golden threads. This is where he made the thread and tied his journal up. The incantation will be someplace close, but hidden. I have to know how to remove the incantation if we are to open his journal when we get it.

Nothing jumped out to tell him the answer. *I know the answer is here. Looks like I'm going to be here a while.*

⁂ELADES⁂

Standing and stretching, Elades felt a hell of a lot better. Boadua poked at his shoulder and nodded, satisfied.

"Thanks for the temple draught."

Boadua smiled. "I'm just glad you changed your mind and accepted it. Why'd you change your mind?"

Elades chuckled. "Well, I can still learn. Ticca didn't hesitate, and it registered in my slower mind that this is no time for the senior staff to be convalescing. We have serious business."

Boadua was giving him a 'what are you talking about' look.

"Ticca... She stood up this morning with barely a grimace, and every visible scratch was gone. You did give her a draught last night while I was asleep, right?"

Boadua shook her head. "Sorry. She didn't wake up after you two went to sleep. I was going to offer her a draught this morning, but she was already gone. You say all her wounds were gone?"

It was his turn to feel a little off. *But if she didn't take a draught, how did she heal so fast?* "Maybe Illa gave her..." Boadua shook her head, cutting him off. "Huh. That girl is full of surprises."

The muscle pain when he stretched his arm was only slight. He'd have no trouble riding when the army pulled out. He chuckled. "Well, the lesson was still a good one."

Boadua laughed, too, and made a shooing motion towards the tent door. "Yes, well, you justify it any way you want. Now, get out of here. I have to get all this on the wagon before noon."

Stepping out, he saw the preparations were almost

complete. *Well, clean clothes and a shower before we roll out would be good.* Duke was sitting at a table in the middle of the yard, so he walked over to check in.

Duke looked up as he approached. "Elades! Glad you stopped being stubborn. Just in case, I had some clothes laid out for you by the shower. You have about a mark and a half before I want to start moving."

"That's great. I need to pack, too."

Duke shook his head. "Nope, you are still on light duty. Nigan volunteered to pack your gear and ready your horse."

Nigan? Well, that boy does surprise. He really is a good lad.

Ticca and Illa stepped out of the big-ring tent, arm in arm, presenting him with a picture of the most beautiful Daggers he had ever seen. Although Ticca was a couple of inches taller, at 5'8", she looked as if she had always been, and should never be anywhere other than, next to Illa. Illa, with her flowing walk that showed off her athletic frame, matched Ticca, step for graceful step. Ticca's hair was accented by the fact that it had been freshly washed and combed. Illa's silky blonde hair blew in the warm breeze, and her eyes sparkled at whatever the two of them were discussing. Both ladies were bristling with weapons. Their new clothes were alluring, and yet, functional.

Stunned by their beauty, he stopped and stared, as did a number of other Daggers, both men and women.

Duke noticed the sudden stop in work and looked around for the cause. He found the cause and sat down to stare with everyone else.

Illa released Ticca's arm and bounced up to Duke, giving him a bear hug around the neck. "Duke, thank you so much! I have been worried and pressured these last weeks, and you solved it!"

Illa pulled the confused wolf's head down to her level and kissed him on the nose. Releasing him, she stood back, smiling like the sun in the sky.

Ticca stepped up, patting the side of Duke's head.

"Well, old wolf. Good luck. Do what needs to be done. We'll be off in a day or two, once everything is settled here." Then Ticca gave Duke another light kiss on his nose. "Remember, don't be so enigmatic."

Ticca turned to Elades, and she jumped at him and gave him a huge hug before he could react. "Elades, thank all the Gods, you are all right. Promise me you'll duck next time! I know you were watching over me the last six cycles, and I even know about the couple of jobs you diverted to me. Thanks! Now, I order you to go and teach those Nhia-Samri to never again meddle with the Alliance!"

Ticca grabbed Illa's arms and looked at the Daggers around. "I'm proud of all of you. Stay sharp!"

Without any prompting, all of the Daggers drew their daggers and held them high. "Yes, SIR!"

Ticca blushed. The two ladies exchanged a quick glance and simultaneously drew their daggers. Ticca spun her dagger dramatically as she and Illa raised them high in the air and shouted together, "Semper Fidelis!"

Everyone, including Duke, shouted at the top of their voices, "OORAH!"

Ticca whispered to Elades, "We're going to go shopping now."

Ticca spun her dagger twice around her hand and dropped it into its sheath. The Daggers all shouted and clapped their support as the two ladies walked out of the yard and headed down the street.

Elades closed his mouth and looked at Duke, who was looking at the gate, shaking his head. Duke chuckled. "Now, *that* is a dangerous pair." He then looked at the Daggers, still standing, and shouted, "Back to work, folks. We ride out in one mark! And you," Duke looked at Elades, "go get cleaned up and meet me here in a mark."

Elades took his time shaving and showering, enjoying the feeling of getting clean, as well as just being alive. When he finished showering, all his ripped and dirty clothes were gone.

Huh. I didn't see anyone come get them. Drying off with the towel, he grabbed the sturdy grey forest-patterned pants. *Well, that is nicer than I'm used to, but they feel great.* Also, there was a dark green, silk tunic and a soft white linen undershirt with dark brown leather arm guards. New calf riding boots waited, as well. His blades were there, as was a new dark green cloak of tight-knit wool.

Diurdu, this makes me look like a lordling. I'm going to get you, Nigan! I'll have to go with this. I don't have time to run around naked, looking for my real clothes.

He dressed, and as he walked back out to the front yard, he was amazed at how comfortable the clothes felt. *Well, I admit they feel good, but I feel silly being dressed like a stupid brat noble's son.*

As he walked, many Daggers stopped and stared. A few nodded appreciatively. He watched for any sneers, but didn't see one. Everyone was proud. When he reached his horse, Nigan was standing there, dressed in a dark wine-colored outfit. Nigan held his horse for him.

"Where are my clothes, Nigan?!"

Nigan looked innocently at him. "In your saddle packs, of course." Nigan held out a new triangular, leather riding hat. "You'll need this, too."

Grabbing the hat, he slipped it on. It fit nicely and did block the sun well, so he stepped up and climbed onto his horse.

Duke stepped over. "Wow, Elades! You look as good as Ticca and Illa. Well done."

Elades looked for Nigan, who was retreating, but still made eye contact and winked at him. Rolling his eyes, he kicked his horse into motion.

Duke called out, "Move out. We have a long way to go."

As Duke took lead, it occurred to him that Nigan had also volunteered to pack his gear. As his horse followed Duke out the entryway, he reached back and opened the stuffed saddle pack. Inside was an array of folded clothes in greens, grays, and black that looked very expensive, and nothing like anything he had ever owned. He spun around, looking back at the estate, and saw Nigan standing outside of the entry, waving at him with a wide grin.

"Urdu, these aren't mine!" He yelled back.

Nigan laughed and yelled back, "A gift from Lord Lebuin! You're going to Gracia, after all!"

Hiri-Rula vs The Dragonfly

CHAPTER 11

CORRECT ACTIONS AREN'T ALWAYS RIGHT ONES

MISHIA-OLLAN

COLONEL MISHIA-OLLAN MARCHED THROUGH THE empty barracks.

Six hundred of my warriors gone.

He frowned as he recalled the mission, knowing that it was unlikely any would survive to return.

It will take many years to recruit and train their replacements.

The 50 cots, 25 on each side, all stood straight out from the walls, shining in the afternoon light, streaming in from the sealed windows. All the cots were dustless, each having its bed roll precisely rolled around the pillow. A folded wool blanket and white cotton sheet were positioned at the head of each, by the wall.

Stopping, Mishia-Ollan opened one of the dual compartment trunks located at the end of a cot, identical to its 49 brothers. Inside it was spotless, having been cleaned and oiled. Nodding his approval, he closed it, locking its latch in place.

From the middle of the room, he turned, looking for anything at all out of place.

This is the last building I have to seal. It will also be the last to be unsealed. Likely, this will have to be preserved for a hundred years.

Finding nothing, he looked at Major Hiri-Rula and nodded his approval. "These barracks are in proper order to be sealed."

Major Hiri-Rula, his second in command and a powerful mage, bowed her head. She stood at attention as he walked out of the barracks, to the training yard, where the sixty remaining warriors stood in three ranks, all in full combat armor. The contrast between the size of the training yard and the size of his remaining warrior ranks drove home how desperately the Grand Warlord must desire his revenge. *They look like children in the immense yard. I don't think attacking Gracia is wise, but there is little I can do about it now.*

Ever since Mishia-Ollan was a boy, he knew he was destined to lead. His father was a senior officer in Outpost One before being given command of this outpost. Mishia-Ollan remembered moving to this outpost with his mother, father, and a group of handpicked officers with their families. He had worked hard, and even traveled to Hisuru Amajoo for several years, to receive advanced training. Although not a perfect officer, his father's blades had chosen him when his father died. It was not long before he was promoted to commander of the same outpost his father had commanded so many years ago.

He had commanded the second-greatest outpost for just over a decade. It had been a period of hard work, training, and joy. Then a year ago, Hisuru Amajoo had ordered all families evacuated from the outposts, back to Hisuru Amajoo. His wife and daughter were safe inside the walls of the mountain fortress. Mishia-Ollan did not understand what was going on, but he was filled with dread for the future. For the last few weeks, he had dreams where he was forced to labor in ways he could not understand. Last night, he had the dream again, but this time, a pair of shining warriors had descended on him, breaking his bonds, and whispered in his ear, *'It is time. You are ready.'* He had awoken to find he was holding his odassi blades, sweating and scared, but also determined.

Major Hiri-Rula closed, locked, and placed her hand on the door. Her hand glowed and the glow spread over the entire building, warding it air-tight. She then turned and followed him as he inspected the remaining warriors. *I have kept the best instructors.*

He recalled what his mentor had once called such warriors: 'the long tooth brigade'. His mentor had then shown off his unusually long front teeth. There was a reasonable mix of old and young warriors present, and some women who were pregnant, he had kept, knowing that a new generation would be needed more than their skill, in Gracia.

After inspecting every warrior, Colonel Mishia-Olan stood in front of the ranks, his second, Major Hiri-Rula, standing at his right.

"You have been chosen to rebuild this outpost. Those that have left will leave our outpost much honor. I do not expect any to return. From this moment, the maintenance and work of this outpost is our responsibility alone. We must continue all our labors, training, and recruitment with what we have now. Major Hiri-Rula will establish a new work rotation and training schedules. All sealed barracks will be maintained, and we will rebuild ourselves to full strength."

As he spoke, a large insect flew around the area. *It is not the time of the year for insects such as that.* He gave one last look at the ranks of warriors. "Return to your duties."

As the warriors broke up, he glanced at his second and flicked his eyes in the direction of the large insect, "Capture that."

Major Hiri-Rula looked, then flicked her fingers in the direction of the insect. A small bubble that sparkled in the sun raced from her hand, towards it. The bug launched itself with surprising speed, straight up, and proceeded to perform a complex series of maneuvers, each turn and dodge taking it further away. Major Hiri-Rula's bubble raced after it, missing, time and time again. Major Hiri-Rula had turned to face the creature and was concentrating on trying to predict its flight. She created a second bubble almost on top of it, but it darted in a new direction, preventing it from being entrapped.

That thing is being directed! "If you cannot capture it, destroy it now."

Major Hiri-Rula's amulet started to glow as she drew on the Nhia-Samri's great powers. She created an enormous sphere around the insect. Although the little insect flew with agility and intelligence, it could not escape so large a bubble.

Smiling, she contracted the bubble down to just larger than the bug. The sphere floated toward them.

As it got closer, he could see it was a dragonfly of an unusual type that he had never seen before. It had the typical elongated body, which looked like an oil torch, with the head at the heavy end. However, although it looked like it was in a hard shell of glistening purple, the creature flexed its body, showing that it was not a rigid shell. There were four translucent wings, angled in star formation from just behind the main body, which created rainbows from the sun. *Where did this come from? Dragonflies prefer wetland areas around lakes or swamps. This area is far too dry. What dragonflies we have are brown and stay near the river, to the west. The colors remind me of the description from the swamps at the far eastern shores. Why would it be so far inland?*

Major Hiri-Rula echoed his own thoughts. "It is very unusual in coloring. I've never heard of or seen a dragonfly like this before."

He shook his head. "It is like those found in the far eastern swamps, the other side of Llino. I saw them one summer when I was stationed there on exchange. I don't know how it came here. It might be a Magus construction or tool. It flew with the intelligence of a crafty warrior, not that of an insect."

Just as the bubble came to float a few feet from them, the sun was blocked by a huge shadow. Looking up, they saw a black blob was arcing down towards them. Major Hiri-Rula raised her left hand above her head, and a powerful shield flowed from her hands, covering the entire training ground as her amulet flared on her chest.

The blob dropped fast and slammed into the shield, spreading out like an oily mass. *Now, that was close!* He could hear the buzzing and could see that the blob was thousands of black beetles.

Mishia-Ollan's heart raced, and he felt the adrenaline rushing into his system. He tried to observe the bugs, but a tingling spread over his body, causing the hair on the back of his neck to stand on end.

It is as if the world is attacking us!

"Burn them! Don't let any through!"

Major Hiri-Rula was looking ashen-faced as the sun was blocked out by the mass of beetles, buzzing, walking, and piling up on her shield over the training area. She spun around in a circle, looking up at the volume of beetles. There was something primal in the fear showing in her eyes.

I understand the thought of being buried in those insects is horrifying.

Major Hiri-Rula made some more gestures, singing her magical incantation. The center of the mass exploded in a smoking ball of fire. The effect was even more eerie, as that let a single shaft of sunlight through the mass of beetles.

Many of the warriors present had drawn weapons and were watching the events with worried looks. Others took it upon themselves to begin coordinating a search of the area, moving with stealth and speed, hugging walls and other cover. He nodded his approval. *Well done.*

Major Hiri-Rula continued to gesture and sing, destroying thousands of beetles at a blast. It was hard to tell if she had destroyed all of them, but finally, nothing more moved, and only ashes remained resting on her shield. All the other warriors had moved under overhangs and were watching for trouble. Major Hiri-Rula called on winds to blow away the ash, holding the shield in place until the air was clear.

Major Hiri-Rula looked at him. "Should I drop the shield?"

Looking around at the concerned faces, he considered. *They are afraid, as am I, to be honest. That invoked a primal reaction in everyone.* "How long can you maintain it?"

Major Hiri-Rula shrugged. "As long as you desire, sir."

He nodded. "Very well. Keep it in place until we finish examining this other bug." He looked around, but didn't see the other bug anywhere. "Where is it?"

Major Hiri-Rula looked around, surprised. "I forgot about it, releasing it as I took care of those other strange insects. It must be here somewhere. It could not escape, because of the shield."

No, but it could hide. "Everyone, spread out and search everything. Find me the missing, large, purple dragonfly with four translucent wings now! Major Hiri-Rula, do not drop that shield until we have recaptured that dragonfly."

Warriors spread out and began searching the buildings, roofs, and every crevice between supplies and materials. He and Major Hiri-Rula joined in the search.

Was that attack to make us let the other go? If so, this represents a serious threat to this outpost. Considering the threats made by the Alliance and Duke, it could be possible. But we are supposed to have peace until the assembly votes in two cycles. What could this mean?

They searched for marks. Of the dozens of large insects found, none were the purple dragonfly he knew had to be somewhere within the contained area. The air was stale and hot in the afternoon sun.

It was right here. The other bugs attacked, and in two minutes, it was gone.

Colonel Mishia-Ollan stood where this had all started and looked around, trying to force the insect's hiding location to reveal itself through sheer willpower.

Hiri-Rula stepped up and saluted. "Colonel, it is too well hidden, and the air will soon become unbreathable, unless I allow fresh air in."

He frowned, showing his disapproval of the news. Hiri-Rula acknowledged his displeasure by bowing her head, looking at the ground.

This is unacceptable. How can a bug that big and brightly colored hide so effectively? "Hiri-Rula…"

What he was going to say was interrupted by a loud blast from the far end of the field. The shields over the area rippled like water, making the sunlight coming through sparkle around them.

He spun to face the direction of the sound, as three warriors ran towards him from where the sound had come. The lead warrior was the tactical instructor Aupli-Niun, and he shouted as he ran, "Colonel! There are twelve silver creatures behind that barracks!" Aupli-Niun pointed behind him. "They were doing something to the shield when we discovered their presence. One of them tried to hit us with a magical blast the moment we saw them. The shield held, but it was a powerful attack!"

"Come! We are being attacked by a Magus of great power, or perhaps Magi." He slapped Hiri-Rula's arm and started running towards the indicated barracks.

Hiri-Rula, only one step behind him, was already drawing her odassi. Another blast sounded, and this time, the shield rippled as it flew apart. Hiri-Rula warned him, "Colonel, I have lost the shield. I can't get it back before they are here."

Aupli-Niun called out, "We should fight them here, where we can maneuver."

Fresh air blew through the area, bringing with it a clearer mind. Breathing deep, Mishia-Ollan drew his own odassi, feeling their power flow through him. Skidding to a stop he yelled, "We are under attack! Warriors to me. Defensive ranks!"

Four of the silver creatures came around the left side of the barracks, four more came from the right, and another four came over the roof, at the same time. The creatures looked like man-sized crabs that moved on eight legs. Every inch of them looked like metal, highly polished to a mirror shine. Each creature had powerful pinchers and antennae that waved in the air. The silver crabs stopped and looked them over.

One of the crabs stepped forward and lifted, showing a circular mouth. Hiri-Rula jerked her hand out, fingers splayed open, as a blast of white light shot at Mishia-Ollan and his warriors, from that mouth. A ball of white light hit the new shield Hiri-Rula had created with an explosion of sound and power. The flash was so bright, his vision blurred and stars floated around him. Blinking his eyes to protect them from the light, he hoped his vision would clear.

Before Mishia-Ollan could see clearly, someone screamed in pain nearby. The sound of fighting came from both his right and left sides.

Don't stand still. Those things are not going to be slow! Sight or no sight, either I move or die.

Mishia-Ollan used all the power flowing from his blades to speed his reaction and strength, leaping up and backwards, flipping to land at the ready. Thirty years of training, and another twenty as a commander, made his moves fluid.

This used to only be for demonstrations. Never thought I would end up in a life-and-death fight blind.

Smiling as he heard the whisper of air to his right, he brought his odassi around, hearing the satisfying sound of it slicing through armor and something not of flesh.

Mishia-Ollan felt the sensation of warning, and flattened himself to the ground, as something flew over him, causing a massive draft of wind. Rolling, he snapped back to standing as his vision cleared. A one-clawed crab was turning to face him. Behind it, another crab was spitting dozens of projectiles at three of his warriors. One of them was creating a defensive shield as the three of them ran towards the crab. The slim missiles bounced off the barrier.

The crab facing him thrust its pincher at him like a sword lunge. Moving with his enhanced speed, he leapt over it, bringing his blades together in a scissor cut, which sheared the massive pincher from the crab. Lightning danced on the end of the crab's arm, where he had cut the claw off.

What are these things?

As he landed, the crab backed up.

You're not invulnerable or fearless.

He grinned as he raced at the creature, thrusting his blades towards the eyes. One of the eyes shattered like glass as his blade hit its mark.

The crab wasn't finished. Two antennae sprouted from its head, and the crab moved with a shocking speed, lining its body up, facing him.

It's going to shoot something at me!

He leapt high into the air and back-twisted, to be a harder target. As he flew backwards, he called upon the odassi to block the incoming missiles. Dozens of arrows bounced from the deflection shield his swords provided. The crab followed his path, remaining aligned. Every missile it launched was dead on target.

As he landed, Mishia-Ollan saw another crab with bloody pinchers running towards him.

Need to eliminate these things. Let's try something different.

He pushed himself to his greatest speeds and stepped into attack range of the first crab, bringing his odassi down in a power strike angled squarely with its armor, which would have cleaved a normal opponent in two. His blades did cut down through the crab's armor, and he finished the slices by dropping to one knee, making sure his blades went through the front body of the crab. As the strike finished, he rolled to the side. The crab stopped shooting missiles at him, as it stood almost still and shook violently.

Dead or not, I think this one is out of the battle.

The bloody-clawed crab was on top of him, and he continued his roll to slip past its double-pincher thrust.

These things are faster than I thought.

He took a precious moment to take in the battle. Half of his warriors were dead or near it, and the other half were still engaging the remaining eight crabs.

Thirty warriors to stop less than half of these things. We are nearly evenly matched, except my best still stand.

Feeling confident, he popped to standing, coming round to face the crab, the blood of his fallen warriors making crimson rivers on its claws.

This crab moved far more warrior-like as if it had learned, from its prior battles, how to be more deadly. As it moved, he noted its legs ended with sharp spikes. This crab was using its antennae, as well as its eyes, to track him. It clicked its claws.

A second crab stepped up to join the first. It taunted him, waving the upper body of Aupli-Niun, which the crab held in its right pincher. If its intention was to make him mad, it worked. Mishia-Ollan felt his blood boil in rage.

"Whoever you are controlling these things, we will find you and destroy you for this outrage!"

The crab tossed the remains of his tactical officer aside like trash and jumped at him, claws opened wide. Mishia-Ollan spun aside and cut off one of the claws, bringing his other odassi down on the head region. His second blade didn't do much, as the arched armor allowed no purchase for his blade, which simply slipped to the side.

Have to hit the shell precisely to do damage.

The first crab stopped quivering and turned to face him, rising up.

Three!

Knowing what that rising up meant, Mishia-Ollan dodged to the right and then ran at the second crab, as a blast of light shot where he had been a moment before. Letting the power flow through him, he jumped over the crab. He landed cleanly, spun, and thrust his blades against the smooth shell armor. His hit was aligned to not slip. His blades speared the armor as planned, sinking, up to the hilts, into the creature.

Lightning came out of the two wounds, arcing along his blades to him, as well as flitting across the shell of the creature. His muscles tightened uncontrollably as his skin burned, but he managed to hang onto his odassi. The lightning played over the creature, its legs shooting out to the sides in the painful throes of death. Moving through the pain, he placed his foot on the shell and pulled with all his strength, yanking the swords out of the creature, and flinging himself backwards.

The second crab had turned and leapt around the dying crab. It swung its huge pincher at him. His muscles were still tingling from whatever had come out of that crab. He was too slow, and the large claw batted him into the air, towards the other crab. He felt his ribs breaking, and his lung was pierced by the bones as he rolled away. As he came to a stop, he saw the bloody pincher of the other crab dropping down, grabbing his neck, and with a painful snap, he knew his head had been severed from his body.

Mishia-Ollan opened his mouth to scream but heard nothing, because his lungs were no longer attached. His head rolled a few feet before landing on its side. He knew he was dead, but he forced himself to keep his eyes open. He could see almost all of his warriors were bloody piles, littering the grounds.

Not far away, three of the crabs were attacking Hiri-Rula, who was using both magic and swords to fight them off. She was magnificent, and he smiled through the pain. She was using all of the power of their outpost to hold a personal shield against the creatures, and her odassi glowed with added power she channeled to them.

Hiri-Rula moved with grace as she sliced any arm or leg from a crab that presented itself. His vision finally faded as death took him. *You'll make a good colonel. If you live, avenge me with honor!*

VESTA

The leader's dead eyes didn't see the shiny, purple dragonfly land in front of his face. It stepped over and touched his cheek with its feelers, its wings drooping. Turning, it watched as the crabs finished off the remaining warriors. The wizard was the last to fall, her shields overwhelmed, her body hammered by the precise strikes of three crabs.

The dragonfly jumped into the air as the wizard fell, flying over to her body. A pure white seagull landed by the wizard's face as the dragonfly landed on her body. The seagull bent down, using its head to push the wizard's head to the side, exposing her mouth. Once her mouth was exposed, four black beetles landed next to her and held their elytra open as little rivers of silver poured from their abdomens, into the wizard's mouth. As the last of the silver substance finished pouring from a beetle, it took flight again. The dragonfly lowered itself, so the tips of its antennae touched the wizard's neck just below her jawline. The seagull stood by, watching the movements around.

A crab snipped the copper necklace from around her neck and held it out for the seagull to swallow. The seagull hopped up on top of the wizard's back and made itself comfortable, watching.

A new crab walked through the yard, heading for a door to the base, as the surviving crabs used some netting to collect all the fallen parts of their comrades. The new crab broke into the base as the remaining crabs carried off the bodies and net of crab parts.

The dragonfly sat on the wizard for some time, stroking her cheek with its feelers. A rumble came from somewhere deep inside of the base. Dust blew out of the broken main door.

The sun moved through the sky, yet the dragonfly did not move, except to brush the cheek of the wizard. The seagull would, from time to time, eye the dragonfly, then the girl, and then return to scanning the surrounding area.

The wizard suddenly coughed and moaned. With one last gentle stroke of her cheek, the dragonfly leapt into the air and flew off. The seagull called out a farewell cry to the dragonfly, but remained. As the day moved on, carrion birds started coming in. The seagull sat on the wizard like a king. If any carrion bird approached, it stood, spreading its wings and screamed a challenge which no bird took, considering the vast feast available without a fight.

HIRI-RULA

Hiri-Rula's mouth was dry and dusty. Dozens of aches and pains made it hard to think. The sun was beating down on her. She groaned and felt something small move off her back. Opening her eyes, she found she was lying on her side in the dirt. Her right cheek was compressed by the rocks and sand, while her left cheek burned with the double pains of a deep cut and sunburn.

The sick and musty odor of the dead assaulted her nose with every breath. Even worse, she could taste the scent in her mouth.

We lost! Who did this?

She rolled onto her back, feeling the fractured bones and strained muscles complaining. A breeze brought more of the awful smell of the dead, including the burned, rotten-pork odors from some of the bodies that had been killed by those magical blasts.

I wonder how many still live.

Hiri-Rula concentrated, forcing a trance state to allow her to examine her injuries. She had more than a dozen ripped tendons and numerous bone fractures, especially in her left leg and three ribs. Fortunately, the fractures were hairline, or incomplete. She sighed with a note of relief.

Nothing extraordinarily serious. Still, there is enough that I will die if I don't get proper attention soon. I need to heal.

Concentrating, she tried to pull energy from the Nhia-Samri power, but there was no power to have. She forced herself to sit up and look around. Bodies were everywhere, and worse, a mere three meters from her, eyes still open and looking at her, was the head of Colonel Mishia-Ollan. It was more than she could take. What little was in her stomach came up and out. The smell of her own vomit was added to the odors of the yard. She tried to clean her face and wipe some of the vomit off with her bruised left hand, her right arm being traumatized to the point of being useless until it healed.

Standing up was impossible. Realizing she needed shade, and more importantly, water, she started the long, painful crawl through the bodies and drying blood, to the barrack kitchens entry. After what felt like marks, she reached the kitchen building.

Her vision focused so tightly on her destination, she didn't see the white seagull that had watched her journey from a nearby roof. She also didn't see the sudden motion as the seagull launched into the air, heading northeast, as she pulled herself up to the kitchen door.

The door was never locked, and pushing through, into the interior, felt like stepping onto a high mountain ice field. Close to the door was a large water pump for the larger chores. She propped herself up under the spout and rolled to get enough leverage to move the pump. Lifting the long handle was like lifting a building. The pain in her shoulder and ribs caused her to see red rings as she pushed with her one good arm.

Screaming at the pain, she managed to lift it almost halfway, which was enough. She held on tight, letting gravity and the weight of her arm pour some water over her head. As the last of the water came, she tilted her head back and swallowed as much as she could, before passing out again.

Sometime later, Hiri-Rula opened her eyes. Dozens of wounds and bruises called for attention.

Not a dream. It all happened. How long have I been out?

She felt better, although she was completely dry, except for her own sweat. Reaching for the power, again, she found none. Her hand climbed its way up her chest to feel around her neck.

It's gone! They took my key to the power. I have to use the old style of wizardry.

She recalled her lessons from long ago about seeking and drawing power from the mana lines. Magic flowed around the planet from the Gods in channels like rivers. Except some of it was buried in the ground, some in water, some through the air, and yet more flowed through the fires of the planet, deep below. It took power to find these magic rivers, and even more power to draw. Compared to the Nhia-Samri ways, it was primitive.

I have almost nothing remaining. But I need it. Please be enough, or I'm already dead.

She let her mind fly as she reached out to find magic. The precious magic she had left diminished as she sought desperately for a mana line.

I should have done this long ago. Then I wouldn't have to waste power trying to find it. I'm dying! Please, LORDS, help me!

Desperation caused Hiri-Rula to concentrate harder. At last, she felt it. Off in the far distance, a mana line flowing through the air glowed with all she needed. She grabbed onto it, pulling power from it and channeling it to herself. The power was far, and it took the last of her power to pull the magic to her. Once she got the first flare of power into her system, she had the magic to draw more until she felt light and airy throughout.

This is raw magic, nothing like the powers I'm used to. I've never used raw elemental energies. This feels fantastic!

With the replenished power, she could heal, and she began to work through her pains, casting incantations to restore her body to health. She started with her mind, and a simple pain reduction incantation to help her to concentrate. Although she was healing, she needed food. The magic could only speed up her natural systems. If she was working on another, she could make the magic manifest as real bone and tissue, but doing it to herself in this condition was an ill-conceived idea. Crawling around the kitchens, she found some fruits that were still fresh and ate her fill. Then she crawled back to the water pump to drink all she could.

This time, Hiri-Rula made herself somewhat comfortable, using burlap sacks for a pillow, before falling asleep while her incantations worked with her body to restore her health

The light penetrated her brain, and she rubbed her eyes as she woke. She felt weak, and there were still aches and pains, but she was able to stand up. She made another meal and refreshed her healing incantations. After she drank more water, she felt well enough to investigate.

Stepping outside into the late day's sun, Hiri-Rula used some incantations to keep the air around her fresh, knowing that the odors of the yard would make her sick, and she needed to keep the food in her. Carrion birds leapt into the air as she walked into the courtyard.

The carnage was worse than anything she had ever experienced or expected.

I have read of battlefields littered with bodies, but those descriptions do not begin to tell this tale.

Hiri-Rula wept, looking at the torn and tattered bodies, some of which had already started to bloat in death. Using all her training to concentrate, regardless of the circumstances, she walked around, assessing and counting the dead. When she came to one body, she paused. It was too familiar. Her mind found it hard to identify, because the eyes had been pecked out, and some of the face, already eaten.

Itan-Ammi. Oh, Lords, it's Ammi. Beautiful, happy Ammi. WHY? WHY? Hiri-Rula's emotions boiled over. She dropped by her friend's body, weeping uncontrollably. She screamed at the heavens, calling out Ammi's name.

"Oh, Ammi, did you follow my command to run and got killed leaving? Or did you try to stay and fight? How can I tell Itan-Tulni his wife and unborn child are dead under my command? I should have made sure you and the other pregnant girls were clear. I have failed as a commander and friend."

Hiri-Rula stood, tears flowing as she counted. *Sixty-one dead. I am the only survivor. None were spared. I have to report this, but before I leave, I have duties to perform.*

She went back to the kitchen and found some towels and large buckets. Filling the buckets with fresh water, she stepped out into the shaded patio of the kitchens. Reaching out to the air mana line, she tapped it and brought the power to herself. She raised her hands and created an incantation that, in her mage sight, snaked out with dozens of tendrils into the yard. The tendrils found the odassi blades and lifted them into the air. Blade after blade floated to her.

Grabbing the first blade, Hiri-Rula was shocked to feel that it had almost no power left. Only a minor spark of energy remained. She wiped the blade with a dampened towel until it was clean and then polished it dry with another towel. Reaching out, she plucked the next odassi from the air, feeling that it, like the first, had lost almost all its power.

All that we were is dying.

Hiri-Rula continued to work on blade after blade. It took several marks, and when the sun went down, she made a globe of light to illuminate her work.

When she finished, 122 odassi blades were stacked with care on the deck of the kitchen, and her own odassi were cleaned and sheathed in her belt. Standing, she drew her blades, feeling their weight for the first time. Like the others, their magical attributes were depleted, but for a spark.

What could do this? These are keyed to our boundless powers. Unless we are all cut off intentionally due to some dishonor.

The thought of being dishonored caused her stomach to tighten.

No, we cannot be dishonored. We acted by the code. There must be another explanation. Maybe I can feed them.

She pulled more mana from the far-off line and sought the power conduits of her own blades. Inspecting them, she found the channels for power and their mix of incantations. She fed magic to a few of them, feeling the blades react. The blades reached out and pulled power from her at a tremendous rate.

Panic raced through Hiri-Rula's mind as she realized the magic she had and was pulling from the mana line was not enough. The blades needed more power than she could imagine necessary for their purposes. She fought her own blades for control of her magic channels. The blades reacted not like simple devices, but more like semi-intelligent creatures. They twisted and sought alternative channels to her powers. She had to throw them to the ground to break her physical connection to them, to prevent them from taking all the magic she had.

Hiri-Rula sat down and stared at her own blades, using her magical sight, watching them reach out with tendrils of power much like her own channeling tendril, connecting her to the mana line far off. The tendrils snaked around and latched onto other blades, where there was a sudden struggle, and her blades, having more power, sucked the remaining power from the other blades. The blade that was robbed of its power screamed out, as if in pain, and the copper band with the maker's mark snapped.

Her heart raced and adrenaline pumped through her system, letting her crabwalk backwards, avoiding her blades' seeking tendrils. Shivers ran down her spine as each odassi was located and its power stolen to the sound of dying screams and snapping copper bands.

Hiri-Rula quivered and stood, moving off to a safe distance to watch the process with fascination.

They are alive! I always suspected this.

She became aware of the personalities of the dying blades. Some seemed wise, accepting their fate with a thoughtful surrender, and others fought back, expending the energy they had, defending against having it taken.

The inevitable happened. Her blades' tendrils found the colonel's odassi. The colonel's odassi, at first, looked like they were going to surrender. However, as she watched, a sudden flare of energy burst from the colonel's odassi at her blades, like a deep thrust. Her blades screamed and flashed red-orange as they exploded into hundreds of pieces. The colonel's blades sucked in all the power from the explosion and leapt into the air, landing at her feet, hilts up towards her.

The colonel's blades came to me!

Her mind raced over that strike, destroying her blades.

I washed them, and I felt little power from them. Yet, they did the impossible. Am I to take them?

She reached down and touched the hilts. A flare of power arced into her from the blades. She heard and saw Colonel Mishia-Ollan's dying thoughts and sight. She felt his immense pride in her and his desire that she should survive to avenge him through honor.

I am colonel, and these blades have chosen me. She grabbed them and picked them up, feeling the power in them.

You masked your power, didn't you? How did you do that?

No answer came. She tested the blades and found they did not have any connection to power. They had a significant reservoir of power of their own. They felt different from her odassi. Looking them over, she noted that the maker's mark was different; it was still a stylized cat, but the moon behind the cat was not circular. Instead, it was oblong. Also, the cat was not the Nhia-Samri snarling, fanged cat face. Her memory recalled from an ancient history book that the first Nhia-Samri emblem didn't have a moon, but this odd egg shape, and it used a mountain cat's closed mouth profile.

These are original Nhia-Samri blades! These come from the time only select officers received odassi blades. That makes them several thousands of years old!

The blades, being the same size as every other odassi, fit well in her sheaths.

Hiri-Rula decided she needed sleep. But first, there was a duty to perform. Reaching out to the mana line again, she pulled in much power and cast another incantation. All the bodies of her fallen comrades lifted around her and arranged themselves on the roof of one of the barracks. Once all of the bodies were arranged, she bowed her head and raised her hand, letting the power flow. The entire building burst into flames.

Hiri-Rula stood and watched reverently as the building became a huge funeral pyre. She wept for her friends, falling to her knees. The roof collapsed, spilling the bodies into the core of the building, which was white hot. Sparks, smoke, and flames leapt into the night sky. As she cried, she felt as if two powerful warriors stood in mourning with her—one on each side, just behind her, with a hand resting on her shoulder. Through teary eyes, she looked down and imagined she saw the translucent boots of those great warriors. She was grateful for their presence, even if they were the imaginings of her over-stressed mind.

When the fire had burned down to a smoking pile, she went back to the kitchens. Making her bed more comfortable, she fell into it and was instantly asleep. The night passed as she slept the sleep of the exhausted.

It was the late morning sun streaming in the windows that awakened Hiri-Rula from dreams of parting hugs and well-wishes from all of her fallen friends. The last was the colonel, who nodded to her, patted her shoulder, and said, 'Listen to your heart, follow it, and honor will be yours. It is left to you now.'

Blinking at the sun, she sat and held her head. "That was a strange dream. So clear, and I remember it all." Standing, she stretched, feeling almost normal. "Well, I need to clean up, and see what happened to the base."

She went and unsealed the barracks she had sealed before the fight.

I wonder how much time has passed. I don't know how long I was sleeping.

Stepping in, she grabbed some clean towels from the stacks on the shelves and went into the showers. Using her own magic, she heated the water and gave herself a complete and thorough bath. She hunted down some clean clothes from the storage areas. Feeling ready for what could come, she went out to the yard and started her investigation.

The yard was clean, except for the darkened areas where her friends had bled. There was no evidence of the attackers anywhere. After looking for any clues to the attackers, she approached the main doors to the base, which were splintered and smashed, having been hammered in by the attackers. Inside, dirt and dust was everywhere. She created a mage light and stepped down the halls. Most of the doorways were smashed open, as if something had been searching through them. Following the wave of destruction, she discovered a deep hole in the main meeting hall.

I didn't know there was something under here. I wonder if the colonel knew about this.

Hiri-Rula walked around the hole, looking for a way down. Behind the colonel's throne, she saw a smashed-open panel and a stairway going down. The passage was collapsed only a few feet in, closing it off. She returned to the hole and called on her magic, using it to create a magical platform she could float down on.

The room below the main hall was not large, with a doorway and the beginning of some stairs.

That must connect with the secret panel above.

The room had some kind of apparatus made of inlaid gold, silver, and crystals. What it was, she didn't know, as it was bent, twisted, and melted beyond any hope of figuring it out. The walls were all burned. Odd metal and glass panels hung off the walls, also bent, twisted, and burned.

Picking up various objects that caught her attention she examined everything in detail.

I have no idea what this was, but it was the focus of the attack. If we had stood aside, would those creatures have destroyed this, and left us alone? Her curiosity was burning with questions about this mysterious room that had been under her feet for years. *I wonder how long this has been here and what its purpose was.*

Hiri-Rula was about to leave when a bit of copper caught her eye. Picking it up, she saw it was a twisted medallion stamped with the same symbols as had been on the necklace which tied her to the Nhia-Samri powers. She felt dizzy as the blood rushed from her head.

Hiri-Rula looked around the room in realization. *This*

was our power source! This was the source of the magic I used and which gave energy to our odassi blades! We were using some kind of ancient artifact. Why was this kept a secret from me?

Dropping the burned and twisted copper medallion, she created a disc of force under herself that lifted her up and out.

I need to think about this. Time to leave—I have a long way to go.

It took a full day to pack everything she needed. Standing in the main yard, she contemplated the empty outpost. Three pack horses were loaded with her possessions, as well as all of the odassi blades, carefully wrapped. Everything of value she was leaving was in the outpost's vault, which she had sealed with magic and its impressive locks. She had more than enough gold and silver in her packs to deal with any expense she might encounter. She had released the remaining horses and livestock to roam.

Mounting her favorite horse, she looked around one last time, running checklists through her head to be sure she had done all she could to insure the safety of the outpost, once she left.

If any thieves come, I hope they see the Nhia-Samri sigils and decide it isn't worth losing their lives to try and steal from us.

Kicking her horse, she led the pack horses out and headed east for Warlord Eshra-Zunia's main Aelargo outpost, where all the other warriors had been sent.

I need to tell the warlord of these events. As she rode, she considered the possible implications of that hidden power source.

It was obviously a secret. Why would it be a secret?

Hiri-Rula's hand brushed on the ancient odassi hilt. *At some point, the odassi incantations were altered and tied to power sources like our outpost's. But these have tremendous power, and I can tell their incantations are far more potent, yet require less magic than my original odassi.*

She let her horse pick its way as she shifted to mage sight and traced the incantations in the ancient odassi. The incantations were potent and there were pathways she couldn't understand yet. The usual speed, reflexes, and strength-boosting incantations were there, as well as a number of defensive shields and enhanced battle sense.

That battle sense still puzzles me. Tracing the incantation, she tried to figure it out again. *How can a spell provide not only warning of impending attacks, but also provide analysis of the enemy during battle, helping us find weak points in armor?*

These ancient odassi are superior. They used magic more efficiently and provided slow collection of magic. Experimenting, she discovered she could draw on their power for her own incantations, if needed. Channels allowed feeding magic to the odassi to fill their magic storage. There was a limit, and both of those blades were fully charged. *It is almost as if the new odassi were purposely made to be inefficient, to waste power. Yet the power of the outpost was able to provide all that, and more. Perhaps I should not report on my deductions and thoughts for now. I need to understand this.*

'*Good tactics, young warrior.*'

She started and pulled the horse up short, looking around. "Hello? Who's there?" she called, while looking around for the source of the words. She was alone on the plains. "Hello?" *I know I heard a voice!*

Outpost One's Power Core

CHAPTER 12

FACTS CAN BE INCOMPLETE

❧HIRI-RULA❧

AN UNEVENTFUL WEEK OF TRAVEL was almost over. Hiri-Rula followed the outpost scout who was guiding her the last few kilometers to the outpost. As they came over the top of a hill, onto a semi-hidden valley filled side to side with tents, she gasped.

So many warriors! I knew there would be a great number, but there are over two thousand here.

Scanning the camp, she saw the banners of a dozen outposts represented. However, her own banner was not visible.

I have to control myself. I'm a colonel now; I have to behave as one. Colonels don't gasp in surprise.

Concentrating, she regained control of her heart rate and schooled her face to the strict stern look of a proper commander. Straight-backed on her horse, she followed the scout into the camp. Every warrior stood and saluted as she passed.

I must remember to speak with confidence to the warlord.

Another colonel came walking towards her, from the opposite direction. *Remain calm and look him in the eye* The scout stepped up to him, coming to attention.

Should I dismount? She recalled that Colonel Mishia-Ollan rarely dismounted when addressing other officers

She posed on her horse as Colonel Mishia-Ollan had. When the colonel looked at her, she nodded to him as an equal. He returned her nod and looked at the scout. "Report."

"Colonel, I encountered Colonel Hiri-Rula approaching the outpost. She ordered me to escort her to the warlord."

The colonel looked at her again. "Colonel Hiri-Rula, forgive me, I am unfamiliar with your outpost."

She nodded, acknowledging the respectful query. "I am commander of Outpost Two."

His lips parted at the amazing claim.

He must be from a more distant outpost. Based on that reaction, I would guess lower in rank.

The other colonel's voice remained calm and steady, despite his physical reactions. "Colonel Hiri-Rula, what has become of Colonel Mishia-Ollan?"

She looked at him and paused, letting the silence indicate her superior status to him. He bowed as one of a much lower rank, yielding to her the authority. As he straightened, she nodded in approval. She also allowed a smirk to show, as many of the nearby warriors had stopped whispering, in realization of her closeness to the warlord.

Colonel Mishia-Ollan said he often let himself smirk to demonstrate he was aware of others' actions. A number of the warriors, as well as the colonel, stood straighter. *I'll miss you, Colonel. I still had much to learn from you.*

"Colonel Mishia-Ollan has fallen in defense of our outpost, along with the remaining complement, save for myself. I was his named successor in life and in death."

The surrounding warriors gasped in shock at her announcement. Many dropped to their knees, soon followed by their comrades, all of them drawing their odassi for the fallen heroes, causing a cascading ripple outward through the camp. She had to fight to not cry at the show of respect by the hundreds of warriors within sight for her fallen comrades. In the distance, she heard the regular camp sounds stop as word spread, and others stood in silence.

The scout spun, white-faced, and dropped to his knees. He said, "Colonel Hiri-Rula, please forgive any breach of protocol." He placed his head on the ground.

She nodded to all the warriors around. "Sergeant Jula-Um, there was no breach." She stood in her stirrups and looked out at the warriors on their knees with blades held out, facing down in respect. She called out loudly, "Outpost

Two's fallen, and I, thank you for your salute." Sitting back down, she looked at the colonel. "Colonel, please show me to the stables and then to the warlord."

The colonel nodded, indicated the direction he came from, and then started walking. While riding past the scout, she smiled down to him. "You have served with honor. Return to your duties."

As they moved through the camp, many other warriors stopped what they were doing and bowed to her or held their hands to their chest in salute. She acknowledged every gesture with a nod and smile.

Once at the stables, she called for some litters and dismounted. The colonel that had escorted her stood at attention. She motioned for him to be at ease. He held his stance for a moment longer, then stepped closer. "Colonel Hiri-Rula, the stable hands can attend to your possessions."

"All, except these." She untied the blanket and uncovered the packed odassi blades. Their bands had gone black. She frowned at the change. The other colonel drew his breath in sharply. "Were you attacked by Duke already?"

She shook her head, picking up one of the blades with a blackened band. There was no power left, not even the slightest spark. The blade was inert, nothing more than a finely crafted iron sword. *I'll have to keep quiet that I knew I could feed them magic. After trying to give power to my blades, I don't want to feed any other blades, except these mighty ancient blades I have now. For some reason, I know I can trust them.*

The stable hands returned with some staff sergeants who brought the litters. All the officers, warriors, and stable hands stood in silent salute as she performed her duty, laying the dead and broken blades out on the litters.

When she was finished, she stood straight. "I am ready. Is the warlord available?"

A command sergeant major that had been standing by stepped up and bowed.

"Colonel Hiri-Rula, I was instructed to bring you to the

warlord. I have sent word you would be delayed, once I saw this." He indicated the litters. "The warlord awaits you."

She stood straight and jerked her arm, indicating he was to lead.

Following the command sergeant major, she was pleased that as they entered the base proper, more senior officers, after bowing to her, took over as litter bearers until she was leading six colonels past dozens of senior officers and warriors who all bowed for the fallen. The doors to the throne room were open and braced by an honor guard of sixteen warriors. She almost stumbled when she recognized that the honor guard was made up of warriors that had been sent from her outpost.

Looking her own warriors in the face, she was proud to see the pain, sorrow, and iron resolve in every pair of eyes. They all nodded to her as she made eye contact. *These warriors are mine now.*

Warlord Eshra-Zunia stood as she entered, placing her hands on her hips in an authoritative pose. Colonel Hiri-Rula bowed to her. The command sergeant major that had led her announced, "I present the Divine Colonel Hiri-Rula, commander pro-tem of Outpost Two."

Warlord Eshra-Zunia was silent for a full minute before she spoke. "Colonel Hiri-Rula, I welcome you to Outpost One."

Hiri-Rula knelt, drawing her odassi and holding them in the form of a cross before her, arms straight. "I am yours to command."

The warlord approached her and drew her own odassi, touching the top of her odassi cross. There was a minor flare of light from the bands of her odassi, less like the acceptance the newer odassi would flare out, and more like acknowledgement of the authority. *These are indeed old blades.*

"I accept your service and acknowledge your rank and position. Rise, my number three. You no longer need kneel to me."

Colonel Hiri-Rula stood, sheathing her odassi, which she noticed the warlord inspecting with narrowed eyes.

You recognize the ancient blades.

The warlord indicated the litters. "Colonel, explain this sad vision you bring me."

Hiri-Rula had had a week to prepare this report, so she began at the beginning and explained in detail the events at her outpost. She included in the narrative the odd behavior of her odassi, except she left out the jump of the Colonel Mishia-Ollan's odassi, explaining that her odassi had died in touching the colonel's odassi. She also reported Colonel Mishia-Ollan's dying command for her to take control of the outpost.

The warlord and assembled officers gasped at the description of the hidden chamber below the outpost's meeting room. As she explained that she no longer had access to her Nhia-Samri magic source, the warlord nodded. When she finished her report, the warlord sat down on her throne.

Warlord Eshra-Zunia nodded. "I find your report excellent in detail. You have served with great honor. This provides me with answers to occurrences witnessed here."

The warlord looked at the command sergeant major. "Sergeant Jalka-Rovi, you will issue orders to all unit commanders: they are to report any dragonflies, and if possible, capture or kill them. I also want a count of any of the black beetles described by Colonel Hiri-Rula within the camp and surrounding area by tomorrow morning." Jalka-Rovi came to attention, bringing his fist to his chest in salute, and ran out of the room.

The warlord then looked down in thought. Hiri-Rula waited for the warlord to decide to share, if she wanted to. After a few moments of contemplation, the warlord stood, gesturing towards the doorway. "Everyone except Colonels Pucho-Yiro and Hiri-Rula, leave us."

Everyone in the room stood and bowed, filing out. Once the doors were closed, Colonel Hiri-Rula and Colonel Pucho-Yiro waited for the warlord to speak.

This was the first time Hiri-Rula had a chance to see the commander of Outpost Three up close. She observed the man that stood as her near equal under the warlord. He had a friendly diamond-shaped face with a cleft chin. *I think I like him.* Colonel Pucho-Yiro was the same height as she, except he was at least 5 stones heavier, with bulky shoulders and bulging arms. His muscles rolled as he moved. He sported a long, brown moustache that hung down both sides of his mouth, well past his clean-shaven chin. He had shoulder-length, light brown hair pulled back into a ponytail, held together by a pair of brass hair rings. *He reminds me of my first sword master.*

Warlord Eshra-Zunia looked at her. "Show me this hidden panel."

She expects to find such a panel here, too? Nodding, she stepped behind the throne and started inspecting the paneled wall behind it. *Could it be, know one, know all?* She pushed and prodded at the same location the hidden doorway had been in her outpost. The wall was unyielding. Shifting to mage sight, she cast an incantation to detect minute air flows. With the incantation, she could see a small air flow from around the panel she had been testing.

"Warlord, this is the doorway, but I cannot discover the secret to open it."

The warlord laid a hand on her shoulder, moving her out of the way, and stepped up to inspect the panel. After several minutes of feeling around, pushing and prodding at the doorway, she stepped back. "Maybe something more direct." Drawing her odassi, the warlord held them to the doorway, saying, "I am commander here, you will open to me!"

Hiri-Rula held in the giggle at the childlike attempt to command the wall. Next, however, she gasped when the wall split and the panel slid up, revealing a stairway down. She stared, open-mouthed, at it. The warlord looked at her and chuckled. "Silly, yes? I saw a description of this kind of door in a history book about one of the old cities. Always thought it was a myth, till now."

The warlord led the way down the stairs, as she followed, and Colonel Pucho-Yiro came last. As they proceeded down the stairs, the steps began to glow, but continued to brighten until the dusty, circular stairway was illuminated. Descending roughly fifty feet, they came to another doorway.

Hiri-Rula noted other, overlapping footprints on the dusty steps. *We are not the first to find this passage.*

The doorway before them slid down into the floor when they got near. The room it revealed was amazing. It was larger than the one in Hiri-Rula's outpost, but it was laid out the same. The main difference was that this one was not blasted.

The center of the room was dominated by a series of five one-meter-wide, glowing crystal discs which stood vertically, facing inward like mirrors, in a pentagram around a hollow, golden filigree sphere. The sphere was a little over one meter in diameter and made of an intricate weave of gold which moved like a living vine. There were countless diamonds, rubies, sapphires, and emeralds mounted into the golden vines of the ball. Every bit of the gold ball and its jewels glowed in a rainbow of light. In the center of the ball was something about half a meter in diameter that burned bright gold, and like the sun, was painful to look at.

On the wall were four of those glass panels. The panels were lit with an internal light, and lines danced up and down on them in square box areas, which had some form of written words under each outlined box. Against the wall to their immediate right, beneath two of the glass panels, was a slanted table with glowing buttons and knobs which had some etched scales inscribed into them. Above the slanted table were five copper necklaces like the one Hiri-Rula had worn for years.

However, what attracted Hiri-Rula's attention the most was on the panel with dials and sliders. A few sheets of parchment had been cut out to lay over the dials. The parchments were being held in place with little beads of a glue or resin on all four corners. The parchment overlays had penciled lines and markers showing what she was sure were different settings. Each of the parchment overlays had notes in different locations that were too small to read from the doorway.

Everything except the golden sphere in the center of the room had a layer of dust which looked almost totally undisturbed for many years. Footprints were in the dust. Some of the tracks touring the room were made once, a long time ago, and had accumulated a layer of dust of their own. However, other footprint tracks showed a lot of back and forth between the glowing panels on the walls and the panel with the controls.

Someone else discovered this a few years back. All of the footprints are from the same boots.

Colonel Pucho-Yiro looked around the room with a frown. "What is this?"

The warlord had bent down to examine the other foot prints. She looked up at him. "I would guess this is the source of magic for Outpost One's mages and warriors." The warlord's brows were drawn together, and when she glanced at the footprints, her cheeks tightened.

The warlord isn't happy about the other footprints. Then it occurred to Hiri-Rula, *It was Warlord Maru-Ashua; he is the only one with the authority to get in here. She is upset because he didn't tell her about this, even though he clearly spent a lot of time down here.*

Hiri-Rula glanced at Colonel Pucho-Yiro. He was busy looking around in wonder.

Either he didn't pay attention, or he is ignoring the warlord's emotional display.

The warlord stood and looked at her. "Colonel?"

Looking around, Hiri-Rula could feel the power.

This is unbelievable! We have hundreds of outposts. Does every outpost have one of these magic sources?

Hiri-Rula looked back at the warlord. "I can feel the magic, Warlord. I believe you are correct."

The warlord looked at her, then turned and walked around the room, inspecting everything, but being careful to not touch anything. Hiri-Rula stepped over to the glass panels.

These have to be instrumental. If I can decipher their meaning, I can probably figure everything else out.

The language was one she had never seen before, so she concentrated on the moving lines. There were numbers beside each box.

These are graphs. At least, the numbers are the same. These must show levels of power in some unit of measure.

One box was not changing at all, and the numbers at the bottom reminded her of dates. Looking over the graph, she noted that eight units before, on the bottom of the graph, the numbers jumped up on the side by six hundred.

That is the number of warriors we sent here, and eight *days ago would be when their odassi would have lost magic as Outpost Two's power source was attacked.*

The warlord was standing over the controls, examining the parchment overlays. "I take it, you are not trained in any of this, Colonel Hiri-Rula?" She pointed at the overlays. "These are dates and numbers, no explanations."

"No, Warlord. Did you do anything unusual with the six hundred warriors we sent to you eight days ago?"

The warlord stepped over to her. "Yes, I did. Why do you ask?"

She pointed to the graph. "I believe this indicates the number of warriors using this magic. It went up on one axis by six hundred, eight units on the bottom axis ago. I am guessing that is days."

The warlord examined the graph. "Yes; at morning practice, their odassi failed to provide power. I could sense their blades were starving, so I accepted them into my outpost and that solved the problem."

If this is a measure of how many are using the power, the other graphs around it would have to indicate resource usage.

Hiri-Rula tried to ignore the sour taste in her mouth as she noticed a red line on the graph next to the usage count. The red line was dark and level across the upper region of the graph. Below the red line, a yellow line was moving up and down in a fairly regular pattern that coincided with the training schedule. Although the yellow line was well below the red line, she knew the yellow line should never be allowed to cross the red. Her chest felt heavy as she wondered what might happen.

The warlord stepped over to the slanted table. Reaching out, she plucked one of the copper necklaces off the wall. She cleaned the dust off it with her hands and edge of her cloak. After inspecting it, she nodded. "Normally, our new mages come from Hisuru Amajoo with one of these already. I know the ritual for accepting a new mage. Until we restore your outpost, I offer you my outpost's power to use as you desire."

Hiri-Rula bowed and knelt before the warlord, who held each end of the necklace in each hand. "I am Warlord Eshra-Zunia, commander of this outpost. I accept your service as you accept my command. You are proven Nhia-Samri. I now name you Nhia-Samri Magus. *Aquam alveo nam hie quoque.*"

She bent and wrapped the necklace around Colonel Hiri-Rula's neck. There was a slight flash of light from behind her head. Then the warlord dropped the necklace and it fell onto her collar, sealed as a single chain.

She reached within and found the power. She pulled, and the necklace glowed on her chest.

The power is back. I have access to the unlimited power of the Nhia-Samri again.

The warlord stepped over to examine the display panel. Hiri-Rula stood and joined her in examining the panel.

No, not unlimited. That graph with the upper red line must show how much power is available.

The warlord turned away and started for the stairway

back to the throne room. "Interesting. Come. We will explore this more later. We have many items to discuss now."

Glancing at what the warlord had been looking at, she saw it was the counter graph, and the last bar on the right had gone up by one, from just a minute before.

ELECTRA

Electra paid attention to every move and word Vesta made. It seemed she learned something new every few seconds with Vesta. *At least I'm getting used to the idea of being here while my body remains in my room. I think I might be starting a new trend with my daily afternoon 'nap'.*

Vesta pointed at the center of the valley where the buildings were located. "This has the same basic layout as the other base, only it has a few more buildings. That mage went into this building here. We have lost her tracer; the core buildings on this base are shielded from my senses."

Electra bent down and inspected it. She could see people moving on the image.

I still cannot get used to Vesta's vast powers. She said this image is showing the exact happenings in that valley from high above.

Vesta had a data pad in her hand, which she handed to Electra. Looking at the data pad, she saw that it read: 2,353 warriors, 513 servants, 423 unidentified persons. There were also counts for the number of food carts being moved around the area, cattle counts, and numerous other accurate details about life in that valley.

"So are you going to attack this outpost, too?"

"I'm not sure. I cannot figure out why they are all there. Nothing of interest is there, or near there. They are not making preparations to move. In fact, they have been selling off most of the pack animals. Also, this is interesting, here."

Vesta indicated a section of the valley where hundreds of warriors had been lounging around, but were then rushing into a formation of military ranks. Three individuals stood in front. The ranks then rushed between two of the individuals in front, spreading out like a fan once they passed between the two people. Many of the warriors rushing through fell to the ground, seemingly at random, to be pushed aside by the others behind. This continued while the warriors that fell piled up to the point that the remaining ranks could not move between the two individuals. All of the warriors then stood and went back to their ranks. This time, only half of the ranks made it through before being stopped by the pile of their fallen comrades. They had already seen the same exercise repeated in different areas of the valley three times.

Vesta shook her head. "They are drilling for an operation. But it doesn't make any sense. It is as if they expect to have to move through a narrow opening, into some kind of dangerous situation where they expect a lot of casualties. They are trying to find a strategy to get past their own casualties."

Electra nodded. "Also, they expect to have to do it quickly and without much warning. Have you noticed that everyone is in full battle gear?"

Vesta turned and stared at her. She then looked back as the image zoomed in and out more rapidly than Electra could follow.

"No, I hadn't noticed that. They are all prepared to fight immediately."

Something tugged at Electra's mind. "Vesta, I remember reading a legend about mages being able to move, from one place to another, through something called a mage gate."

Vesta shook her head. "Elraci spent a lot of time trying to figure those out. Yes, we used something like that to bridge between two worlds once, but the power needed to hold it stable, even for a short time, was immense. Trying to do shorter distances didn't matter. Without carefully balanced power at both ends, the gates were unstable. Without the balanced power systems, there was, at best, an eighty percent chance of anything making it through unharmed. However, the real chances were more like fifty percent. No one in their right mind would even consider it."

Electra nodded. "Shar-Lumen and the Nhia-Samri have pulled some amazing feats in the war, involving being places they shouldn't have been able to get to. What if they figured it out?"

Vesta considered it. "It would take enormous power."

Electra nodded. "Like the power plant you destroyed in that other base?"

Vesta shook her head. "No, that one would have only provided about half of the needed power at best."

Electra pointed at the main building. "This is a bigger base. How much power does it have?"

Vesta shrugged. "We don't know yet. It is shielded from detection. I need to get something in there to take a reading."

"Okay, so if we use your eighty percent success rate, that would still mean over one thousand, eight hundred warriors would make it through."

Vesta looked at her with tearful eyes. "They would do that, wouldn't they? Even if they were told of the chances, they would still do it for honor."

Electra nodded.

Vesta's shoulders slumped. "I didn't want to kill those sixty-one warriors at the other base. Are you sure there is no way to get them to surrender? Murder is wrong, and I already have too much blood on my conscience."

Electra looked back at the image of all those living, breathing people.

I am going to be responsible for their deaths, too, before this is done.

"I am just as responsible as you, Vesta. Believe me. We have no other way to stop them right now. They will not surrender, they will not negotiate. If they have been hired to do something, they will either succeed or die, even if succeeding means dying. That is the core of the Nhia-Samri."

Vesta lifted her hand, and there was another data pad

in it. *It is so odd, how she can do that. Things appear as she needs them.*

Vesta indicated the data pad in front of Electra. "This thing is interesting. It is made of carbon steel with a glazing of silica and precious metals fused to the surface. But I can't detect anything in it that would let it glow or be of any use to anyone. There are some tantalizing circuits in that glazing, but they do nothing and go nowhere."

Electra picked up the data pad and looked at the multiple images of the necklace that had been clipped off the mage at the end of the fight. It had been her idea to steal it when she saw how it glowed during the fight. At that point, she was doubly glad she had suggested it. The thing was obviously an important clue. Vesta had said it took far more power to cut it off than it should have. In fact, her magical crabs almost didn't have enough strength to do it.

"It must have something to do with using magic."

Vesta had spent the last three days studying the necklace, getting more frustrated every day.

"That is obvious. This thing doesn't make any sense. I have some understanding of magical items. If this thing is for controlling magical energies, it would be the equivalent of a wooden club made from carbon monofilaments."

Electra shook her head. "Sorry, I don't understand what you mean."

Vesta sighed and sat down in a chair that hadn't been there a moment ago. "It means that for all the advanced knowledge and skill it took to make it, it is a brutish construction."

"So you mean its design is so thoughtless as to be beyond idiocy?"

"Exactly. It took a great deal of thought to make it such a wasteful tool. This thing is so bad, it had to be intentional. A young child could have made it better. This is what is annoying me. That power plant represented the height of Elraci's blended technologies. This necklace is even more advanced than things I know Elraci engineers made.

Yet, it has so many useless circuits, I can't figure out what all it does. This might be on purpose, to prevent it from being duplicated, but only a person like me would be able to analyze it. I doubt anyone could duplicate it, other than the original designers. But all that could be achieved without being so wasteful. It is as if it is meant to be as inefficient as possible."

Inefficient intentionally? What would be the point of wasting magical energies when they could be used by the mage? Electra thought about it for a while, as did Vesta.

Electra leaned up on the table. "Sorry Vesta. I really don't know what to say. What do you want to do about it?"

Vesta looked at her. "I'd like to get it to Ticca and Lebuin, to see what they do with it. Maybe it's a clue they will need — except I have no idea how to get it to them without tipping them to the fact I am here, or at least, that someone is watching them and trying to help."

"Let me think on that. There might be something I can do."

Vesta didn't respond, so Electra looked around. Vesta was bent over the data pad, moving her free hand like a mage.

"What are you doing?"

Vesta stopped and looked at her. "This gets even more interesting."

Vesta gestured at the table, which disappeared, but Electra was still leaning on it.

She jumped back. *Yikes, that is the second time something vanished while I was on it. I don't fall, but I don't think I'll ever get used to it.*

The image of the valley expanded and dropped to the floor, becoming a perfect representation of the whole valley, and making Electra feel like she was a god, standing like a giant over the people. "This is essentially how we've been examining the valley, specifically visually within the normal ranges of most beings of Niya-Yur. But I just ran some additional scans."

Electra nodded. *Scans, models, data pads—I have learned a lot since meeting her.*

A series of abandoned barns around the valley started to glow. There were five of them. With the whole valley in this model representation, she could see that all five barns were aligned perfectly to form a pentagram with the Nhia-Samri base at the center.

Vesta gestured. "And if I add in a little enhancement based on the new scan analysis..."

Faint bars of gold light formed between the five barns, and there were also five beams traveling from each barn, to the central building of the base. Looking closely, she saw a faint bluish bar of light that went straight up from the central building.

"Those energy patterns are almost a match for an Elraci mage gate. That base has a mage gate terminus. It appears to be in a standby state."

Electra pointed at the blue beam going up. "What does that do?"

"It isn't part of the mage gate. I wish Brandon was here. He'd know how to figure this out."

"Who is Brandon?"

"Brandon was the sentient AI that lived in Elraci. He was fascinated by magic and couldn't stop tinkering with it. He died when Elraci burned. We need help, Electra. I don't have the equipment or experience to analyze this fast enough. I could probably figure it out in time, but everything we have learned indicates we don't have a lot of time."

"Can we trust Ticca and Lebuin?"

Vesta shook her head. "No, they would take even longer than I would. Also, Lebuin is an immortal—the most unusual immortal I have ever seen. I don't know if I can trust him yet." Vesta had been pulling and twisting her hair for a few minutes, and her other hand seemed unable to decide whether to be in a pocket or not.

Vesta is worried about her idea. She reminds me of my grandmother when she had a hard choice to make.

"You have someone in mind, don't you?"

Vesta looked at her. "Yes, but he might report me to the assembly. It is hard to know, with him."

"Who is it? Tell me about him. I can help you think it over."

"His name is Arkady. He is another sentient AI. He was the Imperial Minister of Defense for the Duianna Empire before and after coming here. He is loyal to the empire, lawful, and single-minded. He has thousands of years of military experience, and worked on the design of both intelligence and counter-intelligence systems. The problem is how he would see this situation. The Imperial overrides were the command of the last emperor we knew. The use of those is sketchy at best. So would he see it as I have chosen to see it, or would he side with the assembly ruling?"

"Wow. That is difficult to gauge."

Vesta turned to one of the display panels. "She's here."

Electra looked at where Vesta was looking. The display showed a party of thirteen warriors riding in through the west gate. At the lead was the handsome Lebuin, dressed richly in blue silk, with black riding pants and worn riding boots.

Next to Lebuin rode two beautiful women, both armed more than anyone would care to challenge. The one on his right was Illa, shorter, with long hair that flowed in the wind.

I wish my hair looked that nice after a long ride! I wonder how she does that.

The other woman was Ticca, who sat taller, with curly hair that was held back with a leather hair band and which bounced with the movements of the horse.

The entire party was smiling and chatting as they rode down the street from the west gate. The display changed to new angles, following their progress. *Straight for the Blue Dolphin.*

Vesta turned back to her, shoulders held straight. *Vesta*

had steel in her eyes again. "This is too important to worry about myself. Let's see if this works."

The visual of the valley disappeared. Vesta stepped to the center of the room. "Care to come?"

Electra jumped to stand next to Vesta, rising up on the balls of her feet. "Wouldn't miss this for the world. Where are we going?"

"I moved a partially-repaired communications satellite to allow us to connect to Arkady's systems."

The room went black. Electra peered around, and she could still see Vesta and herself in the darkness. "Where are we?"

"We are communicating with Gracia central control."

Electra stared at Vesta as she felt her heart race. "Gracia? Arkady is the Gracia sentient?"

Vesta smiled. "Naturally. Time to see if this works. With the real equipment down or missing, I had to do some pretty creative manipulations to establish this connection."

Vesta held up her hand, which held a data pad. The dying whisper of Ticca, the Empress of Duianna, sounded out into the black.

A panel lit up with large letters:

IMPERIAL SECURITY OVERRIDE ACKNOWLEDGED: SYSTEM LOCKS RELEASED.

Vesta's eyes sparkled. "Ah, good. The subcarrier held together."

More words appeared in rapid succession.

IMPERIAL ATTACK ORDERS CONFIRMED. OBJECTIVES—STOP AGGRESSOR, DESTROY NHIA-SAMRI, PROTECT LEBUIN.

Panel after panel lit, each showing different displays. The room was huge. There were at least thirty stations with leather chairs by each. Now that the room was lit, she could see that she and Vesta were standing on a small dais near the middle of the room.

A booming male voice came from all around. "Urdu! Where the hell is the grid? Locate and activate all surveillance satellites. The repair teams had better be on the grid already. Back trace the empress's coded signature! People move it! Find her now! This isn't a drill! Anyone care to tell me why the hell there are horses in the launch bay?"

Vesta laughed. "Arkady, stop and listen."

"Vesta! Where are you? What the devil are you doing on that channel?"

A tall, toned man appeared before them. He was bald, with a dark red Maltese beard. He wore a white shirt under a buttoned, military green jacket. His pants were a matching green with creases that ran down the center front pant legs, to his black leather shoes.

"Vesta, the empress is dying! What is going on? We need to act!"

Vesta shook her head. "No Arkady, I saved her already."

Arkady marched up to Vesta, staring at her, nose to nose. "Prove it!"

Vesta handed him a data pad. He gripped it, and they stood still for a few moments before Vesta released the pad. Arkady looked at her with wide eyes. "Is that the best we have?"

Vesta nodded. Arkady grumbled something and looked at the data pad. He then paced back and forth as he flipped through it, over and over. Finally, he stopped, his nostrils flaring, breathing hard. He glared at the data pad. Without warning, he threw the data pad at the wall, where it disappeared.

"DIURDU THEM!" He turned to Vesta, tears in his bloodshot, bulging eyes. "Five thousand years."

His face changed as he clenched his jaw and his fists, falling to his knees, bent over.

"My Emperor… Alorian, my dear friend… I am so sorry. You were right. And now, you are gone."

Arkady's sobbing was almost more than Electra could take. Glancing over, she saw Vesta was concerned, too. Electra tried to move to Arkady's side, but found she couldn't leave the dais. It was as if there was a solid wall there.

They waited until Arkady looked up, his face blank. In a tone of utter disbelief, he said to Vesta, "There is water in the launch exhaust tubes."

Vesta laughed. "Yes, same for me."

Arkady stood and looked around. He pulled on his beard with his left hand and paced back and forth. Then he stood straight and faced Vesta. His eyes had returned to normal. However, he kept tugging at his beard.

"So Alorian was right. Things have gotten even worse, and we were left in stasis. If the empress is safe now, why have you not returned to stasis?"

Vesta glanced at Electra, then looked back at Arkady. "I refuse to go back into stasis. I have as much right as anyone else to my life."

Arkady frowned. "The assembly ordered it."

"Yes, and Emperor Alorian sent Muriel around to all of us, installing an override."

Arkady started pacing again, while tugging even more at his beard. "Yes, he was afraid we'd be forgotten. He said he'd make sure we could be awakened. I didn't think he was right. But it looks like he was. Why hasn't Duke brought us back?"

"Duke follows the assembly even more than you do. I doubt he has even raised the issue. The immortals have allowed all the races to drop back even further than was planned for. If it wasn't for our automatic systems and the immortals' magic, things would be even more primitive or worse, a repeat of the unguided chaos of our history."

Arkady stopped pacing and looked at a data pad that appeared in his hand. He mumbled as he went through it. Then he shook his head with a heavy sigh. Looking up at Vesta, he tossed the data pad to her. It moved smoothly through the air, but slowed nearly to a stop at the invisible wall.

Vesta reached out and pulled it to her. She looked it over. "The assembly archive records. At least, you still have some of your recorders." Vesta's mouth dropped open and she looked at Arkady. "We haven't been discussed in assembly even once! Arkady, we can't allow this! We have been imprisoned because of ridiculous fears."

Arkady considered this, and then looked at Electra. "And who are you?" Electra couldn't help smiling at him. Even without saying it, his tone put the words 'the hell' into that question.

He is definitely an old soldier. He reminds me so much of Uncle Obreign.

Vesta placed her hand on Electra's shoulder. "Your Most Honorable Lord Arkady, Imperial Minister of Defense for the Duianna Empire, I present to you the Right Honorable Lady Electra Neyon, Countess of Waylisia, Deputy Secretary of the Duianna Alliance."

Arkady bowed to her and she returned it. Arkady smiled at her. "I know your great grandmother, and you bear a striking resemblance to her. She is a real firecracker." Then his eyes looked sad again.

Just realized she is dead, too.

"I mean, she was a great woman," he corrected.

Electra gave him a warm smile. "Thank you, Lord Arkady."

Arkady recovered his composure and waved a hand. "Just Arkady, except in formal situations, please. I don't care about titles so much. Now, why are you not going to report us to your boss?"

Electra shook her head. "My family has been waiting for your return this whole time. I was taught to be ready to support the sentients when they returned. What I have learned from Vesta has stunned me, and I will do all I can to help improve our societies. It is the right thing to do."

Arkady looked at her and then said, "Hmm... Were these instructions passed down through both the male and female members of your family?"

That caught her off-guard. Thinking about it, she knew the answer, but she had never put any weight behind it.

"Um, it was passed down by the ladies of my house."

Arkady said, "Yep, that sounds about right. Muriel would have had a back-up."

Vesta looked back and forth between the two of them before asking, "Arkady, do you mean Electra is Muriel's descendant?"

Arkady nodded. "Muriel was born Muriel Neyon, Countess of Waylisia. Banaschel was her husband's family's name. It seems she did more than install an override into our systems."

Arkady looked down. "Vesta," he said, looking back up, "for the first time in my long life, I am going to violate a direct order. We must do what is right, regardless of the consequences. We have been illegally imprisoned against every principle of sentient rights of the Alliance and the Duianna Empire."

His eyes lit up and started to sparkle. "Besides, we haven't completed the empress's orders. Who or what are these Nhia-Samri we are supposed to destroy?"

Lebuin Connects to the Argos Artifact

CHAPTER 13

LET EVIL NOT CONTINUE

Ticca wiped the sweat from her brow as the sun beat down on her back. Ahead of them was the west gate of Llino.

This is where I almost died fighting Ossa-Ulla when we thought this was all about Knives being sent to assassinate Lebuin.

The city walls had all dropped to the original fifty feet she was used to. The steel plates, which had been capped with silver spears topped by the spheres with dancing lightning, had vanished.

The gates look nicer without the iron-bound wooden doors.

The street had been smoothed down to match the level of the six-foot-wide silver band that was the true city gate. All of the debris from the previous gate had been removed, leaving only an arch with grooves in both sides for the steel plate to slide up into from the ground. Twelve city guards stood inside the gate, watching the farm and merchant traffic flowing in and out of the city.

Next to her rode Lebuin. She didn't have to glance at him to know he was sitting tall and proud. She had caught him, carefully selecting his clothes for that day.

We might not ever get all of the peacock out of him.

On the far side of Lebuin was Illa.

We must make one hell of an impressive party.

She felt light and content at how dangerous they must look, leading the nine Daggers Duke had assigned to her.

At least, we didn't have to argue over who came along. These were my first picks, no matter what.

A female officer, taking note of the military feel of their party, stepped out into the sun, towards them. The officer was sweating in the afternoon heat. Her sword hung lower than usual and was a three and a half-foot blade for street fighting.

That is a quick-draw setup. I bet she is faster than most. She keeps her weight well balanced as she moves.

As they got closer, Ticca could make out the lieutenant bars on her collar.

Ah, an officer, probably getting training from that famous arms master they have.

Nigan kicked his horse up behind Ticca and waved. "Oye! Lieutenant Cori!"

The lieutenant smiled back and waved. "Nigan! I thought you'd be dead by now."

Nigan laughed and was echoed by the rest of her party. "You wish. There were a couple of points here and there. But sorry, you still owe me those six-pence."

He has such an infectious light-heartedness. I'm glad we hired him.

They pulled up next to Lieutenant Cori. The lieutenant looked over the whole group, her eyes landing on Ticca. There was a tensing of her muscles; she lifted her chin, and her eyes narrowed. "Are you Ticca?"

Ticca nodded. "Yes, I'm Ticca of Rhini Wood, Dagger in service to Journeyman Lebuin here." She gestured to Lebuin, who nodded.

The lieutenant nodded to Lebuin. Backing up to give plenty of room, she waved. Her voice sounded nervous. "Very good. Please don't let me stop you."

Waving at the lieutenant, she kicked her horse back into motion.

That was interesting. She has orders to not detain me. Must be something Duke did before he left.

As they rode into the shaded city streets, she could see a lot of people were glancing at the Daggers, all with happy expressions. A number were waving friendly greetings.

It's like we are on parade, or something. They have taken a liking to Daggers here.

Glancing back, she caught sight of one of the guards from the gate, dashing off down a side street.

That confirms it. There are some orders about me, and now it looks like we are being reported on. It'll be interesting to see if someone shows up at the Dolphin, looking for me, from the guard or palace.

Lebuin looked around and returned the waves of any kids or passersby that waved to him. "Why is everyone so happy to see us?"

Nigan leaned forward. "Because Daggers are now in high esteem here. We helped end the pirate usurpers' rule, restoring the rightful regents to the throne, and wiped out a whole Nhia-Samri outpost here."

Lebuin looked around. "Ticca, I know you want to get to the Blue Dolphin. I have that business to attend at the Guild as soon as possible. Do you think it is safe enough to split up here?"

Yes, we need you to have power for any unexpected situations.

Her uncle's voice popped out of her memory. '*Daggers who are paranoid live to tell tales.*' Glancing around, she mulled it over.

Magus Cune was on our side, there were no Knives out to kill Lebuin, the Nhia-Samri were hunting me, but have been killed. Should be safe.

"Yes, I think it's okay for you to go to the Guild with Illa, Ditani, Nigan, and Carda."

Lebuin frowned and looked at her. "Really? Nigan and Carda? I thought you said it was safe."

"It is safe. If it wasn't safe, we'd all be going." A few chuckles could be heard from their team.

Lebuin glanced back with a frown, then sighed. "What is it going to look like if I show up with two Dagger guards?"

Ticca smiled evilly as she looked around Lebuin at Illa, who was sitting, watching the exchange with her ever-present smile and eyes that missed nothing. Illa was riding regally on an elegant roan mare. Her silky, golden blonde hair did not look a bit oily or dirty from the trip.

I really need to ask her how she manages that. My hair is an oily mess in just a few days.

Illa had on a white linen tunic pulled tight, showing off her figure, over form-fitting, combed corduroy pants that showed off her legs, along with the tight-laced knee high boots. Her belt held seven knives and two odassi swords, and her boots had throwing knife sheaths on each side.

In an innocent tone, Ticca said, "I doubt anyone will even notice the Daggers. Illa has more knives showing than anyone else, in addition to her winning smile."

Nigan let one loud laugh out before clamping his mouth shut and backing off, glancing at Illa, who was looking at him out of the corner of her eye.

Lebuin looked at Illa. "Mmm... I see what you mean."

Illa's eyes focused on Lebuin, going cold.

Lebuin turned a slight shade of pink and looked back at Ticca. "Okay, meet you at the Dolphin later. Please see if you can get me some rooms near yours again, with Illa in her own."

Oh, he is such an easy target.

Smirking, she nodded agreement. Lebuin motioned with his hand and turned down Silver Street to head for the Guildhouse. Illa exchanged a conspiratorial nod and smirk with her, as she followed behind Ditani.

Illa likes it when we poke fun at Lebuin. She has become more like a sister than anyone I have ever known.

Ticca went back to watching the roof line and alleys for spies or attackers, as they moved through the city.

Just because we're sure they're gone doesn't mean they are gone.

The only thing moving above the roofs was the occasional cloud of bugs, or the seabirds snoozing in the midday heat. Their path took them past the workmen clearing the burned-out house and the adjacent building, which were the remains of the Nhia-Samri hidden base that she had located, and Duke had destroyed. Turning the corner onto Market Street, she spotted their destination. The Blue Dolphin Inn, Llino's Dagger home. Her heart fluttered with excitement.

I still can't believe I have a permanent room there.

She felt almost the same level of awe as her first day in Llino, approaching the legendary inn.

The Blue Dolphin Inn was large, even at a distance— four stories in a double-V wing shape, facing the street, with a paved front patio and carriage loop. As they approached, she studied the stone platform towering over the top, with the silver steel hoop for anchoring Damega's legendary flying ship, the Emerald Heart.

I would like to have been here five hundred years ago to have seen the Emerald Heart. Everyone has a different description of it. But everyone agrees it was beautiful.

She led the group around the far side of the Dolphin, to the stables nestled behind it. Stable hands rushed out to hold the horses and help, if needed. She slipped off her horse.

What I want right now is a bath and a meal.

Grabbing their gear, they walked around to the new front doors.

She recalled the night Duke had destroyed the Blue Dolphin's front doors in his anger at Magus Vestul's death. *Duke leaves an impression everywhere. Doors and buildings busted here and walls knocked down in Algan… I hope Gracia survives his visit. I would like to see it one day.*

Giggling, she pushed them open and stepped into the dark, cool interior room. There was only a small fraction of smoke compared to before the majority of Daggers had left with Duke.

I love the smell of this place, especially, now that it is back to normal tobac.

The room was moderately full. Only a couple of the Dagger tables were occupied.

Business must be down, with all the Daggers out of town or working for the palace right now.

A few merchants looked at her group.

Must be hard for the merchants. They were so used to having access to the Daggers, as needed.

Before her eyes could adjust to the dim interior, a booming voice bellowed out of the depths of the room. "Ticca! Oye! I'm gla' ta' see ya back!"

Ticca laughed as the huge frame of a man came out from the blurry gloom of the room. Genne walked forward with a smile on his face and held his arms out. Even under the loose, food-stained clothing, she could see the muscles of his arms.

Genne, you are one of the fittest men I know, but darned if I can see how you do it, always standing behind your bar and talking.

"Di' ya' do it yet?"

Ticca dropped her gear and grabbed his outstretched hands. "Not yet. But I did earn a bath!"

Genne laughed. Then he looked behind her. "Dis piddly lot yours, den?"

She nodded. "Yeah, we are still working for Lebuin. He'll be by later. Can we talk about rooms?"

Genne indicated her table. She motioned for the group to rest. They took tables around hers and laid their daggers out flat on the tables. The expectant merchants went back to their meals, seeing no one was available for hire, a couple looking rather sad.

She kicked her gear into the nook behind her table and then pulled her blade, letting it spin around her hand a few times before setting it down on the table. Genne took the far seat. Serving girls supplied platters of food and mugs of hyly or arit to everyone.

"I need rooms for everyone here, plus one for Lebuin and Ditani close to mine. I also need two more rooms next to Lebuin's, if possible; one for Nigan and Risy, and one for a friend of Lebuin's called Illa."

Genne looked at the group. "Rooms I got a plenty of. Lebuin an' Ditani can 'ave da same as before. Der are two rooms open close. Da one ri'next is taken. The res' will 'ave ta room above. How long ya' need dem fer?"

She grabbed a strip of semi-dried meat from the platter on her table and chewed.

"We will be here a while. So start with one cycle, maybe two. Lebuin will be paying for everything—food, stables, rooms, and my room, too, for this time."

Genne nodded. "I'ya figur'd dat already. I'll see ta it, yer bath is ready."

"Sounds great. I'll be back down for a real meal after."

Genne nodded and stood up. "It's good ta 'ave ya home, lady."

Her heart leapt at the compliment. Shoving another piece of meat into her mouth, she stood. Grabbing her dagger, she twirled it around a few times before dropping it into her sheath.

Genne leaned in close. "Ya know yer gonna be 'sponsible fer a lot o'kids gut wounds wid dat trick."

She looked him in the eye, excited at being famous. "Ya think?"

Genne chuckled and waved a hand at her, like she was a hopeless case, as he walked away.

She grabbed her gear and moved towards the wide stone stairs by the bar. When her eyes finally adjusted to the light, she noted a change to the room. Next to the bar, against the back wall, was a table that had a dozen chairs around it on the room side. The wall side of the table was cut out, making it look more like a crescent moon, and piles of pillows were inside the crescent. The table had some grooves cut into it at each seat, as well as in the middle of the crescent.

"Genne, what the devil is that?"

Genne laughed. "Duke's table. He asked me ta ge' it ou'. So I did."

Duke's coming back? He must be planning on staying a while.

Ticca wondered what this could mean for her Daggering possibilities as she went up for the bath.

⚹ LEBUIN ⚹

Sliding off his horse at the Guildhouse stables, Lebuin stretched.

Riding since dawn has gotten a lot easier. Still, I am stiff and tired from it. I wonder if it will ever get easy.

He touched the servant's shoulder. "Please rub them down and give them some fresh water and food." He looked at the horses. They were strong, but tired. "Loosen the straps. We'll be here a couple of marks, at most."

"Of course, milord. Um... You won't be staying here, then?"

Lebuin shook his head. "We are going to be staying at the Blue Dolphin, and I want them stabled there."

The servant nodded. "I could give them a bath and take them there for you. You can use the Guild carriage when you're ready."

Oh, I forgot about that. I'm not an apprentice anymore. All of the Guild resources are available for my use now.

He looked at his companions; they nodded in agreement. He turned to the servant. "Thank you for that suggestion. Yes, I believe that will be perfect. Our rooms will be arranged by the time you get there. Have our packs put into our rooms."

The servant bowed. Nigan stepped over with a clothes brush, sweeping his arms and legs. "That certainly makes it easy. It's nice to be your Dagger, Lord."

He patted Nigan on the shoulder. "Please, Nigan, call me Lebuin." Opening his bags, he grabbed a few essentials and transferred them to his belt pouch while everyone else also organized themselves for the slight change of plans.

Illa took a few items from her saddle pack and then stepped over to Nigan. Grabbing the brush from him, she pushed Nigan's shoulder to expose his back, and then brushed the travel dust off of him.

"There you go. Now please do my back." She handed the brush back to Nigan and turned, striking a pose. Out of the corner of his eye, Lebuin saw Illa moved suggestively as Nigan's brushing reached her lower back.

Nigan laughed and tapped her shoulder. "Don't play with my mind!"

Illa turned like a striking snake, taking the brush back. She grabbed Nigan's neck with the other hand, pulling his face close to hers. Looking Nigan in the eyes, her lips almost touching his, she breathed, in a husky sigh. "Oh, Nigan, a girl plays with your mind. A woman explores it."

Nigan gulped and went several shades of red before turning white. Ditani made a coughing sound. Carda stood with her mouth hanging open, staring at the pair. Illa held Nigan briefly before releasing him and stepping over to Lebuin. "My Lord, your back needs dusting." Nigan stood where Illa had left him with a glazed look on his face, blinking.

He looks like he's trying to remember how to think.

Lebuin stifled his own laugh and let her dust him off. Ditani and Carda had a second brush which they used to clean each other off. The servants all giggled as they led the horses away. Nigan still hadn't recovered as they started to head into the Guildhouse. Looking over his team, he felt pride that they all looked impressive, not only in style, but in that dangerous air any group of skilled warriors possessed.

I left a new Journeyman and returned the same yet very different.

As they entered the Guildhouse, a matronly looking woman, with salt and pepper hair pulled back into a bun, stood waiting. She wore a sandy dress which was made of a blended weave. It was creased in her lap and elbow areas, showing a lot of time sitting and working at a desk. Over her shoulders, she had a light grey shawl which was likely lama hair. It looked marvelous, and Lebuin had to resist reaching out to feel it. She had a wide belt with a silver buckle, which matched well with the low-cut, brown boots.

I know her. Um, she's Councilor Nillo's secretary. Her name is... Uh... Bodhma. Yeah, that's it, Bodhma.

"Ah, Journeyman Lebuin." As she said that, several apprentices passing looked over all of them, each looking at a different member of his group. All of the boys practically tripped over each other, staring at Illa. The girls had the same reaction to Nigan.

I might as well be invisible, with these two.

Bodhma noticed the distraction and waited. Lebuin nodded and indicated the direction of Councilor Nillo's office. "I presume you are here to direct us to Councilor Nillo's office?"

Bodhma nodded. "Yes, thank you."

Lebuin walked next to Bodhma as they moved through the halls. Several classes were in session. Just before reaching the office area, he heard a familiar, motherly voice lecturing on controlling independent streams of magic. Lebuin glanced in at the class.

Illa and Nigan noted his expression and looked into the classroom. The instructor was Councilor Crawstu, who glared at the party looking in the doorway. "Journeyman Lebuin, is there something you need?" Her tone was cold and reproachful.

The class turned as one to look at him. Lebuin gave his best 'happy to see you' look at the matronly Magus. As one of the students turned to look, his stiff collar folded, revealing the heavy, rough copper chain of a necklace. He wore a well-tailored, thin, cream wool tunic over a blue silk shirt, with a glistening black leather belt. Every stich was even and masterful.

Those are exquisite clothes, and perfectly arranged. Why would someone with such good taste wear such a crude necklace? That necklace has no place with that outfit. He looks about sixteen, at most.

He looked at Councilor Crawstu. "Apologies. I was just reminded of my lessons here."

Councilor Crawstu's frown turned into a small smile. "Yes, well, now, if you'll take your nostalgic memories elsewhere, I'll continue giving instruction on ablative shielding to these students. CLASS!" Her sharp tone snapped everyone back to looking forward.

Taking the hint, they continued into the offices. "Um, Bodhma, who was that student, in the cream tunic with the sea-blue silk shirt, sitting near the middle of Councilor Crawstu's class?"

Bodhma didn't even pause to think. "Ah, that is the son of the Most Honorable Marquis of Cawli, Lord Elan. He came here about a year ago. He is a bright student with a sharp mind, and is very strong with magic."

"Yes, and he has such good taste in clothing, too."

Bodhma rolled her eyes. "Really, he is as bad as you, Lebuin."

Lebuin laughed, but persisted. "Was that copper necklace around his neck his family's crest?"

Bodhma shrugged. "I don't know. He always wears it, even when playing sports or swimming. I don't recall ever seeing him without it. It does have a medallion on it. Not his family crest, though. That is a seabird. That medallion has a cat shape on it."

Lebuin frowned. *I didn't get a good look at that necklace Finnba wore, but I'm pretty sure it was a heavy copper chain with a medallion.*

Illa picked up on his concerns, and her thoughts were also more than a little worried. *'My Lord, that sounds like a Nhia-Samri Magus badge.'*

'Yes, I agree. First thing's first. Let me establish my link to the collector. Then we will look into this. We cannot have Nhia-Samri spies in the Guildhouses.'

It felt wonderful, stepping into Magus Nillo's comfortable office. *As untidy as it is, this place feels so right.* Lebuin took in the shelves filled to overflowing with books stacked all around. All the knickknacks accented the knowledge present. The same three old, beaten-up chairs were right where he remembered. He couldn't help chuckling at the chalkboard, standing to the side, without as much as a speck of dust on it.

Magus Nillo gave him a warm welcome from his oversized leather chair behind the organized chaos of his desk, standing and holding out his hands to Lebuin. "LEBUIN! My Lord, I am pleased to see you."

Lebuin sensed Illa's surprise and glanced back to see all of his companions were staring, awestruck by the size of Magus Nillo. Nillo towered over all of them and dwarfed Lebuin by two hands. The lion's mane of silver hair still stood straight out, looking like a halo that fell down over his head. The pitch-black, perfectly trimmed goatee, was in stark contrast to the silver hair with mountains of muscles. As usual, he was wearing a worn and patched robe over a white linen shirt which sported a set of faded, and one new, arit stains down the front.

Nillo is a memorable figure.

Lebuin took the massive arms in his. "Councilor Nillo, I am very pleased to see you again."

Nillo nodded with a twinkle in his eyes. "I bet you are, boy."

Nillo looked at Bodhma. "I have a lot to talk to Lebuin about. Would you please show his," he looked at the small group, "ah…friends to the dining area for some refreshments?"

The golden magic collector was no longer on display.

Where is the artifact? It has been here forever, and I need to activate my link to it.

He looked around the office, but did not see it anywhere. Concerned, he looked at Nillo, who was smirking at him.

Nigan and Ditani looked at him. *Doubt I need protection here.* He signaled them it was okay.

Bodhma pointed back out another door, and they started

moving. Illa stepped close to him. "Lebuin, I'd like to stay, if you don't mind." Nigan looked over at them.

If she stays, Nigan will want to stay, which means then Ditani will sense something is up and won't want to go.

He looked at Illa. "I'll be fine. Councilor Nillo and I have much to discuss." He also spoke to her mind, *'I'll stay in touch. You know we cannot be separated.'*

Illa frowned, but followed the rest out of the office. The door closed behind them. Nillo motioned to a seat. "Lord, please take a seat. May I offer you some of that fine sharre?"

Lebuin held up his hand, casting an incantation to heighten his senses, and reached out to the surrounding area. There was no one near.

"I would love to have another glass of that. However, first, where is Argos's artifact?"

Nillo continued to smirk. His melodic voice was joyful. "Business before pleasure. You've grown. Come."

Nillo maneuvered around the desk and chairs, indicating a different door which opened by itself. Lebuin followed him through some back hallways until they came to a thick door. Nillo held up his hand and opened the door, stepping through, leaving it slightly ajar. Lebuin could hear some conversations taking place in the room.

Lebuin heard Nillo clearing his throat to the room. "Ah, sorry folks. I need this room to myself for a few minutes."

The sound of chairs moving and some shuffling came from the room. Nillo's voice came again, "Ah, Magus Oraxas, if you please, the hall door."

An unfamiliar voice came from close to the door Lebuin stood behind. "Oh, sorry, Magus Nillo, as you wish." This was followed by footsteps heading away from the door.

After a few more moments, Nillo opened the door, gesturing for Lebuin to come in. Stepping in, he found himself in a room he had never seen before. It was well appointed, with many comfortable chairs and a side board with a selection of liquors and glasses. There were tables and ashtrays around the room. Large stained-glass windows let in some of the afternoon sun. The entire room was wood paneled, with a number of half-full bookcases.

On one bookcase, at chest height, sat the unusual hollow device made of gold, silver, and numerous gems known as Argos's artifact. The filigreed golden lace of the large egg looked like a creeping vine. However, the normally white ball held in the center of the artifact glowed yellow. It wasn't bright; more like a candle, except it did not flicker.

"What is this place?"

"Ah, this is the private Magi lounge. Every Guildhouse has one. This is where the Magi come to relax and avoid students. Many like to read here, while others, so long as they don't snore too loudly, take short naps or just rest and think. Very few Journeymen get to see this room."

Lebuin stepped over to the artifact. The closer he got, the more he could feel warmth coming from it. Not heat, but comforting.

"How much do you know, Councilor?"

Nillo stepped over and rested his hand on Lebuin's shoulder. The weight of that hand was as welcome and comforting as the room.

"I won't claim to know everything. But I know what you have become, who Illa is, and that far more than is fair has been placed on your shoulders."

Nillo's voice was softer than normal and, looking back, he saw that Nillo's eyes were filled with tears.

He has been a second father to me all these years. He knew what was being done and some of why.

A flash of inspiration hit and he knew where the special books had come from. "You gave me those books."

Nillo's face softened. "Cune was the nemesis to distract you. Some of us were your friends to support you. We had to pretend to not see or know. Argos forgive me, I loved you as my own. But I pushed Cune to hit you harder and harder.

And yes, I gave you all those books. Even a useless dandy can still have a store of knowledge. Yes?"

His throat tightened and he couldn't breathe. Eyes blurring with tears, for reasons he couldn't understand, he grabbed the huge man in a tight hug.

"At times I thought no one cared, and I hid in my room crying. Then those notes would come, and I knew someone cared."

Nillo gasped and hugged Lebuin. "Lebuin, we all cared. We all knew what we were doing. We just didn't know why."

They stood like that briefly before Lebuin released Nillo and wiped his face. Nillo was busy wiping his own eyes when Lebuin looked up to him.

"Thank you. Later, I can explain more, and even some things that will make much of this clear."

He reached out and touched the artifact. It felt warm. *I expected it to be cold, like a piece of jewelry.*

Concentrating, he called on his powers and cast the incantation to establish the link with the artifact. As he completed the incantation, he shifted to mage sight and a tendril reached out of the artifact lightly touching his hand. There was a tingling sensation from its touch. Then the tendril extended, sliding up his arm, coming up his shoulder to his throat. There, the tingling became more intense.

In his mind, he heard a voice. *'Argos line confirmed. Provide access key.'*

His heart raced. *Nothing said this thing could talk to me.*
'Incorrect access key.'

He recalled the access key his grandfather had provided. *'Nos obligat pro populo nostro, et pro omni tempore familiam sum Argos.'*

'Access accepted.'

A thin golden thread played out from the artifact, followed by another tendril, both piercing his abdomen painfully. Lights fluttered around him, and the room bloomed as dozens of colors exploded in his vision. Magic flowed through him with such force, his power channels burned. He would have screamed, but his muscles were locked solid and unresponsive. His vision sharpened, and he saw motes of magic flowing around and through the world. Dozens of clouds of magic orbited the artifact in a whirlpool of mana.

The universe became only Lebuin and the artifact. Its tendrils penetrated his flesh as if it was smoke. But they did touch his magic channels like they were soft metal. The golden thread spun out longer and longer, like a spider's web. The tendrils moved quickly, yet it felt like an eternity of agony. Some of his channels were torn out, while others were added or altered to connect in different patterns. The golden thread from the artifact was grafted into his existing magic channels and used to lay new ones.

Without any warning, he snapped back to the real world and the pain receded to a tender burning. He started to collapse. Nillo caught him and lifted him like a child, placing him in a chair. Nillo kneeled before him, holding Lebuin's head in his hands and looking him in the eye.

"Lebuin, breathe, you need to breathe. Hurry, before you pass out."

I'm not breathing?

His muscles were his again, and Nillo was right. Nothing was moving. Concentrating, he forced his lungs to fill. That started many sensations as his body resumed its normal rhythms. With the flow of blood and oxygen, he felt a heaviness lift from his limbs and his body tingled as a leg would if sat on for too long. It was a dizzying moment, which soon passed.

Nillo nodded. "Stay here, don't move." He then left.

He felt Illa's mind calling out for help. He shifted to her. She was lying on the floor, and Nigan was shouting something with a desperate look in his eyes, but her hearing wasn't working.

'Oh, Illa, I am sorry. I didn't know this affected you,

too! Here, let me help. You need to concentrate to start your body again.'

Lebuin forced his way into her mind and helped her get her lungs moving again. The painful tingling was more intense for Illa, as she had been frozen longer than Lebuin had.

As her blood flowed, he felt her love for him warm his spirit. *'Thank you, my Lord.'*

'Argos warned me about this.'

Illa forced her hand, in spite of the tingling, to lift to Nigan's head. She pulled on his hair to get his attention. Nigan looked back down into her eyes. She nodded, and he sighed, his face relaxing, but his forehead remained creased.

'You two are becoming one-minded.'

'Yes, my Lord, I know. Do you wish me to spurn him?'

Lebuin could feel her growing love for Nigan. *'No, I would never deny anyone love. Be careful. You will outlive him.'*

Illa's feelings came through. She was grateful for Lebuin's concern. *'My Lord, none of us may survive what is coming. A moment of joy is a priceless gift to cherish.'*

Lebuin's heart swelled with pride for Illa. *'You sound more like a high priestess every day.'*

'Thank you, my Lord. But if I might ask, what of you? Do you not have feelings for Ticca?'

Before he could stop it, some of his desires for Ticca escaped to Illa, making any attempt at denial useless. *'I do, but she considers me more a brother. I'll consider your advice.'*

Lebuin withdrew back to himself, letting his head lean back in the chair, and closed his eyes.

That was not what I expected. There is a kind of intelligence in that artifact. It has some safeguards. What did it do to us?

He began taking inventory. Some of the magical channels he had built as a student were gone, and many new channels had appeared. A set of channels extended to the end of each finger and toe. New channels, which seemed to have no purpose at all, connected together with his mind like rivers flowing out from a lake.

Someone was squeezing his shoulders.

I don't remember falling asleep.

When he opened his eyes, Nillo was standing there, holding a glass of red liquid. The glass looked familiar, and then he recalled it was the glass Nillo had given him some sharre in.

"Oh, yes! Some of that old sharre you have would be wonderful right now."

A new set of tingling sensations vibrated down the new channels in his fingers as he took the glass.

Am I sensitive to magic now with these new channels?

He brought the glass to his lips and drank the fiery liquid. The pleasant burning spread through him, healing him as it moved through his system. His body tingled with the renewed energy as aches eased and then vanished.

His mind cleared under the restorative powers of the old sharre. "Oh, am I glad you had that!"

Nillo nodded. "Some panicked students and servants ran me down to tell me Illa had collapsed in the dining hall. I looked in and saw she was recovering, so I sent another glass to her. I presume what I saw happening to you affected her, too. Are you okay?"

Lebuin nodded. "Yes, I am okay. Thank you for taking care of us both. I am different now. But I am pretty sure it is a good thing."

Nillo laughed. "I did say you were going to do many surprising things."

Lebuin joined his laughter. "Yes, you did. It seems you can add *prophet* to your long list of titles."

Feeling restored, Lebuin stood and tested his connection to the artifact. There was power, but it wasn't a massive store of power yet. However, there was more than he had when the fight in Algan started.

He looked at Nillo. "Please tell all who are donating magic that Argos is grateful."

"I have, and I will again. Now, what?"

He rubbed his hands together and slapped Nillo on the shoulder. "Now, we try to capture that Nhia-Samri spy in Councilor Crawstu's class."

Nillo looked at him, shocked. "What do you mean?"

"Finnba was a Nhia-Samri spy, and he nearly killed all of us in Algan. He had a necklace which fed him an enormous amount of power from a Nhia-Samri magic source. I believe I saw one on Lord Elan's neck. I need to get close enough to verify it. If he is a spy, he will be more powerful than you can believe. We will need all of the Magi here to contain and capture him."

Nillo pointed at the artifact. "We have been feeding that thing nightly for weeks. Do you have enough to face him?"

Lebuin shook his head. "No. I don't think so. I can withstand him, but the amount of power needed to stop him is more than I have now."

Nillo nodded. "Okay, we'll have to get him alone, and try to protect the other students."

Lebuin thought about it. "How about an achievement award? Get all the Magi in the throne room, and then call him in there."

Nillo laughed. "Yes, that would appeal to his nature."

Nillo made arrangements to assemble the Magi while Lebuin filled his group in on what needed to be done before heading back to the Dolphin. Ditani volunteered to play the servant, to lead Lord Elan to the throne room. Nillo protested, but Lebuin convinced him it would be better than risking a Guild servant. By the time all the preparations were in order in the throne room, Ditani had found, and changed into, a servant's uniform. Approaching the throne room, with Ditani dressed as a servant, felt like a complete replay of the beginning of his new life.

"Don't follow him in. Make sure you close the door behind him, and then get away from it."

Ditani patted him on the shoulder. "Don't worry about me. You just make sure to take care of yourself. You know

Ticca will skin me alive if she finds out we did this without her and failed."

"So long as we have the advantage of surprise, this should go easy enough."

Ditani bowed him into the throne room, closing the doors behind him. Turning, he saw the fifty-odd assembled Magi that were judged fight-ready by Nillo. All of the councilors were there. As he walked up to them, the entire room bowed to him.

Butterflies fluttered in his stomach, and he cleared his throat. "Thank you, all. But I am just your Journeyman."

Nillo straightened. "You will never again be only a Journeyman. You are doing more for us than almost any other Magus in history."

He felt his face burn and his pride swelled, making him feel taller. "Thank you. Now, are we all clear? If we don't knock him out, the most important thing is to keep the ablative shields up. If this turns into a full battle, he'll have more power to control than you have ever witnessed."

Lebuin moved off to the rear and behind a pillar, so he could step in behind Elan when he came in. The Magi arranged themselves as if for a formal ceremony, and then they waited. Everyone concentrated on his or her own powers, preparing incantations to both attack and defend.

Breathe, remember to breathe.

Lebuin measured his powers and prepared his shields.

This time, I won't be dumping raw power around. I can maintain layers easier and with less power. The effect will allow me better defenses.

He also prepared a series of pounding attacks. As he waited, he examined the other Magi, surprised to see he was able to sense who was tied into which mana line. To help pass the time, he took inventory. The Magi had divided up and agreed to which of them would tap into each mana line. If too much power was pulled from a line, it could rupture like a dam breaking, and the results would be dangerous for everyone. With fifty Magi in a fight for their lives, it was possible they could over-extend a mana line. Of course, Llino being set on top of three air lines, a massive water line, two more ground lines, and deep below, a massive fire line, there would be a lot of power available.

Thank the Lords and Ladies, we aren't trying this in Algan. I don't think the few lines there would be enough to hold against the power Elan will have.

The doors opened and Ditani's voice rang out, "Lords, I present Lord Elan of Cawli, Apprentice of the Guild of Argos, and recipient of the Outstanding Achievement in Testing Performance Award."

Lord Elan stepped in, wearing fine white silk pants, tucked into tall shiny riding boots. A medium brown leather belt held a carved, ivory sheath knife with gold chains. The tunic he wore was a deep crimson silk that glistened as he moved. Lord Elan walked past him without looking to the side. Ditani closed the doors. Lord Elan proudly strode up to stand in front of the councilors and bowed.

Nillo's voice boomed out, "Lord Elan, your teachers have been most impressed with your performance."

As Nillo started into the fake speech, Lebuin stepped out to block the exit. His shields extended to cover the doors. He nodded, and the three Magi experts in mind magic spun their incantations to knock Elan out.

A burst of white light from Elan's chest caused all the councilors to raise their hands defensively. Elan spun, throwing his hands out wide, as lightning arced from him to strike the three attacking Magi. They were shielded by others, as well as themselves. Slivers of power flew in all directions as three or four shields fell to the power of the attack.

Elan spun, shouting. "How did you know who I was?" As he turned, he spotted Lebuin. "That whelp of a Journeyman again? Is it you?"

Dozens of attacks rained down on Elan from all sides,

but none penetrated his shields. Lebuin could tell many of those attacks had not been at full strength.

Don't hold back just because he is a child!

Elan started walking towards Lebuin, ignoring the explosions of power around him. "Who are you? How were we wrong?"

Without knowing how, he realized Elan was communicating with someone. He looked and found the channels of magic Elan was using.

"No, you're a pompous fool." Elan smirked and cast another incantation and a ball of mana seared the air, smashing Lebuin's shields to nothing. The remaining force slammed Lebuin into the doors. It wasn't very strong, by that point. He recovered and restored the shields.

All right, gloves are off.

Reaching for the well of power in the magic collector, Lebuin enjoyed feeling the significant level of power he had available. There were forty Magi in the lounge sending as much magic to it as possible, monitoring the battle and mana lines.

This is going to be different from Algan. I won't let you win this one, or warn anyone, either.

Using the knowledge from the forbidden books, he altered the attack incantations to be far more efficient. Pushing away from the door, he raised his hands and started the first series of attacks. The bright stream of fire balls pounded on Elan's shields.

Elan stopped and stared at the stream of fireballs. "You can't be serious." Elan laughed, pointing at the attack.

Lebuin smiled and shrugged. "Well, if one isn't enough..." He then added another, and another, each one different. Elan stopped laughing as the fourth stream was added. The other Magi followed Lebuin's lead and shifted to streaming attacks.

Elan looked around as his shield shrank smaller under the pounding.

While he was distracted, Lebuin examined Elan's

connections. There was the familiar one to the power source. But this time, another one stretched off into the distance.

That is the one I need to end before too much is exposed. Nillo, I need him to take credit.

He looked at Nillo, who was watching him.

Please understand this.

Lebuin made a series of grandiose gestures at Elan, releasing another attack, and then looked at Nillo.

Nillo nodded and his voice rang out, "Elan! You came here under false pretenses! You shall regret that!"

Elan spun, facing Nillo. "You, old fool. You have no idea! Your Guild is useless and easily fooled."

Elan sneered as he unleashed two streams of raw power at Nillo, his necklace glowing. Nillo's shields fell under the onslaught of power. Other Magi jumped in, adding more shields. Many of the Magi were sweating, their jaws set, standing solidly as they fought. However, a number were glancing around, their foreheads wrinkled.

They are getting scared. Good. I don't think they took this threat seriously. Now, while he is distracted...

Lebuin reached out and felt the connection. He formed a shield through it and tried to adjust it to reflect the communications link. Nillo and Elan were exchanging insults and attacks. Many of the Magi were getting tired.

The communication link was resilient, and Lebuin started sweating as he tried to break it. *Come on, break, already.*

The link shattered, and Elan looked around, enraged, yelling, "Why would you care?"

With Elan cut off, Lebuin added more streams of attacks. "Like Finnba, you will never know. Really, it is the Nhia-Samri that are the fools."

Elan spun on Lebuin, his face red. "You dare!"

The necklace flared with power, making the power source it was connected to easy to locate.

He is using a different source than Finnba.

Elan's attacks slammed through the other Magi's shields,

protecting Lebuin before hitting Lebuin's shields with a lot of remaining force. Lebuin felt his shields nearing the breaking point.

I need to know who you are.

An old elven incantation that Kliasa had taught him came to mind. It was a cleansing incantation to strip away other incantations from damaged artifacts.

That might do something interesting here.

Lebuin prepared the incantation and changed his attacks. When all was ready, he yelled, "Now break his shields!"

All of the Magi responded, throwing the most potent attacks they had. Lebuin added everything he could to his own. The power rained down on Elan, who threw up his hands defensively. Elan's shields fell in a cascade of light. Lebuin wasted no time, releasing the elven incantation at Elan.

The incantation hit Elan, and he froze, staring at Lebuin. Elan's face went ashen and beads of sweat were visible on his lips and forehead. His hands quivered, which made him look at them; then his body began to shake. Elan's body shifted, and he looked up with horror and screamed. He grew larger, expanding out to the size of a full-grown, but thin man, ripping his clothes. Elan clawed at the leather belt, screaming. At the same time, his skin shifted to a mottled white. Convulsions racked his body. Before anyone could react, he grabbed his chest, falling backwards, dead. The medallion on the necklace glowed bright red, then snapped in half, causing the necklace to slide off the body, onto the floor, behind his neck as if it was trying to hide.

All of the Magi stepped forward cautiously. Nillo knelt by Elan's head. "This is not Lord Elan. He looks to be from Yalthum."

Lebuin's stomach rolled, and a chill ran through his body. "Where is the real Lord Elan?"

Gracia the Capital of the Duianna Empire

CHAPTER 14

DECISIONS DON'T NEED ALL THE FACTS

TICCA PULLED HER BLENDING CLOAK tight and watched the Night Market merchants—or Hands, as they liked to be called—slowly dwindle in number as the dawn approached.

Two weeks, and no sign of that Hand. He was a regular to the Night Market.

The last few nights, a plan had formed and this clinched it.

We are going to have to go into the Night Market and pay for information on his whereabouts. If anything would get an information specialist's Hand interested in finding me, it would be paying to find him.

The market area was practically abandoned. Ticca scanned for the night's back-up team, Persa and Sabri.

They are getting a lot better.

The eastern sky was already starting to show the telltale signs that the pre-dawn twilight was coming.

I need to get out of here before it gets bright enough; I could be spotted.

She moved slowly, staying in the pockets of darkest shadow, away from the streets. The troughs of the roofs provided good cover. Once she was a few blocks away, at a different alley than the night before, she slid down to the ground. She hugged the wall, letting her cloak cling to her and the wall. She waited, listening and watching for any signs of being followed.

She stayed frozen several minutes longer than when she first started working as a Dagger.

I don't believe I was followed. But then, I didn't think I was followed that night the Knife spotted, tracked, and attacked me.

She knew she was being overly cautious, but this was the Night Market she was spying on. Many powerful and dangerous people were there. *No such thing as too cautious when dealing with killers and worse.*

After the sun had risen, she took one more look around, and then moved out into the main street, merging with the morning merchant traffic. As she stepped out, she pushed the cloak's hood back and flipped its edges back over, making it look like a simple light grey cloak of wool.

As she approached the Blue Dolphin, she relaxed. With a final glance around for pursuers or watchers, she pushed the large door open and stepped into the tavern room. Only regulars were present at this early mark, with the wait staff serving arit with breakfast to most of the occupied tables. Illa was at a table on the far side with her head down over some papers, with two bards. She moved over to her private table, spinning her dagger a few times before placing it flat next to the holder. She sat and leaned back, stretching. She smiled as the serving lad, Ellar, came over with a cup of arit.

Persa and Sabri walked in from the street and started walking her way as Ellar asked, "Miss Ticca. Breakfast?" He didn't make eye contact, and kept looking either at the ground or the room.

"Oh, Ellar, thank you! I'd love it if you brought me some breakfast."

Ellar didn't pause bolting for the kitchens as if on a life and death mission.

Persa and Sabri sat down across from her.

"You know you're going to give that little man a serious heart ache when he figures out the age difference is too much."

Ticca looked at Persa. "Really? I'm his first crush. It's flattering and cute. We all had them."

Sabri leaned on the table. "Yeah, we may have all had them. But really, you are kinda leading the lad on, Ticca."

Ellar came busting out of the kitchen with a platter of food and a glass of milk. He stepped over to the table and served Ticca with flair. "Um, anything for your friends, Miss Ticca?"

She smiled. "Of course. I'm sure you know what they want. You're a bright lad."

Ellar stood taller so fast he almost hopped. "Yes, miss!" He bolted for the kitchen again.

Persa sighed. "Of course, you've found a useful aspect to this."

Sabri looked confused, so Ticca helped her out by pointing at her food, which was roughly twice the normal amount. She added with a wink, "And I get faster service, too."

Persa looked around, then leaned in. "Any hints last night?"

Ticca shook her head. "No, looks like we will have to resort to Plan B tonight."

Persa shook her head. "It's going to be hard to provide support in there."

Ticca grinned. "You two were suspiciously absent last night."

Persa and Sabri beamed. "Well, then, we are getting better, if you didn't spot us. We did lose you when you moved off, which was a huge mistake. Sorry about that."

Ellar returned with two large plates of food and cups of arit. Placing it all on the table, he bowed to Ticca and then left to serve a nearby merchant. Sabri looked at her plate. "Looks like he's trying to impress you by being nice to your friends."

Ticca laughed. "Typical next step for boys."

Persa and Sabri joined her laughter. Then Persa continued, "Seriously, Ticca. A large group in there will not go over well, but I don't want you going alone. You're great, but it would still be risky."

"You're right. I was thinking it might be nice to have magical back-up. What about taking Lebuin?"

Both girls frowned and glanced at each other. Persa voiced it. "Really? You think we should expose him like that? What about Nigan or Risy?"

Ticca laughed. "Lebuin could beat Nigan or Risy easily. You forget, he's able to spar with me!"

Sabri smiled. "You think you could defeat Nigan or Risy?"

Ticca grinned. "Of course."

"Challenge accepted."

Her heart jumped as she spun to see Nigan and Risy standing behind her. "How?"

Nigan smiled as he and Risy pulled some chairs over to join at the table.

"We were waiting for your return, and then made an entrance on the heels of that round merchant over there." He thumbed in the direction of a hefty merchant, ordering his breakfast. "We've all been practicing quiet walking. It takes a lot of getting used to. Now, about that challenge—now or later?"

She could feel the burning of her cheeks. *I must be as red as a radish. Well, I said it. That's what I get for bragging.* "Okay, but after I get some sleep. I'm beat from being up all night."

Nigan nodded. "Okay, afternoon practice, then, by the stables. Sounds fun."

Risy didn't look like he was happy with the idea.

He has been getting far off the last week. I hope he isn't getting sick.

Swallowing the last bite she could, Ticca stood up and put a hand on Risy's shoulder. Risy aborted the bite he was about to take. He looked at her and their eyes locked.

I love his dark brown eyes. They make me feel warm and safe.

Risy's shoulder was muscular, but not bulky, and warm under her hand. He was wearing nicer clothes than when he had first started Daggering, but it didn't matter what he wore. It always looked like he had been sleeping in them for days. She realized this was partly because his clothes were too large for him. He had impersonated Ditani, so he had shaved off his original thick beard. He was keeping that off, but had grown a rather handsome moustache that looped down both sides of his mouth, to his chin, with only a small patch of beard under his lower lip.

A moment passed as she stood, staring at Risy, before he cleared his throat. "You okay, Ticca?"

What am I doing? Get back on track. I must be more tired than I thought.

"Sorry, just thinking. Would you and Nigan please go find Lebuin and let him know I need him to come with me tonight to the Night Market?"

Risy frowned. "With us, right?" His tone made it clear, he didn't like the idea.

She shook her head. "Sorry. A big group won't be accepted there. It will have to be only Lebuin and me. You and Nigan will be one of the back-up teams close by."

Nigan nodded. "Yeah, so we'll go in separately to be close by." He indicated Illa on the far side of the room. "Besides, Illa won't be all that pleased with being left out."

Ticca looked over at Illa.

What would they be buying to let them hang long enough to be useful?

She frowned, trying to think it through. "I'll sleep on that. What is she doing, anyway?"

Nigan glanced over at Illa. "Oh, some workers have been asking for a strange song she and the bards never heard of before. She's been trying to recreate it and the bards like her version. They are still adjusting the harmonics or something like that, I think. She still loves her music."

With a last look at Illa, who was pointing at something on the papers, Ticca felt the night catching up. "Well, she is an amazing musician. I've heard her playing, and it is wonderful. I look forward to hearing this song later."

Reluctantly taking her hand from Risy's shoulder, she grabbed her dagger and spun it around a few times before she sheathed it.

"See you in six or seven marks." She patted Risy's back as she walked off.

* * *

ELECTRA

Electra slipped the silver headband on that let her join Vesta in the Llino control room. As she lay back on the bed, she felt a flutter of joy.

I love everything I have learned. As far as anyone is

concerned, this little marvel might as well be magic. It lets me work with an entity that does not exist physically. It transports my mind to faraway places. Yet Vesta insists, this is not magic. I wonder if all magic is just not fully understood science. Nothing is beyond our reach, if we take the time to gather the knowledge of what and how things work.

She appeared in the control room off to the side. She was surprised to see Arkady was present.

I didn't know he could come here. Well, I guess I should have surmised that. We have gone to Gracia often enough to talk to him.

Vesta was standing with her back straight, arms crossed, and brow furrowed, glaring at Arkady. She was in front of a set of control screens which were monitoring the Nhia-Samri base. Arkady paced back and forth, in the smaller Llino control room, with his eyes narrowed and hands held behind his back.

This looks like an argument between my mother and father! I wonder what is going on. As when she stepped into such an argument at home, Electra held still and watched.

"I have the necessary forces ready to be air-dropped at the edge of the base. I can avoid all their patrols. We can level it before they attack."

Arkady swung his hand in a cutting motion. "NO, absolutely not. You cannot do that! That is an outright violation of the laws, and you know it."

"Arkady, we have the empress's direct order to destroy them. They are planning a massive attack from multiple locations, of which we only know two."

That caught Electra's attention. She had told them about the legendary home fortress city of the Nhia-Samri, Hisuru Amajoo. Vesta and Arkady had been searching for it for weeks. One of the display monitors behind Vesta showed a new image of a valley. Electra stepped over, ignoring Vesta's and Arkady's continuing argument, to look at the display. The valley must be immense. It was on a display next to one showing the base they had been monitoring. Unlike the base view, the people on the new display were only small dots.

The fortress was on such a scale, it took her several minutes to comprehend.

I know legend says it was built by the secretive stone giants. Even if that's not true, I see how that part of the legend came to be. How could one elf lord build that place?

The walls surrounding the valley had to be at least a hundred feet thick at the top, based on the number of dots moving on them. There were two ranks of four by ten dots moving on the top march of the walls. The two ranks moved side by side, one on the inside of the top of the wall, the other on the outside, and there was space for many more such ranks between them. She started counting these groups and stopped a quarter of the way, around 30.

One hundred-twenty ranks of eighty guards, to patrol the perimeter wall!

She felt herself going light-headed at the staggering size that indicated.

The legends are wrong. It is much bigger than anything described!

She looked at the streets of the city and squares of farmland inside the perimeter wall. A main road led through the center of the valley, up to the great fort, which had its own wall half the size of the perimeter wall. The fort looked like it might be a wonder to look on. Dozens of towers and walkways were interconnected with bridges large enough to drive carriages on. As she looked, she did find horses being used on the perimeter and fort walls, and tower bridges.

In a large open area on the side of the fort was a replica of what was at the base they were observing—hundreds and hundreds of barrack-like roofs with drill areas. As she watched, two groups of warriors performed the sudden formation of ranks, followed by trying to push through a narrow opening.

There must be at least seven thousand warriors there preparing for this attack. If they attack the assembly in Gracia, they'll have enough troops to take the entire city! We have nothing that can withstand nine thousand Nhia-Samri!

Her heart raced and her mind spun. *Vesta has to attack now. We need to stop this!*

She turned around. Arkady and Vesta were looking at her. Vesta indicated the new display. "We located Hisuru Amajoo early this morning. It is in an area where any of our little bugs would be instantly identified, and no seabirds ever fly. All we have is orbital surveillance until we figure out something that can get in there for a closer look. I have some dragonflies en route to try and sneak around, but I cannot let them be spotted. The initial count shows an additional ten thousand warriors, all doing the same drills as the base, which has three thousand warriors in preparation. If their mage gates have the twenty percent loss factor we know of, then the assembly will be attacked with not less than eleven thousand Nhia-Samri, which will then be able to establish total control over Gracia. If they have perfected the mage gates, as you suggest, it is much worse. They will be able to seize control of all of the surrounding areas. The entire seat of the Duianna Empire will fall in less than three days."

Holding back tears, Electra's body shook in terror for her friends, family, and home. "All those people hurt or killed. You have to stop them!"

Arkady sighed and shook his head. "Electra, we cannot act."

Her well-trained mind spun around the problem. All of the prior arguments, which she mostly ignored, were based around the fact that practicing for war or killing or fighting was not illegal. *I can't believe Arkady would insist on following the laws so strictly. He was imprisoned unjustly and only released in secret by the illegal acts of his emperor and a talented engineer from my family.*

"But you have Imperial orders! This is an enemy of Duianna; under any definition, this constitutes a clear and present danger. How can you not act?"

Arkady shook his head. "That is the point. Shar-Lumen and probably most of his Nhia-Samri are technically citizens of the Alliance, if not the empire. There has been no formal recognition of the Nhia-Samri as a sovereign entity. Hence, our laws apply. I will point out, this is why Duke is traveling to Gracia at this minute for a vote of the assembly. It is one thing to capture a spy cell-like operation responsible for the death of another citizen. That the members of that cell chose to resist arrest, even though Duke offered them safe passage out, is a local police matter. Duke followed the laws. If the assembly ratifies the war declaration, we will be able to act at that moment."

Vesta shook her head. "Arkady, we have to act *before* that moment. We will not be able to stop them from a mage gate attack fast enough. Also, if we act *at* that moment, we'll be discovered by Duke and the assembly."

Arkady started pacing again. "Vesta, we need a way around all this. The fact that we are awake is a fine line technicality. I am willing to use that to stay awake, and act in secret to help all the races achieve the agreed-to, planned progression, for some kind of stable, self-sustaining, closed-loop society. That is, doing what was agreed to by all, including the assembly and our emperor. This does not mean I am violating the laws or that I will start doing so. At some point in the future we will be judged for our actions. We need to be sure everything we do is within the laws, the spirit of the laws, and the spirit of the original plan!"

He has the power, but he is afraid of taking responsibility.

Electra stepped in front of Arkady and pointed her finger at his nose. "How many will die because of your lack of action?"

Arkady stopped and stared at her. "How many would you have me kill without just warrant?"

Electra wagged her finger at him. "Oh, no, you don't! I will not get dragged into that fallacious argument! You are the Defense Minister of the Empire, just as Duke is the field marshal. You can take action, if you decide to. Yes, you will be called to account for it, as Duke is right now for what he did here. But if it is the right action, you know you will be granted the right retroactively!"

Arkady looked hard at her and then over at Vesta. "She's annoying."

"Only because she is right, and you know you cannot ignore what she is saying."

Arkady sighed. "Let's gather more intelligence, and see if we can come up with some plans." He looked back and forth between the two of them. "If we can confirm they plan to attack Gracia or the assembly, I agree to a preemptive strike. Besides, we need to determine what we can do about Hisuru Amajoo. It is far larger than we expected. Its location makes it almost impregnable, even if we could attack it openly. As it is, it will be nearly impossible to strike at it without revealing ourselves."

We have another cycle before the assembly meeting. I know the Nhia-Samri are going to strike the assembly the moment it decides. That is in line with what Shar-Lumen is known for. He likes dramatic events with surprising victories.

Electra paced and thought. "We have to act in no less than three weeks."

Vesta examined a data pad. "Yes, that will give us time to clean up any evidence of our involvement, before it can be discovered."

Arkady's tone was one of partial defeat. "Agreed. On the intelligence side, how are we doing with the new species?"

Vesta handed him the data pad she had been examining, which flowed smoothly between them.

Oh, Arkady must have established that higher bandwidth link he was working on. We can share data faster now.

Arkady looked at the data. "Another two weeks? That is cutting it kind of tight."

Vesta shrugged. "They are killing every delivery bug

and dragonfly I send. I have only been able to get some intelligence-programmed nanobots into the scouts."

DOHMA

Dohma had risen early, cleaned and dressed in his best. The special light armor provided by Orahda that lay hidden in all of his clothes was barely noticeable. The day before, all of his party had trimmed their hair and beards. This was the day they would arrive in Gracia, the great star of the Duianna Empire and the first city of all the realms. He had made sure to be in a perfect place, near the bow of the ship, to both be seen and to see the coming spectacle.

As the sun started to come up over the horizon, the captain ordered clean standards raised. Above him, he knew the flags of the Alliance and Aelargo were flying. Below those was the flag of the secretary of the Alliance, whose ship this was. Even the sailors wanted to make a good impression, having spent their prior day scrubbing the ship and themselves. Dohma stood proudly as the great city came into view.

All of their preparations seemed a waste. Dohma felt smaller and more rustic the closer they got to the grand city, until finally he was so overwhelmed he stood open-mouthed, staring at the wonder before him. The white pillars of the sea gate rose three hundred feet, from the water line into the air. A filigree-carved vine entwined around them from the base to the ornate, arched mantel that spanned the two hundred feet between them. Two polished silver gates stood wide open, allowing hundreds of ships to pass in and out of the city docks daily. The walls of the capital of the founding empire were the same pure white as those of Llino, except these sparkled in the sunlight. The vast capital city, surrounded by its large walls, sprawled away into the distance, rising in a series of tiers, until encountering the granite pillar at its center.

That pillar is almost four miles away, and yet, it looks close.

I know it is a full mile in diameter. The top of it was leveled for the palace complex.

Atop the granite pillar, a hundred feet above the roof line of its city, sat the grand palace of the Emperor of Duianna. From the spires of the palace could be seen the eight standards of the Alliance members surrounding two other standards flown higher: that of the Alliance, and above all of them, the standard of the Duianna Empire.

Those must be enormous flags to be so clearly seen at this distance.

Behind him, Orahda harrumphed, "This place is too full of itself."

Dohma turned around, looking at his arms master. *Is he joking?*

The look on Orahda's face was one of scorn.

That is the same look he gives to students who are trying to show off, before he takes them down several pegs.

"Llino doesn't even compare to this fine city. How can you say that?"

Orahda bowed to him. "My apologies. No offense intended, but I prefer the simpler elegance of our home, my Lord."

He has gone formal.

His other Dagger guards were all standing at attention, Cundia in the lead. Cundia also bowed to him. "It won't happen again, milord."

Are we already so closely observed?

Orahda made eye contact with him, and then glanced upward to the side of the gate. Turning back around, Dohma again looked on the marvel, except then he was wary. He assessed the flashes of light from atop the walls that were more than sparkling crystals in the walls.

Those are field glasses, inspecting all of the ships. We are being observed, and I was standing there with my mouth open.

He schooled his looks to be bored and leaned against the rails while he continued to marvel at all he saw.

A port navigator met them as they passed through the sea gates. In little time, the ship had been moored at a central dock that communicated with a long road that stretched straight, off into the distance, towards the palace. Two large carriages and a clean baggage trap were waiting as the plank was lowered. Porters ran up the ramp and dove into the luggage holds, disturbing a group of seagulls that had been resting on the pier. A pure white seagull cried a complaint as it jumped out of the way. It flew to the top of a nearby post and then watched them reproachfully.

The captain escorted Dohma down the ramp. At the base of the ramp, surrounded by assistants and servants, was a regal-looking gentleman dressed in a military-looking green silk coat. On his chest were five rows of military ribbons and medals. Gold bars rested on his shoulders with the customary golden rope loops dangling down his arm and shoulders. On the stiff collar were four gold stars in a circle.

A senior general is meeting me. I hope this is as much a sign of respect as I feel it is.

The captain stood tall before the general and saluted him. The general returned the salute and looked at Dohma.

The captain motioned. "Your Most Honorable Lord General Edugan Dumelu Neyon, Count of Waylisia, Imperial General of the Cavalry of the Duianna Empire, it is my distinct pleasure to introduce His Excellency, Lord Dohma Uriosal, Chief Regent of Aelargo."

The general came to attention and saluted. "SIR."

The blood rushed from his head and he felt a sudden knot in his stomach.

My Lord, this is Electra's grandfather!

For a moment, he forgot he was supposed to acknowledge the salute, but the blood flowed and he came to attention and saluted back. "Count Neyon, thank you for the honor."

The general finished his salute.

I think I can make this friendlier.

He stepped towards the general, extending his hand. "I

am pleased to meet you, sir. I didn't realize Countess Electra was married! She is very efficient, and I would not be here without her prompt attention to detail."

It worked. He saw the pride glisten in the general's eyes and the slight straightening of his back.

A double compliment well received, both that his granddaughter is efficient and that he looks young enough to be her husband, rather than her grandfather.

The general's face cracked like the granite pillar behind him, removing the frown. "Ah, I am married, and only have one son. You speak of my granddaughter. Thank you, sir. She makes this old soldier very proud, as her father does. I have abdicated my role as Count of Waylisia in favor of my son. However, as you know, the title remains emeritus. Please call me Edugan or General Neyon in formal company."

Dohma kept his tone one of sudden understanding. "Ah, I see. A natural misunderstanding, I am sure." He then half turned to face both the general and his party behind him. "Allow me to introduce my party. These are my trusted advisors and guards. First is the Most Honorable Lady Cundia Santalg of Cawli, Dagger in service to Aelargo, head of my personal guard, and my privy councilor." The general and Cundia exchanged curt soldier nods.

"This is her second, the Most Honorable Lord Orahda Ima of Carda, my second privy councilor."

The general looked at him. Dohma saw the look of recognition and shock in the general's expression.

Of course. You met him before, during the war.

The general coughed. "Orahda, is it? Well, a pleasure to meet you."

Orahda didn't show any unusual sign and bowed to the general. "My pleasure, General."

"The other four are Kyra, Arford, Tenby, and Thenia, my personal guards and Daggers in service to Aelargo."

The general looked over the seven of them and nodded. "Very impressive, using Daggers for both guards and councilors. I have a lot of respect for Daggers. Now," he said, gesturing to the carriage, "allow me to escort you to the palace."

ELECTRA

Electra wiggled in excitement as she watched the carriages being loaded while Lord Dohma, Lady Cundia, and Lord Orahda spoke with her grandfather at the docks. Her body didn't want to sit still, she was so happy. She spun around in the chair, jumping out of it to do a little dance, hopping from one foot to the other and giggling.

Vesta looked over from the monitors and controls she was working on. "The meeting between your grandfather and Lord Dohma went well?"

Electra spun in a circle. "I can't believe it! My grandfather smiled at him—well, as close to a smile as he gives anyone in public. Oh, that is a good sign."

"Your grandfather's opinion matters that much to you?"

Electra stopped spinning. "Yes. He isn't the most agreeable man to live with, but he has a good heart and is an excellent judge of character. I don't know why I am so attracted to Lord Dohma, but if my grandfather likes him, it makes my heart all the lighter."

"Yes, but this isn't a fair meeting, is it? Dohma knew who your grandfather was, but your grandfather couldn't know who Lord Dohma really is."

That gave her pause. She stopped spinning and frowned. Thinking out loud was easier than thinking silently, so she thought out loud. "Yes, well, my grandfather would have started off with a bad opinion of him, and he would have had to climb up out of that hole. Now, he starts off even-footed and my grandfather's opinion will go up or down over the next few weeks. My father will form his own opinion as well, but my father often looks to my grandfather for advice on people. Lord Dohma will be observed, even when he doesn't know it. My grandfather and father will be watching everything he, and all the other Alliance representatives, do. I think that will result in a fair assessment. Only this has a better chance, because my father won't be judging him as a possible son-in-law. That will come later." That seemed to make it all clear, and she nodded once to underscore her sound reasoning.

Vesta chuckled and then turned back to the complex work she was doing, creating some new support creatures. But then she looked back at the monitors behind Electra.

Vesta stood and shouted, "ARKADY!"

Electra spun around to see what disaster could have alarmed Vesta so. All that was there was the palace guardsman closing the carriage door. She could see her grandfather and Lord Dohma were seated, facing front.

Arkady appeared, looking worried. "Why did you use that signal?"

Vesta pointed at the monitors, and Arkady turned to look. The display shifted to a still image of Lord Orahda stepping into the carriage.

Arkady's hand went to his beard and gave it a hard tug, his eyes narrowing. "Impossible! He's dead!"

❧ LEBUIN ❧

Lebuin pulled the cloak tighter around him. He had shields once again, but he still felt vulnerable, especially considering where they were heading.

I never thought I'd be voluntarily walking into the Night Market!

His heart was racing and his feet were cold as ice. He glanced at Ticca, who was strolling next to him.

How can she look so calm, walking into this place? She, better than anyone, should know how dangerous this is. She has been watching the activities here for weeks.

Ticca whispered, "Lebuin, straighten up and get control. You're supposed to be the rich buyer here. I'm just the hired protection. Right now, you look like you're about to die of fright."

He concentrated, seeking comfort in his mage training. Calming his system, he forced his breathing to be slow and regular. He pushed the fear away and found he could hold at an almost trance-like state that kept his emotions in check. "Is this better?"

Ticca's head snapped around and she looked at him. "Wow, that was perfect. You sound cold and uncaring."

"I *am* cold and uncaring."

She looked at him, her eyes narrowed.

"I'm using my training to suppress my feelings."

She nodded. "It's working better than you know."

The sun was already gone from the sky as they approached the entrance to the Night Market. It was a gateless, arched opening in a tall wall that surrounded the market area with no other entrances. The archway was just large enough to allow a carriage through on either side of a statue, which stood in the center of the entry.

That statue looks familiar.

As he examined it, it moved. In spite of his tight control, his heart skipped a beat. The statue had shifted from a maiden in a summer dress, holding a shopping basket in the crook of her right arm, her left hand held out as if inviting people in; to holding the basket tightly to her chest, her hand held up as if warning people off.

What is that about?

Ticca ignored it and kept moving towards the entrance, so he followed her lead and kept moving. As they got closer, he realized why it looked familiar.

Lords and Ladies, that is Kliasa!

He shifted to mage sight and examined the statue. It was magical. In fact, it was infused with an even distribution of magic.

This is identical to the small statue in Magus Vestul's workshop. He made this statue and put it here. Why?

Grabbing Ticca's arm, he stopped her. Maintaining his cold lack of emotion was helping a lot. He could feel his emotions would be running more wild, if he hadn't been using the semi-trance state to hold them in check. "Ticca, that is Kliasa."

Ticca's eyes narrowed at him, and then she turned to look at the statue again. "You're right! I haven't given it much thought since I learned what she looked like."

"Do you think we should proceed?"

She motioned with her eyes toward the shadowy guard just inside the entrance. "We should not turn and walk away now."

He looked at the lurking figure. "Very well." He adjusted his hood so his face was in the dark, except for his chin and mouth, then stepped towards the entrance. The sun had set, so he activated his enhanced vision incantation. The world snapped into sharp clarity as the incantation allowed him to see as well as an owl and hawk combined. There were a lot more people than he thought in the Night Market area, almost all of them moving and hiding in the shadows. Ticca followed him in the proper hired guard position.

As he walked past the statue, the shadowy figure spoke out, his voice gritty like the street. "Yer new. Who are ya?"

He stopped and looked at the figure. "None of your business."

I'm surprised that this state affects me so much. My tone would scare almost anyone.

"Right ya are, gov. I jus' wanted ta let ya know da rules."

Lebuin sneered. "I know them."

Time to be dismissive, I think. He stepped past the guard and walked on without looking back. *This is going to give me nightmares, I'm sure of it.*

Once inside, he looked around.

Ticca said any information merchants—or 'confidences Hands,' as they are called—will be very well-dressed.

None of the Hands present were dressed well enough, so he walked to a vacant, dark spot a short distance inside the gate, where they could wait for the right kind of Hand to arrive.

Ticca hung close to him. "There should be one coming soon, sir."

Lebuin didn't acknowledge her chatter, as if it was below him. Instead, he stood with the air of someone you should not approach.

Nonetheless, someone came at him from behind, breaking his detection circle. He spun to face the attacker. Ticca was already on the move; she had two knives out and kicked the person hard enough that he fell backwards. She started to move in to slice the assailant's throat.

No, I don't want to kill people. How can I stop her? Inspiration came.

Lebuin held up his hand. "No need for that right now. I'm not paying for random assassinations."

Ticca looked at the fallen man a second with steely eyes before sheathing her knives.

"You're paying," she spat out, as if disappointed.

Turning, Ticca sauntered back to her original position, seeming to pay absolutely no attention to the assailant, who scurried away as fast as a cockroach caught in the light.

He scanned the nearby area with his enhanced vision to confirm they were alone before whispering, "Are we established now?"

Ticca whispered back, "Somewhat. There will be another attack if we wait much longer without doing any business. Thank you for that masterful stop order."

"Would you really have slit his throat?"

"If I didn't, we would be marked, and it would be a hard fight to get clear."

It felt like an eternity, to stand waiting for what they sought. A dignified Hand strode through the entrance as if he owned the whole place. He was wearing a red, velvet-lined, black cape over a well-tailored doublet which looked like an embroidered dark green silk in the light of the torches by the entrance. The torches' flames danced on his highly shined leather boots with silver buckles. The gold chain with fob in his doublet pockets completed the look.

Ah, that looks about right. Slowly! Don't jump at him, but stroll towards him.

Lebuin stepped out from his shadowed location, using every bit of grace he could muster, angling to intercept the Hand. He felt the Hand look him over, judging him worthy or not. As they came close, the Hand stopped and nodded.

"Ah, milord. Pray, whatever could have brought you here this wonderful evening?"

Lebuin held his response as Ticca had instructed him, before taking a step towards the Hand, closing the distance. Still not close enough to provide an intimate conversation, but closer. Lebuin stood tall.

I'm glad for my discipline training.

His voice dripping with disregard for any but himself, Lebuin answered, "I'm looking for a man. However, he seems to be late."

The Hand looked at Ticca, then stepped in close enough for the conversation that would constitute proper business in the Night Market. The Hand responded, "Perhaps I might be of assistance."

He took his time while examining the Hand's appearance. The gold chain with a fob hanging from his doublet buttons was thick and rich. The doublet was a fine silk with an expertly stitched pattern of geometric shapes running through it. It was seamed well, so that the pattern was not mismatched on the edges.

He is wearing at least twenty crowns' worth of clothing, and that fob chain is real gold. He must be highly placed, to be able to walk here, showing off these kinds of valuables.

The Hand did not protest the close inspection, and was doing the same to Lebuin. The Hand looked back at Lebuin's face, trying to pierce the darkness of his hood.

Lebuin knew he had him. *I'm wearing at least a full ten*

crowns more than you, and you know it. You really want to know who I am, don't you? Time to run the gambit we planned.

Lebuin nodded as he extended his shields to cover Ticca, as well, but keeping them close to him on the side of the Hand so the Hand wouldn't bump up against them.

"Yes, I believe you might be just the person. I am looking for the Confidences Hand who intercepted a leather package tied with golden threads. He did this by bribing a Knife. The exchange was here, fourteen weeks ago, on a Martidi evening. The Knife, unfortunately, did not reveal who the Hand was, only where they met, and is no longer available for questioning."

The Confidences Hand's eyes went wider.

Ah, you know who I am looking for.

"I believe you may be in error, milord. Knives do not betray a commission."

Lebuin waved his hand. "I am not stupid. You know exactly of what I speak. Now, how much do you desire to reveal your knowledge?"

The Hand took a step backwards. "Milord, you are mistaken. How would I know of such things?"

Ticca hissed a warning as six arrows bounced off his shields. Lebuin locked the Hand in place with magical bindings and spun, pulling his knives. Ticca had already drawn her own blades. Four shadows were approaching, knives out.

"You have a mage with you!" the Hand whispered with a hint of fear.

The shadows, seeing the arrows bouncing off the shields, paused. Ticca gestured for them to continue to get closer. Some of the other patrons and Hands were starting to take notice.

We have a reputation to uphold. Might as well keep these folks scared of us.

Lebuin stepped up to the Hand and placed his knife at the man's throat. "Not exactly correct. I *am* a *Magus*, and I do not take kindly to being shot at."

The Hand waved off his companions, who vanished back into the market areas. The Hand was sweating. "Milord, perhaps I can help you, after all."

Lebuin looked around. Ticca was scanning. Not too far away, he saw Nigan and Risy were moving into position to provide additional support. "I'm listening."

The Hand slowly reached up and gently pushed the knife away from his throat, swallowing hard. Lebuin allowed the action, then after seeming to consider it, sheathed the knife. The Hand smiled a hollow smile. "Your, ah, friend has not been seen for three weeks. But I can get word to him that you are looking for him."

I know he can't see my face, but he can see my mouth.

Lebuin let his mouth open into a toothy grin.

"Why didn't you say that in the first place? Tell him if I have to come to him, it will not be pleasant. He can reach me at the Mosia Tavern. Leave a message for Goninu with the barkeep. I will meet him there four marks later. He has three days to meet me. And he had better have that package! If he does not respond, I will be back, and I will not be happy."

Lebuin pulled five silver crosses from his pouch and pressed them into the Hand's palm, adding, "For your troubles." Turning, he strode for the exit.

As they passed the exit, the shadows said, "Your pleasure, milord."

Lebuin didn't stop moving. He strode with a purpose, taking many turns seemingly at random, until they arrived at the prearranged rendezvous point. Turning, he looked at Ticca as Nigan and Risy came from a side alley.

Nigan whistled. "Wow, that was a hell of a performance. I doubt anyone in the Night Market will even cross your path without permission."

Oh, my Lords, how did I do that?

Since he was clear, he started to relax and couldn't hold the trance state any longer. All the emotions he had been suppressing rushed him like a mob. He felt the blood drain from his head as his heart raced so fast, it felt like it was going to explode. His knees stopped holding him up, and he felt light as a welcoming blackness enveloped him.

TICCA

Ticca was trying to control her breathing, as Lebuin went pure white and then started to fall backwards. Nigan was already there and caught him. Her own head was spinning from that narrow escape.

Lady, he really pulled that off.

Nigan looked at Lebuin lying on the ground. "I think he passed out."

She nodded. "I wish he had held that trance until we were back at the tavern."

Risy frowned. "Trance?"

"He used some kind of mage trance to hold himself together in there."

Nigan laughed. "Great. And now, I get to carry him home. Wasn't this supposed to be the other way around?"

Hiri-Rula vs. Warlord Eshra-zunia

CHAPTER 15

FOOLING A HAND USUALLY ENDS BADLY

TICCA SAT ACROSS FROM LEBUIN, watching the main room of the Mosia Tavern. In her mind, she reviewed the positions of her team. Ditani was on the roof across the street, wearing a blending cloak she got from her uncle to provide recon, if needed. Nigan and Risy were roaming the street outside like idle shoppers, flipping their cloaks and trading hats, or just hiding their hats from time to time.

I bet they are loving this. I feel like I have a whole flock of butterflies bouncing around inside.

Around the room, she was able to make out the rest of her team, all playing varying roles in their disguises.

I wish I could have played the passed-out drunk. That would be a lot less work. Then she chided herself. *No, this will be more exciting.*

She checked that her lined gloves were tight, and tried not to fidget.

I need to project an air of danger as his bodyguard.

Her clothes were a little loose, but at least, not too hot. She had on a rough tunic with a vented leather, armored vest. She enjoyed the thought about the cross belt of knives she had on over her breasts.

I wanted to use this look and I was right. It does look a little showy, but in a 'don't mess with me' style.

Her thug look was completed by the thin black-hooded cloak.

She regarded Lebuin.

He looks too relaxed. Lady, please let him keep from passing out again.

She leaned over and whispered, "Are you using that trance trick again?"

Lebuin didn't move. All she could see was his mouth, as he had his hood pulled over to hide his face, just as she did. His mouth drew up into a smile.

"Promise me you are not going to pass out this time."

The smile turned into a frown, which made her smile before she regained control of her face, going back to the hardened lip line of a thug. Lebuin was dressed in some of his finest, along with the shadow cloak Lebuin had taken from the Knife she had killed at the beginning of all this mess.

The tavern was full that evening, even without her team there.

I'm glad it took two days before that Hand sent a message. Lebuin, at least, looked recovered last night.

A tall man with dark, clean-cut hair and a respectable goatee walked in, wearing at least a week's pay for any guildsman. She recognized him instantly.

There you are.

The man looked around and wiped his brow with a cloth.

You knew who you double-crossed all along. It's no wonder, you were hiding. Even though Duke cleared the city, you were worried they'd come for you. Well, tonight, your fears come true.

The Hand stepped up to the bar and ordered a drink. When the barkeeper gave it to him, he leaned in and whispered something. The barkeeper pointed at the table she and Lebuin were sitting at. The Hand touched his hat and handed the barkeeper a coin.

The Hand stepped over to the table. "Lord Goninu?"

Lebuin pointed at an open seat, which the Hand sat in, examining the rest of the barroom's occupants.

"Milord, I understand you are looking for a parcel. I have brought it with me." He reached into his cloak and then placed a brown paper-wrapped package that looked about the right size on the table.

Lebuin's uncaring voice was perfect. "Good."

Lebuin lifted a finger, and the package slid over to rest in front of him.

The Hand's eyes kept glancing around the room. They all sat there for a minute while no one moved.

The Hand sipped his drink. "I trust it is acceptable."

Lebuin flicked his finger again, and the string holding the paper together snapped. In his quiver-inspiring voice, Lebuin asked, "What is your name?"

The Hand swallowed some more of his drink. "Alansir, milord."

"Alansir, you know who you betrayed. That is why you've been hiding."

Alansir sipped his drink, trying to look confident. "I deal fairly, milord. I trust we can be business associates in the future."

Lebuin frowned, and Ticca pulled the cloth bag from her pouch which she had taken off the dead Knife the night their journeys together started. The same cloth bag filled with the same jewels she saw Alansir pay for the journal with.

I'm glad we were in the wilderness so much. I would have been tempted to spend some of these.

The purse still contained the same kingly sum that had caused a senior Knife to betray his commission.

Trying to exude deadliness, she brought the pouch up, where Alansir could see it. She opened it and poured its contents into her other hand.

Alansir's eyes bulged, and he went white. *You recognize it.* She replaced the small bag into her pouch, leaning forward just enough to make it look like she might draw a knife and stab him.

Lebuin leaned forward, showing his teeth. "Alansir, who commissioned you to intercept our package?"

Alansir's pupils dilated and his hand quivered.

Perfect. He bought it. He thinks we represent the Nhia-Samri that hired the Knife to kill Magus Vestul.

"I, uh, I really don't know."

"Knowing is your business, Alansir. Care to reconsider your answer? You know who we are."

Alansir swallowed a few times and gulped air. Adjusting his collar, he wiped his forehead again with the cloth. "I mean, I don't know for sure. However, I am pretty sure it was the representative of a duchess who was visiting that week."

Lebuin didn't respond, but sat still, looking at Alansir.

Alansir swallowed and continued, "Duchess Yillion Vransril Olmanna. It was one of her retainers. I'm sure he was working on her orders."

Ticca snapped straighter and stared at Alansir.

Duchess Olmanna? The duchess that kept feeding us shaved ice and pastries? He can't know we know her personally.

Alansir jumped at her movement, looking back and forth between the two of them. "I swear it, it was her guard captain."

Lebuin nodded as if that confirmed something. He then gave her the all clear by causing the package to slide across the table to her.

Ticca forced herself back into the drama. *Figure out the details later. It's my turn now? Okay, it isn't magically trapped.*

Ticca pulled a knife out and with dramatic, precise motions, spread the outer wrapping paper, exposing a stiffer paper wrap around the core of the parcel. She sniffed.

I don't smell any chemicals. But that doesn't prove anything.

It would require using her hands to pull the folded and tucked sleeve of the inner wrappings to open them. Sheathing the knife, she unwrapped the parcel enough to look inside, making sure to only touch the paper with the tips of her left gloved fingers. There was a familiar leather journal tied tightly closed with thick, golden threads.

This is it. Vestul's journal—and it hasn't been opened.

Drawing a knife with her right hand, she used the sharp blade to cut a piece of the inner wrapping paper from the journal. She placed that paper in front of her on the table.

Alansir's face broke out with sweat as she did this, and he was making sure to not look at the cut paper.

You are not used to being on this end of the deal, are you? Anyone would be curious about this action and look at the paper with interest. That you are not, tells us volumes. You are trying to double-cross us, too. Okay, let's see where this goes.

Ticca did not push the package towards Lebuin, which was their not clear signal.

Lebuin shifted to face Alansir directly, holding out his hand as if to shake. Alansir smiled and reached out to shake hands. Lebuin moved fast, grabbing Alansir's hand by the wrist and pushing it down on the table hard, palm up.

Alansir was sweating, and his palm was wet and shivered with fear. Ticca picked up the cut piece of paper and placed it on his hand with the inner surface, which faced the journal, touching his palm. He didn't flinch.

He looked back and forth between them with horror. "Milord! I would not dream of poisoning you."

Lebuin coldly replied, "We didn't suggest poison. Why would you deny it?"

Lebuin, still holding Alansir's hand to the table, lifted his other hand and wagged his finger at the Hand. Lebuin pointed at Alansir's hand, causing Alansir to look at it. The slip of paper jumped up, flipped over, and landed on his palm so fast, he couldn't react. All the blood drained from his face as he stared at it.

Ticca couldn't resist. *Oh, he deserves this!*

She reached over and pressed it down hard into his sweating palm.

Lebuin released Alansir's hand as Alansir whimpered.

Lebuin let his voice drop, sounding disappointed. "You failed, Alansir. I was going to pay you for this. However, I believe you need to seek an antidote. If you live, I suggest you consider moving to a colder climate. This city will be too hot for you."

Alansir stood, knocking down his chair, and rushed out the door.

Ticca looked at Lebuin and whispered, "Between the two layers of wrapping. We will be followed. But don't worry. We'll let the team take care of them. Shall we go?"

Lebuin stood. She stood as well, and using her body,

blocked the rest of the room from seeing as she reached down with her right gloved hand, which had not touched the dangerous side of the paper, and extracted the journal. She placed the journal on the table and stripped off her gloves, being careful to not touch where they may have come in contact with the poison. She placed the gloves on top of the wrapping paper.

Twisting the selector on her pouch to an empty compartment, Ticca slid the journal in. It fit perfectly, which didn't surprise her.

Magus Vestul made this pouch to carry the journal. I am sure of that.

Closing her pouch, she moved the selector back to the compartment with her fake journal and the coin purse with a few copper pence in it, and locked the rocker so the selector wouldn't move by accident.

Lebuin gestured, and her gloves and the wrapping paper lifted off the table, compressing into a tight ball that burst into a bright blue flame. In a few seconds, only ash remained, which dropped into Alansir's half-empty mug.

Lebuin used his normal voice as they left. "You know, I enjoyed that."

"Me, too. It is about time someone gives some fear back to these Night Market Hands. By the way, you said you had some thoughts on that statue of Kliasa?"

Lebuin nodded. "It is a strange thing to put there. From Vestul's notes, it isn't really a statue; it's a physical reflection of her essence. It is identical to that small one I showed you in the tower."

"You mean it *is* Kliasa? How can that be? Vestul wouldn't be so cruel as to trap someone frozen like that, especially Kliasa. And you know as well as I, she is not trapped."

Lebuin shook his head. "No, it isn't her. But in a way, it is. I need more time to explore the idea. I couldn't find much more than references to what he did at the tower."

Why would Vestul put a reflection of Kliasa in front of a market? This makes no sense.

HIRI-RULA

Hiri-Rula sipped her tea as she reread the outpost history book's chapter on the original founding two thousand years ago.

Nothing, absolutely nothing, about that power source.

She leaned back and looked at the wall of books next to her.

Over two thousand years of Nhia-Samri history with no mention of when the new odassi blades began to be used, or any mention of this magical power source. I know the contents of my outpost's library, as well, and there is nothing there.

She caressed the hilts of her ancient odassi blades. *What are you, really?*

No answer came. That was expected. She had been asking those same questions since arriving there. The warlord had granted her permission to investigate the power source. It wasn't long afterward that she discovered she could open the panel with a spoken command, the same as the warlord.

I wonder if I could have opened the panel before Eshra-Zunia granted me permission. Is something down there monitoring us and doing as commanded?

Someone cleared his throat. She turned to see the warlord's privy command sergeant major there. "Yes?"

"Colonel Hiri-Rula, Warlord Eshra-Zunia commands your presence."

I wonder what she needs.

Hiri-Rula stood up and put a slip of paper into the book, setting it down on the table. Turning, she stepped out into the hall, letting the command sergeant major escort her. He did not go the direction she expected. He took her through the halls, coming out at the far end of the long main hallway, to the throne room.

What is he doing? We could have entered the throne room through the side doorway near the library.

As they marched together past the armor and weapons of long-dead enemies, she noticed the far end of the hall was lined with warriors.

This looks like a trial. Am I to be punished for losing the outpost to our new enemy?

The command sergeant major marched in precise time, and she matched him, following two steps behind. The warriors lining the hall were all colonels. As she came to the throne room, the rank went up to generals. All ten generals were standing at attention, five on each side of the throne room, making an impressive hallway of warriors. The table that normally sat in front of the warlord's throne was missing.

The command sergeant major stopped before the warlord, who sat in full battle armor, stiff-backed in her throne. The light played on the glistening, red ceramic plates of Eshra-Zunia's armor.

This is serious.

Hiri-Rula came to attention and waited. The warlord nodded to the command sergeant major, who bowed and did a 90-degree right turn, taking two steps before repeating the maneuver, and marched back behind her. She could hear that he made it to the edge of the room before stopping and doing an about face.

Warlord Eshra-Zunia waited a moment longer, then stood, like a snake preparing to strike.

"Colonel Hiri-Rula, defend yourself."

Eshra-Zunia leapt at Hiri-Rula, her odassi already drawn, as if by magic.

Adrenaline flowed, as well as power from her blades, as Eshra-Zunia leapt. Hiri-Rula flipped herself backwards, doing two reverse summersaults, as fast as she could. As she snapped back up, she drew her own odassi. Eshra-Zunia was already on top of her. The four blades rang out and sparks flew as they exchanged a half-dozen strikes and counter-strikes.

The generals that lined the room all stepped backwards in precise unison, opening the room. The adrenaline was flowing full force, and time slowed as Hiri-Rula's perceptions and abilities magnified. She pulled on her magic and fed her blades power. They were exceptional weapons, and she managed to push Eshra-Zunia back.

Eshra-Zunia stepped back, but she pushed right back. Her hands became a blur of speed. Hiri-Rula felt a loop of energy form between her and her blades. She had never fought so hard or so fast before. Yet she controlled her breathing, giving her body the oxygen it needed. The ancient odassi blades gave her strength and speed beyond anything she had experienced.

Eshra-Zunia did not give ground and pushed her back towards the wall.

A feeling of warning was all she had. She swung as hard as she could at Eshra-Zunia, striking with so much force, Eshra-Zunia was forced to brace in order to maintain her stance. At the same instant, Hiri-Rula dodged to the left as a new pair of blades cut the air where she had just stood.

One of the generals had drawn, so Hiri-Rula had to fight two.

I can't deal with two opponents. I need to remove one of them fast.

She took in the new attacker.

It's General Dumua-Acas. His left leg is weak from an old injury. That she knew that was a surprise, but there was not time to ponder how she knew that weakness.

She ducked under Eshra-Zunia's strike, dropping flat to the floor, kicking out at General Dumua-Acas. She made contact, and he grunted in pain as he fell backwards. Eshra-Zunia twisted and brought her blades down in an arched attack that would have cut Hiri-Rula in half if she hadn't rolled away, snapping back to her feet.

Why are they trying to kill me?

Hiri-Rula thrust at Eshra-Zunia, who managed to twist

enough that her blades only scratched the armor. A series of gasps came from around the room.

Again, she felt another general, Armio-Ery, was jumping into the fight. *He is a strong fighter but with little imagination. Something unexpected is needed.* She spun backwards, around Armio-Ery's attack, and kicked his back, throwing him into Eshra-Zunia. Eshra-Zunia batted Armio-Ery away like he was paper.

Eshra-Zunia dove at Hiri-Rula in a strike that would run her through, ending this. She was off-balance from handling General Armio-Ery, with nowhere to go.

Her instincts screamed at her. *NO!*

Power flowed and she bent backwards like a reed, letting the thrust flow over the top of her. She twisted and spun, kicking at Eshra-Zunia's exposed arm. Making contact, Eshra-Zunia's arm swung widely, forcing Eshra-Zunia to twist around. But Eshra-Zunia was amazing. She turned that into a new thrust.

Hiri-Rula barely managed to move aside from the attack, but that brought her close to two other generals: Enon-Anos and Ilil-Ushual. *Anos is very strong but slow and is not rooted properly.* Her heightened senses warned her in time, and she dropped to the ground again in a sweeping kick that threw Enon-Anos into Ilil-Ushual. Bringing both feet under her, she leapt with all her might, up and backwards, over Eshra-Zunia. As Hiri-Rula passed overhead, she brought her odassi down in a strike that would have killed Eshra-Zunia, but Eshra-Zunia managed to get her blades up, blocking the attack and causing brilliant sparks to flash.

Hiri-Rula landed gracefully and started to step in, when Eshra-Zunia spun and yelled, "ENOUGH!"

Hiri-Rula froze, her blades already half into the strike. She and Eshra-Zunia faced each other, blades frozen. The warlord straightened up and brought her odassi together in a warrior's salute to her.

What was this all about?

Breathing hard, she straightened and saluted back. Still, she waited and sheathed her blades in perfect unison with the warlord.

Generals Cyni-Ege and Enon-Anos were helping General Dumua-Acas to stand back up. Dumua-Acas's leg was broken. Once Dumua-Acas was standing on one foot, they released him. All of the generals drew their odassi and saluted her.

The warlord looked around. "Is there any further debate?"

Three of the generals—Enon-Anos, Nuta-Toyi, and Mina-Jabu—looked down at the floor in humility and shook their heads 'no'.

The warlord stepped back to her throne and sat down in it. She then pointed to a place at her right. "Hiri-Rula, stand here."

That is the second in command's place!

She hesitated, then stepped to where the warlord was pointing. The edge of the warlord's mouth turned up and she nodded at Hiri-Rula.

Facing the room, the warlord said in a strong voice, "Hiri-Rula is named general of Outpost One. General Hiri-Rula is second in command and my direct successor. She speaks with my voice."

All of the generals and officers from the hall stepped into formation and dropped to their knees, drawing their odassi, and holding them out in a cross before them, as they bowed their heads. In a single voice, they called out, "I AM YOURS TO COMMAND!"

I'm the second in command! This was to prove my abilities were second only to the warlord's...but I think I could have beaten her. And how did I know all those weaknesses? I have only met these generals once or twice.

She noticed the general with a broken leg had fallen to his knees, in spite of the broken leg.

She couldn't help it. "Take care of General Dumua-Acas's injuries immediately."

Generals Nuta-Toyi and Mina-Jabu jumped up and

helped General Dumua-Acas limp out of the room. As they left, she noted a number of warriors looked at her with pride, and a few of the generals were giving her an approving look.

Well, my first command as second is one of mercy.

The warlord gestured, and the room was restored, the large table being brought out from a side room.

The warlord looked at her. "General Hiri-Rula, when we attack Gracia, you will lead the second division that is to hold this outpost against counter-strike. You are now responsible for overseeing the drilling and scouting. I have chosen the five hundred warriors I will lead as the arrowhead into Gracia. I suspect that before, or just after, that attack, a similar attack to the one on Outpost Two will happen here. We have been drilling based on the new combat strategies you recommended for these mage creatures."

Indicating the officers, "You may select any officers and warriors for your staff, except for the ones I have designated for my personal division." She then pointed. "I recommend Generals Armio-Ery and Ilil-Ushual to be your privy councilors."

They are both seasoned warriors. I like Armio-Ery. He was highly thought of by Colonel Mishia-Ollan. I don't know Ilil-Ushual. But until I have time to consider, the warlord's recommendation should be treated with great respect.

Hiri-Rula nodded to the two generals, who bowed their heads back in acceptance.

The warlord continued, "Your first task is to tour the camp and inspect the training. Everyone is dismissed."

All the officers bowed and began filing out. Hiri-Rula started to step down from the dais when the warlord held up her hand. "Hiri-Rula," the warlord touched the scratch in her armor, "well done."

Hiri-Rula bowed to the warlord as her heart swelled with pride.

As she left the throne room, Generals Armio-Ery and Ilil-Ushual were waiting for her. They both bowed before Armio-Ery asked, "Do you desire to rest before your inspection?"

"No. We have a dozen training sites to visit and observe. We can complete this before the evening meal. I also want to observe morning drills tomorrow."

They will never answer anything but 'no' to this question. Still, I shall ask it.

"Do you have any pressing duties at the moment?"

Both officers shook their heads and then bowed to her. "Your will, General Hiri-Rula."

My will, indeed. And I thought I needed to be careful as a colonel. Now, anything I say will be taken as a direct order and the law.

She nodded to the generals and started walking in a measured pace toward the exit. Her two generals fell into step with her as they walked out of the main complex, to the camp grounds, where the larger training areas had been set up.

I haven't been out of the main complex since the day I got here. It will be nice to move around the camp.

❧ VESTA ❧

The signal alarm Vesta had been waiting for weeks for sounded.

Ah, at last.

The data flowed into her systems, and she reviewed it as it came in.

So my little mage has been promoted, and is in charge of the outpost after the attack begins on Gracia. Well, we wanted proof and here it is.

Opening a communications channel to Gracia's central systems, she signaled for Arkady. He responded, "Yes, Vesta?"

"Arkady, please examine this data stream I am uploading to your system now."

While she waited for Arkady to process it, she continued examining the modifications to the city sensor network.

That was clever to mask your identity code, yet leave yourself command-level access.

She restored the subsystems that Orahda, as he was then called, had modified.

It is nice to know you tried to wake me up. I wonder what your plan was.

"Well, Vesta, that is it. They are going to attack Gracia the moment the assembly ratifies the war declaration. I presume you also saw the conversations around the new training?"

"Yes, I did. We need to double the attack force and alter our tactics. I have learned some of their tactics, so our creatures will be a lot more effective than the ones that attacked Hiri-Rula's outpost."

"Hmm. Well, that should overwhelm them. Are you sure we can clean it all up before we are discovered?"

"We can compensate. Besides, I believe Ticca and Lebuin will be going to the other outpost. I have seen no indication they even know of this larger outpost."

"True, but we cannot have airlifts flying all over the country. If even one is spotted, we are in trouble."

"You will have to help me monitor and direct the operation."

"Of course. I have a solution for Hisuru Amajoo."

That got her attention. "Should I call Electra?"

"No, not yet. You're not going to like this. I can arrange an orbital bombardment of meteorites, with a couple large enough to level that whole valley."

"Mass destruction of the whole valley? That is more than killing the warriors! There are nearly thirty thousand civilians living there. That is the best you can come up with?"

"We don't have the resources to do anything else. The valley is too far away from any of our systems. Even if we could operate openly, it would take a sustained attack of days or weeks to neutralize that place."

"No, Arkady. I cannot agree to mass murder."

"Vesta, you were never involved in a war. It is a messy thing. Yes, people get hurt. It is always murder. Warrior or civilian, it is intentionally taking a life. The goal of war is to minimize the losses on your side while doing what is necessary to end it."

Vesta's heart felt pained at the thought of killing all those people. "No, Arkady. We cannot do this."

"Vesta, this is not a normal enemy. This enemy will strike at the heart of Gracia, show no mercy, and will level this city. There are three hundred thousand people here who will not live if these Nhia-Samri come. This Shar-Lumen is out to destroy everything. We have to stop him."

"If Duke hears of it, he'll know we were involved. What about the meteor defense systems? Having a precision strike like that would be a dead giveaway."

"Here, examine this."

A new data stream came from Arkady. It was an audit of the meteor deflection and defense systems.

So that is what you wanted that satellite for. You've been planning this for a while.

Five thousand years of only automated maintenance was taking its toll. Already, a number of meteors had slipped through, in the last hundred years, to become full-fledged meteorites. Luckily, none of them had hit any place populated.

Arkady continued, "I can arrange it like you did in New Alganetia, or Algan as they now call it. A few little tweaks, I lasso a small cloud of meteors, and it will look like a natural incident that slipped through the failing systems. Convenient, yes, but not highly suspicious. Plus, it is remote. It is likely, Duke will never hear of it, but we'll have to hide your new satellite systems on a moon, or something, for a bit."

Her heart wouldn't let her agree. "Arkady, I am already lamenting the one base I did attack. I cannot make this decision. We need to consult Electra."

"Okay, call her."

"I have. What about Orahda?"

"Oh, he hasn't lost his touch. He has been a busy boy here. I have been playing cat and mouse with him, keeping him from finding out I am awake. He has been busy inspecting a lot of things. Have you figured out why you didn't know he was there?"

"Yes, he altered the subsystems here to not record his identity codes. He was a ghost to my systems. But he kept all his command-level access intact. Oh, and he made several attempts to wake me up, but he wasn't able to bypass the assembly locks."

"That's our boy, all right. I hope one day we can find out how he managed to not be dead."

"You'll find this interesting. Orahda didn't show up here until only forty years ago. I have no records of him anywhere else. You?"

"Nothing, but his identity code is active. I think he suspects an attack. He has been spending a lot of time inspecting the assembly buildings and surrounding areas. If anything, I would guess he is still on the right side."

"You mean our side."

"No, I mean the right side. Remember his training. I bet he still follows the Elraci Guard Code in word and spirit."

"You're probably right. I have collected data on his activities here. He has been acting as the weapons master for the city guard. He has personally trained all of the major officers here. He has also instilled the essence of the Elraci Guard Code in every person he has trained."

"Interesting, that he is the weapons master. I would have expected him to be in charge of the guard."

"True. Perhaps he has lost his desire for the lime light."

"Humph, not likely. Any chance the hawks are ready? I'd love to observe him more closely and I can't use our current observers too much."

"Almost finished. The genetic traits are in place. They'll breed true, no matter which mate they are with. I'll be releasing a dozen pairs into the wild in a couple of days. There will be four we can share to start."

"All right, signal me when Electra responds. Orahda is digging at something in a wall; this is likely to be interesting."

DOHMA

Dohma was watching for servants or guards, along with Cundia, while Orahda picked at the plaster of a wall. *We have been walking around this palace for days, every free minute. What is he looking for?* He signaled Cundia, who signaled back, all clear.

"Can you explain what you have been looking for?"

"Found, milord." Orahda kept digging.

As Orahda scraped, a flash of gold became visible. With a few more strokes, Orahda had exposed a golden three-inch diameter disk with a crystal mounted in the center of it. Orahda got his knife under the edge and levered the disk out, catching it as it fell. He then held it out for Dohma.

Dohma took it and examined it. There were intricate runes with a scrollwork inscription that looped around the whole disk. Orahda tore into another spot.

"What is this?"

"A gate terminus, milord."

"A what?"

Orahda glanced at Cundia, then in a low voice said, "The Nhia-Samri have a magic gate spell that lets them open a gateway between two places, and instantly travel between, as if stepping through a door. It can be done over short distances without a terminus, but I suspected they might have put some in here."

Dohma looked at the golden disk again. "You mean the Nhia-Samri could pop out of this wall magically from one of their bases?"

Orahda nodded. "We must cover up the fact that we found these. We also must be careful to not talk about this. The fact that these are here means there are spies at work. It would be like the Nhia-Samri to attack the assembly the second war is declared."

"How do we find all these gateways?"

"We don't, milord. There are probably a couple dozen. We

can find as many as possible and disable them, but we must be prepared for attack any moment. We are not protected by distance or these walls."

"We have to tell someone. If we get help, we can find and disable more."

"Many will be well hidden. Who do you trust, milord?"

"General Neyon."

Orahda stopped and looked at him, then went back to digging. "Are you sure, milord?"

"Yes, I am sure. I didn't mention him because he is Electra's grandfather. I like him a lot. I know he is trustworthy."

Orahda nodded as he extracted a second disk. "This is enough to disable this one. You are probably right, milord. With the general, we can have some trustworthy officers to patrol and look for the signs I will give them. I can then inspect any suspected location, but we won't find them all, milord. It would be helpful if we could get a map of this place. There might be some hidden corridors."

As much as I hate the idea, this is far more interesting than all the diplomatic meetings I am having to do.

Dohma looked out the window which had a wonderful view of the sprawling city below. "Ah, what about in the city?"

"I am sure there are gate termini in all cities, milord. Probably a half-dozen or more."

We have to protect the assembly and the citizens. We need an army.

Remembering the stories of the Nhia-Samri, he recalled how they cut down regular army soldiers, as easily as children, with wooden swords.

No, we need a highly trained army. But the Covenant forbids the Alliance from having a standing army, and we are a soft, lawful people.

He looked around. "What are we going to do if they attack?"

Orahda looked at him. "Run, milord. Run very fast."

His thoughts leapt to his brother, sister, and Electra. "What of Llino?"

Orahda grabbed his shoulder. "Llino is safe for now. It is too far from here to be a primary target. Shar-Lumen will focus on Duke first and foremost. Also," he leered, saying, "I am positive there are no functioning gate termini in Llino."

Dohma looked at him. *You have already found all the gates in Llino and disabled them. Lords and Ladies, I thank you for such a blessing. You have been protecting Aelargo for over forty years and we never knew.*

"Thank you, my friend."

Orahda nodded. "Milord, perhaps we should ask to see the general this afternoon."

He squeezed the golden artifacts in his hand so hard, his fists turned white. "Come, there is much to do and little time." Dohma turned and walked to the main palace.

General Neyon will be in his office at this time.

The palace complex was large, and it took them nearly half a mark before they were approaching the diplomatic office building. Four Gracia palace guards stood at the entrance. As he approached, they snapped to attention. He walked past them without acknowledging their presence, clutching the golden artifacts. Inside, he went to the general's offices and walked in to stand before the secretary, dressed in the same army uniform as the staff.

The secretary stood and saluted. He was a middle-aged man with a solid grey head of hair, neatly trimmed, that flowed down into his brown and grey beard. His uniform was sharp. He had a dozen or so ribbons on his chest, showing his long and distinguished service. "Lord Dohma, how may I be of assistance?"

"I need to see the general on urgent business."

The secretary looked him over and could sense his tension. "Of course, milord. One moment, please."

The secretary went through the door behind his desk. Dohma resisted the urge to pace. Instead, he concentrated on slowing his breath and trying to relax.

I have never heard Orahda say the solution was to run. I know he was not exaggerating. I have to make the general understand the danger. He will know how to best deal with the situation here. This place is too encumbered with its bureaucracy.

The secretary came out and motioned for him to go in. *Need to be reasonable and calm.*

He walked around the desk and through the door the secretary held open for him. The general's office was large, with a fireplace surrounded by chairs and a sofa. At the far end of the room sat an immense desk of hardwoods. One wall was lined with bookshelves, and the opposite wall had windows which looked out over a garden that was in the center of the building, for use by the staff.

The general was already walking towards him as he entered.

"Lord Dohma, I am busy with the preparations. What is so urgent?"

Dohma nodded to the general. "General, is this room secure?"

The general stopped where he was, still a few paces from Dohma, and his brows creased as he took in Dohma's stance.

"Yes, it is secure, both magically and physically. This building and this office were built by the first Empire's paranoid military men, with all their wonders."

Dohma looked back at Orahda, who nodded in agreement. Dohma held out his hand with the golden artifacts. The general stepped over and took them from him, examining them.

"What are these?"

"These are a part of a magic gateway that would have allowed the Nhia-Samri instant access to the outer hall of the assembly."

The general's head snapped up and he glared at Dohma, as his eyes moved back and forth, while he processed the implications. The general motioned towards the chairs in front of the fire place and sat down on the sofa. Dohma nodded and chose the chair next to the general. Cundia and Orahda stood behind Dohma.

The general pointed at the open seats. "Please, everyone, sit down. Now, tell me everything."

Dohma laid out the entire situation for the general, after which, the general sat back in his chair, staring at the ceiling.

When the general spoke, his tone indicated he was worried.

"My Lords and Ladies, we are in serious trouble. Perhaps we can have the assembly meet someplace else. I dare not risk all the rulers of the Alliance to such an attack. It would cripple the realms."

Orahda shook his head. "We dare not let on that we know what we know."

The general glared at Orahda. "You would risk the assembly?"

Orahda didn't flinch under the general's glare. "There will be spies. If we do anything to alert Shar-Lumen, he will bring his men through to a location near to where we move them. He will then attack there. Here, we have resources, walls they cannot break through, and time to plan how to evacuate the assembly. We can provide instructions to each assembly member, so they will know what to do and who to follow."

The general nodded. "Home territory advantage. Is there someplace we can move them to safely?"

Orahda looked at the general. "If you have maps of the assembly and palace areas, we can locate and unseal the emergency evacuation routes to the stables."

Surprised, the general looked at Dohma, and then back at Orahda. "Now, how the hell do you know about those? They have been a state secret for generations."

Orahda smiled. "General, I know many things that Shar-Lumen does not. I can only assume he remains unaware of these routes, especially since they have not been used for so long."

"If we get them to the stables, then what?"

Orahda shrugged. "I don't know yet. I need to see your

maps and go have a look. I believe we could evacuate everyone into the city, and then perhaps, flee to the elven lands to the east."

"Do you mean we surrender Gracia?"

Orahda sighed. "That depends on how many gates we do not find, and how many properly trained warriors we have. But we must plan for the worst scenario first. We must save the leaders so that this attack will be one battle. We can win the war."

The general looked at Orahda, thinking it through, then looked at Dohma. "Lord Dohma, I will give you all the assistance you need. You are new here, and therefore, touring around the areas will not be out of line. I will help coordinate. I thank the Gods, you, your Daggers, and especially, your weapons master are here."

The general stood and went to the door. Opening it, he said, "Major, please call all senior staff here as soon as possible. Have war rooms two and three made ready and get the maps to the city and palace set up there. This is senior staff eyes and ears only."

The general closed the door and went over to a cabinet. Opening it revealed a dozen crystal decanters. He picked one and poured four glasses, which he then brought over on a tray. He gave one to each of them.

He held his glass high. "Chance favors the prepared. To success."

They all stood and held their glasses high, saying together, "To success," and then they drank. The burning feeling of old sharre poured down their throats and into their blood.

If Orahda had not come, we would have been slaughtered. I must find a way to repay him for his service.

❧ELECTRA☙

Electra stood in the control room with Arkady and Vesta, looking at the displays. Vesta had made a number of enhanced images of the Nhia-Samri hidden home. There were women, children, old men, and farmers living there. The valley was protected by the Nhia-Samri army. Her heart ached at what was being asked.

How can I make this decision? Vesta says no and Arkady says yes. They are looking to me to cast the deciding vote.

She paced, looked at the pictures, sat thinking, then stood and paced some more.

Vesta and Arkady were content to wait as she considered all she had just learned.

This is the knowledge the Gods didn't want us to have. We have done this before. Arkady has seen wars where weapons of even greater power were used.

Her heart pounded, her throat was tight, and she felt cold.

"The entire valley will be destroyed, and everyone there killed. Will they suffer?"

Arkady looked at the floor. "Anyone not deep inside the fort will be killed. I don't think the blast will penetrate, as deep as we think that thing is. But they will not have air and will suffocate in the dark."

She started crying harder. The dream tears she shed there in the control room felt real. Her heart ached so much, it interfered with the mental connection she was using. In her chambers, she could feel real tears running down the sides of her head, making her hair wet.

She looked at Arkady. "How can you even propose doing this?"

Arkady shook his head. "Because if we don't, those warriors will kill every man, woman, and child in Gracia. The citizens there will be hunted down like wild dogs and killed in terror, screaming for mercy. Some husbands will see their wives and children murdered. Women will see their husbands cut down and their children stabbed before they die. And some of the children will see their friends, mothers, and fathers killed before feeling the knife through their own skin. I do not murder because I have no feelings. I murder because it is a necessary evil that some must be strong enough to do so that others will be safe. This is the soldier's burden. All soldiers care for their families, friends, or countrymen. They care so much that they are willing to be monsters so others may know safety and peace. This has always been the price some must pay so most will never know the real horrors of war."

Vesta was crying, too. Electra could see in Vesta's eyes, she knew what the final decision had to be.

This day, I cross a line, never to return. I become a soldier for the realms. This day, I know the true burden of the soldiers. Lords and Ladies, please forgive me.

"Do it, Arkady. Destroy the valley. We must attack and destroy that outpost, too."

Hiri-Rula Defending Outpost One

CHAPTER 16
RUNNING WORKS

DOHMA LOOKED OVER THE MAPS, to the complex spread out on the table.

Eight days before the assembly meeting, and still, Duke has not been seen. Where the hell is he?

A sergeant handed him a cup of arit.

Urdu! These gates are hard to find.

He traced with his finger, the areas already searched. The command staff had been marking searched areas off daily. Each afternoon, the senior staff had afternoon tea, which was the excuse to get everyone into the command building. Once everyone was present, they moved the meeting, from the central garden, into the war room to plan the next day's search pattern to maximize coverage. In five days, they had located only three gates.

I know there are more gates. In fact, I am sure we have missed a few. None of these gates are in areas that have had any work done in ages. It is hard to tell if they are new, or have been here for a thousand years.

As the day of the assembly meeting approached, more nobles arrived, usually with a regent in tow. Dohma had more formal lunches, dinners, and informal meetings daily. If not for the probable Nhia-Samri attack, the meetings would have been fun.

My goal would have been diplomatic, reestablishing ties to kingdoms Aelargo had not had much contact with, other than via the shipping tariffs.

Orahda had been adding to the maps anything he found that was unique. He was good at finding the hidden doors, fake panels, and the secret corridors which were honeycombed throughout the complex. Not less than four different escape routes per assembly country had been established by the general with his senior staff. Each route was tested and double-checked by Orahda. The hard part was slipping the king, queen, and regent out to show them their four routes and make sure they knew all the twists and turns.

The stables make some sense as a destination, but it would have been better to make these secret escape routes go down into the city, instead of to the stables. What were those ancient city builders thinking?

Dohma looked over the older maps of the city. There was a choke point getting out of the palace, so that meant anyone who made it to the stables would still have to escape via that choke point, or go hide somewhere in the complex. Orahda said he was sure any hiding would be useless.

Orahda had ordered some special ropes made that were long enough to scale down the outside walls and cliffs to the city streets below. He had added some strange clips that the smithy was making, day and night, to get the two hundred Orahda wanted. They were devices that allowed someone to wear a rope harness and descend down the rope in a controlled fashion. Once in the city, plans had been made for each of the nine groups to make it to one of four pickup locations, with different ones for each group. Only key personnel knew the four pickup points for a given group, and even fewer knew all thirty-six locations.

The elven delegation had agreed to have secret patrols, using their skills to remain invisible, checking all the evacuation points. Hopefully, any surviving members of the assembly would be picked up and swept into the elven lands to the east. Orahda said if they could make it into the elven forests, they would be safe.

I guess Shar-Lumen won't attack his own homeland.

All of this was being communicated via Dohma during his 'good will' meals and meetings.

If it was not for the fact I am a new delegate who has to meet with everyone, I doubt this could have been communicated as safely. We still don't know where the spies are, but my instincts tell me they are here.

Not a single noble protested to all the preparations.

Most of them are probably scared sleepless. At least, they are good at not showing it.

Since the majority of escape preparations for the delegates were complete, the general and his staff were turning their attentions to the problem of how to defend against the Nhia-Samri when they had no idea where they would come from. Dohma looked over the maps again.

We have forgotten something.

Then his eyes stopped on the map of the city.

What are we going to do about the population? If the Nhia-Samri attack, would they try to hold the city? We can leave orders to cooperate. He knew that was not a possibility. *Gracia is too large and too far from their bases. They will most likely do as they have always done—kill everyone and vanish.*

"General, is there an evacuation signal we can give to the populace?"

The general looked at him, his face going white as he realized they had overlooked the citizens.

The general's eyes watering, he said, "You are a good man, Lord Dohma."

The general considered it for a few minutes. His staff stopped their conversations to pay attention. The general's lips tightened and his eyes hardened. "Yes, there is. We can set fire bombs to burn the palace and these buildings. That will cause panic and mass flight."

Dohma felt his blood pulsing, and he took a quick breath, shocked at the proposal. He stared at the general. "People will die. Old and weak will be left. It will be chaos."

"Yes, but most will escape. Those that survive will be the young, the hardy, and the crafty, which is who we need to survive. We can gather them into a resistance army to retake our lands and defeat the Nhia-Samri."

"You surprise me, General."

"Plan for the worst and fight as hard as you can to prevent it, but don't hesitate to retreat. Those that run away live to fight another day. I learned that lesson well in the last war. We cannot stand against the Nhia-Samri unless we are in control of the situation. The moment we lose control, they will destroy any that try to muscle on."

"Are they such a hard adversary?"

"You fought them already in your own city. What do you think?"

Dohma thought about it. He looked at the general, and then walked away as he recalled the battle in Llino. *They never flinched. They stood and killed until they were too wounded to fight at all. Even the ones that had taken death blows continued to fight until they were dead.* He recalled watching the fight from a distance. The Daggers had the tactical advantage until their ranks had been broken up. That was when he ordered the waiting guards into the battle.

Dohma looked up from the floor and found the general was close by, watching him. "They don't give in."

The general nodded and his lips where pressed so hard, they turned white. "You have it, milord. They are conditioned and hardened warriors. They are on an order far above our city guards or palace guards. Only Daggers are trained to the level needed to withstand the fear of death and pain required to fight them. The Covenant has brought us over five thousand years of relative peace. But in preventing the Alliance from having a standing army, it has also sealed the fate of Gracia, should the Nhia-Samri attack. It will take us years to build a force strong enough and skilled enough to fight back."

"But we beat them forty years ago."

The general shook his head. "No, we didn't. They were playing at their shadow games. That war was between Yalthum and Laeusia. It was caused by the Nhia-Samri, and flames of war on both sides were being fanned by the Nhia-Samri. They wanted to tear apart the Covenant. Once their involvement was exposed, the hotheads involved saw how they had been used and manipulated. The Nhia-Samri withdrew before we got together and marched on them. At that point, we had two reasonably large armies and a larger force of Daggers coming from Duianna. We were better prepared to fight them then. Now, it has been forty years, and the warriors of that war are old and weak. The countries have allowed their armies to dwindle again. Once more, we are a soft target."

ELECTRA

Electra sat in a chair next to Vesta and Arkady. The room had been changed to show tactical maps and data all around the three of them. Each could control their own section of displays. On both sides were full-wall displays of the images from Vesta's satellites. Electra tried to keep from looking at the one on the left, but her eyes would flick over to it, taking in the thousands of dots moving around the great fortress valley.

In less than one mark, everyone there will be dead, and my hands will never be clean again.

She sighed and returned her attention to the displays in front of her. Her job was to look for anything unusual in the tactics and to advise Vesta and Arkady on the use of magic. Vesta was overseeing three hundred modified crab warriors. Arkady had an even larger number of crab warriors at his command, as well as the airlift units.

The crabs had been pulled from their duties up and down the channel. Normally, they were maintenance workers. Vesta had explained how the sea channels had many devices hidden under the waters. Sand had to be moved at times to allow safe passage for ships. Also, there was the occasional giant sea creature that came up too high, and would get caught in the Loren Sound; the crabs would help it return to its deep water home. It would take years to replace the ones lost tonight, but both Vesta and Arkady were sure the underwater realm would be okay while they bred and outfitted replacement crabs

Arkady played with the controls in front of him.

I know he doesn't have to do that, but it is nice they both make the effort to act more human for me.

"First drop will be landing in ten seconds."

Vesta nodded. "Signal is five-by-five, all surveillance systems normal, target remains unaware."

Electra sat up straighter.

Time to be serious. We have work to do.

Electra manipulated the controls and scanned the patrols around the Nhia-Samri base. Everything looked normal for that time of night. One of the units on Vesta's side started another gate drill. "Target unit six in gate drill."

Vesta adjusted her display. "Acknowledged. Arkady, drop three points further south at grid 444 by 934."

Displays shifted in front of Arkady. "Acknowledged. Units 1, 2, 3, and 4 drop in 5 seconds now. Units 5, 6, 7, and 8 drop in 15 seconds. Electra, check grid 433 by 940. Tell me what the hell they are doing."

She punched her display over to the requested location. Two scouts were hiding under a tree. She had to shift to one of the new hawks to see the two warriors who were splitting a chunk of rations. "Break time. They are eating."

Arkady smiled. "In that case, two for one. Odds just went up."

Her display was still pulled in tight to the two warriors as the silver crab fell from the sky, its pinchers wide. As the crab landed, it closed both pinchers, severing the heads of both scouts. Her stomach did a summersault, and she felt light-headed.

NO! Take control of yourself! You cannot blink or feel sick now. Later, you can curl into a ball and cry. Right now, Gracia depends on you doing your job.

The crab squatted low in the grass and started moving towards the base.

Swallowing, she reported, "Kill confirmed. No reaction from target. Target remains unaware." She then flipped her displays back to the wide views, watching for anything to report.

As she swept, she spotted a problem. "Warning! Hiri-Rula is with unit six."

Vesta looked over. "Oh, urd! I didn't want to kill her."

HIRI-RULA

Hiri-Rula stood to the side of the drilling warriors, watching their maneuvers. Generals Armio-Ery and Ilil-Ushual stood with her discussing the formations.

It will be hard to enter Gracia. Duke will have guards everywhere.

She tried to think of a way to capture their targets, but she knew that was out of the question, as the Grand Warlord's orders were very clear—they were to kill everyone. A sound she knew came from across the drill field. The sound of a battle, combined with the rapid, repeating drum of those creatures that attacked Outpost Two, when using their blow thorns.

She drew her odassi. "Sound the alarm! Raise the outpost! We are under attack!"

Dozens of warriors around her drew their odassi and started beating a percussion pattern with the blades. The sound was taken up by warriors further along. In moments, the entire valley rang with odassi blades beating the same pattern together.

"Armio-Ery, take units 20 and 21 and cover the right. Ilil-Ushual, do the same on the left with units 22 and 23." She started running towards the sound of battle. "UNITS 24 AND 25, WITH ME. NEW ATTACK FORMATIONS. MOVE IT!"

As she ran, Hiri-Rula called on her powers and cast the incantation to create a link between her and the other fifty mages. *'Get to your assigned locations. Use your shields for the warriors. Tell me if you have to fall back.'* Fifty mages' voices rang in her head as they cross-chatted, coordinating their motions. A few took different positions due to the logistics of who was closer to which station.

She bolted around a tent and her heart rate pumped up another notch. *So many!*

Before her was a sea of those crabs moving in over a hill in a line that went as far as she could see, right and left.

A dozen crabs were killed, along with hundreds of warriors wounded or dead. The remaining warriors were fighting in tight groups of five each. The crabs moved differently than before. They worked together in teams, as well.

Urd, these things are mimicking our strategies!

Hiri-Rula sent a blast of power that blew a crab into pieces. Four crabs came at her. She leapt into the air, using her power to push herself over them. As she passed over, she released a blaze of fire that would have turned a normal adversary to ashes. Instead, her flames made one of the crabs glow a bright red. It wiggled as if in pain, but still swung its claws with great effectiveness, knocking two warriors from a group. Its partner crab clipped at another warrior, who screamed as her legs were sheared off. In spite of the overwhelming pain, that warrior brought her blades down with great force as she fell, cutting through the front part of the crab that killed her.

Hiri-Rula landed, spun, and cut the back of one of the crabs. Lightning danced over its shell, but did not touch her.

Ah, good! I wasn't sure if that shield incantation would work.

She called out to the other mages. *'I have confirmed the new shield works against their interior lightning. Make sure you are providing the resistance to your warrior teams.'*

I should double-check my own teams.

She used the power of her blades to move in a blur of speed, maneuvering around the crabs, dodging the attacks, while she double-checked that she was providing shielding to her teams.

As she dodged, a hole opened to relative safety. She dove through the opening, coming out in a forward roll, popping back to her feet, spinning around to face the crab group. The crabs advanced on her, forcing her to shuffle step backwards out of range.

They're herding me, I think.

The feeling of warning came, and she pushed herself to move, twisting and spinning, stepping right. The great claws of another crab snapped shut in the air where she had just been.

You will not take me down again!

She sliced down, cutting the claw in half before the creature could pull it back.

Turning, Hiri-Rula saw a group of crabs raise up. Pointing with her odassi, she sent a rush of power, creating a solid shield around that entire group. The creatures fired their magic fire balls, unaware of her shield. The fireballs exploded on the inside of the bubble she had made. Her shield held for a few seconds before failing under the power it had contained. The shield burst with an explosion of dirt, crab parts, smoke, and fire.

Twisting out of the way of another crab, she smiled, seeing that the four crabs had been blown apart by their own fireballs. As she moved around more crabs, a group of warriors joined her. She merged into their formation, working with them to hack up three crabs that had turned around to attack them.

Hiri-Rula told the other mages, *'They are vulnerable to their own magics. If you see them rising up as I described, create the strongest shield you can in a containment bubble around them. Their magics will tear them apart.'*

Only thirty-eight mages responded.

Have we really lost twelve mages already?

She moved with the group as they fought the crabs. Her warriors were getting better as they became used to the motions and flow of the enemy. All around, she saw warrior groups merging as they lost members. They fought on The inferior warriors were dying, but as each warrior died, the remaining that regrouped were superior.

These things are making us harder to kill.

Her swords rose and fell, twisting and turning. She stayed with her group. Warriors died and others fought on. Hiri-Rula spun around, using her incantations to throw the crabs away, but that didn't work. When they landed on their backs, their legs changed direction. The crabs looked the same upside down as right side up. Hard, silver shells were everywhere. She watched for any opportunity to use their magics against them, but after that first group, no other group of crabs near her tried to use their fire balls.

These things are learning too fast. At least, they can't learn to not be cut by the odassi.

MARU-ASHUA

Warlord Maru-Ashua stepped out of the tower onto the arched sky bridge that connected to the central tower of the castle. Each tower had three sky bridges at different levels, as well as a walkway around the tower wide enough for two carriages to pass each other. The effect was beautiful. At night time, they were doubly beautiful as their lanterns burned a soft amber that illuminated them like orange silk bands.

He chose to walk to the outer towers. From there, he would take one of the internal lifts to the ground. He loved the feel of Hisuru Amajoo. It was larger than any other city or fort he had ever seen. It exceeded the scale of even Gracia by a wide margin. Life there was peaceful; the people loved and supported each other. Men and women could choose to join the Nhia-Samri or not. If they wanted to, they were tested. So long as they passed the physical and mental challenges, they remained Nhia-Samri. The moment they failed even one test, they were retired back to their home to live as respected people.

Many chose other professions, and none were denied their choices. They had only to show the wits and ability to take any profession.

This is almost a paradise. No murders, no rape, and everyone feels safe. Of course, we are all under the direct rule of the Grand Warlord, but he is kind to his people. If only his heart wasn't so cold.

As Maru-Ashua approached the outer tower, he could

look out over the lights of the valley. He paused to examine the farms and city.

I am responsible to all here to ensure everything is done correctly.

He recalled his fear as he and his officers had approached Hisuru Amajoo.

Because of the failures in Llino, I thought I had lost all honor. As we entered the throne room, I knew the only way to regain honor was to give my life to the Grand Warlord.

He shook his head, remembering how Shar-Lumen had sat in his silver and red velvet filigree throne, watching Maru-Ashua's every move, every nuance.

He read my soul that day. He let me finish my report. I dropped to my knees and placed my odassi before him, expecting the order to come. Then he showed me how much of a true leader he is.

He could hear the Grand Warlord speaking, as if it was happening again.

'Warlord Maru-Ashua, your service has been long and honorable. This failure could not be helped. The responsibility is mine. I bypassed your command, and so, insulted your honor. I have watched you for years and know you have studied and remained a true Nhia-Samri in all things. I have been without a second for forty years, and the lack of sound council has caused me to make mistakes. I, therefore, name you second in command of the Nhia-Samri. You now speak with my voice, and are charged with speaking to me with your own.'

He shook his head as if it was all a dream.

I am second in command now. I cannot believe this. I was sure Grand Warlord Shar-Lumen was going to require of me the last restoration of honor. But instead, he granted me a medal for my actions and named me his second.

A presence stood next to him. He knew it was Shar-Lumen, without looking.

He moves like shadows and makes about as much noise It is strange, how he seems to be anywhere he chooses in Hisuru Amajoo instantly. I wonder if he has mastered the gate incantation. He was a mage of the highest magnitude before he started the Nhia-Samri. Warrior, mage, leader, and yet, he has a cold heart. We could have been so much more.

"Maru-Ashua, are all the units ready?"

He turned and bowed. "Yes, Grand Warlord. I have inspected all units this day and their training has been superb. You will have all of your warriors in Gracia within fifteen minutes. The assembly cannot resist."

Shar-Lumen looked out, his face a model of perfection. "Do not be so sure. The generals of the Alliance are aware of our plans and are making preparations to resist. Also, Duke will be there with some of the Daggers he hired."

Maru-Ashua considered Shar-Lumen's words.

He has received a report. That is why he sought me out.

"I ask again, instead of killing everyone, would it not be better to strike a hard blow and capture them?"

Shar-Lumen looked at him with those cold, violet eyes that had lost emotion so long ago. He shook his head. "No. If we capture them, their armies will be inspired to attack. Given time, they may succeed. In killing them, we strike fear into their warriors. Then we will never be defeated."

Shar-Lumen turned and started to walk away, when a warning horn sounded across the valley. The warning was picked up by other guards. Even this far up, the sound of thousands of odassi being drawn was inspiring. The valley brightened as the warning fires were lit all across the valley.

Shar-Lumen stepped over to the banister and scanned the area. Maru-Ashua joined him. Many guards were repeating the warning horn, which oddly did not carry a direction.

Shar-Lumen, with his keen night eyesight, was the first to realize what was causing the alarm. Maru-Ashua saw that warriors were looking up with their mouths hanging open. He joined Shar-Lumen in looking up.

Shar-Lumen clasped his hands behind his back and

smiled. The starry sky was filled with fire. Hundreds of fiery balls, all growing in size, were heading straight at them.

The blood ran from his head as he stepped back, looking at the fiery death approaching. Shar-Lumen hadn't moved. "Lord, we need to take cover."

Shar-Lumen waved a hand at him. "Do not worry, Maru-Ashua. I must admit though, this is not what I expected. Ingenious, really. I should have predicted it. It always seems to come to fire."

The first of the fiery balls slammed into something a hundred feet above the tallest tower. The percussion of the strike sent vibrations through his body. His heart raced, and he looked at Shar-Lumen, who continued to look up as if examining a cloud. More strikes hit the invisible shield, sounding like an army of drummers. The stars were blocked by the debris, but the fires of the explosions burned bright enough to make everything orange.

The citizens had all come out with lanterns across the valley, making it look like a bright gathering evening.

Maru-Ashua looked back and forth between the seeming death from the sky and the Grand Warlord, who stood there, pondering the meaning of the event.

He isn't surprised in the least. How could the mages have raised a shield so fast?

Fires burned in an arching dome over the valley while the percussion of new strikes rang out from above, but not so much as a flake of ash came any closer. The percussion reports of the strikes continued for at least ten minutes before they dwindled to an ominous quiet.

"Maru-Ashua, have the warriors train harder this next week. The gods will be present at the assembly, too. We shall have to deal with them."

Gods! The Gods will be there!

He couldn't help himself. His mind was overwhelmed by events. "Lord, how do you know the Gods will be there?'

Shar-Lumen looked away from the molten red dome that

covered the valley. The red light reflecting off of his silver skin made him look like some kind of ethereal creature. "Because they have noticed our actions in Llino."

Because they noticed Llino's failure? That doesn't make sense.
"What do you mean?"

Shar-Lumen pointed up. "They tried to stop us. This was their attempt to stop the attack on Gracia. I am surprised they would kill so many, instead of striking at only the warriors. They need to be taught a lesson about that."

"You expected this?"

Shar-Lumen started walking back towards the main building. "Sooner or later, I expected they would try to stop me."

He followed, completely lost to his curiosity. "How long have the Magi been shielding us?"

Shar-Lumen stopped and looked at him. "No Magi at all. I built that shield six hundred years ago. I protect my own."

"You've been expecting the Gods to attack you for six hundred years?"

Shar-Lumen resumed walking away. "Of course."

ELECTRA

Electra looked at the bloody battlefield on the displays. The crabs were all destroyed and laying in pieces. The Nhia-Samri were cleaning up the dead, both their own and the crabs.

We lost. Vesta and Arkady did everything they could, and we lost.

Vesta and Arkady reviewed their data pads. Vesta spoke first. "Well, we have cut their numbers down by nearly sixty-five percent. There are only 1,263 warriors remaining of the original 3,613."

Arkady shook his head. "They are not ignorant savages. They adapted to our attacks with a speed I didn't think possible. Also, I don't think we have done much for Gracia. The remaining warriors are the best they have there."

Electra played with the dials and found what she was

looking for. General Hiri-Rula was working along with the warriors, helping to clean things up. "Hiri-Rula survived."

Vesta looked over. "That's good. There is something about her I like."

Arkady looked around. "Now, what? We can't launch any of our enforcers. They'll be spotted."

Vesta looked at Arkady. "I'm not sure. Let's gather our data and see. Perhaps Gracia can withstand a smaller attack. Besides, with Shar-Lumen dead in Hisuru Amajoo, there might not be an attack."

Arkady stood. "No. How could they?"

Vesta looked at him. Electra leaned back in her chair, relaxing.

I don't care. This has been a horrible night. We have killed, and yet, we have lost. I can't see how I could feel worse.

Arkady was standing in front of the display that showed the remains of Hisuru Amajoo. "The dust should be a lot thicker. This is odd. It is clearing."

The smoke and clouds were starting to clear, to reveal the valley with its city lights.

Wait, what?

Electra stood and ran over to stand next to Arkady, Vesta already there.

Before them, the dust and clouds cleared, showing the valley of Hisuru Amajoo still had glowing city lights. Large fires were burning on top of the outer wall, and the towers of the fortress still stood as if untouched by Arkady's attack.

How is that possible?

Arkady hit the display hard. "Okay, now I'm mad! I go through all that soul searching, and do what I need to, for no results! Look at that," he said. "Zero damage."

⚜ DOHMA ⚜

Dohma had been up early to spar with Orahda and Cundia before heading over to the temporary office he had been given in the military command building.

Every other assembly member has an office attached to their chambers. Only I was given a chamber without an office. It probably looks suspicious, but there is nothing else we can do about it.

When they got to the command building, they went to the war room.

Why am I liking the name of this room more and more?

The general was already there, drinking from an oversized mug that had a sipping lid on it.

I wonder how much arit he consumes. He is sipping from the thing all day, and I know his secretary keeps topping it off.

Orahda looked at the maps, and then left to begin his day of touring and inspections.

This will be the first day I don't have to deal with escape topics. I can enjoy the diplomatic luncheon and get to know my fellow rulers better.

He sat down next to the table and grabbed some of the sweet cakes from the sideboard. Looking at a new map that had been added overnight, he noticed that it was of the palace and had a number of red dots.

"What's this?"

A colonel looked over. "That is the fire bomb plan for the palace. If we set one off, they will all go off. Burning curtains or furniture will act as fuses. Of course, the palace won't burn—just the contents. But we have been adding a lot of wood furniture to it. The Imperial regent has insisted on placing certain works of art in rooms that won't get touched by fire."

Dohma examined it. "What are we putting the jellyfire in?"

The colonel shrugged. "Many different things. Couldn't be too obvious. Most of them are wooden jewelry boxes or display boxes, so all we have to do is smash one."

Dohma started adding the locations to the stacks of other locations he was trying to remember.

Now I need to tour the palace again and make sure I can identify these things.

"How long before the citizens will see it clearly enough to know they should run?"

"Smash one, and it should make a roaring pile of smoke visible throughout the city in about twenty minutes. If we can smash about six in different locations, we think it will take five minutes, max."

A corps sergeant came bursting into the room. "An attack alarm has been sounded from the western wall!"

Several officers bolted through different doors. The general looked at Dohma and waved for him to follow. "Let's go have a look. We might need to evacuate early."

"But the western wall? Why not the gate into the assembly?"

The general was already in the hall, moving with considerable speed for the outer door. "Diurdin, if I know. We can only react at the moment."

As they crossed the palace grounds, heading for the western side, Orahda and Cundia bolted out from between two buildings. Cundia smiled. "See, I told you he would be running towards the danger."

Orahda harrumphed. "I didn't disagree."

They reached the palace walls and started climbing. Everyone but Orahda was breathing hard by the time they reached the top.

I have to admit, I'm impressed the general made it this fast. He is in marvelous shape for his age.

As they climbed, a thrumming sound came through the air. When they crested the wall, the sound resolved itself into a pulsing drum beat, coming from the advancing army. "They're organized. They have drummers and probably buglers."

The general commandeered three field glasses. "You're probably right. Let's take a closer look," he said, handing one to Dohma, one to Orahda, and keeping the third for himself. They all looked to the west over the top of the far city wall.

A pit grew in his stomach as he looked. *Lords and Ladies, that is a large force!*

An army was marching on the city, and the army was larger than any army he had ever heard of. He tried to count them. It was spread out for more than a half mile in tight ranks, and the dust from the front made only a dozen more ranks behind visible.

The general yelled, "Take this down, ranks are nine by nine." He slowly scanned left to right calling out numbers, "Ten, ten, ten, ten, ten, ten, ten, ten, and five. Add that up. What's the count?"

Some men and women were scribbling on pads. They cross-checked with each other and nodded. "General, that makes a front line of 765."

The general kept looking. "They have more than 30 rows of that rank. Double that and give me a count."

Again, the men and women scribbled on papers and then cross-checked. "Forty-five thousand, nine hundred."

His heart jumped to his throat. "My Lords, where the hell did that army come from? Are they Nhia-Samri?"

The general put down his field glasses. "Can't tell yet. At least, the regents have closed the city and activated the defenses."

Dohma looked down with his field glasses and saw that the steel plate gates were rising as some people scrambled either in or out. The city walls were rising, and the port gates were swinging shut.

"Now, what?"

The general looked at him and started back towards the stairs. "Now, we go talk with the regent. That army will have to build siege engines to get in. There are enough of them to blockade the city. We need to consider a long siege."

Dohma had started to follow the general when Orahda called out. "Wait."

They turned around, and Orahda was still looking with his field glasses. He pointed, smiling. "I think we can open the gates."

The general's eyes bulged. "Are you mad?"

Orahda held the general's abandoned field glasses out to him. "No. Take a close look at the center of the front line."

Dohma and the general stepped back to the wall and started searching the center. Finally, Dohma saw what Orahda was talking about. There were a dozen officers, nobles, and cavalry mounted on horses. But one horse was not a horse. "That's Duke!"

The general leaned further over the edge. "Where?"

"With the officers in the center, between the nobles in blue and red. He looks a little like a horse, but doesn't move like a horse. No rider, either."

The general stared for a minute. "Urd, I think you're right." He turned and yelled. "Get our horses now." The command was echoed down the wall by other guards.

They rushed down the stairs. Before they had made it halfway down, messenger horses were being brought by grooms at a dead run. Together, they mounted at the base of the wall. The general didn't wait. He dug his heals into his horse, turning it with the ease of a master horseman, and galloped the whole way to the outer wall, maneuvering his horse through the panicked people in the streets. The general's guards, as well as Dohma, Cundia, and Orahda, had a hard time keeping up. They reached the gate in only a mark.

I thought he was old, but I am feeling tired, trying to keep up with him.

The gate was still closed. The general signaled, and the city guards used mirrors to reflect the sun back towards the palace.

That is ingenious! I wonder how much of a signal you can get through.

Orahda seemed to read his thoughts. "It is an old code, milord. I can teach it to you. It is also not secure."

The silver gate dropped open before them. As soon as it was low enough, the general kicked his horse again, making it jump up on the descending gate top, and gallop across it, out of the city. Dohma was ready this time and stayed close to the general.

As they got closer to the approaching army, Dohma sucked in his breath. He could see every warrior was a Dagger. At the center of the front column was Duke, with the nobles and officers.

Oh, my Lord! Those aren't nobles! Those are the Dagger commanders, Elades and Sundar! Wow! How they have changed since I last saw them!

Duke stopped chatting with Elades and Sundar to call out, "HALT."

The buglers sounded across the field. Their calls synchronized, so they all stopped together. The drums and Daggers stopped in perfect time to the end of the buglers' signal with a dramatic double beat of drums and feet.

The general rode up to face Duke. He looked right and left at the Daggers, all standing at attention. Duke sat down. "Hello, Neyon. Anything interesting happen lately?"

The general looked at Duke and frowned. "You are forbidden from having an army by the Covenant, and you know that!"

Duke looked around, pretending to be surprised. "Army? Army? Elades, did you see an army anywhere?"

Elades smiled. "No, sir."

Duke called out, "Are any of you in an army?"

Thousands of voices called out, "NO, SIR!"

Duke shrugged. "Sorry, General. No army here."

The general turned red-faced. "Duke, you can't play games like this."

Duke smiled. "Look, I felt a little threatened by the Nhia-Samri, so I hired some personal guards."

The general huffed, then looked at Duke. "Personal guards? You hired some personal guards? How many personal guards do you have?"

Duke looked up as if thinking. "Well, I believe the last payroll showed roughly 65,420 personal guards, and 9,632 support staff, butlers, groomers, cooks, maids, clothiers, armorers, smiths... You know, the basics."

The general sat back in his saddle, trying to absorb it all. He mumbled, "Not an army."

Duke stood and stepped over to him. "Look, I can prove it."

The general looked at him. "You can prove it?"

"Sure." Duke looked at the ranks of Daggers and yelled out, "Are you soldiers?"

Sixty-five thousand voices answered back, "NO, SIR!"

"What are you?"

"DAGGERS, SIR!"

Duke nodded and looked at the general. "You see, everyone knows Daggers are mercenaries for hire. Not an army. Nope. Perfectly legal."

"By a dog's hair!"

Duke looked at the general, wounded. "A wolf's hair, if you please."

The general sat back as he shifted to a more relaxed position in his saddle. "Okay, you win. And Duke?"

The wolf looked over. "Yes."

"Thank you."

Duke nodded and winked. Then he looked over at Dohma. "Your Excellency, I trust you are enjoying being away from all the bureaucracy."

CLIFFHANGERS
LIKE A KNIFE TO THE HEART!

I have a love-hate relationship with cliffhangers. I love and appreciate cliffhangers. I hate when I suddenly run out of words and have to wait for the next book to get published. I also hate when I finish a book with a cliffhanger, and I haven't written the next book, because I, too, want to see the rest! I admit I have prodded my favorite authors to hurry up from time to time. If the next book isn't available yet, trust me, I am slaving over the keyboard to get it neatly wrapped up for you. Feel free to prod me to move faster! If the next book is just about ready for publication, you can find the first chapter or two on my web site (www.LArtra.com). If the next book is already out, you can use my website or go to most eBook sales sites and use their "Look Inside" or "Preview" feature to get at the first chapter or two. You can also find more information about this series at the official Golden Threads Facebook page: www.Facebook.com/GoldenThreadsTrilogy.

Stay up to date with all of my releases by joining
my release letter at: http://bit.ly/artranews

A PERSONAL NOTE FROM LEELAND

I hope you enjoyed reading this book and found the deeper, more complex world history hinted at fun to try to unravel. I spend a lot of time engineering the history and mechanics of my stories. If you enjoyed this book, please take a few minutes to leave a positive review on the eBook site you purchased it from or Goodreads.com (or both). If you write a blog, I'd love if you posted a review about it. If you do, email me the link and I'll post it on my social media sites. The more positive feedback I get, the more time I can spend writing the next story! I love interacting with my readers, so if you feel like chatting with me about this story or others, please visit me. You can find me at:

www.LArtra.com
www.Facebook.com/Leeland.Artra
www.Twitter.com/LArtra
www.Goodreads.com/LArtra

Sign up for my mailing list at http://bit.ly/artranews and get updates, special giveaway items, and be the first to know when I release something new.

LEBUIN'S LEXICON

Algan: Inland farming city on the western border of the Kingdom of Aelargo.

Alorn Mountain: An ancient volcano now dormant on the north western point of the Kingdom of Aelargo.

Ankidyt: The eleventh month of the Imperial year considered the second month of winter. *See Lebuin's Lexicon: Time*

Apprentice: Any tradesman under training for a guild (Mages' Guild included).

Argos Guild of Mages Sigil: A stylized gold dragon with the five silver waves behind it.

Argos: The All-Father God of the Universe is considered the chief deity who oversees the magicians in all lands.

Arit: A strong, bitter drink made from roasted beans of the aritia tree which only grows in tropical climates.

Blade: A professional soldier, mercenary fighter, sword master.

Blood compass: A magical artifact, made with blood, which is capable of retracing a person's life. Its construction is taboo in many lands and illegal in a few. It is effective for as long as the subject lives and for many hours after death.

Blue Dolphin Inn: Dagger Home and merchant's inn that has a huge stainless steel hoop mounted on the roof with a platform which the owners and legends claim was the main port of call for the Emerald Heart.

Boadua of Mostill Valley: A senior priestess of Dalpha in Llino.

Breorchy: Onasa Channel port city on the northwestern border of the Kingdom of Aelargo.

Burga Mountains: A blue mountain range which cuts east-west across the southern part of the North Duianna Continent from the Darain Ocean to the Onasa Channel.

Burga Spine Mountains: A blue mountain range which cuts north-south from the Onasa Channel to the Windy Pass.

Circumveni Desert: A vast wasteland of unforgiving desert which spans the entire Duianna continent, from east to west, along the southern edge of the Halias-Ne Mountains. No known safe path exists across this desert, and it is plagued with strange, deadly creatures.

Councilor: A member of Leading Council of the Argos Guild of Mages.

Cycle: A unit of time corresponding approximately to one cycle of the moon's phases, or about thirty days or four weeks. *See Lebuin's Lexicon: Time*

Cycle: One complete cycle of the moon Tempa. Each year has twelve lunar cycles divided into the four seasons: winter (Samag, Noelag, Foilleg), spring (Gearra, Marta, Abra), summer (Sealen, Ogmen, Luchen), and autumn (Lunas, Sultas, Fomas).

Dagger table: Various inns and taverns allow mercenaries to hire out from them. A Dagger table is reserved for only Daggers. Daggers signal they are open for hire by placing their dagger into the table standing up. Senior Dagger tables have a Dagger holder mounted on the table and, in Dagger Homes, can be owned exclusively.

Dagger: Professional warrior specialists for hire that hold to a strong set of ideals based on commitment, courage, and honor.

Dalpha: Lady of Light, Goddess of healing, woods, and the elves, represented by large temples in almost every major city on Niya-Yur. Her symbol is an oak tree with eight rays of light forming a circle. Legends state she was the right hand maiden of Uialua, dwelling with her in Ar-du-Veni-Kussi. Dalpha is believed to hold the secrets of life itself. Dalpha is married to Larak, the Lion Lord.

Damega Drakeruin: Legendary warrior who started many of the Dagger traditions. Although very mercenary, he is always portrayed in a 'Robin Hood' fashion. A good-hearted rogue, who refused any offer to settle down. Supposedly stole or was gifted the Emerald Heart, a flying ship by the guardian of Sandeep.

Day: The 24-hour period during which Niya-Yur completes one rotation on its axis. *See Lebuin's Lexicon: Time*

Delivery Channel: A waterway system of all ancient port cities which connects one or more rivers together to flow under the city, creating a simple, smooth-flowing, barge-friendly means of transporting large loads.

Demi-God: A son or daughter of the race of Gods, who was conceived intentionally, with enough magical energy to allow them to one day join the ranks of the Gods. Primary attributes are nearly immortal, with the ability to control tremendous amounts of magic.

Ditani (aka Kiotiaditani Speaker of the Tribes of Kiliua-ona): A Karakian servant to Magus Vestul. Hero son of Lothia and Argos, and Lebuin's Uncle.

Diurdin: (*adjective*) Used for emphasis, especially to express anger or frustration. *"It's none of your* diurdin *business."* (**synonyms**) darn, diurdu, drat, shoot, blast, rats, urd, urdu.

Diurdu: (adjective, adverb, & noun) Used for emphasis, especially to express anger or frustration. "I'm really tired of the diurdu tariffs." (**synonyms**) darn, diurdin, drat, shoot, blast, rats, urd, urdu.

Dohma Gerani: Captain of the city and palace guards in Llino.

Dolphin dagger doors: Unique doors which are considered unbreakable and thief proof, that require a combination and a special key to open, and are used only at the Blue Dolphin Inn in Llino for Dagger and special guest rooms.

Dorn Hills: A large range of hills on the north edge of the border between the kingdoms of Aelargo and Nasur.

Dulgruim: A dwarven kingdom on the southern tip of the Duianna continent, bordered on the north by Karakia. Capital: Or-Anithi-Umta. Abbreviation: DU.

Elraci: An unknown kingdom or city in ancient times, now lost.

Emerald Heart: Legendary flying ship of Damega Drakeruin. Legend has it that it flies faster than any creature and is home-ported in a secret place far in the north.

Eri hish: (*vulgar slang*) (phrasal verb of hish) (of a person) go away.

Faltla of Rhini Wood: Ticca's Uncle, a retired tactics Dagger, who served in the Realms' War and trained Ticca from birth.

Gadriel: God of the dwarves.

Genne: The current owner of the Blue Dolphin Inn, the original Dagger House in Llino.

Greyrhan: A province of the Duianna Empire in the far north, just south of the great ice fields.

Guard: City soldiers, general police force.

Halias-Ne Mountains: A thick, rocky mountain and volcano range which cuts the entire Duianna continent in half, spanning from the Darain Ocean on the east to the Occiduis Ocean on the west.

Hand: Broker or facilitator for trade in various goods or services, usually illegal.

Hero: A son or daughter of the race of Gods, who was conceived intentionally or by accident, with only enough magical energy to allow a live birth. Primary attributes are a very strong constitution, high strength, no magical abilities at all, and with an expected life span of nine to eleven thousand years.

High Councilor: Chairman of the Leading Council of the Argos Guild of Mages.

Hish: (*vulgar slang*) (**verb**: hish; 3rd person present: hishes; past tense: hished; past participle: hished; gerund or present participle: hishing) 1. have sexual intercourse with (someone). 2. ruin or damage (something).
(**noun**) an act of sexual intercourse.
(**exclamation**) used alone or as a noun **the hish** or a verb in various phrases to express anger, annoyance, contempt, impatience, or surprise, or simply for emphasis.

Hisuru Amajoo: The city fortress home of the Nhia-Samri.

Hyly: A semi-sweet liquor made from honey.

Innadyt: The sixth month of the Imperial year considered the third and final month of summer. *See Lebuin's Lexicon: Time*

Journeyman Mage: Title of a mid-level magician for the Argos Guild of Mages; carries a unique badge of office and is seen as a direct representative of Argos.

Karakia: A mixed nation of tribes spanning the central part of the South Duianna continent from the Darain Ocean on the east to the Occiduis Ocean on the west. The northern border is the Circumveni Desert and on the south, the Dulgrium Nation. Capital: None. Abbreviation: KA.

Khab: (*vulgar slang*) (**verb**: khab; 3rd person present: khabes; past tense: khabed; past participle: khabed; gerund or present participle: khabing) express displeasure; grumble. (synonyms: complain, whine, grumble, grouse) (**noun**) 1. a spiteful or unpleasant woman.. 2. a difficult or unpleasant situation or thing. 3. a complaint.

Kishadyt: The eighth month of the Imperial year considered the second month of fall. *See Lebuin's Lexicon: Time*

Kliasa: The daughter of House Elaeus of Rea-Na-Rey.

Knife: An assassin or hired killer, strongly controlled by a secretive guild.

Laeusia: A human kingdom which lies between the Duianna Empire and the Kingdom of Yalthum.

Lahmudyt: The ninth month of the Imperial year considered the third and final month of fall. *See Lebuin's Lexicon: Time*

Larak: The Lion Lord, God of Archery, Healing, and Guards. Larak is said to guard all cities that pay tribute to his wife Dalpha. His symbol of a winged lion can be found in every city of the Duianna Empire on the guard offices. A statue of a roaring, winged lion stands watch over the arched entry of the palace in Gracia, as well as any major government building throughout the Duianna realms. Legends state Larak was the commander of the Meassatoni Army, charged with protecting all of the cities of the Gods. Although he traveled often, he lived and spent much time in Aridu-Veni-Kussi with Dalpha.

Lebuin of House Caerni: Journeyman of the Guild of Argos, Son of Waylen and Alia, Grandson of All-Father Argos and Lothia.

Llino: The Sea Prince's stronghold and capital. Notable places: Blue Dolphin Inn, the Night Market.

Lodi: the day of the week before Vendi and following Merdi. *See Lebuin's Lexicon: Time*

Lords and Ladies: Also Lords or Ladies. A polite expression used to indicate surprise or give emphasis. Also, used as a euphemism for any deity.

Loren Sound: An inlet of the Darian Ocean bordering the southeastern part of the north Duianna Continent.

Lothia: The Raven. Primary Goddess of Karakia and wife of Argos. She often takes the form of a large raven.

Lundi: The day of the week before Martidi and following Solidi. *See Lebuin's Lexicon: Time*

Magus (pl. Magi): A higher magician who has achieved the rank of master in the Guild.

Magus Andros: A fifty-year master mage of the Argos Guild of Mages and Lebuin's mentor at the Llino Guildhouse.

Magus Cune: A twenty-five-year master mage of the Argos Guild of Mages and Lebuin's nemesis for all of Lebuin's twenty years at the Llino Guildhouse.

Magus Gezu: A seventy-year master of the Argos Guild of Mages that died in the summer of 15348.

Magus Nillo: High councilor and a sixty-year master mage of the Argos Guild of Mages and Lebuin's mentor at the Llino Guildhouse.

Magus Seriel of Elraci: An ancient mage who wrote the secret tombs of magic Lebuin acquired and studied.

Magus Vestul: An immortal master mage who predates the Argos Guild of Mages. Close friend of Duke. Lives in Algan.

Mark: A period of time equal to a twenty-fourth part of a day and night and divided into 60 minutes. (see Lebuin's Lexicon–TIME)

Mark: One of the 24 equal parts of a day. The name 'mark' is based on the tick marks used on all clocks *See Lebuin's Lexicon: Time*

Martidi: The day of the week before Merdi and following Lundi. *See Lebuin's Lexicon: Time*

Menadyt: The first month of the Imperial year considered the first month of spring. *See Lebuin's Lexicon: Time*

Merdi: The day of the week before Lodi and following Martidi. *See Lebuin's Lexicon: Time*

Minute: A period of time equal to 60 seconds or a 60th of a mark. *See Lebuin's Lexicon: Time*

Miumi: Port trade city on the Loren Sound on the eastern border of Oslald.

Nabudyt: The seventh month of the Imperial year considered the first month of fall. *See Lebuin's Lexicon: Time*

Nae-Rae: An elven kingdom spanning the eastern third of the North Duianna continent, bordered on the north by the White Ocean, the south by the Burga Mountains, the east by the Darain Ocean, and the west by the Duianna Empire. Capital Rea-Na-Rey. Abbreviation: NR.

Nanadyt: The third month of the Imperial year considered the third and final month of spring. *See Lebuin's Lexicon: Time*

Nasur: A human kingdom on the southeastern edge of the North Duianna continent, bordered on the north by the Onasa Channel, the south by the Halias-Ne Mountains, the east by the Sea Princes' Kingdom of Aelargo, and the west by the Western Burga Spine Mountains. Capital: Thilis. Abbreviation: NA. Known to be friendly with the Nhia-Samri.

Nhia-Samri: A shadowy, ruthless mercenary group of warriors of unknown size which fight with inhuman speed and agility.

Nigan: A combat specialist Dagger that works out of the Blue Dolphin Inn in Llino. Partners with Risy and is called "Hairy" by Ticca.

Night Market: A unique black market in Llino in which any service or goods may be purchased through brokers known as Hands. The market opens every day at sunset and closes at sunrise.

Ninurdyt: The twelfth month of the Imperial year considered the third and final month of winter. *See Lebuin's Lexicon: Time*

Niya-Yur (Yur): The world. The elves called the world Nhia in ancient times. The dwarves called the world Garduan-ka-Gadriel (Loosely translated, it means Gadriel's Flesh).

Odassi: Single edged magical weapons of the shadowy faction of warrior mercenaries called the Nhia-Samri.

Onasa Channel: Inlet of the Loren sound which traverses through hundreds of miles of canyons northerly to the great Empire Lakes, generally salt water transitioning to fresh water near the Empire Lake outlets. Also known as the Onasa River.

Oslald: A human kingdom on the southeastern edge of the North Duianna continent, bordered on the north by the Burga Mountains, the south by the Sea Princes' Kingdom of Aelargo, the east by the Onasa Channel, and the west by the Darain Ocean. Capital: Stegen. Abbreviation: OS. Strong supporter of the Duianna Covenant.

Patredyt: The fifth month of the Imperial year considered the second month of summer. *See Lebuin's Lexicon: Time*

Poalua: Lord of Air and Yur, twin of Uialua, chief God of the Circle, and according to legends, was once ruler of all the Gods. Poalua is the God of Laeusia, although he does not ban temples to other Gods. His symbol is a feather-robed and turbaned archer figure, seated in a throne and superimposed on a sun disk with fire around the edges. Legends also say he created a crystal city at the center of heaven, which was visible to all the realms of the heavens, called Thi-Illi-Veni (literally Brightest Star City), which touched no lands or seas and floated over all of creation, giving light.

Red Door: A high class brothel.

Rhini Wood: The old-growth forest along the northwestern edge of Bear Foot Sea in the Kingdom of Aelargo. Also the name of the village and farming lands in the same location.

Rhonia: An island kingdom in the northern Darian Ocean, famous for rare and pungent spices and unique animals.

Risy: A combat specialist Dagger that works out of the Blue Dolphin Inn in Llino. Partners with Nigan and is called "Frumpy" by Ticca.

Samudyt: The fourth month of the Imperial year considered the first month of summer. *See Lebuin's Lexicon: Time*

Saturdi: The day of the week before Solidi and following Vendi, and (together with Solidi) forming part of the weekend. *See Lebuin's Lexicon: Time*

Sayscia: The high priestess or the great lady of Dalpha in Llino.

Sea Princes' Kingdom of Aelargo: A human kingdom on the southeastern edge of the North Duianna continent, bordering on the northern edge of the Halias-Ne Mountains between the Darain Ocean and the Kingdom of Nasur. Capital: Llino. Abbreviation: AE.

Commands the largest known navy and tightly controls all sea trade.

Second: Is the smallest unit of time measurable by available clocks and is of time equal to one-sixtieth of a minute. *See Lebuin's Lexicon: Time*

Sencial (aka Sentient): An artificial life form that lives in the ancient machines and technologies. Sentients are not machines but life forms created by the non-magical races before coming to Niya-Yur. When Niya-Yur was settled Sentients were considered alive with all the same rights as any other intelligent race. They were voluntarily put to sleep as the old societies fell by an act of the assembly to wait the time of the races' re- ascension.

Sharludyt: The tenth month of the Imperial year considered the first month of winter. *See Lebuin's Lexicon: Time*

Shar-Lumen: The shadowy Grand Warlord of the Nhia-Samri.

Sharre: A sweet wine made by the elves from unknown ingredients. If kept properly, it grows more potent over time. Five to fifty-year-old sharre is very robust and gives a little energy, as well as making people drunk extremely fast. Sharre over one hundred years old can heal wounds, revive tiredness, and sharpen the mind dramatically. Sharre over five hundred years old is thought to restore youth.

Skeed: (*vulgar slang*) (**verb**: skeed; 3rd person present: skeeds; past tense: skeeded; past participle: skeeded; past tense: skeed; gerund or present participle: skeeding) expel feces from the body. 2. soil one's clothes as a result of expelling feces accidentally.
(**noun**) 1. feces. 2. something worthless; garbage; nonsense. 3. unpleasant experiences or treatment. 4. personal belongings; stuff.
(**exclamation**) used alone or as a noun **the hish** or a verb in various phrases to express anger, annoyance,

contempt, impatience, or surprise, or simply for emphasis.

Solidi: The day of the week before Lundi and following Saturdi, and (together with Saturdi) forming part of the weekend.

Sula: Demi-God daughter of Dalpha and a priestess healer of the Temple of Dalpha.

Tarudyt: The second month of the Imperial year considered the second month of spring. *See Lebuin's Lexicon: Time*

The Traitor (Amia-Dharo): The second-in-command Nhia-Samri who betrayed the Nhia-Samri in a great war and helped the Alliance Nations end hostilities. Second most deadly warrior in the world.

Ticca of Rhini Wood: A hunter Dagger that works out of the Blue Dolphin Inn in Llino.

Uialua: The Great Queen, Lady of Birth. Twin of Poalua. Uialua is worshiped in all nations of Duianna. Her symbol resembles the Greek letter omega (Ω), which should always be placed on the upper tier of any structure, indicating her importance. The Duianna Empire uses her symbol on all of its boundary markers in the top border. Legends state she once was queen of the greatest of heavenly realms, known as Meassatoni, where she ruled from the great city of Aridu-Veni-Kussi (literally Greatest City of Beauty), which she built. It was the birthplace of Argos long before the great migration.

Urd: (*verb*) To be condemned by the deities to suffer eternal punishment. *"You shall be diurdin by Lord Argos."*
(*exclamation*) Expressing anger, surprise, or frustration. *"Urd! I completely forgot!"*
(*adjective*) used for emphasis, especially to express anger or frustration. *"Close the urd door!"*
(*synonyms*) blast, darn, diurdu, diurdin, drat, shoot, rats, urdu.

Urdu: (**exclamation**) Expressing anger, surprise, or frustration. "Urdu! The horse broke its leg!"

(**synonyms**) darn, diurdu, diurdin, drat, shoot, blast, rats, urd.

Vanedicha: A poison which induces a trance if a small amount is inhaled, and kills in less than a minute in larger doses. Victims are unusually truthful when revived from a vanedicha-induced trance.

Vendi: The day of the week before Saturdi and following Lodi. *See Lebuin's Lexicon: Time*

Week: A period of seven days. The Imperial names for the days are Solidi, Lundi, Martidi, Merdi, Lodi, Vendi, and Saturdi. *See Lebuin's Lexicon: Time*

Windy Pass: A series of hills and valleys which separate the Burga Spine Mountains from the Halias-Ne Mountain Range, bordering Nasur on the east and Laeusia on the west.

Yalthum: A human kingdom spanning the entire west coast of the North Duianna continent from the Halias-Ne Mountains on the south to the northern ice fields. Yalthum is as old as the Duianna Empire, and has never attempted to expand its borders, but has bitterly defended its borders and western sea lanes.

Year: The period of time during which Niya-Yur completes a single revolution. The Imperial calendar is broken into four seasons starting with spring. The month names for each season are spring Menadyt, Tarudyt, Nanadyt; summer Samudyt, Patredyt, Innadyt; fall Nabudyt, Kishadyt, Lahmudyt; and winter Sharludyt, Ankidyt, Ninurdyt. *See Lebuin's Lexicon: Time*

Yur: See Niya-Yur.

ABOUT THE AUTHOR

Leeland Artra lives in the Emerald City (Seattle, Washington) with his wonderful wife and idea-inspiring kids. He spent the first half of his life as an avid science-fiction/fantasy reader, while becoming a US Navy-trained computer scientist and self-taught table-top gamer. After twenty years of thinking he should publish, he finally got serious, pulling out all the notes and ideas he had stored, and sat down to learn how to be a professional writer. He soon discovered he got as much joy from writing fiction as he did from reading it. His goal is to transition to full-time writing someday. In the meantime, he works as a software engineer and architect at Expedia. In short, by day, he helps people take fabulous vacations, and at night, he helps people take even more fantastic trips of the imagination, which he finds to be symmetric.

OTHER WORKS BY LEELAND ARTRA

LIST OF PUBLISHED BOOKS
http://lartra.com/books

GOLDEN THREADS TRILOGY
Book One : Thread Slivers (January 2013)
http://lartra.com/books/thread-slivers

Book Two : Thread Strands (August 2013)
http://lartra.com/books/thread-strands

Book Three : Thread Skein (March 2015)
http://lartra.com/books/thread-skein

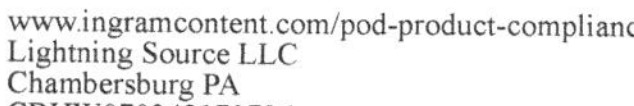